WRITTEN ON THE TIDE

Also by Julia Bryant

WAITING FOR THE TIDE

WRITTEN ON THE TIDE

Julia Bryant

Hodder & Stoughton

First published in Great Britain in 2000
by Hodder and Stoughton
A division of Hodder Headline

10 9 8 7 6 5 4 3 2 1

British Library Cataloguing in Publication Data

Bryant, Julia
Written on the tide
I. Women and war – Fiction 2. Bereavement – Fiction
3. Sailors – Fiction
I.Title
823.9'14 [F]
ISBN 0 340 75107 X

Typeset by Hewer Text Ltd, Edinburgh
Printed and bound in Great Britain by
Mackays of Chatham, plc, Chatham, Kent

Hodder and Stoughton
A division of Hodder Headline
338 Euston Road
London NW1 3BH

For my daughter Kerry
and Rory, her seafaring husband
With Love

ACKNOWLEDGEMENTS

My thanks are due to many people who very generously gave me their time and advice:

Mr Don Baker of Mead Mill Water Gardens, Romsey
Mr Barry Thomas, Writer and Naturalist
Jo Hayes, nature lover
Mr William Kentish Barnes, Golden Threads
James Cramer, Police Historian
Ken Hampton of Portsmouth Police and Fire Service
Angela Rabbitts of G. Andrews and Son Funeral Directors
The staff of the Royal Naval Museum Library
Mr Peter Goodwin, Keeper Curator of HMS *Victory*
The staff of Portsmouth Central Library and the Records Office
Chris and Margaret Seal of Sealpoint Computers
As ever, Mr Peter Rogers, Local Historian
Michael Staniland of the Royal National Institute for the Blind
Mrs Pat Arnold of St. George's Church, Portsea
and last but not least, Janice White, my earliest writing friend.

'It was my sixteenth birthday when I waved my green shawl to Michael, already an indistict blur, on the deck of HMS *Lister*. As it steamed off to the China Station I wondered, what will have happened to all of us by the time the ship returns.'

Lily Forrest
5 June 1921

Chapter One

Easter Saturday March 26 1921

Dear Michael,
It's going to be such a strange day, full of endings and beginnings.
I wish you could be here to share it with me. Writing isn't half
as good as touching is it? Paper kisses are not a patch on the real
thing. I'd like to swap my pen for a magnet that would haul you
back across the sea to the pew beside me in St Georges Church.

Lily Forrest looked up as her grandmother tapped on her open bedroom door. How elegant she looked in her grey two-piece and mauve blouse, her silver hair combed into an elaborate bun. So different from the Gran of every day – with her cross-over apron studded with pins and her specs sliding down her nose as she sewed the stack of sailors' collars. Gran had been her rock from earliest childhood and Lily so wanted her to be happy. 'Do you love Uncle Albert as much as you loved Granddad?' she asked.

Gran chuckled. 'That was a young woman's love – all urgency and fizz. I haven't forgotten what desire feels like, not by a long chalk.'

'But what about Uncle Albert?' Lily said, blushing at Gran's frankness.

Gran's dark eyes shone. 'Albert's the only person ever to call me Beatrice. He always gave me the respect of my full name, from the first day that I started as his mother's scullery-maid.'

'So when did you know that you really loved him?'

Gran helped Lily into her new dress before saying, 'It was after that falling-out we had last year. I realised how much I missed his company and when we eventually made our peace we knew that things had changed between us.'

Lily smoothed down the skirt of her dress before kissing Gran on the cheek. Something had changed between them, too, in the last few minutes. In sharing such confidences with Lily, Gran had acknowledged her growing up.

'Oh, before I forget,' Gran said, 'I want you to look after something for me and keep it safe till I get back from Romsey. Can't take it next-door now, Albert will be there. Once we've all set off for the church I want to know this house is locked safely with nothing left behind.' She went across the passage to her bedroom and reappeared with a little wooden box which she set down on the dressing-table.

Lily recognised it at once as her grandfather's ditty-box. Every sailor had one in which he kept his private possessions such as letters and family pictures. Lily ran her fingers over the name, Joseph Forrest, stamped on the tin label nailed to the side. She wondered in how many different ships it had been Grand-dad's little piece of home.

'What's inside?' she asked.

'Our letters, mine and your grandfather's,' said Gran. 'We poured out our hearts to each other, as well as putting down the little everyday bits of living. Paper lives, we called it.' She looked unseeingly past Lily, as if her mind was years away.

Lily wondered if she would have Michael's ditty-box filled with letters when she became an old lady.

The clock on the mantelpiece chimed one and the mood was broken.

'Where was I?' said Gran, collecting her thoughts. 'The ditty-box. If you could take it next-door and keep it safe 'til we're back from Romsey, I'd be much obliged.'

'Of course I will,' said Lily.

Gran gasped. 'My stars, look at the time. We need to be setting off in a couple of ticks. Just let me have a look at you.'

Lily blushed.

'It's a work of art, my duck,' said Gran. 'I love the scalloped edging on the bodice and the way it buttons onto the skirt. Your apprenticeship at Denby and Shanks has put a real skill in your fingers.' Gran kissed her on the cheek. 'That red colour sets off your lovely dark hair and eyes. Albert was saying that you put him in mind of one of those gypsies in a Spanish painting. A real beauty. Enjoy it while it lasts.'

They stood together, for the last time, in Lily's bedroom, their arms about each other. Then Gran chuckled and the moment was gone. 'It's not many girls that get to be their grandmother's bridesmaid.'

'And not many sons that give their mothers away,' laughed Dad, standing unnoticed by them in the doorway. 'Ma, you look a treat,' he said, crossing the room to her. 'Like the Royal Yacht dressed over all with flags. Need any advice before you take the plunge?'

'Alec Forrest, you can stop that flannel right away,' snapped Gran. 'Lily, fetch your little sister. The car will be here soon. Your Dad and me are going to walk.'

'But Gran,' protested Lily, 'the car's especially for you.'

'Not another word,' said Gran, drawing on her gloves.

Dad winked at her behind Gran's back. 'You look beautiful, Lily love. We must get someone to take your picture so you can send it to that Michael of yours. Off you go, tell Uncle Albert the Queen of Sheba's on her way.'

Lily winked back at her father before hurrying downstairs with the ditty-box. It wasn't only Gran's wedding, it was the day they moved out of 27 Lemon Street, her home for as long as she could remember. It meant the end of her life alone with Gran. When they moved next-door, to number 25, Uncle Albert would be with them.

'You all right, Ma?' said Alec as the door closed behind Lily.

Beattie swallowed hard. 'My nerves are tight as fiddle strings.'

'You've known Albert nearly all your life, even before Dad,' said Alec, his dark eyes full of concern.

'Yes,' she admitted, 'from the age of fourteen.'

'So why the butterflies? You're only moving next-door. It's like a game of musical chairs. Miriam, me and the kids move out of Albert's to Sandown and you move in.'

Beattie tapped her chest, 'It's in here. That's where the changes are. I've been on my own now twenty years, almost as long as I was married to your Dad. Belonged to myself, called my body my own.' She blushed. This wasn't at all the conversation she'd meant to have with her son.

'Ma,' said Alec gently, 'It'll be for you and Albert to find your own path.'

Beattie took her handkerchief from her sleeve and blew her nose. 'You're right, son, of course.' She couldn't tell him about the glimpse caught of her body earlier in the day and her sharp disappointment at its sagging contours. What did she expect at sixty-five? Moving into an older body didn't suit her at all nor did taking custody of swollen ankles. Vanity, vanity, she chided herself.

'Albert's a poor frightened bachelor marrying an experienced widow who's going to take advantage of his innocence,' laughed Alec.

'Your mother should have brought you up to be more respectful,' she snapped, slapping him on the hand.

'That's better,' he said. 'Now, Lily said something about flowers in the scullery.'

'Samuel and Olive sent down some violets and primroses from the farm at Romsey,' said Beattie, shaking the water off the smallest buttonhole and pinning it to the lapel of Alec's petty-officer's uniform. 'I don't suppose I'll see you again in uniform, son, now that you're going to be a landlord in the Isle of Wight.'

'The Lord Tennyson sounds a bit too grand for a little pub in Sandown, doesn't it?' laughed Alec. He took the other buttonhole and pinned it to Beattie's suit.

She glanced in the mirror, tilting the grey flower-pot-hat back on her head and admiring the mauve pleating around the top. 'Well, son,' she said, 'in case I don't get the chance later, I wish you and your new little family the best of luck.' She kissed him on the cheek. 'Now, we must be off. Mustn't keep the bridegroom waiting.'

They stepped out into Lemon Street, one of many of the dockland backstreets of Portsea, her home for the last forty years. Beattie had been into nearly every house: helping to bring babies into the world or wash the dying, taking soup, lending money, laughing or crying. She said hallo to the Vine children outside 23.

'We're coming to the church,' shouted the youngest child. 'We're goin' to throw 'fetti at ya.'

'Poor kids,' said Alec, 'what with their mother in the asylum and Dad always down the pub.'

'Clinging to the wreckage, that's what they are,' sighed Beattie.

'Ma, come on now,' chided Alec. 'It's Easter and the war's over. Even in these little streets there's signs of spring.'

And there were. Green leaves budding on the elm trees in Curzon Howe Road, little pots of daffodils sitting on tables at front-room windows. The pale winter sunshine seemed as tentative as the Peace. There were queues of men in shoddy, demob suits trying to get work. The dockyard, Portsea's main employer, was on short time, and strikes and rationing were a constant reminder of things not back to normal. Yes, she thought, I'm ready for Easter, we've been in Calvary too long.

'Remember the last time we walked out together dressed in our best?' said Alec squeezing her arm.

'Last year,' she smiled. 'Your wedding, when I gave you away to your lovely Miriam. You're a lucky fellow, Alec, getting a second chance like that. I've got a special place in my heart for your wife and little Rosie and Joseph.'

'Talking about lucky second chances,' laughed her son, 'what about you and Albert?'

Her reply was drowned out by her little granddaughter's cries of excitement.

'Nanny Forrest, look at me, look at me,' four-year-old Rosie shouted, rushing out to her from the church porch. Her toffee-coloured curls bounced in her excitement.

Beattie laughed. 'You look as pretty as a fairy on a Christmas tree. What a lovely red dress.'

'Daddy's two princesses,' said Alec, smiling and kissing his daughters as Lily joined them.

'Ready, Gran?' Lily asked.

Beattie smiled and rested her hand on Alec's arm as they entered the porch of St George's Church. Lily and Rosie formed up behind them. They stood beside the font, filled with an arrangement of daffodils, narcissi and pussy willow. Her senses were overwhelmed by the scent of the flowers and the smell of Sunday suits and church polish. The congregation of friends and relations turned to look at her before they were engulfed in the sound of the organ booming out the Wedding March.

Everything merged into the background as Albert stepped from his seat and turned towards her, his dear face shiny with joy. The four of them, Alec, Beattie, Albert and his brother Samuel stood before the Reverend Merchison as he cleared his throat and twitched his rusty black surplice.

He began a rambling introduction to the service, which

included mention of Canaan of Galilee, brute beasts of the field and avoidance of fornication, most of which floated past her. And then she began to listen.

'Thirdly it was ordained for the mutual society, help and comfort that the one ought to have of the other, both in prosperity and adversity.'

Yes, that was what she and Albert could offer one another. Their arms were just touching and she could smell the faint scent of the pomade he used on his hair. They looked at one another and smiled.

'Beatrice,' he whispered. But when asked whether he would, 'Love her, comfort her, honour and keep her in sickness and in health?' his voice could have been heard at the back of the church.

'I will,' said Beattie with equal conviction.

And then they were holding hands and making their vows.

Samuel took the wedding-ring out of his pocket and laid it on the prayer book with his large freckled hand.

'With this ring I thee wed,' said Albert, sliding the ring down over the pale stripe on her finger once covered by the ring that Joseph had given her, now consigned to her right hand. He looked directly at her as he said, 'With my body I thee worship, and with all my worldly goods I thee endow.'

They knelt together on a little wooden stool, hand-in-hand as the Reverend Merchison offered a blessing on their behalf. She looked up at the altar at the stone texts of the Creed and the Lord's Prayer, the words blurring through happy tears. She signed her name, relinquishing Forrest and accepting Pragnell and then it was done. As they walked down the short aisle together Beattie realised that she was suddenly very hungry.

It seemed an eternity spent greeting friends outside the church, smiling for the photographs and being pelted with confetti by the Vine children. At last, shivering a little, they were ushered into a beribboned black Daimler for the short ride home. Beattie sniffed the rich smell of leather appreciatively.

Albert turned and kissed her on the cheek. 'Are you happy, Beatrice?' he asked.

She looked at her husband's square face, tanned from sitting painting in the open air, his clear grey eyes and white hair just that shade too long. 'Yes, you old Bohemian,' she whispered, 'and I shall be even happier when I'm sat in front of a plate of boiled ham.'

Albert laughed. 'We're ready, now, driver,' he said, tapping the glass partition.

The Daimler purred away from the kerb and out of St George's Square along The Hard and passed the dockyard into Queen Street, with Beattie sitting upright, one hand in Albert's and the other clutching a leather strap by the window. As they drew to a halt in Lemon Street the neighbours clustered round to greet the bride and groom.

Lily and her best friend Dora Somers bustled about passing around sandwiches, pouring drinks and exchanging greetings to everyone crammed into Uncle Albert's kitchen. Beattie sat beside him in a happy fog.

Alec and Miriam barely had time to toast the happy couple before the taxi arrived to whisk them and the little ones to the Harbour Station to start their journey to the Isle of Wight. Most of the guests spilled onto the pavement to wave goodbye.

'I'll write, I promise,' said Lily, hugging her Dad fiercely and kissing Miriam. 'I'll miss you,' she said to her little brother and sister.

'Be happy, Ma,' Lily heard Dad say as he hurried into the car.

There was a lull in the general rejoicing. Some friends and relations drifted away then the happy couple rejoined the feast.

The Vine family had never left it for a second. Gradually the snowy grandeur of the wedding table was transformed into a wine-stained gutter of bread crusts, half-eaten cake and spilled pickles.

Fourteen-year-old Mary chewed steadily at her beef sandwich. Blyth, her brother, crouched, his arms forming a defensive wall around a plate of jam tarts. Faith and Mercy, the ten-year-old twins, skinny and chalk-faced, stood on chairs in front of the mirror painting their mouths with slices of beetroot.

'You like our lipstick Dor?' they chorused, jumping off the chairs and catching hold of Dora's hands.

As the fiancée of their brother Harry, Dora was being drawn into the Vine family. Looking at the chaos around her, Gran's face was a picture.

'Sit down Beatrice,' said Albert, 'the car's not coming for a while. Why don't we have a little concert.'

'Who shall be first?' asked Beattie.

'I don't mind,' said Dora, her hazel eyes bright with excitement. She strutted about in front of them, her little bird-like figure assuming the big-bosomed bravado of Marie Lloyd as she sang, 'I'm one of the Ruins Cromwell knocked about a bit.'

The twins clapped loudly. 'That was ever so good, our Dor.'

'Bobby Shaftoe,' said Blyth, getting to his feet.

Lily watched Mary looking at her little brother. There was no calculation in her feelings, only a fierce protective love. When she smiled at him, tall, skinny, freckle-faced Mary was transformed. Her boot-brown eyes shone with pride and for once she wasn't biting her nails. He was a beautiful child with his blond curls and blue eyes. His voice was high and breathy and he accompanied the words with gestures to mimic the rolling of the ship or the combing of Bobby Shaftoe's hair. At the end he was kissed and hugged by all his sisters before going to sit on Dora's lap.

Lily smiled at her friend sitting among the family that would soon be hers. Poor Dora, she thought, so kind and so willing.

'Our turn, our turn,' shouted Faith, breaking into Lily's thoughts. She dragged Mercy off her chair. 'Song about a sailor.'

'Who's that knocking on my door, who's that knocking on my door? Cried the fair young maiden,' warbled Faith.

'It's only me from over the sea,' barked Mercy, 'said Bollicky Bill the sailor.'

Gran looked as if she would burst.

'I'll come down and let you in, cried the fair young maiden,' continued Faith, oblivious of the response of the audience.

'I drinks me whisky, while I can, whisky is the life of man,' barked Mercy, red in the face by this time. 'Whisky in an old tin can, said Bollicky Billy the sailor.'

Lily had never seen Uncle Albert laugh so much and Gran looked a lovely mixture of pretended shock and hilarity.

Blyth leapt off Dora's lap and strutted about, shouting 'borricky, borricky' at the top of his voice.

'We 'aven't finished,' shouted the twins, shoving him out of the way.

'Don't you 'it' im or I'll wallop ya,' cried Mary, jumping to her feet.

Lily took Blyth down the yard to the lavatory away from his warring sisters. When they returned, the Vines, weighed down with bags of cake, took their leave.

'From the sublime to the ridiculous,' said Uncle Albert quietly.

Gran smiled at him. 'I could do with a good cup of tea,' she said, 'my mouth's as dry as the bottom of a bird's cage.'

'I'll put the kettle on,' said Dora.

There was a loud rapping on the front door and Albert got to his feet. 'I'm sorry, my love, but I think it's our car. We'll be in Romsey in no time. Olive and Samuel will be waiting to welcome us.'

'Have a lovely, lovely time, Gran,' said Lily, close to tears.

'I will, my duck,' said her grandmother, hugging her tightly.

'Goodbye Lily, my dear,' said Uncle Albert, kissing her on the cheek. 'We'll see you late on Easter Monday. And thank you for everything.'

Once the Daimler had turned the corner of the street, Lily grabbed Dora and danced her round and round the pavement.

'We're free, we're free,' she cried. 'We got the whole blooming Easter to ourselves.' Arm-in-arm they went indoors and set about the washing-up.

'How d'you feel about living here with your Gran and Mr Pragnell?' asked Dora as she tied an apron round her waist.

'Well, I could have gone to the Island with Dad and Miriam,' said Lily, 'but that would have meant leaving work and finding something else and there wouldn't be anything much in San-down. Gran is my real family. But, it just won't be the same sharing her with Uncle Albert.'

'Sharing's not your strong point, from what I know of you,' teased Dora, flicking Lily with the end of the tea-towel.

'You've got that beady-eyed look,' said Lily crossly, splashing her with washing-up water, 'you always have when you're telling me something I don't want to hear.'

'Well, what about all the carry-on over Michael's mother wanting to wave goodbye to him?'

'All right,' said Lily sulkily. 'Don't overdo it or I'll begin on you.'

'Where shall we start?' said Dora. 'There's my not standing up to Mary, screaming at my batty old Gran and not swiping Harry's Dad when he . . .' She put her hand to her mouth.

'When he what, Dora?' Her friend had blushed and looked away. Lily took her by the shoulders and tried to turn her back so that they were facing each other. 'You can't not tell me, now you've got this far.'

'It was nothing,' said her friend, staring down at her hands.

'Dora!' demanded Lily, 'tell me or I'll think the worst.'

'He tried to kiss me.'

'What do you mean, kiss you?' said Lily eyeing her closely.

Dora squirmed. 'Well properly like, with his mouth open and . . .'

'Blaah!' Lily scrubbed her mouth with her hand. 'Didn't try anything else did he?'

'Course not.' Dora was red-faced and indignant.

'D'you think he was drunk?'

Dora shook her head. 'I was in the house on my own, 'cos he'd sent the kids over the shop.'

'So it wasn't like a joke or anything?'

Dora shook her head.

'Harry would go mental,' said Lily indignantly.

Dora shrugged, 'I'll just have to keep out of Fred's way.'

'Don't go round there anymore.'

'I've got to,' insisted Dora. 'Harry sends me money for the kids and I like to see them, they're fond of me, except Mary, of course.'

Lily sympathised. Although she had a sneaking admiration for Mary she knew she could be difficult. Mary was prickly and defensive and hugely jealous of anyone she suspected of being a rival for Harry's affection.

'Here,' she said, 'I'll make us some cocoa and we'll fill the hot-water bottles.'

'We'll be like them girls in those books you used to tell me about,' said Dora, crunching a pickled onion in her teeth. 'Having midnight feasts in the dormitories.'

'Oh, "Monitress Merle" and such like,' said Lily, rubbing her stomach. 'I'm full to bursting.'

'Me too,' said Dora, yawning sleepily.

'Andrew would have loved today,' Lily said, suddenly thinking of her brother drowned off Jutland. 'He'd've been twenty-one.'

'Might have been a dad by now,' said Dora, 'or gone off to Australia. All those boys what I knew at school, all of them gone.'

'All with their dreams,' sighed Lily. 'Big things like getting married or apprenticeships and little things like watching Pompey win the cup.'

'What are your dreams?' asked Dora.

'It was being a teacher until I couldn't take up my scholarship. Now?' Lily shrugged. 'Finishing my apprenticeship and maybe taking up Gold Wire work. Mrs Markham says I've got sharp eyes and nimble fingers, besides, it's much better paid than tailoring.'

'I just wants to leave home and marry Harry and for the rest of his family to, I don't know, to dissolve or something.'

Lily felt a sudden wave of affection for her friend. Dora lived with her two brothers and parents behind a bicycle shop near the dockyard. Her father was an anxious hectoring man and her mother faded and meek. In the attic lived Dora's demented grandmother who screamed and banged on the ceiling with her stick. The Vines and the Somers were like the blades of a pair of scissors with Dora caught between them.

'You said you was writing every single detail of the wedding to Michael,' said Dora, as they stood in the front bedroom undressing by candlelight.

'I just hope he remembers we've moved to twenty five. I wouldn't want his letter laying about in an empty house or the new people reading it.'

'I wonder who they'll be,' said Dora, yawning.

'The house belongs to Ma Wheeler. She packs people in, we could have all sorts.'

'The woman who comes round in a car, to collect her rents, wearing a fox fur?'

'That's her,' said Lily, sleepily.

'Shall I blow out the candle?' asked Dora.

'I'll do it,' said Lily in a fit of generosity.

The next morning they lingered over their breakfast still in their nightclothes – wickedly slothful – the whole day spread before them. 'We could do lots of things,' said Lily, curling her bare toes on the bottom rung of the chair. 'Dress up and go to church or the Easter Fair on the Hill.'

'Weather doesn't look that good,' said Dora, looking out the window.

'Oh bother!' said Lily, getting to her feet, 'there's someone knocking on the front door. Nine o'clock on a Sunday morning, who it can be?'

It was Sergeant Wilkes with his police cape shiny with rain. 'Is Mr Pragnell at home?' he asked, 'or is your Gran about?'

Lily blushed at being caught in her nightie, especially by a policeman. 'They're away on their honeymoon.'

It was then Sergeant Wilkes' turn to blush. Was it seeing a young woman in her nightclothes or the mention of the honeymoon that embarrassed him, she wondered.

He cleared his throat noisily. 'It's the Vines I'm after. I've knocked at their door and can't get a peep out of them. Dolly has died up at the asylum. Fred's needed up there to sort out the formalities.'

'I'll get dressed, then go over the back and give them a message,' said Lily, wishing Gran was home. 'I'll get Mr Vine to come and see you.'

'No,' said the policeman, 'you're a sensible girl. You break the news and get him up to the asylum.' He tipped his hand to his helmet. 'Things to do at the station.'

Lily felt a rush of resentment as her holiday plans evaporated.

'I'll go and tell them,' said Dora, lacing up her shoes, when Lily had told her the depressing news. 'I'm almost family, after all.'

'D'you want me to come with you?' asked Lily, pulling her nightdress over her head and standing shivering in her vest.

'No,' said Dora firmly. 'You best sort out some grub for me and the nippers, in there. Get a good meal going, it'll give me something to look forward to.'

Lily watched Dora's resolute little figure walking down the yard and felt a guilty surge of relief that she had only the dinner to deal with. Listlessly she washed and dressed and wandered around the kitchen. Noticing a dirty wine-glass on the floor she bent to pick it up and saw Gran's gloves under the chair. Intending just to take them upstairs and put them on her dressing-table, Lily hurried into the main bedroom. As she set the gloves down on the polished oak surface she noticed a little glass dish with a few coins in it, a packet of peppermints and a brass key with a little green tassel. Lily recognised it as the key to Granddad's ditty-box. She knew that she should go downstairs and leave the key in the dish. Boredom and curiosity struggled for mastery. Why should she put it back? Because Gran trusted you, answered her conscience. She picked it up and held it in her hand. What else was she going to do all day? She could throw a meal together of leftovers in half an hour. Nobody would know that she had opened it. Perhaps she was mistaken. If it wasn't the key, no harm had been done, and if it was, well, she'd just make herself put it back. She went downstairs into the front bedroom. Her hands were shaking as she lifted the box onto the bed and turned the key in the lock.

Chapter Two

'Beatrice, come to bed my darling,' he said, holding out his arms to her.

Beattie shivered. It was years since anyone had seen her naked. Then it had been Joseph who knew her body almost as well as he knew his own.

Nervously she slid between the covers.

After kissing her tenderly Albert whispered,' Take off your gown, let's be as Adam and Eve.' He ran his hands over her body and nuzzled his face into her neck. Whispering endearments, stroking and kissing, he thoroughly aroused her then held her in his arms until she fell into a blissful contented sleep. 'Where did you, a bachelor, learn to be such a good lover?' she asked teasingly, the next morning.

'Put it down to my Sea Dad,' he answered.

Beattie was mystified.

'Older sailors take raw recruits under their wing and guide them in the ways of the world. My Sea Dad took me to see Madam Cheng and her young ladies.' Albert chuckled softly. 'It was humiliating. My companion was quite exquisite. When she saw me naked with my manhood exposed she couldn't stop giggling.' He joined in Beattie's laughter. 'I learned a lot from Madam Cheng's establishment.'

Beattie had tried to be shocked but like Madam Cheng she couldn't help giggling.

Now it was Easter Sunday, their first morning together and she was richly content lying in his arms listening to his heart steadily beating.

'When I woke up earlier and found you beside me, this poem came into my head. *'Who would have thought my withered heart could have recovered greenness? It was gone quite underground as flowers depart, And now in age I bud again.'*

'Have I brought you back to life,' she asked, hugging him tightly.

Albert chuckled. 'An abundance of life,' he whispered.

They dozed happily in each other's arms until they were awoken by the barking of a dog. Through the window of the cowman's cottage they watched a young, ginger-headed lad opening the field gate and shooing the cows down the lane to the dairy.

'Oh, look at that one over there,' laughed Beattie, 'the little one with the caramel coat, isn't she pretty?'

'That's a Guernsey,' said Albert, 'the rest are Short-horns. They keep the Guernseys for their creamy milk.'

'I'd have her just to look at.'

'And be penniless within the month,' he laughed.

'Do we have to go to church, this morning?' Beattie asked, 'I'd like to have a walk about and see everything.'

'We're free agents 'til one o'clock, then we must show ourselves to Olive and Samuel.'

'We'll have to wrap up warm,' said Beattie looking at the young lad's breath, smoky in the morning air as he talked to his dog.

'By the time we've had our breakfast and dressed, the day will be a bit older and warmer,' said Albert, taking her hand and drawing her away from the window. 'What shall it be, a pot of tea, an egg and brown bread soldiers?'

'Fit for a queen,' laughed Beattie, later, as he set down a well laden tray beside her. 'I don't know,' she said tapping the turquoise shell of the duck egg, 'it's only twenty or so miles down the road from Portsmouth and yet it's like a foreign land to me.'

'I've always loved it,' said Albert pouring them both a cup of tea. 'Did you know, Mother came from around here, a place called Nursling. Often, as a small boy, I came out to see my grandparents. Mother loved sketching and she was like an encyclopaedia about plants and animals. I once thought of settling here. But, beautiful as it is, I knew I'd grow tired of it. My roots are in the town with the sea and the ships.'

'Have you ever done any painting around the farm?'

'Only rough sketches.' He shrugged as he stirred the sugar in his tea. 'Nothing that ever amounted to much.'

'I'm ready for anything, now,' said Beattie, gathering up her dressing-gown and towel. 'You stay up here and I'll have a wash in the kitchen, in the warm.' As she stood at the sink and soaped her face and arms she smiled to herself. At this moment, standing on the flagstones by the window, she knew herself to be truly happy.

After clearing away the dishes and dressing warmly in stout shoes, gloves and scarves they set off for their walk. Rarely had Beattie ever been out in the countryside. Nervously she clutched Albert's arm, overcome by the emptiness of the landscape. The air was cold and a breeze tugged at the edges of her scarf. She jumped at the sudden clatter of rooks as they carried twigs up to their nests in the tall trees.

'Let me help you over this stile,' said Albert, approaching the field where earlier she'd admired the little Guernsey cow.

'We're not crossing it are we?' she asked, looking anxiously at her husband. 'It's full of animals.'

'Beatrice, we shall be of no interest to these young ladies whatsoever,' smiled Albert leaning down and helping her up onto the stile and then into the field. 'They're just gossiping about the milker's cold hands this morning. All you have to do is avoid treading in any cowpats.'

'Where are we off to?' asked Beattie, stepping gingerly onto the grass.

'I thought a turn around Squabb Wood and perhaps a little further on if the ground is not too swampy. It'll give us an appetite for dinner.'

Arm-in-arm they crossed the fields with Beattie casting nervous glances towards the cattle and Albert whistling cheerfully. She felt conspicuous with all the space of fields and sky around her.

'We're on the verge of spring, with everything crouched underground ready to burst out at any moment.' He squeezed her hand. 'I think there might be a few surprises later on.'

The fields had patches of squelchy mud and Beattie had to grasp Albert's arm firmly to avoid slipping over. Gradually she began to lose her nervousness and notice her surroundings. 'Look Albert, catkins,' she cried delightedly, 'and there's pussy willow.'

'A real sign of Easter, some people call it palm, don't they? I wonder if it's because it's usually out by Palm Sunday or because you see it among church flowers at this time of year.'

At the entrance to Squabb Wood a robin sat on the gate, his head to one side watching their approach. They heard someone give a sharp commanding whistle and two muddy dogs burst on to the path putting the robin to flight.

'Ajax, Achilles,' shouted a man in a long tweed overcoat and deerstalker hat. 'Good day to you,' he snapped at Beattie and Albert, before going out of the gate with his dogs bounding behind him.

'Posh names for a couple of mongrels, they should have been Rusty and Spot.'

Albert laughed. 'Sorry the ground's so boggy. We'll just have to watch our steps.' He gave her a pleading smile. 'We can turn back now, if you like, but you'll have missed a magical sight if you do.'

'How can I resist, you old charmer,' laughed Beattie, stepping carefully on to a dry patch of the path ahead.

Their breath streamed out ahead of them and they chatted easily. Albert named the trees and birds they passed on their way and Beattie looked about her with interest. Her only memory of being in woods had been on a Sunday school treat in summer with the trees in full green leaf and being tormented with midges. There was a damp earthy smell almost spicy in character.

'What's that funny, rattling chirring sound?' she asked.

'A little wren fiercely defending her territory,' said Albert.

'And who's that singing those lovely, liquid notes?'

'A blackbird. Look see these tiny little white flowers with a pink tinge – they're wood anemones.' Beattie was almost totally absorbed in avoiding squelchy patches of mud and setting her feet on dry earth. Gradually she began to look about her and notice the different trees budding into leaf. The wood was full of different sounds: the wind through the branches, the trickling of water in a little stream, birdsong and the alternate crunching and slithering of their own footsteps.

'Now, my love,' said Albert, 'the best is yet to come. I want you to close your eyes and catch hold of my hand, I won't let you trip or fall.'

Trustingly she followed his lead. When she felt she had been stumbling after him for what seemed an age, he stopped.

'Happy Easter, my darling, open your eyes,' he said, and waved his hands like a conjurer.

Following the scallop-edged banks of the little stream were star-petalled celandines and then beyond them primroses in pale profusion. 'Oh,' Beattie cried clapping her hands together in delight. 'Oh, Albert.' Their numbers astonished her and their delicate, creamy petals seemed to glow in the dense, dark wood.

She drew in a draught of cold air full of the smell of new things bursting through the earth. 'I don't know what to say,' she gasped. 'Such beauty. I'll never, ever forget this.' Beattie stretched out her hands and pulled Albert's face towards her. It was some while before they noticed the rain falling in the puddles at their feet.

'We'd better make haste or we'll be soaked,' said Albert, taking her scarf and tying it over her head. 'Pull up your collar, that's it. Are you ready for the off?'

'Before we go,' she said, 'I want to say thank you, for bringing me here, I shall never ever forget this time in the woods with you.'

'It's been magical,' he said smiling at her, 'and now, one last kiss before we drown.'

It seemed hours later that bedraggled, wet and muddy they presented themselves under the thatched eaves of Samuel's farmhouse. They were welcomed in by Olive who offered them old slippers to change into and warm towels to dry their wet faces.

'You look like drowned rats, the pair of you,' she laughed. 'Go in and sit by the fire and let Sammy pour you a glass of sherry to warm you up.'

'Something smells wonderful,' said Beattie handing back the towel.

'Leg of lamb and new potatoes,' said Olive. 'I hope you've worked up an appetite. I can't abide picky eaters.'

Beattie smiled at her. Strange, she had always dismissed this woman, on the rare occasions that she met her, as dark-haired and dumpy, with little to say for herself. But she realised that Olive, in her own kitchen with its huge black-leaded range and gleaming copper pots, was the confident mistress of her own domain.

'Ha,' boomed Samuel, coming into the kitchen, 'it's the lovebirds. Come in, come in.'

He was a genial, sandy-whiskered, toby jug of a man as broad as he was tall. His face, weathered by the wind and sun, beamed at her. 'Beattie, come through and sit by the fire. Lord, your hands are frozen. What can I get you, sherry, brandy, rum?'

Tea would have been more to her taste. She could have warmed her fingers around the cup but she didn't want to trouble Olive who was busy with the meal. 'Sherry would be lovely,' she said, smiling shyly.

'Rum for you, brother?'

'With a dash of water, Sammy please.' Albert settled himself almost inside the fireplace on a padded leather stool.

Beattie perched on the edge of a plump chintz armchair. She looked around her at the cosy sitting-room. The huge oak mantlepiece gleamed with polish and was crammed with little china figurines and brass bells all grouped around a framed photograph. The young man in the picture was the image of Samuel. He sat in his Sunday suit beside his curly-haired wife in her dress with a lace collar. Three little boys, between the ages of five and nine, Beattie guessed, smiled up at their proud parents.

Samuel drew a little table towards her and set down her glass of sherry. He followed her gaze. 'Matthew and Sarah and the grandchildren,' he said. 'We miss them dreadfully. Been in Rhodesia six years now. Haven't even seen the youngest. Still,' he sighed, 'only blessing, he missed the slaughter over here. Lucky, nowadays, to have a son at all. War cut a swathe through Romsey. Had to have schoolchildren bring in the harvest and help with the beasts. Them and the old-timers.'

'Farming must have been different when you went to Canada, as a young man,' said Beattie, anxious not to dwell on the war.

'Glory, yes,' her brother-in-law answered as he poured Albert's rum. 'I'll never forget my first sight of the wheat fields in Manitoba. On and on they stretched filling the horizon. No hedgerows dividing up the fields. A land of opportunity it was in the eighties, when I was a young man, and still is.'

'What brought you back?' asked Beattie.

'My Olive,' he said, smiling fondly in the direction of the kitchen. 'We were both youngsters when I went off on my adventures but she used to write to me.' Samuel sighed happily. 'Such letters they were, brought the countryside around here to me in every detail: birds and flowers and what was happening in the fields, little drawings, pressed flowers. In the end I grew so homesick for her and England I spent the money I'd been saving for a farm out there on the fare back home. Never, never regretted it. I got the tenancy of this farm on the Ashley estate and we're happy as bees in clover.'

Olive stood in the doorway with a tea-towel in her hand smiling at her husband. 'We're ready everyone. Come and take your seats.'

'This looks a feast,' said Albert, 'thank you, both of you.'

'It's a joy to us to see you settled at last, Albert,' laughed Olive. 'We thought you were fated to be a lifelong bachelor.'

'Big changes for you, too, Beattie,' said Samuel, taking up a knife and beginning to carve the joint. 'You'll miss your Alec and Miriam and the little ones.'

'Well,' Beattie held out her plate, 'there's still Lily, of course and we've not moved far. But yes, I shall miss young Rosie and Joseph and Miriam. She's become very dear to me over the last few years.'

'I should think you'll be free to go with Albert on his painting jaunts, now. After all you won't be tied to the children or the collar-making,' said Olive, heaping Beattie's plate with vegetables.

'I'm looking forward to showing her something of England and France,' said Albert, handing her the mint sauce.

Beattie felt a spurt of anger. 'I haven't decided anything, yet,' she said, no longer smiling. 'They're decisions we'll make when the time comes. I still have Lily to consider.'

Albert looked taken aback.

'I hope we haven't trod on your corns, Beattie,' said Samuel, seeming amused by her huffiness. 'We wouldn't want to cause a lovers' tiff.'

Olive blushed. 'I meant no harm by what I said, I'm sure.'

'Please, please,' now it was Beattie's turn to apologise, 'you just took me by surprise. I suppose with the wedding and everything we haven't given much thought to what comes next.'

'Beatrice, my dear,' said Albert, looking suitably contrite, 'if I've taken anything for granted, I do apologise. It won't happen again.'

She looked at the three of them as they sat expressing varying degrees of amusement and discomfort and laughed. 'Yes it will. Of course it will. It's just that I've been on my own a long while and grown used to making my own decisions. We've both got a lot to learn.'

Albert flashed her a grateful smile. 'This lamb is delicious, so tender, and the potatoes, you don't get the same flavour in the town.'

'Straight out of the earth, they are,' said Olive, 'and the carrots.'

The tension eased between them and the meal progressed with talk of the weather and farm prices. After a pudding of apple pie and clotted cream, the men retired to the sitting-room and Beattie helped Olive with the washing-up.

The two women fell into an easy rhythm of working. While Beattie hung the damp tea-towels over the range Olive poured the water into a large brown pot. They took the cups and saucers into the sitting-room and were greeted by their husbands' combined snores.

'Poor Sammy,' said his wife indulgently. 'He gets so tired. I'll be glad when the new cowman and his family arrive.'

'Albert's got no excuse for snoring,' laughed Beattie. 'He's just eaten too much.'

'Oh, I don't know,' said Olive, smiling mischievously, 'If I remember rightly honeymoons can be very tiring.'

'I wonder what Lily is up to,' said Beattie blushing furiously. 'Not listening to a couple of old codgers snoring their heads off, that's for certain. I bet she and her pal Dora are having a whale of a time.'

Chapter Three

Dora crossed over the two low walls into the Vines' back yard, her legs heavy with reluctance. Towser, their smelly old mongrel, his eyes milky white, blundered towards her. Dora patted him and he waddled on down the yard. 'Anybody home?' she called, stepping through the scullery and into the kitchen.

Mary was sitting at the table in her nightdress eating wedding cake. 'Hallo,' she said unenthusiastically. 'What do you want?'

'Didn't you hear the policeman at your door just now?'

'No. Anyway Dad's blotto. Bound not to be anythink we wants to know,' she snapped. 'What's it about?'

'He came along to Mr Pragnell's house to Lily and me. Given me a message for you. Wants your dad to go up the asylum.'

'What they want?' she challenged.

Dora swallowed hard. 'It's your Mum.'

'What about her?' Mary asked, her eyes narrowing with suspicion.

'I'm really sorry,' gulped Dora, 'but she died earlier this morning.'

Mary turned her head sharply away then bent over her plate and chased the cake crumbs with her fingers.

Everything seemed unnaturally quiet. Dora would have been

grateful for the ticking of a clock or even Towser's laboured breathing. She couldn't bear the silence and Mary's determined lack of response. She reached out and touched the frayed sleeve of the young girl's nightdress. 'I'm ever so sorry,' she said lamely.

Her hand was instantly flung aside and Mary leapt to her feet overturning the chair and sweeping the plate onto the floor. 'Liar,' she shouted into her face, 'bleedin' liar. Dad said she was gettin' better. He said, he said.' She ran screaming out of the room.

Dora's heart thumped painfully against her ribs as she tried to swallow down her panic. She wanted to cover her ears to blot out the savage sound. Only the thought of Harry kept her standing there. She closed the door into the passage cutting off the sounds of banging and screaming from overhead. Anything could be coped with once she'd distanced herself from Mary. After drawing a few trembling breaths she stirred up the coals under the range and filled the kettle. Dora sorted out some clean cups and set them on the table as the door was pushed open and Blyth came into the room in a grubby vest and socks, trailing a piece of grey blanket behind him. He stood looking around him.

'Mary crying,' he said. 'Why she crying?' He began to look alarmed as the screaming and banging showed no signs of diminishing.

Dora searched around and found some trousers and a crumpled jumper on a chair. They smelt of Towser. She helped Blyth into his boots sitting him on the corner of the table to lace them up. 'You go down to the lavatory and when you come back I'll make you some bread and sugar,' she said, holding the back door open for him. Once he was on his way she hurried up the stairs. 'You're frightening Blyth,' she shouted.

Deaf to all reason, Mary continued to beat on the back bedroom door.

Suddenly it swung open and her father stood there holding up his pyjama trousers in one hand and his head in the other.

'Jesus,' he wailed, 'can't a man have some rest of a Sunday. What's all the carry-on about?' He glared at Mary then took his hand away from his head and dragged her off the door by the back of her nightdress. 'For Chrissake, shut up and tell me what you're caterwauling about.'

Gulping and sniffing Mary's sobbing came to a shuddering halt. 'It's Ma, she's died up at the 'sylum, Wilkes come and told Dora.'

'Oh my Lor,' said Fred, going back into his room and sinking onto the bed. 'My poor, poor Dolly.' Tears leaked out of the corners of his faded blue eyes and ran down his stubbly cheeks. He made no attempt to dry them and they began to make dismal trails down his neck onto his vest. 'My poor Dolly, dead and gone. No, oh no,' he wailed.

Dora stood in the doorway trying not to breathe in the stale odours of sweat and unwashed sheets. She was close to panic. First there'd been Mary's silence, then her screaming and now Fred's watery collapse.

'Dora, little Dora, what are we going to do?'

She wanted to hit him, to smash some response from this weak, shambling excuse for a father. 'Blyth wants you,' she said, touching Mary gently on the shoulder. 'He's frightened,' she added.

Mary turned her blotched, tearstained face towards her before trailing miserably down the stairs.

'What we goin' to do?' repeated Fred, dully.

'I'm going downstairs to make some tea and toast. We're relying on you to get dressed and go up the asylum to sort things out.'

'Oh, I dunno about that,' Fred's voice trailed away.

Dora backed down the stairs. 'You're their Dad,' she said, trying to keep the disgust from her voice. 'I'm just trying to help you all for Harry's sake. But you're the head of the family, you must decide things.'

She found Blyth sitting on a chair and Mary still sniffing as she made him a slice of sugar bread. Pouring the water on the tea and slicing a stack of bread she set it down on the table. Half-past nine and already Dora felt weary and ineffectual. How was she going to stop everything just disintegrating? There was Mrs Vine to bring home, a funeral to arrange and she couldn't even get them all seated around the table for breakfast. The twins were still in bed and goodness knows how they were going to be when they found out about their mother. Tears started behind her eyes. Why did Harry have to go away? Why did he have to leave her with this family that pushed her to the edge, seeming to deny her even space for breathing? She poured three cups of tea. 'Mary,' she said cautiously, 'there are things that have got to be done. Your Dad must go up to the asylum and sign a certificate, there's arrangements to be made about bringing her home and the funeral.'

Mary said nothing.

'If you don't help me, I'll go home and leave you to it,' said Dora desperately. 'Your mother will be buried on the parish. No hymns, no flowers, no nothing.' She pulled Mary around so that the young girl in the skimpy nightie had no choice but to listen.

'I'll get dressed. Me and Dad'll go up the asylum. You get the place sorted and the kids,' she said dully. 'I'll tell the twins.'

'Thank you, Mary,' said Dora, gratefully holding a cup of tea out to her. 'Lily's going to make us all some dinner for later.'

With excruciating slowness Fred Vine got himself together. Dora stayed waiting in the kitchen while he slocked about in the scullery, washing and shaving. He then padded about the kitchen rolling a cigarette, drinking tea, alternately coughing and crying till she could have screamed at him. When she'd almost given up hope of anything being achieved that day Fred and Dora said they'd go off to the asylum. The twins after initial tears settled down to their breakfast and even helped her clear away and straighten the house. She cajoled the two of them to take Blyth out for a walk before dinner to give her time to straighten the front room in preparation for Mrs Vine's body being brought home. Standing in the front room she wondered what to do next. This was Mary's bedroom where she and Blyth slept. The mattress would need to be taken upstairs and all the family wedged in together for the next few days. Had it occurred to Mary that they would keep her mother's coffin in the front room, Dora wondered? She remembered how delighted the girl had been to take over the front room when Harry went away. How would she feel about sleeping there again once the coffin had been removed? Dora found she was clenching her fists as she steeled herself to cope with whatever the Vines demanded of her.

She jumped in alarm as she heard the key rattle in the letter-box. It was Mary and Fred, back to borrow a shilling for tram fares to the asylum. As she hurried next door for some money she wished desperately for Harry to be there to help her. If only she could pour out all her fears to him. But Harry was thousands of miles away.

In spite of knowing that she was completely alone, Lily got up and shut the door before opening her grandfather's box. Her mouth was dry and her heart thumped against her ribs as she took out the tightly packed bundles of letters and laid them on the bed. They were all in yellowing envelopes, some with her grandmother's large round writing and others with her grand-dad's beautiful copperplate script. At the bottom was an envelope in her father's handwriting, the postmark dated October 1904, just a few months after her birth. It was the time of her mother's mysterious disappearance. A subject that Dad and Gran found very difficult to discuss with her. Perhaps if she read the letter she would find out why. Sliding the pages out of the envelope she smoothed them flat and began to read.

Dear Ma,

I parted from you and my babes with such a heavy heart. All the shock of Mary going missing and then the policeman at the door with the terrible news. It has been the worst time of my life. And then to top it all, to really twist the knife, I had to face your not believing me.

The sight of that body and what the sea had done with it will haunt me all my days. It had to be Mary. I've never been so cold and frightened. The sergeant looked at me and I nodded then rushed out to be sick in the yard, couldn't stop shivering. I don't know how I managed to go back inside and sign my name to say that I had recognised Mary's body. All I wanted to do was crawl away somewhere and lose myself in sleep.

I felt hounded by you making me swear on the Bible. And still you called me a liar.

I know our marriage had gone bad but I didn't want her dead.

Ma, we must put these terrible days behind us, make our peace and look after Lily and Andrew.

If I have identified Mary mistakenly, surely she'll come back, if only for the sake of her children, and I will make my peace with her, as well.

Your Loving Son Alec.

The words leapt from the page at her like flames burning away her childhood certainties. Lily stared at them horrified at what they described. It was no new discovery to learn that her mother had drowned. This she had known as a small child. But she had not imagined that the body had been found, or that her father had been forced to see and identify it. To her, Mary Forrest, her mother had just floated away, never known and rarely thought of until Dad wanted to remarry. Gruesome as these new facts were they were not what appalled her most. It was the doubt that now began to eat away at her whole security. Even when he had sworn on the Bible, Gran had not believed him. Why? She would not have said that lightly. It was a terrible accusation. Gran had thought that Dad had lied to free himself of a wife he no longer wanted. And if she were right did it mean that her mother was still alive somewhere? Bitterly she regretted ever having opened the letter. Even if she now replaced the contents of the box she could not cancel the secret she had learned. It had confirmed fears that she had never consciously admitted to herself, sweeping away all her security. She had discovered a vital part of a jigsaw which made up a very different picture of her childhood than the one she was familiar with. But it could never be satisfactorily completed because of the missing pieces.

Lily began to cry. She sat on the bed, amid the yellowing packets of letters, with her arms around herself rocking backwards and forwards in her distress. There was no one to whom she could turn. Gran was part of the dreadful secret and if she told her she'd have to admit to opening the box. Dora had worries of her own and Mary had her own mother to grieve for. But at least she had known her, thought Lily, in a sudden spurt of anger.

No, she couldn't be still alive and not have come to see her children. Not let all their childhood pass away without some contact. Gran must have been mistaken. And if Dad had any doubts about his first wife's death, surely he would never have married Miriam. It would be more than he dared do. It would have been bigamy. He'd have risked going to prison.

Poor Dad, poor Miriam and Rosie and Joseph. The room in which Lily was now standing had once been Miriam's, when she first came as Uncle Albert's housekeeper. It had been shared by her and Dad when they married. In this room Lily had knelt on the floor, in front of Miriam, and helped little Joseph into the world. No, no it couldn't be true. There was too much for all of them to lose. But a worm of doubt gnawed away at her. Gran knew her son through and through, if anyone could tell if he were lying it would be her.

Why had Dad never really talked to her about her mother? Why were there no pictures of her? Once Gran had shown her a yellowing snapshot and given her a pair of her mother's gold earrings. Lily had gazed hungrily at the small heart-shaped face with the beautiful dark eyes and mass of long black hair. It had been like looking in a mirror. But there had been a row with Dad afterwards and the picture disappeared. Perhaps it was upstairs in the dressing-table in Gran and Albert's room. But she had lost her appetite for spying. She could almost hear Gran saying to her, 'If you pry into other people's secrets, you must live with the consequences.'

'Lily, Lily, where are you?' It was Dora calling her from the kitchen, any minute she would come into the bedroom and catch her spying. Hastily she thrust the remaining letters into the box, turned the key in the lock and slid it under the bed.

'What's up?' she said as she forced her father's letter back into its envelope and put it into her skirt pocket along with the key. She was brushing her hair by the time Dora put her head around the door.

'I need to borrow a shilling,' she said, 'so's Mary and her Dad can go up the asylum and see to her mum's arrangements.'

'How did they take the news?' Lily asked, as she took her handbag off the handle of the door and found two sixpences from her purse.

Dora shuddered. 'Ooh, that Mary, screamed her head off. It gave me the willies. Still they're all calmed down a bit now. The twins have taken Blyth out so while Mary and her dad's away I'll try and get the place a bit straight.'

'Tell you what,' offered Lily, desperate for distraction, 'I'll stick some spuds in the oven for all of us, then I'll give you a hand.'

'Lily, you're a real pal,' said Dora, putting the money in her pocket and giving her friend a quick hug. 'See you in a jiffy.'

Lily knew she must return the key to the glass dish. But what was she going to do with the piece of paper in her apron pocket? She'd throw it away, that's what she'd do, and never look at it again. Resolutely she went back upstairs. As she dropped the key into the dish she noticed that the green tassel was missing. Would Gran notice when she came back and sat at the dressing-table? Where was it, where was it, she fretted. Well there wasn't time to look for it now, Dora was waiting. Lily glared at the gloves lying innocently beside the glass dish. If only they stayed unnoticed until Gran returned. Uselessly her mind tried to unpick her actions as if they were careless stitches. What she must do was busy herself. Almost running she dashed down into the scullery and hauled some potatoes from the sack under the sink, scrubbed them, pricked them and put them inside the range to bake.

Stepping across the yard of her old home and into the Vines' scullery she found Dora bundling up a pile of dirty washing.

'I don't know what to do for the best,' she said. 'They'll be bringing Mrs Vine home before the funeral and they'll put her in the front room. I don't know whether to move Mary's mattress out or not. What d'you think? I don't want to interfere but if I do nothing it'll all be a muddle. The poor woman's got to have somewhere to be put decent for people to pay their respects.'

'Well,' said Lily, 'I think we'll take it upstairs and lay it in the twins' bedroom, then clean and straighten this room ready for the funeral people. They may not come 'til tomorrow but they won't want to hang about with the coffin waiting outside.'

'Right you are,' said Dora briskly. 'I'll just put this washing under the sink and deal with it tomorrow.'

'I'll nip back next-door and get a duster and some polish,' said Lily. For the next hour or so she lost herself in busyness, hauling the mattress up the stairs and helping Dora sweep and tidy the front room.

Her friend stood away from the mantelpiece over the little tiled fireplace and looked about her with satisfaction. 'Not half bad, now we've cleaned the mirror and polished everywhere. We ought to open the window, it smells a bit of wee. I don't know whether it's Blyth or that old dog.'

'I'll make us a cup of tea,' said Lily, 'I'm really parched.'

'You're a pal,' said Dora. 'Shall we bring the grub in here and eat it or have it in your place?'

'Let's keep them on their own patch,' said Lily firmly, 'I want to have my place nice for when Gran comes back.'

Barely had they created enough space in the Vines' kitchen and laid the table than the twins were back with Blyth and Towser hobbled in from the yard.

'In't 'arf cold,' said Faith, as she threw her coat off and stood with her arms crossed jigging about.

Mercy took off her coat and Blyth's and added them to the growing heap of assorted garments in the corner of the kitchen. Towser settled himself on top. Without waiting to be invited they dashed to the table and began pulling slices of meat off the the dish and cramming them into their mouths.

'Here,' said Dora sharply, 'you're not savages. Wait a minute while I set it out proper. There's your Dad to come and Mary.'

'He'll be up the pub,' said Faith, reaching for more meat and being slapped back by Dora. 'Besides our Mary wouldn't wait for us.'

'You're going to eat your dinner with us proper or we'll take the food next-door.'

Lily was amazed at Dora's firmness and the sudden obedience it produced. Soon she had set aside a plate for Mary and her dad and joined them all around the table where they ate in some degree of order.

'Blyth, you're a big boy now,' she said. 'Here, use this fork, that's better.'

The key rattled in the front door and there were footsteps in the passage. Whoever it was took their time about coming into the kitchen. Lily heard the front room door slam and Mary burst in on them. 'What's 'appened?' she demanded. 'Who's taken my bed? What you been doin', Dora?'

It was one thing to sort out the twins but facing their sister was another matter entirely. Lily watched her friend square her shoulders, get up from the table and turn towards the furious Mary. Sometimes little mousy-haired Dora could persuade her onlookers that she was twice the woman they thought she was, like she did with her Marie Lloyd imitations. With Mary her courage seemed to fail her and she was anxious and placating. 'I've been doing what your brother Harry would want me to do,' she said, avoiding the girl's furious stare. 'I've made the front room ready for when your Mum's brought back here.'

'That's me and Blyth's room,' said Mary, jabbing Dora in the ribs with her finger. 'Where we goin' to sleep?'

'Our Mum's dead,' said Mercy, 'we don't want to see her dead.'

Faith began to cry. Blyth leapt from the table and wrapped his arms around Mary's waist.

Lily felt sorry for Mary as she clung to her brother and stroked his hair with her fingers. Her hands with their bitten nails were those of a child. Her brown hair hung about her face in greasy strips and the coat she wore was too short with only one button hanging from a thread.

'Where's your Dad?' asked Lily, firmly. 'Never mind shouting at Dora.'

'Some bloke up the asylum was going to the funeral place and give 'im a lift in his car. Dunno when he'll be back.'

'I saved you some grub,' said Dora. 'Come and sit down. Here, Blyth, you can have a biscuit.'

'Why's our Mum comin' back here when she's dead?' asked Faith, rubbing her sleeve across her nose.

'So's you all can say goodbye to her,' said Dora quietly. 'It won't be for long. Then you'll have the funeral and it will all be over.'

'Will you come with us, you two?' asked Mary, her earlier fury forgotten. 'When we goes into the front room and sees her in her coffin?'

"Course we will,' said Dora, before Lily could protest.

Who would have thought yesterday when they were all laughing at Gran's wedding that in less than twenty-four hours she would have uncovered a terrible secret and be plunged in death? Lily smiled sourly to herself. She was like a heroine in a melodrama. 'Yes,' she said firmly, 'of course, I'll be there.'

'Wish your Gran was here,' mumbled Mary, voicing Lily's unspoken wish.

'Well she'll be back tomorrow. Meantime we'll just have to do the best we can. There's some daffodils growing in our old back yard. Why don't you go with Blyth and pick them after dinner and we can put them in a vase in the front room. It'll make it smell nice and look pretty.'

Mary nodded and then sat and picked at her food.

'What happened up at the asylum?' asked Dora from the scullery where she was filling a kettle.

'Dad had to sign papers. They said Mum died of satic monia or summink. Give him this bag wiv all her things in. Just her old clothes and shoes what she went in with and letters from Harry, what she never opened and others what she tore up in little pieces. He took it wiv him.'

Lily touched her apron pocket and the letter crackled under her hand. The words seemed to pulse through her fingers. *Called me a liar, I swear to you, back for the sake of her children.* She gripped her fork and tried to eat a slice of cold ham. It was thick and salty and seemed to rise up to the roof of her mouth and stay there blocking her throat when she tried to swallow.

'Faith and Mercy you come upstairs and help me make some space for Mary and Blyth,' said Dora, breaking into her thoughts. 'Lily, could you do the washing-up and Mary and Blyth you get the flowers? By the time your Dad gets back we'll be nice and straight.'

'Fat lot he'll care,' sniffed Mary.

As she swallowed the meat and began on the dishes, Lily wondered how early she and Dora could decently leave the Vines and salvage some time to themselves. If the coffin was brought back tomorrow they had promised Mary they'd be with her but surely, with a bit of luck when Fred returned from the undertaker they could disappear. She was hanging up the tea-towels over the fire-guard by the time Mary and Blyth came in with the daffodils.

The little boy was shivering and went straight to the battered old armchair and curled up in it by the fire. He began to cough and his sister cast him an anxious look. 'Don't you feel well, my babes?' she crooned kneeling down beside him. Blyth shook his head.

'We'll rub some camphorated on your chest and wrap a nice warm sock round yer neck.' Blyth nodded, his face flushed.

'I'll fetch a lemon and some honey from Gran's house and we'll make you a nice drink,' said Lily.

Dora washed a cracked glass vase and began arranging the daffodils while Mary fussed over her brother. After drinking Lily's hot lemon drink, having his chest rubbed with campho-rated oil and being swathed in a blanket Blyth dropped into a wheezy sleep.

They were all startled by a loud rapping on the front door and Mary hurried to answer it.

'If it's Fred we'll make ourselves scarce,' whispered Lily to Dora. 'We've done about as much as we can.'

White-faced, Mary hurtled into the kitchen. 'It's the funeral man with the coffin. What we goin' to do?'

'Is your Dad with them?' asked Dora hopefully.

Mary shook her head. 'Man said Dad told him he was comin' ahead to get things ready. He's buggered off to the pub, don't care about us.' She looked at the two older girls, her eyes pleading with them. 'You gotta do sommink,' she said.

Lily and Dora looked at one another as if trying to draw a collective decision from the air. The clock ticked and Blyth wheezed and snuffled. Mary bit her nails. Lily wished desperately that Gran would come home.

The three girls started with fright at the sound of someone clearing their throat. They turned around to find a man in a black coat standing in the passage. 'Mr Vine not here?' he asked looking irritably about him. 'We really need to leave the deceased here, now. Got another client to go to.'

Mary looked at Dora and Lily. 'What we goin' to do?'

Dora blushed and said hesitantly, 'The front room is ready. I suppose you could leave the . . .' Her words trailed away.

'Couldn't you come back tomorrow' asked Mary, 'when our Dad's here?'

The undertaker shook his head. 'I really would like to finish my job here, now.'

'What do we need to do?' asked Dora, straightening her shoulders.

Lily looked at her friend. It was obvious she was frightened but her loyalty to Harry overrode everything. How brave she is, she thought. I hope I would do so well if it was me.

'You just show me into the front room, young lady,' said the undertaker reassuringly, 'then take everyone into the kitchen. I'll let you know when we've finished.'

'I'll come with you,' said Lily. 'It's the least I can do. Mary, you get the twins down with you and Blyth. We'll see you in a minute.'

Dora's eyes flashed her thanks.

'This'll do fine,' said the tall undertaker, smoothing his moustache. 'Now hold back the front door and I'll get the trestles set up.'

Lily stared at the vase of flowers on the mantelpiece as the two undertakers carried the small coffin into the cold bare room. She thought of her father having to stand in the mortuary while they drew back the sheet. What had he really hoped for? Had he wanted her mother dead? What had gone wrong between them?

The two men, their coats shiny with rain, manoeuvred the coffin onto the trestles. As the shorter one passed around to the head of the elm box, Lily caught a whiff of violet cachous overlaying the smell of beer. 'Now, we'll remove the lid, ready for you to pay your respects.'

'Would you have time for a cup of tea in the kitchen, afterwards?' asked Dora, backing towards the door.

'That would be very kind,' said the tall undertaker, smiling mournfully. 'We'll leave the lid up against the wall, over there. You two young ladies can see to the tea. We can manage now.'

'Oh, I was so glad you was with me,' gasped Dora, as they hurried down the passage together.

Mary and the twins looked at them fearfully as they opened the door into the kitchen. Blyth was still asleep with the old dog curled up beside him.

'What we gotta do now?' asked Mary, looking at Dora with none of her usual antagonism.

'Nobody has to do nothing, 'til your Dad gets back,' said Dora as she set out some cups. 'The men have set everything straight. It's up to you. We can all go and see your Mum, together, if you want. Then you can tell your Dad what we've done and he can pay his respects on his own later.' She shrugged her thin shoulders. 'Up to you.'

Again they were startled by the coughing undertaker. 'Thank you kindly,' he said, taking the tea from Dora. The shorter man poured his tea into his saucer and began to blow on it, before slurping it noisily into his mouth. Faith and Mercy watched him closely.

'I'd like to extend to you children my deepest sympathy,' said the tall man. 'Tell your father, we'll be back Tuesday at midday to secure the coffin and to proceed to Kingston Cemetery for the funeral at one o'clock.'

Lily thought he was like an actor playing the part of an undertaker, trotting out the words, with the same counterfeit sympathy for each performance. The front door slammed behind the men and seemed to vibrate through the house.

Mary and the twins looked anxiously at each other.

Lily swallowed hard. 'Why don't we all go together, now, before your Dad gets back and while Blyth's asleep? Thinking about it'll only make it worse.'

'What d'you think?' asked Dora looking uncertainly at Mary. 'We could all hold hands. And you need only do it once. That way Blyth won't have to see his mum at all.'

The mention of her brother seemed to make the decision for her. She looked over at him as she began to chew her fingers. 'My little boy more'n ever he was hers,' she mumbled. 'Faith, Mercy, you hold Lily's 'ands and I'll go in front with Dora.'

It seemed that they all willed each other through the door. The coffin dominated the room. The twins gripped Lily's hands, their eyes darting about like those of frightened animals. It was Dora who first approached the still figure of Dolly Vine. She dipped her head over the side of the coffin and kissed the dead woman's face. Mary gave a quick intake of breath then, still holding Dora's hand, she kissed her mother. Had she not been holding hands with the twins Lily would have recoiled in horror. The person lying in the coffin bore no resemblance to Dolly Vine as she remembered her. The wild, red-haired, shouting, dancing neighbour, always on the move. The absolute stillness terrified Lily. Death had taken all the softness from Dolly's features causing her cheeks to sink in and her nose to sharpen. She seemed bleached. Her hair was dull and grey and her face had a washed-out yellow tinge. As Lily bent to kiss Dolly an overpoweringly sweet stench wafted up into her face, a mixture of stale breath and something she couldn't identify. Holding the twins' hands lent her a sliver of courage. If it had not been for them she would have run screaming from the room. Faith dug her nails into Lily's wrist as she bent to touch her mother's face, then Mercy stiffened and with clenched jaws swooped at her mother then back again, before running from the room.

'She's really dead,' she sobbed, 'really, really gone.'

Mary curled herself into the armchair around her brother's sleeping body. Faith and Mercy, still crying, trailed out of the room and up the stairs.

Lily looked at Dora sitting at the table and pleating the edges of the crumpled cloth between her fingers. 'I never knew your Mum,' Dora said to Mary, 'but Harry said she was ever so pretty.'

Mary sniffed and nodded her head.

Lily felt Dora looking at her trying to coax her into some response.

'She had goldy sort of hair, curly it was, and blue eyes like Blyth,' she said.

'Loved dancing,' mumbled Mary, 'used to swing us up in her arms when we was little and sing to us.'

'That's how you got to picture her now,' said Dora, re-pleating the cloth. 'When she was happy and smiling.'

'I can't hardly remember that,' said Mary, chewing her nails.

The sound of the key being pulled on its chain back through the letterbox halted any further talk between the girls. They sat listening to the uncertain footsteps making their way to the kitchen. The door opened and Fred Vine stood there shivering and crying.

Lily turned her head away unable to look at him.

'They brought my darlin' girl home yet, 'ave they?' he whined.

'No thanks to you,' snapped Mary. 'You just left us to it. No, don't you smarm round me.' She leapt to her feet and pushed away his attempts to kiss her. 'She's in the front room. No, no you're not going in there all pie-eyed and stupid.' Mary dragged him away from the door. 'Get up them stairs and sleep it off.'

'Mary, my little sweetheart, it's your Dad talking to you.'

'Well I wish you wasn't my Dad. I wish you'd just go away and leave us alone.'

Fred stood in the doorway, skinny, unkempt and reeking of drink. He smiled foolishly at Dora.

'You'll have to give us hand gettin' him up the stairs,' said Mary, 'else 'e'll fall down and hurt 'isself.' She hauled his left arm around her neck and indicated to Lily that she should take the right.

'Dor', you come behind, else we won't manage.'

Trying not to inhale the stink of sweat and booze, Lily nerved herself to loop Fred's arm around her neck. Pushing, shoving and swaying the three girls heaved him up the stairs.

'You 'ang on to him, Lil, while I gets the door,' gasped Mary.

Crabwise, Dora and Lily edged across the room and deposited Fred on top of a tangle of frowsty sheets. For a few seconds the scene teetered on the edge of comedy reminding Lily of the cavortings of Charlie Chaplin.

As they were about to creep from the room Fred opened his eyes and grinned foolishly at them. He waved his hand in time to an imaginary tune. 'So goodnight, pretty ladies, goodnight,' he warbled.

The three girls went down to the kitchen where the sleeping Blyth had been joined by the old dog. 'Poor little boy,' sighed Mary, 'he don't know what's 'appening.'

'Well, he's got you, Mary. That's all that counts with him,' said Dora.

'We'd better go back to Gran's and tidy up,' said Lily, anxious to make her escape.

'You sure you'll be all right?' asked Dora.

Mary nodded. 'I'm going to lock the front room. Our Dad

can go in there when he's sobered up. Don't want Blyth to get frightened or nothin'.

Lily felt ashamed of her eagerness to leave. She and Dora could climb over the back wall and slough off the problems of the Vines like so much dead skin. Mary was stuck in the mess created by her shiftless parents with no escape. No wonder she got jealous and ratty.

'Look, if you're worried about Blyth's cough or anything, send the twinnies down to us,' said Dora.

Mary nodded. 'Bye,' she said turning back into the kitchen.

'I don't know about you,' said Dora, as they let themselves back into Albert's house, 'but I'm fit to drop. It's not the cleaning up and cooking it's all the geeing them up all the time. Trying to set them straight. And Mary just seems to draw out all my energy. Lil, whatever's the matter. What you crying for? Anyone would think it was your mother what had been taken.'

'Yes,' sobbed Lily, 'I feel as if it was.'

Chapter Four

Her time away with Albert had been wonderful but now she wanted to go home. 'Treats are not treats if you have them all the time,' she said. 'It's the rareness that makes them special.'

'So you wouldn't enjoy strawberries in December or sprouts in July?' teased Albert standing at the bedroom window of the cowman's cottage with his arms around her waist.

Beattie leant back against him delighting in his closeness. 'Quite right,' she said. 'Look what Samuel was saying about his cows. They're in the barn out of the cold in the winter and then come spring they go back into the fields, almost dancing to be in the air and at that fresh green grass. Change and contrast – that's what makes life interesting.'

'I suppose I'm being selfish – I want to cling on to you a bit longer. Once we're back in Lemon Street you'll be swallowed up in everyone's concerns.'

'And won't you be itching to get at your painting?'

'Well,' he said consideringly, 'I have got a few ideas for the Marine Artists' Competition next year.'

'There you are,' she said briskly. 'Now if we're going to catch the eleven-thirty train we'd best get ourselves in the rig of the day.'

'Shame about the Daimler,' said Albert, 'I so enjoyed treating you like a duchess.'

'And I revelled in putting on the swank,' laughed Beattie, 'but I'm a Pompey sparrow not a peacock. Besides I can't remember when I last had a train ride. I've stood on many a station in my time holding back the tears. Now we'll take our time, look out the window and steam into the harbour station all refreshed and ready for the next chapter.'

The shrill of the whistle and the hiss of the steam almost drowned out their goodbyes to Olive and Samuel.

Beattie hugged her sister-in-law. 'Thank you for making me so welcome,' she said, 'and please don't wait for a wedding or a funeral to drop down and see us.'

'We'll come down before haymaking,' Olive said, 'I like a drop of sea air.'

'Bye Sammy, old man.' Albert shook his brother's hand before holding the carriage door open for Beattie.

'We're going home, we're going home,' the words chugged in her head in tune to the swaying of the train. Beattie shifted her position and looked up at the picture above the seats opposite. It was a watercolour of Sandown Pier in the Isle of Wight. The colours were muted, lemon sand and pastel blue sea with children in straw hats paddling in the shallows. A young girl laughing and clutching the arm of a sailor got on the train at Bursledon reminding her of Lily. For the first time that day Beattie wondered how she and Dora had fared with the house to themselves. She hoped they'd enjoyed themselves, Dora especially. Beattie had grown fond of the girl. She was so warm-hearted and eager to please.

'Look Beatrice,' said Albert pointing out of the window at the clumps of primroses growing on the banks by Swanwick station.

At the market town of Fareham halfway to Portsmouth another young sailor got on and leaned out of the carriage window kissing his young wife and baby until the whistle blew.

'We're going home, we're going home,' chugged the train as they passed Portchester and Beattie got a sighting of the castle and the first view of the sea.

'Portsmouth Harbour, Portsmouth Harbour,' announced the guard.

Exultantly Beattie clutched Albert's arm. 'Don't call a taxi yet,' she said. 'Let's just stand here a minute and drink it all in.'

On either side of the bridge leading to The Hard with its pubs and hotels were wide stretches of mud.

'Good old Pompey stink,' laughed Albert, 'seaweed, cockles and Brickwood's Beer.'

'Come on lady spare us a tanner,' called a lanky mudlark in a spattered cap with a broken brim.

'They've put up their prices,' Beattie said as she fished a coin from her pocket and flung it over the bridge. 'I carried on top ropes to Lily and Andrew when they tried their hand at this lark. Sent them to bed with no supper and put their takings in the poor-box at St George's.'

Albert laughed. 'Always were bossy.'

Beattie laughed up at him. 'It was a lovely holiday, Albert,' she said, 'and a wonderful start to our marriage but oh, I'm glad to get home.'

'What is it that charms you so about Portsea?' he asked. 'It can't be the golden sands and it's certainly not the beauty of the buildings.'

'Well it's not my birthplace, as you know,' said Beattie. 'I was washed up on the beach like so much flotsam, tucked in a sailor's oilskin. Often wondered if he was my dad. But it became home. I've survived and put down roots. The first sound I heard was the sea and it's beat in my ears ever since. Brought up in a town of survivors. Especially the women. Against the odds all of us eking out our lives with bits of sewing, corsets, sailors' collars, officers' epaulettes. Grubbing for firewood, collecting rags and jam-jars, even some women on their backs. Living between the tides of men at home and men at sea. Waving and waiting. Trying to keep our love alive in letters and pictures, existing on pecked fruit and paper kisses.' She took his hand and drew it through her arm. 'You know last year, on Lily's birthday when we went down to Clarence beach and we all stood on the shingle waving Michael's ship away, I had this strong feeling of, well you'll laugh at this.'

'Try me.'

'Of almost standing in the footprints of the women that had gone before us, waving their men off to Trafalgar, and the Crimea and the war with the Boers. Miriam and Lily and me leaving our footprints for the women who'll come after.'

'Beatrice, you're an artist,' said Albert, squeezing her hand.

'How d'you make that out?'

'With words. You've brought it all so vividly alive for me.'

Beattie glowed. 'You're an old charmer, Albert Pragnell,' she said. 'Now let's take a handle each of this bag and get ourselves home.'

The early April afternoon wind was chill and they hastened their steps. They passed families strolling in Queen Street, some going up to the harbour and others down to Victoria Park with its statues and flowerbeds. The mothers and daughters sported new Easter hats or at the least some fresh ribbon trimmings. Young women giggled as they passed groups of sailors who whistled appreciatively.

'It's a new chapter for both of us,' said Albert as they turned the corner into Cross Street. 'I've been a bachelor all my life. I've had Mother to cook for me and then of course young Miriam. But I'm a novice at marriage. That's where I shall be under your instruction.'

Beattie chuckled. 'I shall be tender with you,' she said, laughing with him. 'But, then, I've been a widow for twenty years or more. I'll have to find myself afresh. No need for me to sew sailors' collars anymore. There'll be plenty of young women glad of the chance. Lily will be up and away, once Michael Rowan's back home.'

Albert laughed. 'You know those old novels they have with a title for each chapter?'

Beattie nodded.

'Ours will say – "Wherein Albert and Beatrice set their feet on a new path on the journey to the Celestial City".'

Beattie tapped him playfully on the arm. 'I know why I married you Albert – because you're full of nonsense.'

As they turned into Lemon Street they saw the curtains twitch at number 25. A few seconds later the front door opened and Lily hurtled down the street towards them. 'Gran, oh Gran, I'm so pleased you're back.' She rushed into her grandmother's arms almost knocking her to the ground, then burst into noisy tears.

Beattie was astonished.

'Give me the bag, I'll go ahead and put the kettle on,' said Albert, taking the key from his pocket.

'Let me get indoors and gather my wits, Lily love,' gasped Beattie, thoroughly alarmed. After Lily's outburst she was relieved to find the house still standing and afternoon tea laid on a spotless white cloth. She hung up her coat and settled herself in an armchair by the fire. 'Just pour me a cup of tea and then you can give me your news with both barrels.'

'Would you rather I made myself scarce?' asked Albert, making towards the door.

'Certainly not,' said Beattie firmly. 'This is your home, you sit yourself down, Albert. Lily will pour us all a cup of tea and we'll take it from there.'

'Oh Gran it was awful,' she burst out the moment they were settled. 'Mrs Vine died up at the asylum and Dora and me had to cope with everything. Getting the front room ready and showing the girls how to pay their last respects. And Fred was drunk and we had to help him up the stairs. Our Easter was ruined.'

'I don't expect Mary, Faith and Mercy had much of a time either,' said Beattie, 'poor kids.' She took Lily's hands in hers. 'It sounds to me like you were two young women to be proud of supporting them all.'

'I felt so frightened and so did Dora. I'd never seen a dead person before,' sniffed Lily, reaching into her pocket for a hankie and dabbing her eyes. 'She was so still and cold and didn't look a bit like I remembered her. I wanted to run away, but well,' she shrugged her shoulders, 'we couldn't just leave them.'

Beattie put her arms around her granddaughter and let her cry out her distress. When she became calmer she said, 'There'll be other Easter holidays, love. Neighbourliness is never wasted. Besides it will give you something to put in your letter to Michael.'

Lily gave Albert an apologetic smile. 'I'm sorry Uncle Albert, to spoil your homecoming.'

'What have you spoiled?' he asked, passing her a buttered scone. 'A lovely meal awaiting us and the house spick and span. Now I shall go and pay my respects to the Vine family and see you in a while.'

Beattie watched her granddaughter. There was something else, something she was hiding. What was it? 'Where's Dora?' she asked. 'It can't have been much of a break for her either.'

'It was worse for her because of Harry. They seem to think she's family already and draw her into everything and sort of swallow her up.'

'Is she still next-door?'

'We told them we had to tidy up in here today otherwise Dora wouldn't have had a moment. I took her breakfast in bed and we just stayed in here talking. Went home about an hour ago.'

'You'll have to keep an eye on Dora,' said Beattie, pouring herself another cup of tea. 'She has a poor valuation of herself.

Always working to earn approval. She'll get overburdened if she's not careful.'

'It's good to have you home,' said Lily, cutting in. 'I'll go and fetch Granddad's box. Where do you want it putting?'

'It can stay where it is, for the time being,' said Beattie, 'it's not eating anything. It'll take Albert and me a week or two to get our things settled. There's no rush is there?'

Lily shook her head. 'I'll just wash up and then I'll go and write to Michael.'

'I'll see to the dishes,' said Beattie, 'it'll give me something to do.'

After an hour or so, Albert came back saying that he would help Fred to finalise the funeral arrangements in the morning.

'I'll call in tomorrow and see what's needed, but tonight I just want to sit by the fire and gather myself.'

Lily came back from her bedroom and she and Albert settled to a game of draughts.

Beattie watched her granddaughter. After her initial outburst she seemed normality itself as she laughingly took a king from Albert. Of course the first sight of a dead body was bound to be upsetting especially someone you knew. And the absence of any responsible adult didn't help one iota. Fred Vine was neither use nor ornament.

Later when she sat at her dressing-table combing her hair Beattie noticed the gloves she'd been searching for just before they left on honeymoon. She was certain they'd been downstairs by the armchair. Lily must have brought them up, but why? They could have been put in the dresser drawer. What could she have come up for? Beattie looked at the various items around her: a hairbrush, a handkerchief, a powder-bowl, a glass dish with hairpins, a packet of cachous, a few coins and the key to Joseph's ditty-box. She held it in her hand twisting it absentmindedly in her fingers. And then it came to her, the little green tassel was missing. What had Lily done with it?

Chapter Five

The only sound in the room was the scraping of her father's pen over the card leaving a trail of misshapen letters. Beside him the wreath of daffodils and laurel leaves exuded a green earthy scent. The ash on the end of his cigarette fell on the words: 'In loving memory of my wife Dolly from Fred and the children.'

'Why couldn't you put Mum's proper name?' Mary demanded.

He put down the pen and stared at the table saying nothing.

'Has Mummy gone to heaven?' asked Blyth sliding off her lap and going to stand beside his father. The words hung unanswered in the air along with the overpowering reek of camphorated oil seeping from Blyth's vest.

Dad stared out of the window his jaws clenched and tears glinting in his eyes. 'Gone for an angel,' he gasped. A tear splashed onto the card, making the ink run. 'It'll have to do,' he flung at his daughter before going back upstairs.

Mary knew he felt belittled by her, his fumbling efforts made worthless by her silent scorn. 'Go up and give your Dad a cuddle,' she said.

Her brother rubbed his sleeve across his nose. 'It's cold and stinky up there.'

'Give me my coat, there's a sweet in the pocket.'

Blyth began laboriously to pick the fluff off the pear-drop.

'Please babes, just for a tic,' she pleaded. 'Call you down ever so quick, I will.'

Reluctantly Blyth went upstairs after his father.

Mary took down her much-prized fountain pen from the dresser shelf. Snatching up an old envelope she practised thin upstrokes and thick down ones. Licking her chapped lips she began to write on the reverse side of the card: *In loving memory of Dorothy Vine from her husband Frederick and children, Harry, Mary, Faith, Mercy and Blyth.'* As an afterthought she added, *'Born April 1st 1882 died March 27th 1921.'* When the ink was dry she threaded the card onto the wreath and tied the ribbon in a small bow. Taking the key off the dresser she unlocked the front room and set the flowers on a chair beside her mother's open coffin before darting out the door.

Ever since Mum had been taken away screaming into the police ambulance Mary and her brothers and sisters had lurched from one crisis to another. At first her brother Harry had been sent home from his gunnery course. Lily's gran had helped the pair of them to set the place in order. Mary and her brother had worked well together and got things running reasonably smoothly. Apart from visiting Mum, who sat blank-faced, her eyes like the windows of an empty house, tearing paper and gibbering, those six months before Dad came back had been happy. She knew where the next meal was coming from and what was to happen the next day. Blyth had stopped wetting the bed they shared and his talking galloped ahead. Really, he was her little boy. The twins had each other and she had Blyth.

Dad's return had tipped them into chaos. It had been a wonderful rackety first few weeks with more presents than they'd ever had, but then everything had fallen apart with Dad and Harry rowing all the time. Then Harry got all moony over Dora and worse still he was sent out east for another three years. Grudgingly, Mary had to admit to herself that Dora had been kindness itself to all of them. Without her and Lily setting things straight they wouldn't have survived the last few days. The twins loved Dora and so did Dad. Blyth would have loved her too, but Mary wouldn't let him.

Shrugging her narrow shoulders Mary went into the passage and called up the stairs. 'Cup of tea down here for you two.' It was twelve o'clock, dinner time. The twins would be back from school any minute, ravenous as usual. Mary shrugged, they'd all have to make do with toast and broken biscuits.

Dad and Blyth hurriedly came downstairs and settled themselves by the fire as the twins burst in from the front door. They flung their coats in a heap in the armchair. 'What's to eat?' demanded Faith hitching up her skirt and standing in front of the fire.

'Drippin', toast and biscuits. Here's the toasting-fork, I'll pour the tea.'

'Miss Lavender sends her condiments,' said Mercy nudging her sister away from the fire.

'No it was convalescences,' snapped Faith.

'Don't matter what it was, she said she was sorry for our loss,' said Faith taking a piece of ginger biscuit out of the bag.

'Where's your mother's flowers?' asked Dad, perching on the edge of the armchair and holding out his hands to the fire.

'In the front room,' said Mary, spooning sugar into his tea.

'I'd best go and pay my last respects,' he said and shuffled to his feet.

'No, it's all tidy in there now,' protested Mary. 'I've cleared the beer out of the cupboard and given it to Lily's gran. She's goin' to get a tea ready, later, in case anyone wants to come back with us.'

'Daddy, you makin' me toast?' wheedled Blyth handing him the fork.

Resignedly her father sat down again and began threading a slice of bread onto the toasting fork.

'I wonder if Gran and Auntie Betty'll come down from Yorkshire,' said Faith, warming her hands on her cup of tea.

'She'll get sent off again with a bloody round turn,' said Dad fiercely.

'Like she did after Jutland,' said Mary, smiling at her father.

'What Jutland?' asked Blyth, his face flushed by the fire.

'Before you was born, my young sprog,' Dad chuckled. 'Your Ma and sisters was all coming back from the Memorial Service in the park, a-weeping and a-wailing, thinking I was drownded. And blow me down I'd been rescued and was sat outside our house bold as brass waiting for all of you. Poor old Towser was leapin' about fit to bust, your Ma was laughin' and cryin' both at the same time. Then along comes your gran, poison-Ada. Pitches into me good and proper. Real disappointed I hadn't been lorst at sea. I chased her down the street and threatened to tan her backside.'

It was one of those good moments with her dad when Mary forgot the rows and the lies and the misspent money. Moments she wanted to stretch out to cover the other times of drink and disappointment. In those good moments she loved her father suddenly and fiercely.

'Dad, Dad, you're burnin' the toast.' Mercy snatched the fork and blew out the flames.

'Here, let Faith do it,' said Mary, putting a cup of strong sweet tea into her father's hands.

'Shall we take Blyth into Granny Pragnell's? That's what she wants us to call her, now,' said Faith.

'No,' said Mary, 'she's coming in here to get the tea ready and everything. You might as well go back to school.'

'See ya later,' said Mercy reaching for her coat.

'Hark! there someone at the front door,' said Dad. 'Most likely it's the undertakers for the coffin. Won't be any mourners. I 'spect vinegary Ada and Betty's goin' straight to the cemetery.

Mercy, you go and show them into the front room while I get myself ready.'

Mary reached up and took down the clothes brush from a hook on the dresser.

'Let's give you a bit of a brush off,' she said to Dad as she straightened his collar. He was in his number one naval uniform with its bell-bottomed trousers, tight jersey and striped collar. After twenty years in the navy he was still only a three-badge able-seaman. He had been promoted to Leading Hand more than once always to be demoted again for lateness, missing items of uniform or drunkenness on duty.

There was a tap on the kitchen door and a tall man in a top hat with a crepe ribbon stood in the doorway. He coughed respectfully. 'Mr Vine,' he said. 'We need to put the lid down, now. Would you like a moment with your wife, before we do so?'

'Come with us, gal,' said her father taking her hand.

Unwillingly she followed him.

As they entered the front room the two black-coated pall-bearers stood aside to allow Mary and her father to approach the coffin.

'You first,' said Dad.

Mary bent over the side and kissed the cold cheek of the figure who had once been her mother.

'Bye, Doll,' croaked Dad, barely able to get the words out. He wiped the tears away with his fingers then glanced at the wreath waiting on the chair, holding up the card to read Mary's swirling copperplate writing and perfectly spelt words. For a moment he met her eyes and she knew that she had shamed him. He stepped back into the passage looking shrunken and defeated.

'If you just go back into the kitchen for a few minutes, we'll let you know when we're ready to set off.'

Mary brushed her short brown hair away from her face and tied one of the twins' red wool scarfs around her head before putting on her coat.

'Thought you'd be staying home with Blyth to get the tea ready,' said Dad, shuffling his feet.

'No, said Mary, 'I'm coming with you. Mrs Pragnell can sort that out.'

Dad gave his nose a resounding blow into a ragged handkerchief. He held out his arm to her. 'Thanks, gal,' he said.

They stepped out together into the street. All the curtains were drawn and the neighbours stood in their doorways with their heads bowed.

Mr Pragnell came out of his house and shook their hands before taking his place behind them in the funeral procession.

Nobody said anything as they set off, walking behind the coffin in its open wheeled carriage and the pall-bearers in their tall black hats and crêpe ribbons. The only sounds were the clopping of the horses and the rattle of the harness. Mary slipped her hand through Dad's arm feeling him trembling with cold in the chill April wind. They walked down Queen Street past the two naval barracks, officers on one side and ratings on the other, and crossed the town on the long walk to Kingston cemetery.

How long ago it seemed since her mother had been with her, really present in her life. Ages before she ever went to the asylum. When was is that she had last felt safe and had known that her mother would look after her? Mary frowned. It must have been when the twins were small before Harry went off as a boy seaman to Greenwich. Slowly as her childhood had progressed her sense of safety had ebbed away like water down a plughole. Always she was being urged to be a big girl and told that 'Mummy's relying on you.' She was the one who told the tally man that Mummy wasn't in, or put the twins to bed because Mummy was tired. At eight years old she hadn't wanted to be a big girl; she didn't much fancy it now.

Thank goodness Blyth seemed more confused than upset by everything.

Understandable really, thought Mary, his mother had been in

the asylum for most of the last year. When she had been home she'd never been more than a spasmodic figure in his life. She smiled to herself. 'Mary' was the first word he'd said, and it was to her and not his mother that he held out his chubby arms.

'Christ, I'd forgotten about them. What in God's name have they come for?' snarled Dad, making Mary jump.

Outside the cemetery gates stood Grandma Scovell and Auntie Betty dressed head to foot in black like a pair of mournful ravens. Skinny Gran and fat tearful Betty.

'Can't of come for the pickings. But they're after something,' said Dad.

Mary couldn't tell him what childless Auntie Betty had come for. It didn't bear thinking about.

'I'm sick to my back teeth with hearing about the Vines,' roared her father when Dora rushed home at dinner time to get her black hat for the funeral. 'Taking time off for a woman you've never met – losing money. Here's me slaving to keep you while you charge around after that feckless tribe.'

'But Dora pays her keep here and is always helping,' said her brother Barney quietly.

'What gave you the right to chip in,' snapped her father. 'Who pays for your dockyard apprenticeship I'd like to know?'

Dora tried to flash him a grateful glance but he was staring angrily at the tablecloth.

'George, don't upset yourself,' said her mother nervously.

'Dad,' said her older brother Mark, from the doorway. 'Chap in the shop come to collect his bike repair. Wants to speak to you, specially.'

'Can't you deal with anything on your own?' snapped his father, flinging down his knife and fork and slamming down the stairs.

'Mum, sit down and have your dinner. I'll put Dad's plate in the oven,' said Dora moving towards the kitchen.

Mum's face was creased with anxiety. 'It'll get dried up and upset his stomach.'

'Please, don't let me be like you,' Dora prayed, 'scuttling about apologising all my life.'

'I'm off now,' said Barney, 'walk down the road with you?'

'Bye, Mum,' said Dora. 'Don't save me any tea, I'll have something with the nippers after the funeral.'

'Poor little scraps,' her mother sighed, 'give them my best won't you?'

'Dad makes me so wild,' said Barney as they shut the front door. 'I know he's fretting about the shop losing money but taking it out on us won't help. What with them and batty Gran . . .'

'We should take a leaf out of Mark's book, all he worries about is himself,' said Dora, thinking of her elder brother lounging behind the counter with a newspaper.

'Marry your Harry and sail away,' said Barney, kissing her on the cheek.

'Bye, and thanks for sticking up for me,' said Dora, waving after him. She hurried up to Commercial Road and just managed to catch her bus for St Mary's Church. After the tears and strains of the weekend she was dreading Mrs Vine's funeral and being dragged further into the family's affairs.

As she stepped off the bus the church clock struck one - she was late. Panic-stricken she began to run up the road to Kingston Cemetery. Breathless and sweating she hurried through the large wrought-iron gates. The cemetery was overwhelming. The central tree-lined path seemed to stretch forever with not a soul in sight. She reached a drinking fountain and held her hand under a trickle of water to quench her thirst. Looking up she saw, in the distance, some black horses harnessed to a carriage at the top of one of the side paths. As she drew level Dora saw Fred, Mary and Mr Pragnell with their heads bent, standing beside a priest reading from a prayer book. The coffin was being lowered into the ground. It took her some time to gather her breath and hear what was being said due to the noise of a train passing by on the other side of the cemetery wall. Mr Pragnell nodded to her and Mary stared unseeingly ahead.

' *"The days of man are but as grass: for he flourisheth as a flower of the field. For as soon as the wind goeth over it, it is gone: and the place thereof shall know it no more"* ' the vicar intoned.

Dora stood behind two women and wondered who they were. Harry had mentioned a grandmother. 'A right old tartar' and his mother's sister Auntie Betty who was 'Loony about Jesus.' As they lived miles away in Yorkshire she had paid little attention to his descriptions, not expecting ever to see them. Strange that they had come all that way for the funeral and yet had never, to her knowledge, visited when Dolly was ill and could have done with their help.

Fred scattered some earth on the coffin and then it was Mary's turn. She continued to stare ahead and threw wildly. The earth fell short of the grave all over Fred's shoes.

The vicar shook hands with everyone and the undertakers moved off, followed by Mary and her father. Mr Pragnell accompanied the mysterious women and Dora hurried uncertainly after them.

' 'Ello Dora, love,' said Fred. 'Good of you to come.'

She felt a rare glimmer of sympathy for him as he stood shivering with his daughter clutching his arm. Always he disappointed people, unable to meet even their smallest expectations. Perhaps that was why he drank so much, disappointment with himself, she thought.

As they reached the main path the younger, fatter woman suddenly lunged at Mary and wrapped her in her arms. 'You poor, poor, child,' she wailed.

'Geroff, geroff me Auntie Betty,' shouted Mary, pushing her away. 'Dad, come on, let's leave them and go home.'

'I've ordered a car to take everyone back to Lemon Street,'

said Mr Pragnell, turning around to face them. 'Mrs Scovell, do you and your daughter want to be dropped off at the Town Station?'

'No thank you,' Mary's grandmother snapped. 'We've got business back at the house with Mr Vine.'

'That's news to me,' said Fred, glaring at the small spiteful-looking woman. 'You can't 'ave come for Dolly's leavings 'cos there ain't none.'

'Mary knows what we've come for don't you my dear?' said Aunt Betty.

The car drew up at the cemetery gates and Mr Pragnell raised his arm to the driver. 'I suggest we all get inside before anyone gets a chill,' he said. 'Whatever business you have can be done over a cup of tea.'

'I'll catch the bus,' said Dora, 'and see you all back at the house.'

Mary clutched her arm and whispered urgently in her ear. 'You gotta come wiv us. Sommink terrible's goin' to happen.'

Wedged between Mary's grandmother and her father, Dora could feel the antagonism between them. Mrs Scovell exuded soap, starch and order while Fred reeked of sweat and slovenliness. At Lemon Street, Mr Pragnell got out quickly and held open the door for everyone.

Dora felt a surge of relief as she saw Beattie standing in the open doorway of the Vines' house, smiling at everyone. 'Come in Fred, and Mrs Scovell, Betty, such a long time since I've seen you,' she said, sweetly. 'Take a chair, you must be chilled to the bone. There's tea or a glass of sherry. Albert, pour Fred a rum: he must be shrammed with the cold.'

'Where's Blyth?' asked Mary, tugging at Beattie's hand.

'I've slipped him upstairs to his bed. That cold of his is going to his chest.'

'Fred, dear chap,' said Albert. 'We'll have a drop of Nelson's blood together, you and I.'

'Now ladies, which is it to be?' asked Beattie.

'We'll have tea, don't believe in intoxicants,' said Ada Scovell, glaring at Fred.

'We've business to attend to.'

'Right you are,' said Beattie briskly, 'I'll pour the tea and then I'll leave you, if you don't mind. I've things to do indoors.'

Dora's heart sank. Beattie would have been a welcome buffer between the warring parties, now there was only herself. She cast about for some excuse to leave when Mary nudged her sharply. 'You gotta take this,' she said, 'and read it out to everyone.'

Flustered, and feeling all eyes on her, Dora took the piece of paper that Mary passed her under the table and slid it into the sleeve of her blouse.

'I'm going up ter see Blyth,' said Mary.

Betty rose awkwardly to her feet, 'I'm sure the little lad would like to see his auntie,' she said, looking ingratiatingly at her niece.

'He don't never want to see you,' Mary snapped.

'You mind your manners, miss,' said her grandmother, her voice icy with disapproval.

'Dad,' said Mary, 'you gotta listen to the letter what Betty wrote. Dora's goin' to read it. If you don't do sommink I'll hate you forever.' She slammed out the room.

Dora blushed at suddenly being the focus of attention. 'Please, Mr Vine,' she said, trying to pass him the letter. 'It's none of my business.'

'That's my letter,' said Betty, looking flustered. 'I don't think I put it very well, it would be better . . .'

'You're family, Dor,' said Fred firmly, 'more to my kids than this old crow and her lardy daughter. Go on, fire away. Lost my readers anyway.'

'Before you begin your business,' said Mr Pragnell, 'I'll take my leave of you.'

Dora felt abandoned. Nervously she licked her lips before smoothing out the paper and beginning to read.

My Dear Little Mary,
    I was heartbroken to hear of the death of your dear mother.
She was a wonderful sister and I shall miss her dreadfully.

Fred blew a derisive raspberry, 'Miss her my backside!' he
snorted. 'Oh, sorry,' he said to Dora 'Carry on, carry on.'

    You must be very worried especially with a father who can't
be relied on. Of course you are old enough, now, to go out to
work yourself but it is little Blyth that worries me and your
Uncle Herbert.

'Now we're getting to it,' said Fred, menacingly.
    Swallowing nervously Dora continued.

    We could offer him a fine life in up in Yorkshire and would
want to make him our own little boy. Once he is with us it will
be easier for him to settle if all contact with his old family is cut.
You are a big girl now, and I'm sure you will see it is for the
best. I've put in a ten-shilling note for you to get some flowers
from me and your grandmother.
    Your loving Auntie Betty

Dora sat staring at her hands waiting for someone to break the
silence.
    As everyone drew breath the twins dashed down the passage
and into the room. They looked warily at everyone and at the
untouched food.
    ''Allo my gals,' said their father. 'What d'you think? Auntie
Betty's come down to take your brother away with her.'
    'What for?' asked Faith, taking a cheese sandwich from the
plate Dora held out to her.
    'She ain't got no kids of her own so she's come to steal
mine.'

'That's not fair,' whined Betty. 'I'm offering the little chap a new start in life, far better than he's got here with you.'

'We don't 'ave to go do we?' asked Mercy, in alarm.

'No, she don't want you or your sisters, it's Blyth what she's after.'

'But 'e blongs to us,' said Faith.

'What can you give him?' snapped Ada Scovell getting to her feet.

'We loves 'im,' said Mercy, glaring at her grandmother.

Ada looked scornfully at the battered furniture and then at her son-in-law. 'This place is going to rack and ruin. And you, Fred Vine, couldn't even clean your shoes for your wife's funeral.'

Fred stared past her to a spot on the faded wallpaper, his jaw tight with anger. The moment she paused to draw breath he was out of his seat and facing her. 'Why don't you cut out my heart? Why leave me with anything, you cruel bitch?' He struggled to keep control of himself, gasping and holding his hand over his eyes. 'Blyth's my little nipper and I'm his dad,' he said in a fierce whisper.

'But Fred,' wheedled Betty, 'you've got the girls. Me and Herbert have not been blessed with children.'

Wailing loudly the twins rushed towards the door. 'Mary, Mary,' they screamed, 'Auntie Betty takin' our Blyth.'

Unnoticed by the warring factions, Dora grabbed the back of Mercy's dress, and dragged her into the scullery. 'Over the back and get Granny Pragnell, chop, chop,' she commanded.

'Christ! You two puts me in such a rage.' Fred was shouting into Betty's face.

'Where were you when my Dolly was ill? Where were you when the kids was bare-arsed and snot-nosed? Only time you roused yourself when you thought I'd copped it off Jutland.' He gave an ugly mirthless laugh. 'As for your precious Herbert, what shot his finger off just before the call-up. 'E should of shot 'is dick off for all the good it's done you.'

Dora watched Betty flush an angry red, her chins trembling like turkey wattles. She glared at Fred.

'Vulgarity, that was always your way, Fred Vine,' snapped Mrs Scovell. 'But we're Dolly's flesh and blood. And don't think you can just sweep us out of the way. We've taken advice on the matter. Almoner up at the asylum said I could get a welfare report done. We've not finished not by a long chalk.'

Faith and Mary with Blyth in her arms, stampeded down the stairs and into the room.

Mercy dashed in from the kitchen and kicked Betty in the shins.

Ada swung out wildly at her and hit Mary instead.

As she gasped under the impact of the blow Betty tugged at Blyth and wrenched him out of Mary's arms. She grabbed her brother and a wrestling match ensued with Blyth, suddenly woken from sleep, screaming in terror.

Dora's heart was hammering against her ribs. She wanted to run as far and as fast as she could. But what would Harry think of her if she abandoned his family and Blyth got taken away?

On the edges of the turmoil, Beattie Pragnell stepped into the room. Quickly taking in the scene she bent and picked up a paper bag off the top of a cupboard and began to blow into it. Around her the screaming and tugging continued unabated. As Fred aimed a punch at Ada Scovell there was a loud bang.

Blyth, joggling about in Betty's arms, was promptly sick all over her. Sobbing hysterically Auntie Betty collapsed into an armchair and Mary wrenched her brother out of her arms.

'What in heaven's name is going on?' said Beattie, glaring around her.

Everyone spoke at once.

'They're stealing my kid,'

'She hit me, the old bitch.'

'Lardy witch, lardy witch,' shouted Mercy jumping up and down.

'Crow face, crow face,' screeched Faith.

'Silence,' Beattie commanded. 'Mary take Blyth out to the scullery and clean him up. Dora get a cloth and help Betty to tidy herself.'

'If you don't leave my house this minute' stormed Fred,' I'll throw you out, the pair of you.' He moved menacingly towards Betty.

'You touch a hair of her head and you'll be summonsed,' squawked Ada. 'Then who'll look after your children?'

'Fred,' snapped Beattie, 'you're playing into their hands. If the police get involved you could well lose your nipper. For pity's sake take hold of yourself. Mary, change your brother's clothes, give him a drink and take him back to bed. That little boy is not fit to go anywhere. Tonsillitis if I'm not mistaken.'

'Reckon the police'll want to know how often you've been to see my little lad,' said Fred sulkily. 'Be surprised to find 'ow he's hardly set eyes on the pair of you.'

'Oh look at my blouse,' wailed Betty, 'it'll stain, and the smell! We've got to go back to London tonight. I can't sit on a train like this.'

'If that's all you're worried about you can come next-door and I'll lend you one of mine,' said Gran shortly. 'Bringing up a child, you'll need to develop a strong stomach.'

'You haven't heard the end of this,' snapped Ada. 'I shall contact the authorities, reports will be made.'

'I'm sure we can help Mr Vine to get professional advice,' said Beattie quietly. 'After all he is the child's father. There must be plenty of orphans up in Yorkshire, certainly enough soldiers came from there.'

'Just let me come over and change my clothes,' said Betty. 'I must get out of this house.'

'Best thing you've said all day,' snapped Fred.

'Right ladies,' said Beattie getting to her feet. 'If you and Mrs

Scovell come with me, we'll leave Mr Vine and his children alone. I think they've had enough upset for one day.'

Dora watched the three women walk towards the front door and wondered when she could safely make her escape.

Fred went out into the yard.

Mary and a calmer, cleaner Blyth came back into the kitchen. 'Fetch me a vest and drawers for him,' she said to the twins. They scurried up the stairs.

'I'll make a fresh pot of tea and then I'll be off,' said Dora.

The twins came back and flung the clothes at Mary before sitting themselves at the table and making short work of a plate of jam tarts.

'Lardy witch,' giggled Faith, spraying her sister with pastry crumbs.

'Crow face,' shrieked Mercy.

Dora let out her breath in a long sigh. The disorganisation and squalor of Harry's family overwhelmed her. Their grabbing at things, trampling over each other's feelings, their noise, it was all too much. The three girls fell on the remains of the sandwiches while Blyth stood naked and shivering, his clothes heaped on the table beside the remaining jam tarts. Dora picked them up. 'Come over here, my pet, let me put your things on.'

The little child was hot and trembling.

'Let's get you dressed and you shall have a nice glass of lemonade.'

He banged the heel of his hand repeatedly against his head.

'Got a headache?' she asked. Blyth nodded.

Dora sat Blyth in the armchair and then rushed into the kitchen and poured the water in the teapot before running a flannel under the tap and fetching the little boy a cup of lemonade.

The three girls continued eating.

Dora sat on the edge of a chair with Blyth on her lap. She settled the cup on the floor and sponged his face with the flannel.

He started to cough hoarsely and then with no warning vomited all over her.

Mary leapt from her seat her eyes wide with alarm. 'He's proper sick ain't he?' she cried. 'D'you reckon e's got dipfeeria?' She looked imploringly at Dora.

Fred came back into the room.

'You sit on your Daddy's lap and I'll get myself cleaned up,' Dora said. 'I reckon you should go for the doctor, Mary. Probably tonsillitis, like Mrs Pragnell said.'

She stood at the sink trying not to inhale the sour smell of sick as she sponged it from her dress. Behind her she could hear Fred crooning to his son.

'Dad we needs half a crown for the doctor,' said Mary almost dancing with impatience.

Fred produced a shilling and a sixpence.

Wearily Dora searched in her purse and produced the necessary shilling that was snatched from her hand. 'I'll be off now,' she said, trying to summon up a smile. 'See you all later on in the week. Bye darling,' she whispered to Blyth, kissing his hand.

'Sure you won't stay and finish the grub,' said Fred, waving at the table. 'There's plenty to spare.'

'Bye everyone,' she said, hurrying up the passage before any further disasters could happen.

As she slammed the front door Mary, who had been rushing down the road, ran back to her. 'You don't reckon they could take him away, do ya?' she asked anxiously. 'Nobody reckons much to us 'cos Mum was mental and Dad's a boozer.'

'I'm sure Mr Pragnell would stand up for your dad. And people would take notice of him bein' as he's a naval officer' an all.'

'Think so?' asked Mary.

'Sure of it,' said Dora firmly. 'Besides you didn't see your auntie's face when Blyth sicked up all over her.'

'Thanks our Dor,' said Mary, giving her a rare smile before racing away.

A temporary truce, thought Dora. By my next visit it'll be forgotten. Out in the street, the early evening air was fresh and cool to her skin. Gratefully she drew in a slow steadying breath. Earlier she'd promised to pop next-door and see Lily but now she felt too tired and stale-smelling even for the sympathy of her best friend. As she walked down Queen Street the Town Hall clock struck six. Was it only five hours since she'd run down the road to the cemetery gates with a stitch in her side? It felt a lifetime ago and there was still the letter to write to Harry. How could she describe what had happened that afternoon to someone hundreds of miles away?

Directly she walked into the kitchen and saw the envelope on the mantelpiece Lily's spirits lifted. A letter from Michael.

'Tea is a bit of a picnic, today,' said Uncle Albert smiling at her, 'your grandmother's been busy with the funeral. There's watercress or fish-paste sandwiches but still a sliver of wedding cake. You make your choice while I make us some fresh tea.'

It could be left until later as far as Lily was concerned, all she wanted was peace and privacy and Michael's letter. But she knew that if she refused Uncle Albert's tea and company, at least for half an hour, Gran would be mortally offended. 'How was it? The funeral, I mean, did Dora manage to get there in time?'

Uncle Albert sighed. 'We were a meagre gathering, I'm afraid. But I was touched by young Mary's courage, you know, Lily. She walked the whole of the way to the cemetery hand-in-hand with her father. The aunt and grandmother came down from Yorkshire and, yes, Dora, just scraped in at the last minute.'

'Did she call in afterwards?'

'Not that I'm aware of. When I left them some while ago, she was there still.'

As Lily nodded she stole another look at the envelope then caught Albert watching her and smiling.

'How can my company compare with that of a young sailor,' he laughed. 'Why don't you lay yourself up a tray and take your tea in your room?'

'Thank you, Uncle Albert,' she said, helping herself to a plate of watercress sandwiches and a slice of cake.

'I shall tell your grandmother it was my idea,' he said as he handed her a cup of tea. 'I know she doesn't want you to neglect me.'

Lily blushed. 'Uncle Albert I'd never . . .'

'Fiddlesticks. You and I have known each other too long to bother with the niceties. Shoo, shoo, off you go.'

Laughing, Lily picked up her letter and took the tray with her. After a gulp of tea and a mouthful of sandwich she peeled back the flap of the envelope.

Penang February 1921

Darling Lily,

Thank you for the lovely letter about your grandmother's big romance. I look forward to the next one about the wedding. I'm sure it will be a wonderful day. I can't see Mr Pragnell leaving your Gran at the altar like Miss Havisham. And even if he did I'm sure she wouldn't spend the rest of her life in a moth-eaten wedding dress or have mice running in and out of the cake. I'm so glad you gave me, Great Expectations. I love Joe Gargery and Biddy. How about Mr Jaggers do you think he's supposed to be like Pontius Pilate because he's always washing his hands.'

Lily laughed to herself at the spectacle of Gran as Miss Havisham. What lovely letters Michael wrote. It was almost as if he were with her.

Today we have arrived in Penang on Prince of Wales Island off the Malayan coast. To me it smells awful. Some of the older hands say that each place in the East has its own peculiar pong. But it seems that we smell awful to Chinese noses, too.

Harry and I went ashore to the botanical gardens and saw some wonderful butterflies. Honestly Lily, they were the size of tea plates. I wish I could have painted a picture of one amazing blue one. It was baking hot so we sat under a palm tree sipping iced drinks listening to a waterfall. The next day there was a tropical shower. I kept watch in my bare skin with the warm rain water trickling down my back.

Lily tried to picture Michael naked in a tropical rain storm. It was a very disturbing thought. On first reading she had muddled the words together and had wondered what a bare watch was like, perhaps one without a glass covering the face or minus its hands or numbers even. Then she saw he had said bare skin. She could visualise the water rivuletting down his back but could not, in her mind, turn him around. Maybe because she had never seen a man naked. She wished that their kissing and holding one another had progressed further and that she was as familiar with his body as she was with his thoughts. What if she had been there with him and they had stood together in the warm rain, what would it have felt like, skin to skin? Had he written about it because he wanted her to picture him in that way. She thought of Gran's words, 'all urgency and fizz', and sighed. Her face was hot as she picked up the letter and continued to read.

The sky is so huge out here. The sunrises and sunsets seem to fill the whole horizon. Lily, the stars are magical. I wish you could see them with me.

We have now arrived at Ding Dings on the Crocodile River. It sounds like a story book place doesn't it? Somewhere between the mountains of Chanclibore and the Bong Tree Forest. To tell

you the truth, it's a scruffy little place with only a few
ramshackle buildings on the edge of a tropical forest. A few miles
away are rubber and tea plantations.

It is difficult to think of you all in Pompey still wearing your
coats and gloves while we're sweating away here in the East. It truly
is a different world out here with baking heat and wild storms. On
the one side are awful tropical diseases and many, many poor people
and on the other great beauty in the wonderful beaches and trees and
flowers. I wish that you could be with me to see it all. I try to
visualise you in a silk dress carrying a paper parasol walking arm in
arm with me along a stretch of white sand. The two of us collecting
shells never ever seen in England.

Lily sighed: if only that was possible. She told herself that she
was managing their separation quite well but under the surface
content was an intense loneliness often made worse by his letters.
His writing brought him so close, his thoughts and feelings so
like her own. Blinking the tears away she returned to his letter.

What a long time it is before I see you again. All I have to
remind me is a picture. Please, please send me another or I shall
wear this one out with looking at it. Such endless days, nights and
months to be got through. But, on the bright side, there's almost a
year gone already. I really miss you, Lily and so look forward to
seeing you again. Take great care of yourself.
All my deepest love, Your Michael.

P.S. If you have any spare time do call across the street to see
my mother. Honestly, Lily, she would love to see you. I know if
you got to know her you would find her very interesting and she's
a book worm, too, like us.

Michael's postscript about his mother brought her other secret
letter painfully to mind. As she sat on her bed, unlacing her work

shoes, Lily was once more overcome with doubt. She should have thrown it away, torn it up, forgotten it. But she had kept it. Was her mother out there somewhere? Had she been somehow prevented from seeing her? Had Gran or Dad stopped her? There must be some way of finding out.

How about Aunt Hester, over at Eastney? She had been fond of her mother, had once told her how interested she had been in her garden. Lily decided next Sunday she'd go over to see her and Uncle George. One way or another she had to find out the truth.

Chapter Six

'Sailor, for the Lord's sake stand still. The last thing I can deal with is you wandering off.'

The voice was coming from the street just below her window. Beattie slid to the edge of the bed, her feet searching for her slippers. What on earth was the time? Putting on her glasses she peeled back the edge of the curtain and held the little carriage clock to the light. Only six o'clock, what in heaven's name was going on?

Once more she peered out of the window, and after a few moments acclimatised herself to the early morning gloom and made out the shape of a handcart. On top, wedged between various knotted handles of what could be bedding, was the sleeping form of a child. Holding one of the handles was a man wearing an able-seaman's uniform and a straw hat. Issuing the orders was a large woman in a long coat.

'Peeping Tom,' accused Albert, creeping up behind her.

'They woke me up,' said Beattie, giving her husband a good-morning kiss. 'Who are they d'you suppose? Are they our new neighbours?'

'It's very early to be moving in and where is Mrs Wheeler? She doesn't normally trust new tenants with the key. Wants to be around to lay down the law, the moth-eaten virago.'

Beattie chuckled at his apt description of her former landlady.

He let go of the curtain and took his trousers from the chair pulling them on over his pyjamas. 'Now we're awake I'll fetch us some tea.'

Beattie lit the lamp and sat at the dressing-table fully alert. She took up her brush and began to put her hair to rights. If that odd trio on the pavement were going to live next door she and Albert were in for an interesting time. Were they related? It was difficult from a distance and in poor light, to gather much of an idea as to their ages or anything else about them. She surmised that they had flitted owing the rent and felt a wave of sympathy. The stories every night in the *Evening News* told of families packed into one room, husbands and wives having to live apart. Beattie sighed. Everything had been disconnected by the war and as yet there were precious few signs of repair or recovery.

'Gran, open the door, I've brought your tea, and some hot water. Uncle Albert's gone next-door to turn on the water for the new people,' said Lily, breaking into her thoughts.

'Come in, my duck,' she called, putting down her brush. 'Did the new neighbours wake you, too?'

'They look a very funny lot,' said Lily, 'from what I could see from my window. The woman is huge and the old man is blind.'

Beattie put down her brush. 'I thought I noticed a child asleep in the cart. Did you see one?'

Lily went over to the window and parted the curtains. 'Oh yes, the woman's lifting him off, now,' she said, 'he looks about Blyth's age.'

'I must get into the rig of the day and see what's wanted,' said Beattie, pouring the jug of water into the basin. 'Oh yes,' she said turning to Lily, 'there was something I wanted to ask you. Something I've lost track of but it'll keep until later.' Was she mistaken or did her granddaughter look guiltily relieved?

'See you downstairs,' said Lily, closing the door.

Beattie took up the cake of lavender soap and lathered it

between her hands. She needed to be sure of her ground before asking questions. As she dried her face she put the matter to the back of her mind; timing was everything, in dealing with Lily.

'They had the front door open by the time I went out to them,' said Albert as Beattie came into the kitchen. 'I said we'd run them in a tray of tea to tide them over. The woman said there was no hurry, they'd had an early breakfast before they left.'

Lily gulped down her tea, kissed Beattie and Albert and rushed out, saying, 'I'll catch up with everything later.'

'Oh, good luck with your new job,' called Beattie to her departing back.

'Thanks Gran,' called Lily slamming the door behind her.

'She's gone to the Epaulette Room for a trial period,' said Beattie in answer to Albert's enquiring look. 'It's all the decorative stuff, the gold lace and spangles and such. Highly skilled according to Lily. Anyway that Mrs Markham reckons she's got the aptitude so we'll see.' She hurried through the breakfast anxious to meet her new neighbours after Lily's description.

'You go off and be ambassadress,' said Albert, taking the tea-towel from her hands. 'I'll make short work of this.'

'What did you make of them?' she asked her husband as she set up the welcoming tray.

'They look as if life has dealt rather harshly with them,' said Albert. 'All their things smelt charred. The old man is totally confused. But the woman is a battler, she won't let Ma Wheeler get the better of her of that I'm certain.'

'Curiouser and curiouser,' said Beattie, buttoning her coat. She went out of the front door and tapped on the knocker of number 27. Stepping over the back wall and walking into the kitchen would come later when she and her neighbour had taken the measure of each other.

The woman startled her. She seemed to fill the doorway with her tall, solid presence. Her faded floral dress looked as if it had been slept in and her hair was scraped off her face and tied with a length of string. Oblivious of her bedraggled state she held out her hand and said, 'Dahlia Carruthers, pleased to meet you. My neighbour, I believe?'

Beattie smiled back as much in amusement as friendship. What an amazing name. The voice was a surprise too, rich and cultured like a duchess. Not an accent often heard in Lemon Street. 'I'm Beattie Pragnell, pleased to meet you,' she said, realising that this was the first time she had called herself by her married name. 'I thought a tray of tea and some cake might come in useful.'

'We meet at a low ebb in our fortunes,' said Mrs Carruthers, taking the tray from Beattie. 'I hope you have time to take a cup of your tea with us.' She turned and walked back into the house.

Wild horses would not have dragged her away. There was a story here well worth listening to. Beattie was glad she'd left the old furniture behind; by the look of the handcart earlier her new neighbours had brought little with them.

It was strange to be sitting as a visitor in her old home, without the familiar landmarks such as family photographs and her old sewing-machine in the corner. But she was not left long with her memories.

'Sailor, Algie, come here and meet one of our neighbours,' called Dahlia as she set the tray on the table.

There was sound of footsteps coming down the stairs and along the passage. An old man and a young boy came into the kitchen hand-in-hand. The man looked like a sailor from the Victorian Navy in his wide-brimmed straw hat and silvery beard. The boy was like a plant kept in the cellar, pale and weedy with legs like straws. His jumper was felted from frequent washing and his trousers were miles too big.

'Pleased to meet you,' said Beattie, reaching out to shake his hand.

The old man smiled vaguely in the direction of her voice.

'Good morning, Missis,' he said gruffly before their hands connected.

'Algie,' said Beattie, 'welcome to Lemon Street. Welcome all of you.'

The boy, whom she judged to be about six years old stared solemnly at her. It was a calculating adult look which made her shiver beneath her bright welcoming smile.

'We're the flotsam,' said Dahlia guiding Sailor to a chair. 'Hopefully we shall find a safe anchorage here.' She met Beattie's eyes unflinchingly.

'Fine cake,' said the old man after Algie had placed his fingers around the plate, 'made for a celebration.'

Beattie laughed. 'I'm a newly-wed. One week married to a man who waited forty years for me.'

'Congratulations,' Dahlia said, spooning sugar into her cup.

'A drop of winter sunshine to warm old bones,' said Sailor smiling to himself.

'Yes, that's how it was.' Beattie felt a sudden warmth for this odd little family. Wafting across to her from their clothing was the smell of charred paper or singed material that Albert had mentioned earlier. Covertly she glanced about her looking for its source and then saw Dahlia watching her with equal curiosity. Flustered she asked, 'Is there anything I can lend you until you get yourself settled? Or if you want any shopping—?'

'A penn'orth of bones, some pot herbs and if you could be so good as to loan us a screw of sugar and tea we would be much obliged,' said Dahlia. 'We'll unpack and look around the house and see what's needed elsewhere.'

'Your grandson looks to be of school age,' said Beattie, 'he'll be able to go along to Drake Street with the nippers next door.'

'Algie,' said Dahlia, 'ah, he's mine by choice not by birth. Rather fell into my hands at the death of his mother. Yes, school is on my list for next week but there are other priorities for today.' She got briskly to her feet, putting the cups and plates back on the tray.

Beattie felt herself to have been dismissed. 'I'll see you with your shopping later,' she said, stepping back across the doorstep.

'Much obliged,' said her neighbour, disappearing behind the door.

'Well, they're a mysterious crew,' said Beattie, to Albert as she sat at the kitchen table making out her shopping list. 'I'd bet a pound to a penny that Ma Wheeler doesn't know a thing about them. Though how they got in beats me.'

Albert shrugged. 'Seems a very resourceful woman.'

'And quite a beauty at one time. Did you notice her eyes? They were really green. And her confidence! She stood there in rags and talked to me as if she were royalty. Funny that, isn't it, Albert? Most of us put on the confidence from the outside; wearing nice things give us an armour. Hers is inside, a sort of belief. It'd a take a lot to rob her of it.'

'You surprise me, Beatrice,' he said, smiling at her. 'I've always thought that you were a confident woman, who knew her skills and her worth.'

This was a new thought. 'I don't know as I would call it confidence. Worth perhaps. I have as much right to respect as anyone and I try to give other people their dues.'

'Well, they've had a narrow escape whoever they are!' said Albert, settling himself at his desk.

'What's your programme for today?' asked Beattie as she picked up her purse and shopping-bag.

'I must go through the ledgers and see what arrears there are before I collect the rents. And, of course, while I'm doing that there will be fresh tales of repairs to be done,' he answered, seating himself at his large oak desk. 'See if there's room anywhere for more tenants. Seeing those people next door makes me think of all the other hundreds of souls looking for rooms.'

'How many properties have you got?' asked Beattie, realising that she knew very little about the business side of Albert's life.

'Twenty-five, spread over Lemon Street and Cross Street. They don't bring in a fortune but coupled with my naval pension they'll keep us comfortably afloat.'

Beattie smiled at her husband, knowing full well that Albert's kind heart and ready sympathy meant he never collected all that was due to him. 'How long will all this landlord business take?'

'Two or three days I shouldn't wonder. I'll be at my desk most of the morning. And what's your agenda?'

'Shopping and I'll call into Goldstein's and tell him I've done with sewing sailors' collars. There might be one of your tenants as would be glad of the job.'

As she walked down the street Beattie realised it was the first time in over a week that she had been on her own. Much as she enjoyed Albert's company she needed time to herself to think her own thoughts and get back into routine. But there was no routine established yet between her and Albert, it was all new and uncertain. Her husband had his own established pattern to his days and she'd had hers. Suddenly she was uneasy. What would she do with her time? She couldn't fill it entirely with cleaning and cooking. Leftover time. It was a luxury she'd never had before and the thought filled her with acute anxiety.

She strolled down to Queen Street with none of her usual urgency. First stop Goldstein's, one of the twenty or so naval tailors, past Zeffert's Hat and Cap Company, Shimbart's, Baun's and Moseley and Pondsford. The bell tinkled over the door and Beattie stood waiting for Isaac Goldstein to step through the dusty velvet curtain at the back of the shop. She pulled up a chair to the counter looking down through the glass top to the gold cap badges, naval ties and brass buttons displayed underneath. Behind the counter were numerous polished oak drawers. She could hear the busy whirr of the sewing-machines from the workroom at the back of the shop.

Getting up again she opened and closed the door setting up another tinkling of the bell.

Isaac hurried in full of apologies. 'Beattie, my dear, sorry to keep you. A new machine giving trouble. How many collars you taking? Three dozen as usual?'

Beattie shook her head. She smiled at the old tailor. 'How long do we go back, Isaac?' she asked.

The little man spread out his hands and shrugged. 'Thirty years or more, just after my Samuel was born. He's got his own shop now. Many many years, Beattie.'

'Well, today I'm signing off, so to speak. I've remarried as you know, so I shan't need the sewing money.'

'Good news for you and sorrow for me. Always your work was immaculate. Always on time.' Again he shrugged. 'But as you know there will be some young woman eager to take it on. I have a couple of addresses already. I'll get my daughter Rebecca to sort that out.'

'D'you mind if I try and find someone for you, first?' asked Beattie. 'There's a new neighbour might be interested.'

'Of course, my dear. But let me know by Friday. I can't afford to fall behind.'

Beattie nodded. 'I shall miss coming here every week and seeing you, getting my money and setting the world to rights.'

'Don't be a stranger,' he said, coming around from behind the counter and shaking her hand.

Their talk was interrupted by a young woman trying to manoeuvre a wooden mailcart into the shop with two babies wedged in it head to toe. They were clutching a large brown-paper parcel.

'Here you are, Mr Goldstein,' she said, lumping the parcel on to the counter.

Beattie smiled at the babies. One of them thrust a jammy crust at her which landed on the floor to be trodden on by the young mother.

'I'll drop in next time I'm passing,' said Beattie.

Isaac nodded to her before undoing the parcel and minutely examining the collars inside.

Another bit of the past over and done with she thought as she left the shop. Gradually she filled her shopping-bags not forgetting Dahlia's requests. The day had warmed up and all the different smells of Queen Street wafted out onto the pavements: fried fish, hot pies, cooked beetroot, beer from the brewery near Bonfire Corner. Beattie suddenly felt hungry. As the Town Hall clock behind Victoria Park struck eleven she turned towards home. Her hand was raised to knock on her new neighbour's door when out of the corner of her eye she saw Ma Wheeler steering her car up to the kerb.

As Dahlia Carruthers opened the door Ma Wheeler sprang on to the pavement.

'Get out of my house, whoever you are,' she shouted, flinging her fox-fur scarf around her neck. 'You're trespassing and I'll set the lor on ya.'

Beattie stepped out of her path. She'd had dealings with her old landlady before and knew the strength of her temper. Arguments had been known to end with punching, kicking and hair-pulling. It was really none of her business; she should by rights go indoors to Albert and leave tenant and landlady to settle their differences. But curiosity got the better of her.

'Are you addressing me?'

The coolness of Dahlia Carruthers' reply seemed to rob Ma Wheeler of the advantage. She took a step backwards and fixed her glasses more firmly on her nose. 'What you doin' in my house?' she snarled.

As Dahlia stepped onto the pavement to confront Ma Wheeler, Sailor stood behind her in the doorway. 'We're taking refuge, Queenie,' she said.

Startled at the use of her Christian name, Ma Wheeler looked about her.

It was dinner-time and the street was full of neighbours coming and going. Fred Vine with Blyth perched on his shoulders crossed over from Ma Abraham's shop. Chippy Dowell came into view pushing his mother in her bath-chair. Vinegary old Mrs Perks stood in her doorway arms akimbo watching the action played out at number 27.

'You gotta nerve calling me Queenie,' said Ma Wheeler, looking distinctly rattled but determined to bluster it out.

'The name's Dahlia Carruthers. It should be familiar to you.' Her words had an astonishing affect.

Ma Wheeler collapsed like a burst balloon. She tried to slide past Dahlia and into the house away from the avid interest of her other tenants.

'You once sought refuge with my family and now it's my turn,' said Dahlia, standing stolidly in front of her.

'Yes, well, Mrs Carruthers,' whined Ma Wheeler, 'that was in different circumstances.'

Dahlia swept out her hands to include her new-found neighbours. 'I'm sure your tenants here would be most interested to know what those circumstances were,' she said, her voice carrying down the street. 'No?' she asked.

Ma Wheeler shook her head.

Beattie wished she'd had a camera at the ready to capture the scene. Fred was agog with curiosity and Mrs Perkins had her neck craned in an effort not to miss anything.

'I think you should step inside and perhaps we can work out some compromise,' said Dahlia as if she were the landlady.

Ma Wheeler, giving every impression of the cringing tenant, head down and fingers worrying at her fox stole, slunk over the doorstep.

Beattie chortled to herself; ooh, this would make a good tale to share with Albert. But when she opened the door and called his name there was no reply. She felt a twinge of disappointment. It was dispelled instantly by the sight of a letter on the table with an Isle of Wight postmark. She delayed the opening of it until she had unpacked her shopping and made herself a fresh cup of tea. Spooning the sugar into her cup she seated herself by the kitchen window and tore open the envelope.

The Lord Tennyson
Hope Street
Sandown
Isle of Wight
11th April

Dear Mother,

I am sat here in our little bedroom above the pub early on Monday morning writing to you while Alec and the children sleep.

I feel I must write now, when Alec wakes we shall be up to our eyes. The journey to Sandown was lovely, watching the island slowly getting nearer and nearer as the ferry steamed towards Ryde Pier. All those little white houses nestling between the trees and the lovely stretches of golden sand. Rosie was full of excitement jiggling about in Alec's arms. 'Are we still in England?' she asked us. Joseph missed it all as he slept from start to finish.

The little train was waiting on the pier for us and the trip to Sandown was so pretty past all the little villages with their farms. The sidings were a mass of primroses. I couldn't quite make the best of the journey as I was sick with nerves. Having to take over the pub straight away, with two little ones to settle at the same time was no easy undertaking.

The Lord Tennyson is a large five bedroomed square white building set back on the cliffs. You can walk from our pub all the way along the cliff path to Shanklin. Though when we shall get the chance to do that I don't know.

When we got there the old landlord and landlady were in a rush to leave. We were only half an hour away from opening up time so I was in a panic. But luck was on our side. The landlady's sister Mabel offered to stay the night and help us settle in. She was a Godsend, I can tell you. Her usual hours are the lunch-time trade but I think she was charmed by Rosie rushing up and kissing her or it could have been my look of terror that made her stay.

The customers are mostly holidaymakers and locals — not a single naval uniform as yet. On top of them we have two rooms for bed and breakfast people. It's all a terrible rush in the morning what with seeing to the children and getting the bacon and eggs on the table, then there's the changeover at the weekends when the new visitors arrive. Last Saturday I went to clean this room and there was a terrible smell. Alec and I searched and searched to find where it was coming from. We opened all the windows and then in the bottom of the wardrobe was a heap of seaweed. I scrubbed out the wardrobe and tipped some eau de Cologne inside. Now we've got a notice about leaving buckets and spades in the yard outside.

My biggest worry is making sure we have a bit of family privacy and that the children are kept out of the pub. Mabel is a great help in all this and I am taking on a young widow for evening work. She has a young baby but he can be put in the children's room to sleep so all in all it's working out quite well.

Everything looks tired and needs a clean from top to bottom. The curtains are faded and full of dust. I'm itching to get at it but just keeping things ticking over takes allo my energy. Mabel says at the end of the season there'll be the whole of the winter to worry about curtains and suchlike.

Beattie sighed. In all the flurry of the wedding and the honeymoon Alec and Miriam had been put to the back of her mind. She blew her nose noisily. If only she could wave a wand and find herself at the Lord Tennyson she'd roll up her sleeves and pitch in with her daughter-in-law. But that would never do. Miriam must make a new course for herself without the interference of her mother-in-law, as she must adapt to being Albert's wife. Nobody could make the transition but themselves.

None of the recent changes to her life had been marked in her diaries, Beattie now realised. It had been a habit of hers since she was a young girl at the orphanage. She would get up before anyone else was stirring and confide all her joys and woes to those little penny notebooks. There were now dozens of them and not even Lily's prying fingers had uncovered their hiding-place. Now they were secure in an old hat-box in her locked wardrobe.

Since becoming a grandmother Beattie had seen them as something more than her random thoughts. They were a record of times and people long gone but linked by ties of blood and friendship to Lily, Rosie and little Joseph. Perhaps now time was less pressing she would be able to sort them into some sort of order. When Albert lost himself for hours in his studio she could now absorb herself in something of her own. With a feeling of satisfaction she returned to Miriam's letter.

> *Although I feel a bit anxious as to how things will pan out for us at least Alec and I will face things together. No more separations or waving from the shore.*
>
> *We were talking about you and Lily coming down to see us in the summer and Albert of course. He was so kind to me and so respectful.*
>
> *Write to me quickly Mother, I need to hear from you.*
>
> *With love Miriam, Alec, Rosie and Joseph.*

Beattie kissed the names then folded the letter back in its envelope. Busyness, that was the cure. If she didn't stir herself she'd be bawling her eyes out. Besides it was gone twelve and if she wasn't quick Albert would be back to an empty plate. Well, it would have to be cold meat, pickles and mashed spud.

She was startled by a tapping on the window. It was Algie.

'What can I do for you, young man?' said Beattie, stepping out into the yard.

The boy jigged about from one foot to the other. 'Could Mother have her shopping, please?' he said.

'Yes, of course. I got sidetracked with one thing and another. Come in, come in.'

Algie perched in the doorway as if ready for flight. He looked a mite cleaner and his hair had been combed but, my God, she thought, he needs feeding up. She gathered up the shopping and added a few things of her own including a jar of jam and a few treacle toffees. 'I used to have a boy like you,' she said, trying to get some response from Algie. 'His name was Andrew.'

'Gotta go,' said the boy dismissively.

As she shut the back door footsteps sounded in the passage. 'Hello Albert,' she called, 'I'm like the cow's tail, this morning, all behind.'

'Don't fret, Beatrice,' he said, putting a cash bag and the newspaper down on the desk. 'I can reckon up my rents and read the paper. There's no hurry.'

As she began to peel the potatoes he said, 'There's evidently been a huge fire over in Tipnor. Bayley and Whites the timber yard has burnt to the ground. It will put over a hundred men out of work. A couple of lodging-houses nearby were damaged but they think everyone got out in time.'

'Poor souls,' said Beattie thoughtfully.

Chapter Seven

'Girl wanted for kitchen duties for naval household in Lancaster Terrace. Must be used to hard work. Apply with references to Servants' Registry Gibraltar Road.'

Armed with a glowing testimonial from Mr Pragnell and a reasonable offering from her old headmaster Mary Vine trailed up the stairs to The Servants' Registry. The office was housed in a dingy room at the top of a large building separated into various businesses. It was hot and airless and the May sun glared through a skylight at the women and girls sitting on the hard wooden benches. There was a smell of stale sweat and anxiety. Mary glanced at her fellow applicants, at their red hands and patched clothes. Some of them seemed worn and ancient with barely a day's work left in their bent grey-haired forms. A pale young girl coughed persistently.

Mary looked around at the high brown roll-top desk, the black telephone, and the woman seated there shuffling filing-cards in a box. She wore a white blouse with a string of jet beads and a black skirt the tightness of which caused her to take tiny scuttling steps. What fascinated Mary was her grey hair parted in the centre and arranged in deep waves. They had the ridged regularity of railway lines. How had she achieved this uniform appearance? Was it a wig?

With numbing slowness the morning passed, each interview punctuated by the woman ringing a small brass bell. At last it rang for Mary.

She swallowed hard before peeling her skirt from the bench and approaching the desk.

'Name?'

'Mary Vine, Miss Snelgrove,' she said, reading the name from a wedge-shaped wooden block on the desk.

'Application form and references.'

Mary handed them over. It seemed an age while Miss Snelgrove adjusted her glasses and studied the papers.

'What are the duties of a scullery maid?' she asked.

'Working in the kitchen under the direction of the cook,' Mary recited from memory from *the Forsyth Book of Household Management*.

'Bone-handled knives, how are they cleaned?' Miss Snelgrove demanded to know.

'Put them blade first into a jug of hot soapy water. Don't get the handles wet or they'll go yellow and split.'

'What are the first items to be washed?'

'Glasses and fine china.'

'I see you have no experience of domestic work, Miss Vine.'

'I haven't never been paid to do it but I been doing house-work since I was little. My dad been away in the navy and my mum been sick a long time. She died a few weeks ago.'

'Very sorry, I'm sure,' sniffed Miss Snelgrove.

'I'm hard workin' and anxious to learn,' Mary said, as Lily's gran had rehearsed her.

'That's as may be. There are three other girls after the position at Lancaster Terrace.'

'Bet they ain't as deservin' as me,' pleaded Mary, speaking for herself. 'They ain't got a family dependin' on them.'

'They have professional experience.'

'I can be experienced if I gets a chance,' said Mary, holding Miss Snelgrove's assessing look and refusing to drop her eyes. Her head itched under her straw hat and she was desperate to go to the lavatory.

'Come back after dinner at two.'

'Thank you. Very Christian of you,' Mary said sweetly, playing her last desperate card.

Miss Snelgrove gave a wintry smile. 'You've worked hard to impress me, young woman.'

'And have I?'

'Have you what?'

'Impressed you?'

'Come back at two sharp and collect your references.' As she rang the bell she said, 'Take nothing for granted, Miss Vine.'

Mary rushed down the road to Victoria Park and the public toilets. After thankfully using them she filled one of the cracked basins with water and splashed her face and neck. The roller-towel was wet and grimy so she dried her hands on the skirt of her petticoat. Every few minutes as she strolled between the flowerbeds, Mary looked up at the Town Hall clock, visible between the trees, its black hands creeping with aggravating slowness towards two o'clock.

Her stomach rumbled with hunger. With the minute hand on the eleven Mary hurtled back to Gibraltar Road. She arrived as Miss Snelgrove was pulling up the blind on the front door. Already a queue had formed of women and girls clutching papers in their hands and eyeing each other speculatively.

'Come in, ladies, and take a seat, I shall be with you presently. Miss Vine, sit by the desk. I won't be a moment.'

Mary tried to distract herself by thinking about the Chelsea bun she'd have whatever the job outcome. It would either be a glorious reward or a sweet consolation.

Miss Snelgrove took her seat behind the desk and picked up

the receiver of the black telephone and began to dial some numbers with the rubber end of her pencil.

Mary was fascinated. How did the voices get carried back and forth, she wondered. Harry had once tried to explain it to her but she hadn't taken it in, preferring to think of it as magic rather than wires and air waves.

'Oh, good afternoon. May I speak with Mrs Mullins. Ah, yes, Mrs Mullins this is the Servants' Registry here. I shall be sending you a girl on Monday, at what time would you like her to arrive? Oh, yes, the references are satisfactory. Seven o'clock, good, and a month's trial wasn't it? Thank you, good afternoon. Oh, I'm sorry,' she said as she was about to replace the receiver, 'her name is Mary Vine and she is fifteen.'

'Oh, thanks ever so much,' gasped Mary, flushed with heat and excitement.

'Don't let me down,' said Miss Snelgrove, 'here, take your references and take them with you on Monday.'

Mary sat on a park bench by the fountain with the black-and-white plaster swans and unrolled a strip of Chelsea bun. She relished the gritty sugar and plump sultanas; would it have tasted as sweet if she hadn't got the job, she wondered?

Scullery maid, it wasn't nothing special when she thought about it, just skivvying for other people and she wouldn't be able to boss them about or swipe them one, like she did at home. Still there was half-a-crown a week and Sunday afternoons off. Dad said she could keep a shilling for herself so it wasn't half bad when you thought about it. She stood up and brushed the crumbs from her skirt: time to go home and share her triumph with Dad and the nippers.

It seemed no time at all since she'd gone home on Friday and now she was setting out at half-past six on Monday morning to her first day at work. As she passed the front doors of the houses in Lancaster Terrace young maids on their knees were scrubbing the front steps. She went into the back entrance of number 15 and rapped smartly on the door.

'What you want?' a skinny freckle-faced girl asked. She stood in the doorway clutching a floorcloth, almost overwhelmed by a large sacking apron.

'Come for the job,' said Mary staring back. 'I'm Miss Vine, I got me references.'

An older woman, harassed and red-faced glared at her as she snatched the papers out of Mary's hands. 'Get in, 'ang up your coat and get yourself over to the sink.' She turned to the other girl and snapped, 'Cissie don't stand there gawpin' go and finish the steps.'

Mary stared at the woman, determined not to be cowed by her.

After rapidly scanning the references she handed them back. 'Mrs Mullins, cook, and who might you be?' she demanded in an angry, rapid-fire way of talking.

'Mary Vine,' she said, staring back at Mrs Mullins.

'You've got a bold eye,' the cook said, 'I hope you're strong and willing.'

'Do me best,' answered Mary, determined not to be bullied.

Mrs Mullins strode to the stove and began furiously stirring a pot.

Thank goodness Lily's Gran had given her a bit of a rehearsal of the sorts of jobs she'd need to know as a scullery maid.

'Everything in its place. Side plate on your left wine glass on your right. Cutlery arranged as you need it working in from the outside. Dessert spoon and fork at the top, spoon facing left and fork below facing right. Washing-up we've talked about,' she said. 'Glasses first, then cups and saucers. Roasting-tins are put to soak then scoured with powder later.'

'Everything with toffs is such a palaver,' Mary had burst out.

'Just think of the half-a-crown at the end of the week,' Mrs

Pragnell advised. 'Be polite. If you don't know how to do anything ask. And for pity's sake, keep your temper.'

Gritting her teeth, Mary rolled up her sleeves and began washing the cups, saucers and plates and stacking them on the wooden draining-board. She looked for a jug in which to soak the knives.

The cook rattled about the kitchen and Mary was just congratulating herself on making good progress with her task when she was suddenly pounced on.

'What in God's name have you done with that bacon fat from the frying-pan?'

'Poured it down the sink,' said Mary.

'Christ almighty! You'll have it blocked up and it'll be the devil to clear.' She nudged Mary aside with one of her beefy arms. 'Out of my way. Over there at the stove, fetch the kettle. Move yourself.'

The black kettle full of boiling water took all her strength to lift and carry across the kitchen. When she reached the sink the cook took it from her grasp and disappeared in a cloud of steam. Behind her, Mary heard a clanking as Cissie came in from washing the steps and set the bucket and floorcloth outside the back door.

'Cissie put yourself to rights and you can run the breakfasts up to the nursery. And you can set up the table for three,' said Mrs Mullins. 'We'll get ours down us while there's time to breathe.'

Mary began to set the cups and saucers that she had just washed and dried on to the table.

'Not them, not them, they're the family's china,' barked the cook, 'put them on the dresser. Kitchen's china in the cupboard under there, under there.'

Mary was almost crying with temper as she bent to fetch the thick white plates. How was she going to last out the day let alone the week?

'Sit yourself down,' snapped Mrs Mullins, 'don't stand about idle.'

The three of them sat at the table each with a bowl of porridge and a plate of hot buttered toast. Cook passed Cissie what looked like a bowl of wet sand and the girl sprinkled it over her porridge. Mary did the same. It turned out to be sweet like sugar. It was the first time she'd tasted porridge made with milk and without lumps and she relished every mouthful. While cook was occupied with her breakfast Mary took the chance to look around her.

You could have got their little kitchen, at home, several times into this one in Lancaster Terrace. The floor was covered in black-and-white tiles and a wooden dresser ran floor to ceiling along one wall. It gleamed with willow-patterned china, water jugs, copper jelly moulds, egg cups. Above the glass-panelled door leading into the rest of the house was a row of bells with the names of the rooms printed above them. Suddenly the one under drawing-room jangled loudly.

'That'll be her ladyship,' said cook, taking off her apron and smoothing back her hair. 'Wantin' to look at the week's menus.' She glared at the two of them. 'Have this place spotless by the time I get back. Mary you can start on the veg and Cissie you go and get the crocks from the nursery.'

'She always such a narky old bitch?' asked Mary as she finished her toast.

'Cripes,' gasped Cissie, 'keep your voice down. She'll skin you alive.'

'But is she?' Mary persisted.

'Worse of a Sunday after she's been up the pub the night before.'

'Why d'you stick it?'

'Ain't got nowhere else. I come here straight from 'ome. Dad died in the war and Mum got took with 'flu just after. On me own, now.'

This was a new experience for Mary, finding someone worse off than herself. While she digested this new piece of information she sprinkled more of the brown sugar on her toast. 'What's the family like?'

'Don't hardly see them,' said Cissie, standing at the stove eating the remainder of the porridge out of the saucepan. 'Lieutenant Clements'e's tall with blue bolgy eyes and a beaky nose talks loud and lah-di-dah and Lettice, that's Mrs Clements, she's got fair curly hair she's little and laughs a lot.'

'Wah!' exclaimed Mary, 'she can't be called Lettuce.'

Cissie giggled. 'They don't say it like that, it's Leteece.'

'What's their nippers called, Radish and Beetroot?'

Cissie was now almost helpless with laughter, 'no, you soft hap'orth, Miles and Charlotte. He's four and she's nearly two.'

Once more a bell clanged, this time from the nursery. 'That'll be Nanny Harker.'

'What's she like?'

'Tell you later,' said Cissie, hurrying out the door. 'You better look lively, Cook'll be down in two shakes.'

Mary had cleared the table and had almost finished the fresh load of washing-up by the time Mrs Mullins burst back into the kitchen.

'Leave that, leave that for Cissie,' she snapped, 'you go in the larder and fetch out that sack of potatoes. Here fill these two saucepans with water, little one for mash for the nursery, and the other for boiled for the dining-room. Spread some newspaper on the table and take this bowl for washing them.'

Mary began her task while Mrs Mullins prowled around the kitchen pulling pans and roasting dishes out of cupboards and then slamming out the back door.

'Cripes,' said Cissie as she set down the nursery tray, 'them spuds looks like marbles, you better peel 'em thinner than that.'

The back door crashed open again and Mrs Mullins once more foraged in the larder. 'Dratted boy,' she snapped, 'didn't bring me the shin of beef.' She glared up at the clock. 'I'll need that casserole in the oven by half nine or it'll be tough as old boots.'

She looked speculatively at the two girls and then she noticed the thick curls of peel and the pan of puny potatoes. 'Jesus girl,' she yelled, fetching Mary a swipe around the neck with the flat of her hand, 'can't you do nothin' right?'

Her face burned and her hands instinctively balled into fists.

Cissie jerked her away from the cook by the back of her apron. 'Mary'll run round there,' she said, not letting go. 'Marshall's in Green Road. Tell them it was left off Mrs Mullins' Saturday order.'

Mary bolted down the street with tears of temper running down her cheeks. Rotten, rotten moody old cow. She'd pay her back. By the time she was in Green Road her temper had cooled to be replaced by a steely determination not to stay in Lancaster Terrace a minute more than was absolutely necessary.

But she'd got plans that needed money to fuel them. They were just beginning to find their feet again after Mum's passing. Blyth had bounced back from his tonsillitis and went most days across the street to be looked after by Mrs Rowan, Lily's boyfriend's mother. The twins were back at school and Dad had got a job as a porter at the Sailors' Home Club. She and Blyth now shared the big bedroom and Dad was downstairs in the front room.

Dora had got three pounds saved from Harry's money that she was going to give her towards getting a couple of beds. And Miriam had left a big blue curtain with gold moons and stars on it that she would hang down the centre of the room giving her and Blyth their own separate quarters.

Everything hinged on her and Dad hanging on to their jobs and both of them keeping their temper.

By the time she'd reached the butcher's shop Mary was gasping with a painful stitch in her side. She stood outside waiting for the pain to pass. The window display was a wonder to her. Shiny silver trays of meat divided each from its neighbour by a hedge of green paper, necklaces of sausages hung from hooks suspended from a central ring, white sheets of sweet-breads, rows of rabbits with little buckets hanging to catch the blood from their mouths, and attached to each tray a hand-written copperplate label denoting the contents. The gleaming white-tiled walls had pictures of plump pigs and well-fattened cattle and fleecy lambs. The bell over the door jangled merrily as Mary stepped into the shop onto a floor thick with clean sawdust. A butcher's assistant immaculate in striped apron and straw hat leaned across the marble counter.

'Yes miss,' he said, 'how can we help you?'

'Mrs Mullins, 15 Lancaster Terrace says you left off her shin of beef on Saturday's order.'

The butcher disappeared into the back of the shop and Mary turned and spotted a little glass kiosk in the corner, with the title 'Accounts' picked out in white letters.

Seated inside was a woman in a starched white coat, busily writing in a ledger. From time to time she paused in what she was doing and took money from a customer and rang the amount up on a large brass till.

'Beryl,' said the butcher, 'check Mrs Mullins' order. Make sure there's two pounds of shin down on it.'

The woman in the white coat took several bills off a metal spike and shuffled through them. 'Yes,' she said in a thin nasal voice, 'down here, two pounds five shillings.'

Mary watched the woman minutely.

'You want something,' said Beryl, looking disdainfully at Mary's crumpled apron and flushed face.

'Only to say you got two labels in your window what you 'aven't spelt right.'

'Oh, yes,' sniffed Beryl.

'Cutlets, you got it spelt with an "i" and sweetbreads, you got sweetbreeds.'

'Well thank you very much, I'm sure,' snapped Beryl frostily.

'Here you are,' said the butcher handing her a white paper parcel. 'You better make tracks or that Mrs Mullins'll 'ave you in the pot along with the stew.'

Triumphantly Mary swept from the shop, her eyes shining.

Back at Lancaster Terrace Mrs Mullins snatched the meat from her hands and set about it with a large knife.

'Those three onions peel and slice them, when that's done wash your 'ands and you and Cissie can clean the drawin' room and dinin' room and lay the table up there.'

'Certainly, Mrs Mullins,' said Mary sweetly.

The cook glared suspiciously at her. 'What's your game?' she snapped.

'Nothin,' said Mary, but it wasn't true. Everything had changed since she'd seen the inside of 'Marshall Brothers High Class Family Butchers'. She had found the perfect job for herself. All she had to do was last out a couple of months in Lancaster Terrace and dislodge that snooty Beryl from behind the glass kiosk. She could almost feel the starched white coat fitting snugly around her shoulders.

'Welcome to the beehive,' the forewoman, Freda Hatcher, had said to Lily on her first day. Looking around the tiny room high up in the roof of Denby and Shanks Lily thought it an apt description. Its walls were lined with hundreds of tiny wooden drawers and it smelt of dust and wax polish. There were four of them including herself sat around a table working away at their individual tasks like bees in a honeycomb.

Although Lily considered herself a good seamstress, watching the women around her demonstrated how much she had to learn. Freda was the undoubted expert who oversaw all the sewing. She had a leather-bound notebook crammed with precise pencil drawings of all the ornamental items likely to be required. They ranged from the relatively simple rings of gold lace to be sewn around an officer's sleeve to the intricate band master's shoulder cords, sword knots, cocked hat tassels and Household Cavalry aigiulettes. She and Nesta Armitage, her second-in-command, would discuss the progress of the work each morning and what new orders had come in. The final member of the beehive was Clemmie Ivers, a tiny white-haired woman who kept account of all the stock in the many drawers and cupboards. She perched on a stool pulling out one drawer after another unfolding all the precious threads and laces from their wrappings of acid-free tissue-paper. They were supplied by Benton and Johnson Ltd, a London manufacturer of gold and silver wires and threads. It all sounded quite medieval to Lily and she would not have been surprised to be asked to swear an oath of secrecy. The names of the threads passed through her head like a magical litany: Pearl Purl, Peak Gimp, Fine Gold Tambour, Russia Braid, Shamrock Lace and Rococo. The three women addressed each other by their Christian names but Lily was called Miss Forrest and returned the courtesy.

Working in the beehive was a recognition of her developing skills but Lily missed the companionship of Dora and Mrs Markham, even the bitter humour of Ruby Froggat.

Freda, Clemmie and Nesta were all well over forty. Their talk was of the price of food, the lowering of standards and looking back. They were all part of the shop choir which rehearsed in the lunch hour and the highlight of their life was the invitation to 'sing in the new year,' at Admiral Shanks' house in Southsea every December.

Lily sat next to Freda and laboured over making sleeve curls for a sub-lieutenant's uniform.

'Two and a half per cent gold in naval work, only two in army uniforms. Why d'you think that is?' the forewoman asked her.

Lily couldn't think. 'I don't know,' she said honestly.

'The sea, the sea, it's the salt in the air you understand. It corrodes the metal.'

Under Freda's guidance she left the space of a sixpence in the centre of each curl and struggled to make the pleated edges lie flat. In the first few weeks she could think of nothing but getting the stitching right. Slowly and surely she became more adept and began to notice what the other women were making.

Nesta was making a Royal Navy sword-knot and was in deep conference with Freda. 'Haven't made one of these for ages,' she said.

'You'll need gold gimp and blue silk, round the lower mould twice, then over middle and round the top. Take up Becket Stitches and work from waist upwards. Miss Forrest, you'll need to get a notebook and copy all these drawings. You'll be able to practice them at home.'

'Is this all right?'

'Miss Forrest,' snapped Freda. 'We have only one standard here and that is perfection. Your pleating falls far short of the mark.'

Red-faced, Lily unpicked her stitches and reset the curl.

'Did you see those letters in the *Evening News* about Palmerston Road?' asked Nesta.

'Oh, complaining about all the fruit barrows and the sandwich men? They was quite right. It's beginning to look like a market. Used to be so select.'

'Then there's that creature in the doorway selling newspapers,' said Clemmie. 'He gave me quite a turn. Got no legs and shuffles about on a little wooden platform. Shouldn't be allowed.'

'What d'you mean?' asked Lily, greatly daring but indignant at Miss Ivers calling the man a creature.

'Ought to be put away somewhere out of sight.'

'Did you see his medals?'

'That's as maybe, miss,' snapped Clemmie.

'Used to be a footballer before the war,' said Lily. She had no idea whether that was true but suddenly wanted to shame the narrow goody-goody little woman.

Clemmie flushed an angry red. 'Hardly my fault, I'm sure, I'm as sorry as anyone.'

'You'd better make the tea, miss,' snapped Freda, 'twenty-five to eleven already. If you applied yourself more to your sewing instead of keeping chipping in to the conversation your needle-work would be a sight better.'

'I'll not let you humble me,' she thought angrily as she lit the gas-ring and filled the large black kettle. 'I am going to learn this craft in spite of you.' It was all such a contrast between the beautiful work produced by these women, the precision and delicacy of their stitching, and the carping ugliness of their words. Please, please, please let there be a letter for me from Michael. Let there be something to look forward to.

Almost two and a half hours to dinner time. After washing the teacups Lily settled to master the golden curl. She composed a story in her head as she bent over her work. It concerned three mean-spirited spinsters and an interloping beetle who'd toiled up to the attic from the coal cellar trailing soot all over the women's fine stitchery. Admiral Shanks the owner of the shop was so furious when he found the ruined needlework that he had the spinsters cast out of the beehive and condemned to sit in the cellar sewing onion sacks with string for the rest of their lives.

'That's better,' said Freda when Lily handed her the com-pleted sleeve, 'a bit of concentration was all you needed. Now off you go to dinner. There'll be the other sleeve waiting for you when you gets back.'

Lily sped down the stairs, glad to be free. She was halfway home before she remembered that she had wanted to drop into the workroom and leave a message for Dora. Never mind, she'd pop in after dinner.

She flung her coat on her bed before going down the passage

to talk to Gran and Uncle Albert. On the dressing-table was a letter from Michael. Lily's joy was tinged with guilt. Gran had been into her room. Had she noticed the apron on the floor and the letter from Dad in the pocket? She sank to her knees and searched under the bed, in the dressing-table drawers and in the bottom of the wardrobe.

A tap on the door had her leaping to her feet. 'Who is it?' she called her voice sharp with alarm.

'It's Albert. We thought we'd heard you come in. Hurry up, my dear, your Gran is just dishing up now.'

Was it her imagination or did Gran avoid meeting her eye?

Lily went into the scullery to fill her glass with water. The back door was open and hanging on the line was her apron blowing in the late spring breeze.

Hong Kong February 31st

My Dear little Dora,

I miss you like anything and wish I could wake up and find you snuggled up beside me in my hammock and all my shipmates thrown to the sharks. You can't believe how cheesed off we get with each other. Only 27 more months my sweetheart and HMS. Lister will be steaming home to Pompey and yours truly will leap ashore and hold you in my arms and kiss you breathless.'

For a few seconds Dora forgot it was Monday morning. Even the chill gloom of the Denby and Shanks cloakroom with its chipped sinks and backless chairs failed to intrude on her happiness. Even her sore throat and pounding head ceased to matter. Harry still loved her. Eagerly she scanned the pages.

I am writing to you from the sick bay. I'm here suffering from sun-stroke. Trust me to fall asleep on the upper deck. When I woke up I had a blinding headache and was sick as a dog. I've

*spent all my time in here sleeping and drinking gallons of water.
Got a real roasting from my Divisional Officer saying as I was
irresponsible falling asleep in the sun and making myself unfit for
duty. Good thing most of the sunburn is on my back so I can lie
on my front and write to you.*

Dora bit her lip, she couldn't bear to think of Harry being ill.

*What's happened to Mary? I miss getting her news of the
family. Can you gee her up a bit? No letters from Dad as per
usual. At least not expecting nothing from him I don't get
disappointed. You didn't say anything about Ma in your last
letter. I don't know what good it does visiting her or what
difference all them pills make.*

*Then there's the kids. If it wasn't for you keeping an eye on
them I'd be worried sick. Sorry to blather on about things. It's
being cooped up in here that's getting me down.*

Once more the knot of anxiety tightened in her chest. Harry
hadn't got her letter yet about his mum. And why hadn't Mary
written to him? The joy of hearing from him was clouded now
with other concerns.

*Sorry to have missed a couple of days. We are now anchored
in Hong Kong Harbour. Another world from Pompey. Me and
Michael stepped ashore and got ourselves caught up in a Chinese
Funeral. Very quaint affair, it was. Around the dead bloke's
coffin was all this cooked rice and candles. They were lit to keep
the evil spirits away. Someone handed out cigarettes to all of us.
Then the procession moved off with boys carrying blooming great
banners with pictures of Chinese Dragons on them.*

*Lots of cooking stalls out in the street. You'd be amazed Dora at
the way people live. The harbours is choked with these little boats
called Sampans. Thousands of the ordinary Chinese live on them*

and hardly ever step ashore, sleep, eat, breed and die on them they do.

Nasty shock as we were on board the other day we looked into the water and the body of a little girl floated past. Out here women have a thin time of it. The family needs a dowry to get a daughter married off and sometimes the poor girl is sent to a state brothel to earn her money or to pay off a family debt.

It all seemed unreal, to Dora, as if he were writing from another world. Abroad there was change and difference to make the time pass more quickly. Letters never kept pace with life. It was now a fortnight since Mrs Vine's death and it would probably be over a month before Harry got to hear about it. By the time he wrote to her about his mother she and his family would be plunged into the next crisis.

Michael and me are doing well as torpedo men and the instructor reckons that torpedoes are the weapons of the future. He was talking to the pair of us about volunteering for the submarine service. It's much better money and the main base is only across the harbour in Gosport.

You and me could get married and get ourselves a couple of rooms across the water away from both our families. It's another two years and more 'til I get back and by that time they'll have sorted Ma's head out and Mary will be at work and little Blyth at school.

How easy it sounded on paper. Tears gathered in Dora's eyes. Soon he would get her letter about his mother and all his hopes for her would be dashed.

Write back quick and let me know what you think, my sweetheart. We could be hitched directly I get back you'll be way over twenty one then well able to please yourself.

All my hugs and kisses,

Your Harry

Hastily Dora slipped the pages back into the envelope. It was a lovely, lovely better full of plans for their future. If only she could draw that cheerfulness off the paper and make it her own.

Last night she had looked at the photograph they'd posed for the week before he'd sailed. How happy and carefree she'd looked then. Her eyes shining her hand in his. They'd glowed with confidence. Harry had called her his little 'nut brown maiden'. This morning a girl with dull hair and shadows under her eyes stared back at her from the mirror. She turned on the tap and cupped her hands and tried to drink a mouthful of water. Her eyes filled with tears at the pain of swallowing. After taking a few steadying breaths she straightened her shoulders and walked into the workroom.

She nodded to her workmates before settling down at her chair to start the buttonholes of an admiral's jacket. The air was dry and smelt of scorched cloth as Mr Savours wielded the flat irons. It was so hot she felt that she would faint at any minute. Perhaps she was going down with tonsillitis like little Blyth.

The voices of her workmates rose above the whirr of the sewing-machines.

'The Prince of Wales is coming to Fratton Park to watch Pompey play,' said Ivy, a mousy-haired nervous girl.

'Where'd you hear that?' asked Ruby scornfully.

'In the *Evening News*. He's coming on the thirteenth. Ooh I reckon he's ever so handsome.'

Ruby chuckled. 'Fancy your chances do ya?'

'Don't be so silly,' protested Ivy, 'I only said as how . . .?'

'Gone all red you 'ave. Rather have John Gilbert any day of the week. What d'you say Dora?'

Dora looked up at Ruby, red-haired, raucous and full of life. She wished she could summon up even an ounce of the other girl's spirit. She swallowed painfully before saying, 'Haven't thought about it.'

'What's up with you?' said Ruby, peering down at her.

'Sore throat,' gasped Dora.

'Whaa, your head's burning. Miss Pearson come and have a look. I reckon she got a fever.'

The forewoman's hand was cool on her head. 'Miss Somers, you certainly don't look well. Do you think if you splashed your face with some cold water and I'll send out for some lemonade . . .'

Dora could see the anxiety in Miss Pearson's face. Today Admiral Fawcett was going to the shop for the last fitting of his new civilian suit. She had the jacket in her lap finishing off the buttonholes. Admiral Fawcett was legendary for his gimlet-eyed inspection of any garments made for him, and for his temper when they failed to meet his requirements. She nodded her willingness to try and carry on. Putting down her sewing she made her way to the cloakroom.

It was as if she had a wire feather trapped in her throat continually rasping and irritating. She stood at the sink holding a wet hankie to her head. Could she last out until dinner-time? There was only this last buttonhole then the jacket could be pressed and delivered. Perhaps if she could go home and lie down and sleep.

Miss Pearson came in with a glass in her hand. She put it on the edge of the sink and pulled a chair towards Dora and helped her into it.

'Sip it slowly, my dear,' she said. 'Hot lemonade and sugar. You must go home at dinner-time but if you could just finish off the jacket I would be most grateful. You're my best apprentice, so methodical and painstaking.' Sighing Miss Pearson shut the door behind her and went back into the workroom.

She was quickly followed by Ruby. 'You don't 'alf look bad, Dor,' she said, 'Don't let old Pearson run you into the ground. Regular slave driver she is.'

Dora nodded and smiled while Ruby combed her hair and prinked and posed in the spattered mirror. When she was satisfied with her appearance she gave Dora a wink before slamming out of the door.

Sitting sipping the lemonade Dora began to feel cooler and calmer. Back in the workroom she forced herself to focus on the grey worsted jacket and managed a few more stitches until the necessity to swallow rasped again at her throat.

As the dockyard bell chimed the dinner-time break she handed the jacket to Mr Savours for pressing. The silver-haired old tailor hauled the fourteen-pound flat-iron off the gas jet as if it were half its weight. 'You go steady, my dear,' he said kindly. 'No good overdoing it. Denby and Shanks will still be here tomorrow.'

'There's lots out of work,' said Dora anxiously.

'Reliable girl like you, good timekeeper and good needle-woman. You've got no anxieties.'

'Thank you,' Dora managed to gasp.

'Off you go, Miss Somers, and thank you,' said a relieved Miss Pearson. 'Let me know if you can't come tomorrow. Perhaps I could send some work to you for over the weekend. We'll see.'

Dora nodded goodbye to everyone and walked slowly down the stairs out into Half Moon Street. Outside the dockyard gates opposite there was the usual surge of bicycles as maties cycled home to their dinner. Some men lit their pipes from the wall lighter and the pavements were crowded with sailors. She decided to call into the chemist at Cross Street, near Lily's house, and get herself some medicine. Perhaps someone there could give Lily a message. Now her friend had been moved to the Epaulette Room she really missed her.

They had become good friends, in the two years since Lily had been a nervous young apprentice at Denby and Shanks. Now with both their boyfriends away they'd grown especially close. Dora had been drawn into Lily's family and her gran had been ever so kind to her. But since Harry's mum's death and Lily starting working in the beehive something had been lost. Perhaps they both needed to make more of an effort keep the friendship going. Lily had always been warm and kind but sometimes she got so caught up in her own concerns that she didn't notice Dora trailing anxiously in her wake.

With her throat burning and head throbbing she snailed along the pavement towards Mr Donald's shop. The act of walking took all her concentration and she was startled when an angry voice accosted her.

'Watch out you dozy mare, where you think you're going?' cried an exasperated woman as Dora stepped in her path. Potatoes, carrots and onions rolled across the pavement.

She knelt down, her head spinning, and began to pick up the scattered veg. The task was beyond her. Dora clutched hold of a lamppost and sunk down onto the pavement.

'You all right, gal. You looks proper poorly,' said the young woman, helping her to her feet. 'Sorry I shouted at yer. You was lucky not to get run over not looking and that. 'Ow far you gotter go?'

'Unicorn Gate,' Dora managed to gasp between bouts of shivering. It seemed an impossible distance away and yet was only a few streets further into the town. Above her voices rose and fell and then, amazingly, she heard her brother calling to her.

'Dor what you doing? It's okay Missis, it's my sister. I'll see to her.'

Mark leant the shop bike against the kerb and helped his sister to her feet. At the sight of a familiar face Dora burst into tears.

'Never mind the waterworks, let's get you back home. Here stow the bag in the basket and slip your leg over the cross-bar. Catch hold of the handles, that's it.'

The journey was a blur of traffic noise and dizzying swoops between trams and other bicycles. For once her father didn't scold or nag but helped her up the stairs. Her mother put down the saucepan on the table and drew Dora into her arms. 'Come here, my lamb, let's get you into bed. Mark, you run that tray up to your grandmother. Barney, you and your father will have to see to yourselves.'

Dora stood shivering in her bedroom while her mother undressed her and helped her on with her nightdress.

'I'll make you up a sage and vinegar gargle that'll soothe that throat of yours. Then you can have a good sleep. Barney can drop off a message to that Miss Pearson. You won't be back there 'til Wednesday at the earliest.' The gargle was followed by a cool lavender compress. Mrs Somers settled herself with her knitting beside her daughter's bed.

A blessed feeling of being taken care of, of being safe, stole over Dora. Gratefully she dropped down into sleep. For the next few days she floated in and out of consciousness alternately burning and shivering, her throat throbbing with pain. Her mother brought her bowls of soup, swathed her neck in bran poultices secured with a crepe bandage. At first they were wonderfully soothing and then cold and clammy. Even her father came and sat with her reading her bits out of the paper. But that was something of a mixed blessing.

'Seventy men let go at the yard,' he sighed, 'reckon it'll be at least fifty a week for the foreseeable future. Talking of closing down altogether at Milford Haven, now. Then look at this,' he jabbed his finger at another gloomy forecast, about slipways in the dockyards being inadequate for construction of new capital ships.

'Stop reading the paper, Dad,' she said taking his hand in hers. 'It only gets you all het up and it doesn't change things.'

'I've always provided for my family,' he said staring past her and pulling his hand away. 'What if the shop goes under. What'll we do?'

With a shock, she realised that her father was frightened. Dad who had spent his whole working life in this shop. Who got up at five to take all the dockies' bikes into his shed and stood there in afternoon handing them out again never to the wrong owner. Who stayed late at night doing bicycle repairs. He'd taken on his business from his father and wanted to pass it on to his sons.

'Look, Dad,' she said, 'I'll finish my apprenticeship in September and be on good money, at least thirty shillings, Barney will be earning well when he's done his time. Even Mark could get a good job at that motor cycle place in Gosport. A young lad could help you here. Be less money and probably do just as well.'

Her father sprung off the bed and glared down at her. 'What d'you think I've been slaving for all these years, the shop's for Mark. He's just got to set his mind to it.'

It was tempting to cling to her invalid status to relish the spoiling. Even Faith and Mercy called with a crumpled bag of barley-sugar. 'Our Mary's got a job in one of them posh 'ouses workin' as a maid. Dad don't reckon she'll last five minutes what wiv her temper. He says she'll even 'ave to empty their chamber pots.'

Faith chuckled, 'She won't like that.'

Dora smiled. It would do her good to do something she didn't like for a change and learn not to answer back. Although Mary was the last person she wanted to see, she felt hurt that she had not called or even asked after her well-being.

'We brought you this dress of our mum's, thought you could make us both a blouse from it. What'ya think?' Dora nodded and smiled.

'Gotta go now. See ya later.' The girls kissed her and ran quickly down the stairs. On the Wednesday Miss Pearson came. She brought her a bag of purple grapes.

'Just a couple of jackets,' she said apologetically, draping them over the back of a chair. 'I hate troubling you Miss Somers, but we're very hard pressed at the moment. You're the only one I can rely on. I'll drop in on Friday morning if you're not at work by then.'

Dora nodded and smiled.

Miss Pearson was followed by Lily who brought her a tiny bottle of eau de Cologne and a copy of *My Story Weekly*. At first she enjoyed her visit as Lily read to her about, 'The man who let me down' and 'Confessions of a Mill Girl.' Then she began to feel tired and achy again. Lily said there was a secret she must tell her. Something about finding a letter and how her mother could still be alive. Dora was confused and couldn't seem to make the right response to what Lily was saying.

'Surely she'd have come to see you, I can't believe she'd let all this time go without trying to find out about you.'

She closed her eyes and Lily's voice drifted on and then when she opened them again she was gone. Barney got her some paper and envelopes so that she could write to Harry but the words wouldn't come. What she craved was just to be left alone, to sleep and have nothing expected of her.

The next day when she was sat out of bed trying to sew one of the uniform jackets her mother came in. 'Dora, love,' she said, standing at the door in her coat and hat, her face creased with anxiety. 'Could you run up a glass of stout for your gran? I've to get her medicine from Queen Street and I'm running a bit late.'

Dora nodded. She couldn't bear that hounded look and the helpless hand-wringing. Alternately she wanted to gather her mother into her arms or give her a good shaking. How had she let herself become such a cringing shadow?

She drew a blanket around her shoulders and carried the brown glass bottle up the stairs. Her grandmother was leaning on her stick, peering out of the window.

'Gran, I've brought your stout. Shall I open it for you now?' she said loudly.

The little wizened old woman creaked around to face her, like a worn mechanical toy. She pulled her shawl more tightly over her shoulders before peering at her granddaughter. 'What you doin' up here? I don't want you, I wants Myrtle.' Her voice was rusty and accusing.

'Mum's gone out to get your medicine, she'll be back soon.'

Granny Somers tapped her stick on the floor. 'Never here when I wants her,' she moaned. 'Oh, yes, open it, open it and I wants a bit of bread. Fetch me a slice.'

Dora hurried down to the kitchen and cut a piece of bread and slapped it on to a plate before going back up to the attic.

'About time,' said her granny as she sat herself at a small rickety table.

Dora opened the stout and poured it into a green ribbed glass before setting it down beside the plate. 'What you doin' still in your night-clothes? Looks slatternly to me, very slatternly.'

'I've been home sick. I've got . . .'

'I never had time to be ill when I was a young maid. You been indulged and mollycoddled, that's your trouble.'

'I'll see you later,' said Dora, hoping to make her getaway before she lost her temper.

'Could stay and talk to your granny. You young ones got not an 'ap'orth of kindness.'

Firmly Dora shut the door and returned to her bedroom. The earlier feeling of being cared for had evaporated. After the first day when her mother had brought her cool drinks and sat with her Dora had increasingly felt herself to be a nuisance, an added burden to everyone. Dad only wanted to unload all his concerns on her, the twins wanted new clothes and even Lily wanted advice that she was incapable of giving.

Resignedly Dora took off her nightdress and began to dress in her work clothes. She folded the jackets neatly in the Denby and Shanks box. Home had ceased to be a refuge.

Chapter Eight

Beattie studied Lily's face as she took her seat at the kitchen table. She looked like a child caught pinching sugar. Poor kid, she almost felt sorry for her. For two pins she'd give her a good telling-off for prying into things that didn't concern her and get the air cleared between them. But it wasn't that simple.

If only Lily had tucked the letter away in a drawer; if only she'd not left her apron on the floor. When Beattie took the pile of freshly ironed clothes into Lily's room it had been the most natural thing in the world to pick up the apron and take the rustling paper out of the pocket before bundling the garment up for washing. Finding that letter had been a sickening shock. It had brought back all the pain and distress of those weeks when her son had walked the streets searching for his young wife and Lily, a baby not yet weaned, cried for her mother. She thought those times were gone forever – locked fast in her memory. The very last thing she wanted was for Lily to prise them loose. Alec and Miriam were now well and truly settled with two young children needing love and stability. No, she would not allow her granddaughter to open that wound again.

Life went forward, not back. Lily had so much to look forward to: getting a real skill behind her, the return of Michael and perhaps making a new life together. One day the raising of a family of her own. The past was a treacherous place with many false turns and blind alleys. As an orphan herself Beattie knew only too well how easy it was to deify a missing mother. It did no good, all this harking back. History could not be rewritten. The present moment was all you had and by God she was going to live it.

'Shall I serve up the dinner, Beatrice?'

Albert startled her into action. 'No, no I'll do it. I'm sorry, I was wool-gathering. Two sausages, Lily, spring greens and a bit of mash?'

'Oh, yes Gran, that will be fine.'

'Did I notice a letter addressed to you this morning?' asked Albert smiling at her. Lily blushed and patted her pocket, still not meeting Beattie's eye. 'It's from Michael. I shouldn't think he's got the news about the wedding yet. Dora's worried about whether Harry has got the news about his mum.'

'The same for me too, my dear,' said Albert, handing Beattie his plate. 'That's the trouble with letters,' he continued, 'they're always out of kilter. By the time you reply to something another event has taken its place.'

'Where is he now?' asked Beattie, trying to keep her voice casual yet interested.

'Hong Kong still, I think.'

Beattie ransacked her brain for something else to say. She picked at her food and noticed Lily doing the same. 'Why don't you go and read your letter, ducks?' she said. 'You must be dying for news from that handsome young fellow. I'll warm up your dinner for tonight. I'll bring you a cup of tea and a biscuit later.'

'Thanks, Gran,' said Lily, hurrying up from her chair and out of the kitchen.

'I can understand Lily playing with her dinner,' said Albert quietly, 'but what's wrong with you, Beatrice? You've hardly touched a thing.'

Always she had found it easy to be honest with Albert but

today the words wouldn't come. She wanted time to sort out her thoughts. If she kept calm the crisis might go away. 'A still tongue in a wise head' – wasn't that what Albert's father always said? Beattie smiled reassuringly at her husband. 'Can I tell you later, my love? It needs thinking about, it's all fragile at the moment.'

'Why don't you sit out in the yard for a spell?' he said. 'Feel the sun on your face. I'll fetch you out a cup of tea later. I've got a challenging afternoon ahead of me. Sailor and I are going to have a game of draughts.'

'How are you going to manage that?' she asked, glad of a diversion to her troubling thoughts.

He went over to his desk and returned with a chequered board and box of draughtsmen. 'It's all very experimental, of course,' said Albert. 'I've made the edge raised to stop the pieces falling off and sunk the white squares so that Sailor can distinguish them.'

'Very clever,' said Beattie, 'but how will he know the black pieces from the white?'

'The black are smaller with one raised ridge and the white have three.'

'That's so clever, Albert,' she said smiling at him. 'I should think the old salt'll be delighted.'

'I'm sure he will be. After I've made you a cup of tea I shall nip over the wall and we'll test out the game.' Albert made a shooing movement. 'Off you go and sit out in the sun. I won't be five minutes. I'll be out soon.'

Beattie sat in an old armchair by the honeysuckle growing between the houses. This idleness took some getting used to. Not that she missed sitting toiling over the collars for Gold-stein's. That was a labour she was well rid of. What she did miss was time with Miriam and the children. Seeing the day-to-day changes in baby Joseph, miles away in the Isle of Wight: she would miss his first steps and first words. What a help she could be to Miriam if she were down there: taking the little ones off her hands for a few hours, giving an eye to the cooking, even serving behind the bar. Still, Albert had said they would visit in the summer and with that she must be content.

The back door across the yard opened and Dahlia helped Sailor over the step. She lowered the washing-line and hung his walking-stick over it and then by means of sliding the stick along the line he was able to guide himself down the path to a rickety wicker chair.

'Afternoon to you both,' called Beattie.

'Mrs Pragnell, good day to you,' said Dahlia, as she carried a card-table out and set it beside the old man before pulling up another chair.

'Afternoon, Missis,' called Sailor gruffly. 'Is your good fellow about?'

'He'll be with you in a few minutes,' said Beattie smiling at him. She knew he couldn't see her but felt that in some way her voice might carry the smile. 'I hear you're going to have a draughts match.'

'According to the Admiral,' laughed Sailor wheezily. 'He reckons to have devised something to make it possible.'

'You'll excuse me,' said Dahlia, 'I've a tap that needs fixing.'

Beattie nodded to her as she went back into the house. The woman intrigued her. Since they had moved in next-door she had gleaned very little about her new neighbours beyond the fact that they were totally unrelated to each other. Dahlia had never paid her for the shopping Beattie had bought for her that first morning, and it was difficult to see how they managed for money. Thinking to be helpful she had suggested that Dahlia might like to take on her collar assignment.

The woman had been almost scornful. 'Not at all in my line, Mrs Pragnell,' she'd said. 'Give me a box of spanners and it's a different story. My father was an engineer and would have turned me into one if Mother hadn't interfered. However, I mustn't keep you,' she had said, walking Beattie towards the door.

Albert came into the garden carrying a tray of tea.

'Has Lily gone back to work?'

'Yes, she said not to trouble about tea as she'll call in to see Dora and probably get something there.'

'Ready for the draughts are you, Sailor?' called Albert as he stepped over the little dividing wall. 'I think it'll be something of a dry run.'

'Sea trials, as you might say,' laughed Sailor, stretching out his hand to his neighbour.

Beattie barely heard what they said; her thoughts were all of Lily. She was avoiding her. Why couldn't she have left the apron where it was? Had she done nothing Lily's interest would have eventually waned, commonsense telling her that a mother who disappeared so long ago was unlikely to reappear. Poor Lily, she couldn't broach the subject without admitting that she had been spying. It was down to her grandmother to open the subject and the sooner the better. A scarcity of information would be eked out by dangerous imaginings if she wasn't careful. But, the truth, the truth . . .

She was startled back to the present by the howling of a dog. It was a sound full of panic.

Albert sprang to his feet and picked up a bucket before rushing into the Carruthers' kitchen.

'Jesus, Squire,' said Sailor, 'what's the rumpus? You've knocked all the pieces on the deck, just as we was getting the hang of it.'

Towser, the Vines' old dog, staggered and half fell over the small wall into the yard. His tail was black and singed.

'My Gawd, what a pong,' said Sailor screwing up his face in disgust. He turned his face to Beattie. 'What's going on, Missis?' he asked.

'Somebody's set fire to Towser's tail,' Beattie cried, as Albert sprung over the wall and flung the water from the bucket over the terrified animal.

'The wretch,' he gasped, 'who could have done such a thing?' After the soaking the dog subsided in a whimpering heap. 'I'll find him a blanket. I just hope the shock won't be too much for him.'

'Poor beast,' said Sailor. 'No prizes for guessing who's done that – the evil little tyke.'

Beattie was mystified. It certainly wasn't any of the Vine children. They loved their mangy old hound. And then she saw Algie creeping back from the Vines' yard and throwing a box of matches in the hedge. 'That was a wicked, wicked thing to do,' she cried, shocked at the boy's wanton cruelty.

'What's he done?' cried Dahlia striding out into the yard.

'Set fire to the neighbour's dog,' said Sailor. 'A good thrashing that's what he needs.'

'I'll fetch the belt,' said Dahlia,' he'll not do it again.'

'He's only a child,' gasped Beattie, 'surely to God . . .'

'None of your business,' snapped Dahlia, rushing back into the house with the white-faced Algie in tow.

'Jesus, Sailor,' Beattie cried, 'can't you do something? He's only a little lad.'

'No, no,' screamed Algie, 'it weren't me. No, no, no.'

Beattie felt sick as the boy continued to scream. However much she condemned his action she could not bear to hear his cries of terror.

'Got to be stopped afore he kills someone,' said Sailor, as if reading her thoughts.

'Terrible what he done, just terrible.'

'You're right,' said Albert, 'but children don't think of the consequences. He was curious rather than wantonly cruel, I'm sure.'

'It was all the spur of the moment,' said Beattie, sickened by the swishing of the strap and the little boy's screams. 'Surely to God, he's been punished enough.'

The screaming ceased abruptly to be followed by the sound of sobbing. Beattie was sure the crying, now, was coming from Dahlia.

All the pleasure of the afternoon in the May sunshine had evaporated.

'I'm sorry you had to hear that rumpus,' said Sailor. 'Mrs Carruthers has got to check him. Not the first time that lad 'as played with matches.' The old man got to his feet and after some fumbling looped his walking-stick back onto the clothes-line. 'Albert,' he said, 'can you step over and pick up these pieces for me. We'll have another game some other day. Need to see how the game hackles when you put one draft atop the other to make a king. Tell you the truth I haven't the heart for it now.'

Chapter Nine

Dear Harry,

   Next time you wants me to write to you don't go whining to Dora. Sunning yourself out there you got no idea. It was horrible: me and the kids havin Mum's coffin in the front room, Dad legless, then Auntie Betty wanting to take our Blyth away. Dad gave her a right roasting. Blyth was sweaty with fever but is okay now. Goes over most days to Michael's mum.

   I've been a month now in this rotten job in Lancaster Terrace working for these toffs. Bleedin helpless they are. Even have to empty their po's. Makes such a palaver they do, a plate for this and a plate for that no wonder they needs Cissie and me and Mrs Mullins to fetch and carry all the time. She's a great fat raging old mare. I'm biting my tongue and all for a purpose.

   Harry, I found just the job I wants. Cashier in a butcher's shop. Spose it won't sound much to you but I really, really want it. You have to sit at a desk and have a big brass till and a starched white coat. It's all separate in a little glass kiosk. Just one snag, I got to winkle this Beryl woman off her perch. Get them butchers to see that I'm really suited to it.

   Things is changed round a bit at home. Dad is down stairs in the front room now and me and Blyth up in his old bedroom. Don't know where you're going to sleep when you gets home.

Spose you'll be out with Dora all the time. She's all right, quite good with the kids and that but I miss the time when it was just you and me. So long as she don't get Blyth on her side.

Things is going good for all of us. I'm crossing my fingers, scared it won't last. Dad is gettin on all right with his job. Reckons the other porters are a lot of fussy old buggers. You know what he's like just as we're sat pretty he's got to pull the cloth out and send everything crashing. Like he's got to trip himself up and us along with him.

Mary stared out of the window into the street. It was Sunday afternoon, her only free time away from Mrs Mullins. It was nearly three o'clock before she managed to finish the dinner-time washing-up: all those vegetable dishes and pots and pans. Her greatest hatred was reserved for the meat-tin where deposits of fat set like concrete in the corners. She rubbed her fingers raw with the wire wool and scouring powder.

When she'd given up hope of ever escaping, the cook had snarled at her, 'Go if you're going. Don't hang around on my account.'

High as a kite with her freedom, she'd flown along to Green Street to walk past the butcher's front window. It was empty save for a few rows of paper grass and steel tongs and skewers. Tomorrow she promised herself another look when perhaps she could spot a few more of Beryl's spelling mistakes. It had become a crusade to discredit the disdainful cashier and insinuate herself into the gleaming glass kiosk.

Again she looked down on Lemon Street where Blyth was being pulled up and down the pavement in a wooden cart made for Algie by Mrs Carruthers. Her brother was laughing and calling out, 'Faster, faster.'

She didn't really take to Algie. He wasn't at all like a seven-year-old, more an old man in a young boy's body. Always watching and waiting. She'd seen him take money out of Sailor's purse when he was asleep out in the yard. When she challenged him he kicked her in the shins and called her a 'nosy bitch'.

She'd slapped him hard across the face making his eyes water and leaving a red mark across his cheek. He'd stared at her defiantly, challenging her to hit him again.

'Faster, faster,' called Blyth and Algie swooped up the street, letting go of the guiding rope inches before the cart crashed into the lamppost and tipped Blyth into the street.

She rushed down the stairs but the twins were coming up the street and swept their brother up into their arms then all three came laughing through the door.

> *Got to go now, me and the kids is going down the pier to listen to the band. Dad as per usual of a Sunday is snoring is head off behind The News of the World. Still he did cook the dinner. Twins said it was all right. I had mine at work. Mrs Mullins does really good roast spuds, for all she's a moany old cow.*
>
> *Write soon. Love Mary.*

'Did you like my mother?'

Aunt Hester stopped making the trellis for the sweet peas and turned towards her, twine in hand. 'What's put that in your head?' she demanded, her voice sharp with suspicion.

Lily had slipped the question in among innocent queries about the garden. 'I wonder about her sometimes,' she said, rubbing her sweating palms down the skirt of her dress.

'Well,' Hester said consideringly. 'Didn't see much of her. She was a pretty little thing, bright and lively. Had your Dad spellbound to start with.'

'But, did you like her?'

'Yes I suppose I did. Felt sorry for her in a way.'

'Why?' asked Lily, handing Hester the scissors.

'Like a plant in the wrong soil and climate. As if she were starved of something and put in the wrong pot.'

'Wasn't suited to life with a sailor,' said Uncle George, settling himself on a stool beside her and sliding his braces off his shoulders. 'Couldn't cope on her own. Wanted to be off out enjoying herself.'

'Married too young the pair of them. Her sixteen and Alec only just eighteen.'

'Have you got a picture of her?' asked Lily. She sensed their reluctance to talk and wanted to seize the opportunity before they changed the subject.

'I suppose I have somewhere, I don't know whether I could put my hand on it now,' said Aunt Hester doubtfully.

'Oh, please Auntie. I'll wash some flowerpots for you.'

'Always was a determined little miss,' she muttered, handing the twine to George.

Her uncle got his stick and shuffled to his feet and continued threading the twine up the trellis.

Lily reached out to the tray of lemonade and poured herself another glass. 'Would you like some more, Uncle?' she asked.

'What I'd like,' he said, turning towards her, 'is to fathom out what you're up to.' Lily blushed.

'Why didn't you ask your Gran for a picture? She's more likely to have one to hand than your Auntie.'

'She doesn't like talking about her. I don't think they got on. I think Gran was glad she disappeared.'

'You're thinking too much if you ask me. Taking liberties, that's what you're doing and behind your Gran's back and all.' Easy-going Uncle George with his bleached blue eyes and walrus moustache was looking at her in a way that made Lily uncomfortable.

'I was out fighting in India when your mother was drowned. Can't say as what your Gran felt about it. Your Auntie was in hospital after losing our child. Your Dad was having to leave for China.'

'I know all that,' mumbled Lily.

'That's where you're wrong, Missie,' said Uncle George. 'You can have no idea what any of us felt. Hester alone in that hospital with no one of her family with time to visit her. Me wanting to come home and comfort her. Your Dad losing his wife and having to leave his little kids. And your Gran a widow suddenly having to take on two motherless babies. That's one thing I'm certain of, Lily. You haven't the foggiest notion of what any of us felt.'

'Why are you being so angry?' she asked.

'Because you're going behind your Gran's back. If you just wanted to see a picture of your mother you'd have asked her and she'd have shown you. But you've got something else up your sleeve.'

Lily stared at the little sweet-pea plants in the wooden seedling tray. What would Uncle George say if he knew she'd opened Gran's box and read her letter? The low opinion he had of her, this afternoon would be even lower.

'All your young life ever since you was a baby hasn't your Gran been good to you?' When Lily said nothing Uncle George reached forward and tilted her face towards him. 'Well hasn't she?' he demanded.

Lily nodded.

'Mother and Grandma all rolled into one.' He smiled at her and his voice lost its angry edge. 'Don't lose what you got, our Lily, for some fancy notion or other.'

Too tearful to speak she nodded again.

'Well, I'm off to the Glass Bible,' said her uncle, patting her on the shoulder. 'I've worked up a proper thirst. Give my regards to your Gran.'

'Gone off down the Three Marines, I spose,' said Aunt Hester as she walked down the path towards Lily, an envelope in her hand. 'At least he had the grace to finish the trellis.

'Here you are. Might as well keep it. No use to me.'

It was what she had wanted so badly and now the envelope was in her hands she couldn't open it.

Aunt Hester set out a worn mat and settled back on her knees. 'Pass us those plants one at a time, there's a good girl,' she said, making a hole with the trowel and watering it with a large chipped jug.

Lily watched the old woman with her faded auburn hair and freckled, knobbly, arthritic hands. Aunt Hester working contentedly in her garden was a different person to the Aunt Hester who came to Gran's on a visit. She'd be all dressed up and nagging the life out of Uncle George. The two women brought out the worst in each other. Hester carping and critical and Gran angry and defensive. Perhaps Aunt Hester had been jealous when her brother Joseph married Gran. Like Mary Vine with Dora.

'They'll make a lovely show down here in this little corner, and the scent! That's the thing with sweet peas, you get double delight: perfume and colour.'

'I better be going, Auntie,' said Lily when the last seedling had been planted. 'It's an hour's walk back home.'

'It's been nice to see you Lily,' said Hester struggling to her feet. 'Tell your Gran not to be a stranger. And put the kettle on, on your way through the kitchen, there's a dear.'

As she came out of the front door in Cromwell Road she looked up at the clock-tower of the Royal Marine barracks opposite. Half-past four, by the time she got home Gran would have tea laid.

She walked along the sea-front, the yellowing envelope Auntie Hester had given her seeming to burn a hole in her handbag. The crowds were thinning along the promenade as she reached the South Parade Pier. She was less than halfway home. Lily stepped on to the beach and crunched over the shingle to the water's edge. After tossing a few stones into the water and listening to the satisfying splash she opened her handbag and drew out the envelope.

There was one photograph. It was of her mother with Andrew standing beside her in a sailor suit and herself as a baby in her mother's arms. She gasped with shock, tears filling her eyes. She hadn't been prepared for this. Seeing Andrew, her brother as she first remembered him, with his round freckled face and wiry red curls. Andrew who had been lost at Jutland just before her twelfth birthday. The pain felt as fresh as on the day the telegram arrived. No, no, she'd not expected this stabbing misery. She could hardly see the picture through her tears. Lily reached into her handbag and found her hankie and dried her eyes. Taking a deep breath she took another look at the photograph. It was like seeing herself in a mirror. The same long black hair and dark eyes, even the high cheekbones and pointed chin. What had she expected to feel? Satisfaction at seeing her mother at long last? A gleam of pleasure at having achieved her ends behind Gran's back? Certainly not this pain and loss. Gasping and shuddering she turned the picture over and read the inscription on the back. '*To Daddy from your loving Family, Mary, Andrew and Lily. Don't forget us.*'

But they had forgotten her, all of them. She was never mentioned. Only on that day when she'd had her ears pierced and Gran had given her the earrings that her mother had left for her. She had shown her the photograph, the first she'd ever seen, and then Dad had come in and snatched it away from her. There'd been that terrible row between her and her father about him and Miriam and little Rosie being her sister.

Lily put her hand to her mouth and bit her finger until the pain distracted her from the other larger distress. After a while she put away the photograph and dried her eyes. The sound of the sea lapping at the shingle, the sucking retreat and surging advance slowly entered her consciousness. She watched the little pebbles being drawn into the water and the foaming crest of the waves as they ran up the shore. Lily tried to think of a word that imitated the sound of the sea. Surf, suurrff, sssuuurrrfff, she whispered, elongating the word, saying it in time to the movement of the water. Gradually she began to feel calmer. She dipped her hankie in the water and after wringing it out held it up to her eyes. The last thing she wanted was for Gran to notice she'd been crying. There had been an uneasiness between them since the episode with the apron. She wasn't ready for questions, not yet.

The twins were enchanted with themselves. They stood smiling into the cracked mirror hung above their bed. 'They're ever so pretty Dor. You ain't arf clever,' said Mercy, jumping off the mattress and giving her a sticky kiss.

Dora felt richly rewarded by their genuine delight. She had sat up until one in the morning making the two pink floral dresses from their mother's old frock. It had taken ages to unpick, wash and press the material, measure the twins' straight little bodies and create a pattern from some brown paper. At the market along the dockyard wall she'd managed to pick up glass buttons and satin ribbon. Looking at the girls walking past each other swirling their skirts she felt proud of her efforts. It was Sunday the 29th of May, their tenth birthday. She and Lily were taking them for a picnic in Victoria Park.

'What we going to eat?' asked Blyth jumping up and down.

'It's a surprise,' said Dora, smiling down at his excited face.

'Anyone at home? Cooee, anybody there?'

'Lily, we're here,' called Faith, 'come on up.'

'Come down and see what I've got for you,' called Lily.

The twins hurtled down the stairs followed by Blyth bumping down the steps on his bottom.

Faith and Mercy tugged at the two paper packages.

Dora felt a surge of happiness. The picnic had been her idea and Blyth and his sisters were so excited at the prospect of a treat. She was anxious to get away from Lemon Street before Fred rolled out of the pub or Mary got back from work. The children were relaxed and happy when they were alone with her. She felt a bond of affection growing between them.

'Look Dor, what Lily give us.' The twins held up two little pink satin drawstring bags, each with an initial embroidered on it.

'Let's go to the park,' urged Blyth, 'I wants the picnic. We got lemonade and cake and stuff?'

'Right,' said Dora, 'we got everything, bread for the pigeons, a ball and the skipping-rope?'

'Where's Mary?' asked Lily, as they swung along Queen Street with two string bags full of sandwiches and cake.

'Got this friend where she works, Cissie, I think. Gone out to the sea-front. Cissie's Gran come down from Guildford on a charabanc, reckons she'll be back later. Glad she's gone,' said Dora. 'Kids are lovely on their own. We're a real little family.'

Lily squeezed her hand. 'You're so good to them. Harry's really lucky to have you. I hope he knows what a bargain he's got.'

Dora laughed. 'Makes me sound like seven oranges for the price of six.'

'Oh, eight at least, you're selling yourself short' Lily laughed, too. 'Seems ages since we were out for an afternoon. Used to be every Saturday. Why don't we do something next weekend. Go out in the country, just the two of us.'

'Could borrow a couple of bikes from Dad,' said Dora entering into the excitement. 'We could cycle to Droxford woods if we left early enough. They must be full of bluebells.' She gave a little skip. 'You've given me something to look forward to,' she said smiling at her friend.

'Goldilocks' house,' shouted Blyth as they passed the little fling cottage at the entrance to the park.

'Andrew and me used to call it that,' smiled Lily.

They walked up the main path past naval monuments and the goldfish pond with its fountain and black plaster swan.

'We gonna give fish some dinner?' asked Blyth trying to take the bag from Lily.

'Let's go over on the green patch and have our picnic first,' insisted Dora, 'then we'll see what we got left.'

The twins raced ahead and plumped themselves down in a clear space between two other families. 'Ere Dor we forgot the blanket.'

'Just as well it didn't rain last night. Now settle yourselves that's it. You're all eating the sandwiches first and then the cake. Let me get the cups out, who wants a drink?'

'What in the sammages?' asked Blythe kneeling beside Dora.

'Bloater paste or blackberry jam,' said Dora taking out two brown paper bags and setting them on the grass beside her.

'Ooh don't they taste different out in the open air?' said Lily.

'Pass us the lemonade,' said Dora, 'I'm parched.'

'Cake time, cake time,' chimed the twins.

'What about them crusts I saw you hiding back in the bag?' demanded Dora. 'Eat them up first then I'll see about the cake.'

Blyth pointed his finger fiercely at his sisters. 'Auntie told ya,' he said.

Everyone laughed.

'How come you're Auntie, all of a sudden?' asked Lily.

'One of the nippers down the street got an Auntie what brings 'im stuff. Reckons he's one up on Blyth so I'm Auntie Dora, now.'

'We've eaten our crusts, Auntie,' said Faith, her cheeks bulging with bread.

'You got the knife in your bag?' asked Dora, as she untied the string around a plump brown paper parcel. After a lot of persuasion and great secrecy her mother had been persuaded to make the twins' birthday cake. Feeling the pent-up excitement she slowly peeled back the paper.

'Waah!' gasped the twins, their hands to their mouths in delight and astonishment.

It was a large sponge cake decorated in white icing with the names, Faith and Mercy, picked out in silver balls.

'We aint never had a birthday cake before,' said Mercy.

'Waah!' said Faith.

'Sing, we gotta sing,' insisted Blyth.

'Happy Birthday dear twinnies, Happy Birthday to you,' sang Dora.

Everyone laughed and clapped. The cake was passed around on the paper serviettes Dora had sneaked out of the cutlery drawer. A long sticky silence fell on the group. The Vines' licked the last bits of cake from their lips and rubbed their hands on the grass.

'Oh, I wish we had a camera to take a picture,' said Lily. 'They all look so happy.'

Dora nodded. 'That's all I want,' she said softly, 'everyone to be happy.'

'But, Dora, it's not all up to you. You can't make everyone happy all the time. And Harry wouldn't expect you to.'

'Don't you think so?' Dora asked, a familiar feeling of unease stirring in the pit of her stomach.

'You lot,' said Lily, 'go and wash your hands under the drinking fountain and when you come back I got a sixpence from my Gran for ice-creams.'

Swinging Blyth between them the twins hurried away.

'Look, Dora,' said Lily firmly. 'Harry's family are Fred's problem – it's up to him to be a good Dad to them. And if he's not, it's not your responsibility. You just got to dole out Harry's money to them as you think right and pop in and see them once a week. Blimey, Dora, you'll be saying next that it's your fault that men are being laid off at the dockyard. It's your fault that man over there lost his leg in the war.'

'Now it's you that's being daft,' said Dora smiling at her friend, and wishing that she could deal as briskly with the Vines as Lily suggested.

'I am being daft, but in a different way,' said Lily tugging at a stalk of grass.

'How come?'

'You remember when I told you I read this letter of my Dad's where he said that he'd identified my Mum's body and that Gran didn't believe him. That she thought Mum was still alive?'

'But you don't think that, Lily, do you?' said Dora watching her friend's face carefully. 'Wouldn't she have tried to see you and Andrew? Surely she would.'

'I wish I'd never read that letter. I went and saw Aunt Hester and got a photo of my Mum. Uncle George said I was sneaking behind Gran's back. Made me feel as if I was being ungrateful for all she's done for me.'

'We come for the ice-cream money,' said Blyth, holding out his hand.

'Here you are,' said Lily handing him a sixpence. 'Enough for three cornets.' She took out another coin. 'D'you want them to fetch us one each?' she asked.

Dora shook her head. 'Hot day like this they'll be all melted by the time they got over here again.' She was glad of the interruption. Lily's quest for her lost mother seemed pointless to her. A storm in a teacup. There she was with a gran that had always loved and cared for her and a nice dad. On top of that there was Michael who wrote every week and thought the world of her.

'Why can't you believe your Dad?' she said. 'After all nobody's seen her since she disappeared, have they?'

'No, not as far as I know,' said Lily doubtfully.

'Don't you think your Gran would be really hurt if she thought you were doing all this digging about? Make her think you'd not felt properly loved?'

'I suppose so. Only when I saw the picture of her with me and Andrew it made me feel so sad.'

Dora reached out and touched Lily's shoulder. 'I expect it

did. But you got such a good life, Lily. So much to look forward to. Best thing you could do is get on with here and now.'

Lily smiled. 'Any more cake left?' she said.

'Just a sliver,' said Dora, relieved to change the subject. 'Must save some for Mary and her Dad else they'll carry on top ropes.'

'Auntie Dora!'

'Blimey,' she exclaimed, 'looks as if they're wearin' that ice-cream. Got more on their faces than ever went inside them.'

After playing ball with Blyth and turning the rope for the twins the afternoon melted away. It was after five by the town hall clock when they all packed up and headed back to Lemon Street.

'Bye Lily,' said Dora as they stopped at her door. 'Thanks for coming with us.'

'It was a treat for me, too,' said Lily hugging her friend. 'It was good to see you enjoying yourself. Don't forget to fix up about the bikes for next Sunday.'

Dora nodded.

'Hallo my sweethearts, Happy Birthday,' said Fred Vine, standing in the doorway of number 23. 'Had a good time have you? I got a little something for the pair of you.'

The girls jiggled excitedly around him.

Dora's spirits plummeted.

With much delay, to whip up the excitement, Fred produced two tiny gifts wrapped in shiny pink toffee-paper and waited with soppy pride while they were unwrapped.

'Waah, two-bob bits,' they cried delightedly.

How easily you've bought them off Dora thought sourly.

'And something for his nibs,' said Fred, giving Blyth a silver threepenny-piece.

'Got some cake for you, Daddy,' said Blyth, leaping up into his father's outstretched arms.

'I'd best get off home,' Dora said, handing the bags to Mercy.

'Stay, stay, Auntie Dora,' pleaded Blyth.

Swallowing hard Dora nerved herself to walk past Fred and into the kitchen. She was tired now and wanted to go home with the glow of the day about her. Going indoors would soil things.

'Had a good time 'ave ya?' Mary almost pounced on her as she set down the bags on the kitchen table amid the clutter of greasy plates. 'Bet you aven't saved me no cake or nothing.'

'We had a smashing time,' said Faith, 'and there's lot of cake left because Dora said we gotta leave some for you and Dad.'

'That's all right then,' muttered Mary sulkily.

'I'll put the kettle on,' said Dora. If she could just set out the tea and the cake, maybe she could sneak away.

She pushed past Fred to get to the tap in the scullery. He was dressed in a vest and trousers and she tried not to breathe in the smell of sweat and beer as she passed him. The stale disorder of the house oppressed her. Whatever efforts she made to improve things they always fell apart. What was the point?

'Let's skip in the yard,' said Mercy, 'come on Faith.' The twins disappeared outside.

'I'm commin with ya,' said Blyth.

Dora made the tea and unpacked the picnic bag. She sliced up the remains of the cake and set it on a plate after clearing away the remnants of Fred's dinner. If she could just last out for another half-hour or so may be she could then make her escape.

'I forgot the twinnies' presents,' said Mary,' I'll go up and get them.'

Dora edged towards the door after Mary.

Fred swayed to his feet and stood between her and escape.

'Must go,' said Dora staring at her feet, 'Mum'll be expecting me.'

'That's not very friendly,' slurred Fred, putting his hands on her shoulders and pushing her against the wall.

Dora turned her face away from him and tried to push against his chest. 'No. No please, I got to go.'

Fred took his hand off her shoulder and held her face,

turning it towards him. He planted a wet slobbery kiss on her mouth.

Dora felt sick. It wasn't even as if there were any genuine affection in his touch. It was just the beer swilling around his fuddled brain. Vainly she tried to struggle against him but his weight was firmly set in front of her. She hated herself for her weakness.

'You sneaky cow,' Mary suddenly shouted at her, rushing in from the door. Fred melted into the yard.

'Mary I wasn't,' protested Dora, scrubbing at her mouth with her hand. 'You can't think I was . . .'

'Just push off and leave my family alone,' raged Mary, her face ugly with spite. She grabbed Dora's arm and shoved her towards the front door.

Dora wandered home dragging the empty picnic bag, sick at the injustice of everything. All the happiness of the day was soured. She longed for Harry to be home. For him to hold her and tell her he loved her. To be given care and affection. Not to be always having people wanting things from her. Not to be always falling short.

As she approached the shop she was met by her parents with Gran between them in her bath-chair fast asleep.

Her father looked flushed and exhausted. 'That's the last time I let your mother drag me out with that chair,' he gasped. 'Next Sunday you can go. About time you did something for this family.'

Dora helped her father lift Gran out of the chair and carry her up the stairs. As her mother shut the front door the happiness of the day faded as if it had never been.

Chapter Ten

Dear Beattie,

Hester is agin me writing to you reckons I'm shovin me oar in where it's not wanted. Lily was over to see us last Sunday. I had the feeling you didn't know about the trip specially when we got to the reason for her coming.

Beattie licked her lips nervously. She'd never had a letter from George in all the long years they'd known each other. Not even when she'd written to him about Hester's miscarriage years ago. Her stomach gave a lurch of alarm, must be something serious. She picked up the letter again: better read it, no good surmising, it didn't do a happorth of good.

Seems she wanted to know all about her mother and even got her Auntie to search her out a snapshot. I gave her a right roasting saying as she should be grateful to her Gran for all the love and care what you give her and not too give way to all her airy fairy notions. She went home with her tail between her legs. Shouldn't think you'll be hearing anymore about it.

Hope I've acted for the best.

Say nothing to Hester you know how aireated she gets.

Best love,

George.

Beattie sat on the bed in her best coat not knowing what to do. She'd found the letter on the mat as she was on the way upstairs to get her hat. Albert was taking her out to visit the museum followed by a picnic down at Portsmouth Point so that he could do a bit of sketching. The letter couldn't have come at a more inconvenient moment. Albert was eager to take her to see a painting by a friend of his, in the museum. It was to be a day to themselves away from the aggravations of Lemon Street. The last thing she wanted to do was put a damper on it.

'Are we ready for the off?' Albert called up the stairs.

Beattie slipped the letter into her handbag and shut the bedroom door behind her.

'This is a rare treat,' she said with forced cheerfulness. 'A visit to the museum and lunch out with a naval officer all on a working day, too.'

'Have you left something for Lily?' asked Albert.

'A cold collation,' said Beattie laughing. 'I remember when I was working for your mother. Couldn't have been more than fifteen. "Beatrice", she said, "Dr Pragnell and I will be out to lunch. Perhaps you could tell Cook. We shall only require a cold collation this evening." I thought it was some wonderful new animal or foreign vegetable. When Mrs Frostick told me it was just a light meal of cold things I was really disappointed.'

'Poor Mother,' smiled Albert, 'We used to tease her about her fads and fancies.'

Walking up the street they passed a neighbour, Chippy Dowell, hurrying over to the shop. 'Ma wants some picalilli. Awful partial she is to it. Won't never 'ave her corned beef without it.'

Beattie smiled at the skinny elfin-like Chippy, more child than man.

'Poor fellow,' said Albert, when they were out of earshot, 'the Lord knows how he will survive when his mother dies.'

'That won't be long by the look of her last week,' said Beattie, 'wheezing away like a pair of leaky bellows. Must be nearly eighty now.'

'Let's strike a bargain. Once we get to the end of the street it doesn't exist until we return this afternoon.'

'Agreed,' said Beattie smiling up at him.

Arm-in-arm they strolled down past the dockyard gates and on to The Hard. Sailors sporting their summer uniform white cap-covers, passed them talking and chiaking each other. Passengers hurried over the bridge to the trains at the Harbour Station.

'It seems more fun to have a trip out when most of the world is working,' said Beattie as they turned into the High Street in Old Portsmouth.

Albert laughed as they passed the grey barrack-like grammar school. 'Just think of those poor inky-fingered boys poring over their Latin Verbs.'

As they strolled towards the museum Beattie marvelled to think that these few streets leading down to the sea had once been all there was to Portsmouth. The High Street didn't seem very impressive now, with its shabby bow-windowed shops and pubs, and yet it had once been packed with history. Nelson had spent his last night ashore in the George Hotel a few steps away and the Duke of Buckingham had been stabbed to death at his house just past the grammar school. And then they stopped.

'Well,' she said, looking up at the museum, 'this is grand enough for anyone. Do you know Albert, I must have passed it hundreds of times but I've never crossed the doorstep until now.'

It was a stone building with a triangular top resting on four stone pillars and supported by three great arches. Running across the front of the second storey was a large balcony.

'Let's see if the interior lives up to outside,' said Albert, holding the door open for her.

The room made her think of gravy with its shiny brown floor and mass of brown tables. She was overwhelmed by the number of glass cases and pictures on the walls. Her eyes flittered around not knowing where to settle. There was a vast wooden table with strange animals, such as she had never seen before, carved on the legs. In the glass cases were a strange collection of objects bearing no relation to each other: a heap of blackened Roman coins, two large dried-up Cuban cigars, a beautiful model of a galleon carved in bone by a French prisoner-of-war, yellowing manuscripts and – grisliest of all – a mummified finger of a local villain.

She sniffed. 'Wouldn't give you five bob for the whole kit and caboodle,' she said, 'save the galleon.'

'You're such a stern judge,' laughed Albert, his voice seeming unnaturally loud in the high-ceilinged room. 'Come and have a look at my friend Vicat's painting,' he urged, taking her arm. Among all the huge canvasses of naval battles, seascapes and belligerent-looking admirals was a gold-framed country scene. It was called 'A Hampshire Woodland'. Beattie was entranced. Here was something worth looking at. She started with the wonderful gradations of colour in the spring sky, the little girl with a necklace of flowers, the richness of her purple smock, the mass of ferns with their green fronds and dry brown edges, the flash of bluebells here and there, a ribbon-like stream. It was all so fresh and vibrant and joyful. 'A real tonic,' she said squeezing Albert's arm. 'That's lifted my spirits.'

She stood gazing at the picture while Albert roamed around looking at the other exhibits. After ten minutes or so she had seen enough. 'Albert, I'm done with history it's old and brown and dusty.'

'Right ho, my dear,' he said, walking towards the door and holding it open for her. 'Tell me again what we have for lunch.'

'Cheese and picalilli sandwiches.'

'You and Granny Onslow,' he laughed, 'women with salty tastes.'

Beattie chuckled. 'I've catered for you as well. There's the last of the boiled bacon and some seed cake.'

'What are we washing it down with?'

'There's a flask of tea and and a bottle of lemonade.'

'No wonder this basket weighs a ton.'

It will be all right, thought Beattie as they walked past St Thomas' church to the end of the High Street. Albert will set it all into perspective, he always does. But not quite yet. They'd have their picnic first and she'd share the letter later. They stood at the end of the High Street looking through the Sally Port archway in the old town wall where Nelson left for Trafalgar and where hundreds of Portsea families walked onto the beach. The sea sparkled in the July sun. 'Spice Island,' she said, as they turned into Broad Street and strolled down to the harbour entrance. 'I wonder why this little stretch got that name?'

'Beer, rum, unwashed bodies, chamber-pots emptied out of windows, the reek of fish. That will do to be going on with.'

Beattie chuckled. Arm-in-arm they walked down to the harbour entrance and parked themselves on a low wall outside the Still and West, an old bow-windowed pub.

They sat eating their sandwiches looking out over the sea. On the Portsmouth side were three great grey warships tied up at King's Stairs. A little ferry chugged its way to Gosport and a yacht sailed past, so near that Beattie could almost touch its beautiful flapping sails and gleaming wood and brasswork. Across the harbour was Fort Blockhouse, the submarine base.

Albert followed her gaze. 'That's the young man's navy — underwater warfare.'

'The mere thought of being all wedged together under the sea makes me feel queasy. Like being in a tin of pilchards,' said Beattie with a shudder.

'Well you've got the old Navy right next door,' he said, pointing his binoculars at HMS *Victory* anchored nearby. 'Your Joseph and I started out in the days of sail, barefoot recruits, holystoning the decks.'

'It's all moving so fast, isn't it?' she said, biting into her sandwich, 'cars and telephones, electric light and as for aero-planes . . .'

'Young people have a wonderfully exciting future before them,' said Albert, as he pulled a small sketch-pad out of his pocket. 'Harry Vine and Michael Rowan, Mary, Dora and Lily. It's a matter of taking the best of the past with them into the future.' He took out a pencil and began to draw. 'Why don't you read that letter I saw you tuck into your handbag,' he said, 'while I get a few things down on paper.'

'I've read it,' said Beattie. 'I didn't realise you were spying on me,' she said.

'Don't be so foolish,' said Albert mildly. 'I just happened to come out of the kitchen as you picked it up off the mat.'

'Do you want to know what it says? Am I to have no privacy?' she snapped.

'Beatrice,' he said closing his sketch-book and putting away his pencil. 'Where has all this erupted from? I just thought you might be bored while I was sketching. Do what you will, my dear. I've no wish to provoke you.'

To her intense annoyance Beattie began to cry.

'Beatrice what on earth's the matter? My dear, what is it?'

'Oh! Albert, Lily's found out something that could sink us all.'

'I'm no good at riddles. Just tell me simply what's upsetting you. Whatever it is we'll face it together, I promise. Here,' he said, 'have a sip out of my brandy flask.'

Gratefully she took the little silver bottle and gulped down a mouthful. It made her cough and splutter but also warmed her through. 'Fancy shivering in July,' she said.

Albert took her hand.

'I don't know what to do for the best.' She took another smaller mouthful of brandy. 'You remember, just before Alec and Miriam got married, I found out something.'

Albert nodded. 'I shall never forget your face, Beatrice.'

She took his hand and held it tightly. 'You were so kind to me, Albert. You calmed me down and showed me that no good would come of telling anyone what I'd found. I haven't thought about it for months. Having made that decision, somehow I felt it was all boxed away for good.'

'How have things changed, Beatrice? Tell me.'

'It's something and nothing really,' said Beattie, finding her earlier panic beginning to subside. 'Lily had charge of Joseph's ditty-box while we were away in Romsey. Seemingly curiosity got the better of her and she found the key and opened it. There was a letter inside that Alec had written me just after Mary was found drowned and he'd had to go away. As you know we'd had a bad falling-out with me accusing him of lying when he identified her body.'

'Has Lily told you this?'

'Heavens, no! She'd have to admit opening the box. Admit she couldn't be trusted.'

'So how have you found out about this letter?

'I went into her room for some reason, I can't remember what it was, and her apron was on the floor. I picked it up meaning to take it for washing and I found it in the pocket. After all,' she said defensively, 'it was addressed to me.'

'Where is it now?'

'I tore it up.'

'Having read the letter Lily will now feel that there is doubt about her mother's death. A real possibility that she is still alive somewhere?'

'I think it's stirred up a hornet's nest. And the worst of it is she won't feel that she can ask me about it. Do you know, she went over to Hester's and asked for a picture of her mother. George gave her a right telling-off about being disloyal to me. Poor kid, she must be so confused.'

'Why did you take the letter?' he asked her. 'If you'd left it where you found it Lily's curiosity may well have faded.'

Beattie squirmed under his gentle probing.

'I suppose I wanted to get the situation under my control. Both Lily and I know it's been found but it will be up to me when I broach the subject. As I said, guilt will prevent her from ever mentioning it.' She sighed. 'And I've bought myself some time to think what's best to do about it.'

Albert took her face between his hands and kissed her. 'Before you rush into anything, my darling,' he said slowly and quietly, 'consider the consequences. Whatever you tell Lily cannot be taken back later. It's like dropping a pebble in a pond, the ripples or consequences will be so far-reaching. And not just to Lily. You say that she's confused. That's nothing to what she will feel if you say that her mother is still alive. And what about Alec and Miriam? If the authorities found out he could well go to prison for bigamy.'

In spite of the sun glaring on the water Beattie shivered.

Chapter Eleven

Around Dora the Vines laughed and chattered while they dipped in and out of the sea. A few paces away were Mrs Carruthers, Algie and Sailor. Words were flung across her but Dora could not make herself a part of the Sunday outing. As she watched the sea withdrawing itself she stared at the wet abandoned stones. They were stranded like her. The sun was hot on her head but the effort to find her hat was too great. The stones were digging into her and she needed to change her position but felt unable to move. She was thirsty but somehow the effort of slipping the bottle of lemonade out of the basket was beyond her.

Since having tonsillitis a few weeks ago her energy had never fully returned. She fell into bed exhausted each night and felt just as tired in the morning. Even the simplest task became an effort. Nothing was of any interest. It felt as if a glass barrier had grown up between herself and other people – as if she were becoming invisible. But even as she felt herself disappearing their demands increased.

'Dora, those nippers are relying on you. They don't have much fun, the least you could do . . .'

'Take your Gran her breakfast. Can't you see your mother's exhausted? Surely to God she deserves a lie-in on a Sunday.'

'If you could just take this jacket home with you, Miss Somers. I know I can rely on you.'

Dora love, what's up with you? It's weeks since I got a letter. I'm depending on you.'

Tears of weakness leaked beneath her lashes and down her face. She stared at the sea, afraid that someone would ask her why she was crying. Blyth, hobbling over the stones, flopped cold and sandy into her lap. When there was no response he wriggled around and looked up into her face. He traced the tears down her cheeks with gritty fingers then flung his arms around her holding her close. Dora felt a brief moment of reprieve. Around them the three sisters swirled and chattered, pulling their picnic out of the string bag. As suddenly as the little boy had landed in her lap he was hauled away by Mary.

'Get off her,' she snarled, snatching him from Dora's arms, 'go back in the water and wash yer 'ands.'

Lily arrived and flopped down beside her. She reached over for Dora's hat and slipped it on her friend's head. 'You'll be getting sunstroke if you don't watch it,' she said.

'What you got in your sammiges Lily?' asked Blyth, going over and kissing her.

Lily laughed. 'You are a proper cupboard lover, that's what you are. Here have this one, it's banana and sugar.'

Dora wished she could be like her friend – so full of enthusiasm, always looking forward to things. For herself, everything was an effort. Even Harry's letters failed to interest her. They were just another intrusion, another demand for her attention.

'Here, Dora, have some lemonade,' said Lily passing her a bottle, 'you look like a lobster, you must be parched.'

She sat trying to summon up the energy to prise the wire and glass stopper off the bottle and take a drink.

Lily got up and brushed the sand from her dress. She looked around her. 'Who wants some winkles?' she asked.

'Me, me, me,' the Vines chorused.

Dora felt her heart thumping with anxiety. She was supposed to be at home looking after her grandmother. Mum and Dad had gone out for the Sunday. When she had taken up her breakfast the old woman was slumped in her chair, her mouth drawn down to one side. The room was filled with the sound of her snoring and the smell of stale urine. Terrified, Dora slammed down the tray and rushed out of the room. She should have stayed and sent Mark or Barney for the doctor. Instead, she washed and dressed and ran from the house. As she wandered about the silent Sunday streets she kept looking over her shoulder fearing that someone would call her back.

Increasingly she felt herself to be on the run, pursued by people who professed to love her but who devoured her with their demands. Eventually, too tired to walk any more, she had found herself at Old Portsmouth and had wandered through the Sally Port arch and onto the beach. At first she had sat there staring at the sea, soothed by the sound of the waves lapping the shingle. She must have been there some hours but it only seemed moments before the Vines found her and stole her peace.

Anxious questions teemed in her head. Should she go home? Gran could be dead by now. Dad would never forgive her. What would she say when he asked her why she had left the old woman sick and alone? Again she looked at the sea: it glittered invitingly. Around her families were intent on their sandwiches. Trippers were queuing at Victoria Pier for a boat cruise around the harbour. Lily was at the winkle stall. Nobody was concerned about her at all.

Dora took off her shoes and got to her feet. The pebbles were hot and sharp in the mid-day heat but she didn't mind. It was a small price to pay in order to reach that cool, empty greenness beyond. Slowly she walked into the sea feeling her clothes clinging to her and the sounds of the bathers receding behind her. People called to her but she refused to answer. Something drew her deeper. Soon, soon she would feel the water closing over her head and she would gone from them. All those people who wanted something from her.

Blyth kept tugging at her arm nearly spilling her lemonade. 'Watch out will ya,' Mary yelled at him, crossly.

'Dora, Auntie Dora,' he was shouting now and pointing down the beach. 'In the water.'

'So what.'

'Sea going up to her neck.'

Idly Mary looked up from her drink. It took her some seconds to realise that Dora was not on the fringes of the shingle with the other bathers. She was ahead of them, fully dressed, wading out into the sea.

Mary was paralysed with fright. She hated the sea. She'd only come to the beach with the kids because she didn't want to be on her own at home. Steadily the water rose around Dora's shoulders. Mary clutched Blyth to her and looked around in panic. The twins began to scream. 'No,' she cried, 'no, oh, no.'

Mrs Carruthers, who had been asleep beneath a parasol opened her eyes. 'What's the matter,' she said sharply. 'Tell me child.'

'Out there, Dora's drowning,' Mary cried.

Dahlia didn't waste a moment. 'Out the way, out the way,' she shouted as she charged down the beach thrusting people out of her path. At the water's edge she flung aside her hat and dragged off her shoes before wading into the sea. By now Dora had disappeared. Suddenly aware of some crisis picnickers left their food and gathered in anxious knots at the water's edge.

Mary drew the twins into her arms. Blyth clutched at their skirts. It couldn't be happening, Mary couldn't believe that Dora had gone from them. It couldn't be true. Tears streamed down her face. Harry would never forgive her.

Dahlia plunged beneath the water her large purple-clad bottom reappearing briefly followed by her feet. Ripples spread outwards. Mary held her breath. There was a lot of thrashing about and then Dahlia emerged clutching Dora around the waist. She struggled to change position and to hitch the lifeless girl over her shoulder. Dora's long skirt was weighing her down and it took some time before Dahlia was able to get her safely positioned and to wade out of the water with her. Bystanders unravelled and surged towards Dahlia.

'Get back, get back,' she cried. 'Smelling-salts, anyone, fetch them quickly.' She dragged Dora's hair off her face and shook her roughly as if she were a dog. Someone rushed up to her with a small brown bottle. Dahlia snatched it from her fingers and waved it repeatedly under Dora's nose. The body remained lifeless.

'What's amiss, for God's sake someone tell me?' demanded Sailor. 'What's all the panic about?'

'Ma's gone in the water with all her clothes on,' said Algie, examining his sandwich.

'Young girl tried to drown herself, old chap,' said a man in a deck-chair. 'Your missis fished her out and is trying to bring her round.'

'She'll do it, will Dahlia,' said Sailor firmly,' you can bank on it. Now Squire, I wonder could you give us one of your ciggies?'

Mary wanted to scream at him: 'How can you think about fags when Dora could be . . . ?' No she couldn't say it in case it made it true. She hauled Blyth up into her arms and she and the twins hobbled barefoot over the stones. They stared at Dora as she lay on the beach, her sodden clothes moulded to her body, her hair strung out like seaweed. Mary was terrified by Dora's still, pale face and blue lips. Mrs Carruthers straddled Dora's body and began lifting the girl's arms rapidly up and down. Jesus! What if she couldn't save her? Panic-stricken, Mary shoved her sisters aside and ran up the beach. No, no, no, she couldn't lose anyone else.

At the sight of Dora, Lily dropped the pots of winkles on the sand. Blyth and the twins clung to her incoherent with fright. She wanted to cry out to Dahlia, who was hooking her fingers into Dora's mouth, 'Don't be so rough, you're hurting her', but what did roughness matter if it brought her round? Please, please God, bring her back to us, she prayed.

'Quick,' said a young soldier, 'Surgeon's up at the barracks. No time to waste.' He hauled Dora over his shoulder and almost ran up the beach, his boots crunching over the stones.

Without argument, Dahlia followed. As he made his way through the Sally Port Arch there was a choking sound and Dora vomited down the back of his uniform.

Lily was crying with relief. Sailor clutched at her sleeve, the twins and Blyth whimpered and Algie dodged between all of their legs. 'Quick,' shouted Lily, grabbing Dahlia's handbag, 'get all your stuff together.' She fumed with impatience as they scrabbled to obey her. Minutes later they followed her, a rag-tag little party, festooned with bags and soggy towels.

At the other side of Broad Street they stopped outside the guard-room of Point Barracks. Dahlia was waiting for them.

'She's over the worst, now. You wait outside with Sailor and the children. Don't let Algie out of your sight.'

The soldier disappeared inside with Dora and Dahlia. Outside in the street the sun beat down remorselessly.

'Is Dora goin' to be all right?' whimpered Mercy.

'She'll be better soon,' said Lily, guiding Sailor with one hand and clutching Algie's sleeve with the other. 'Where's Mary?'

'She went off roaring and crying,' said Faith, 'ain't never seen her like that before.'

Lily felt a surge of rage. Trust Mary to land her with her family. It was mostly her fault that Dora was so unhappy. She wanted to slap her so hard. Instead she snarled at Algie who was trying to slip from her grasp. 'Stay with me or I'll wallop you.'

Algie kicked and writhed.

Faith grabbed his wrist and twisted it savagely. 'Do that again and I'll give you another Chinese burn,' she snarled.

Lily was tired, thirsty and anxious. She wanted to be rid of the lot of them.

'I gotta do a wee-wee,' said Blyth, walking towards the gutter and pulling down his trousers.

'He's peed all over 'is shoes,' said Algie sniggering.

Lily wanted to scream.

A soldier came out of the guard-room and said, 'You lot better come and wait on the bench inside, unless you wants sunstroke.'

It was blessedly cool inside the bare stone room. The soldier sat at a large table and behind him was a glass-fronted cupboard filled with rows of keys on hooks. On the wall opposite was a framed copy of the King's Regulations.

Lily sat down with Dahlia's handbag between her feet. Algie opened the clasp and made a grab for his mother's purse. 'Algie put that purse back,' she hissed, abandoning all attempts at patience.

'Do as you're told you thievin' little tike,' roared Sailor, hitting out with his stick and fetching Algie a wild swipe on the neck. The boy roared with pain and anger.

'Pipe down,' snapped the soldier at the desk, 'or I'll put you in irons.'

Mercifully his outburst had the desired effect. Algie slunk on to another bench and sat there snivelling.

Lily approached his desk. 'Excuse me,' she said, softly, 'It's my sister they've taken inside,' said Lily, praying the twins wouldn't contradict her. 'She had an accident in the water. I'm waiting to see if she's all right. Could I go in and see her? Oh please,' she begged, 'the others can stay outside.'

'Since you're a relative suppose it's all right,' said the soldier. 'Down that corridor over there. Ask for the sick bay.'

'You stay here 'til I get back,' she demanded. 'You all do what Sailor says.'

'Nobody's goin' nowhere,' said the soldier glaring around him. 'I'll see to that.'

She was shown into a smaller barer room. In the corner behind some screens she found Dora lying swathed in blankets on a high iron bed.

'Oh, Dora,' gasped Lily, tears welling in her eyes. 'Dora are you all right? I was so worried.' She sat on the bed and put her arms around her friend. She smoothed the wet tangled hair away from her face and kissed her on the cheek. Dora opened her eyes and stared at Lily as if she were a stranger. There was an acid smell of vomit on her breath. Lily took her hands and gripped them tightly. They were small and neat like a child's hands. Lily wanted to cry.

From behind her someone said, 'I'll go and get Captain Lewis and clean myself up.' Lily turned at the sound of his voice and saw it was the soldier who had carried Dora up the beach.

'Thank you. You and Mrs Carruthers,' she said, noticing Dahlia standing beside him. 'The two of you saved her life.'

'Training, ma'am,' he said, 'nothin' to do with kindness.'

'This Captain Lewis,' asked Dahlia, 'would that be Owen Lewis of the Seventh Hampshire Artillery?'

'The very same,' said the soldier. 'He'll be with you in two shakes.'

'Most grateful,' said Dahlia.

'How is she?' asked Lily, looking anxiously back at Dora who had once more closed her eyes.

'Well,' said Dahlia, brusquely, 'she's in the land of the living but we must get these wet clothes off before she gets a chill. The orderly gave me a shirt to put on for the moment. Once she's got that on and has seen the doctor you can go back to your grandmother's and fetch her something to go home in.' Dora's half-conscious body was awkward to move and Lily felt a sense of invasion in stripping off her clothes. How thin she was, how pale. Poor little Dora. After a struggle she managed to get her arms through the sleeves of the shirt and her head through the neck. Once she'd pulled it down over her chest she undid her skirt and pulled it slowly down over her feet. She took the garters and stockings off noting her pale almost white toenails. As she and Mrs Carruthers were pulling off her drawers Dora suddenly stiffened.

'No, no,' she murmured.

'Dora, it's me Lily, you've been in the water.'

'No,' said Dora pushing her hands away.

'But, Dora I just want . . .'

Lily looked up to see Mrs Carruthers shaking her head.

'Let's just get the gown on and cover her over.'

The screens parted and Lily looked around to see a handsome moustachioed man in military uniform.

'What have we here, a drowning I believe?' He turned from Dora to exclaim in surprise, 'Dahlia, my God it's you.'

Mrs Carruthers laughed. 'Yes, Owen, it's me. The girl is coming around now.' As she said this Dora turned to one side and vomited violently again, over the floor.

'That's the way, orderly, bowl and towel please,' he called, stepping back hastily to avoid any splashes on his immaculate brown boots.

Again Dora's eyes flickered and then flew open. They stared out of her chalk-white face.

'Dora, oh Dora,' Tears were streaming down Lily's face she sat on the bed and held her friend's hand, chafing warmth into her fingers. Never had she been so frightened. She sat on the bed willing her friend to open her eyes, to reassure her that she was all right, now, and that the danger was passed. From behind her she heard the doctor talking to Mrs Carruthers.

'We'll let the orderly clean her up and then I'll check her over.' He turned to smile at Dahlia. 'Last time I saw you was in the mud at Cambrai with a wheel-brace in your hand. God, Dahlia you're soaking. Let me take you to the mess and get a gin down you and find you some dry clothing. I think we'll let the young woman sleep a while.'

Lily stood uncertainly at the end of the bed.

'Do you want to wash her?' said the orderly.

'Yes, please,' said Lily.

'She's past the worst, now. Here you are, drop the cloth in this bucket. I'll fetch it in a minute.'

'Oh, Dora,' said Lily, as she washed her friend's face, 'I was so worried.' She sponged the vomit from Dora's neck and hair. Already the pallor was fading from her skin. But Dora was still in a drowsy state. She almost looked as if she had just awoken from sleep. Lily's mind shied away from the possibility that her friend had seriously wanted to kill herself. Even attempted suicide involved the police and the newspapers. It was a terrible disgrace and could result in the victim going to prison. She couldn't bear to think of little Dora being exposed to such harshness. Lily rubbed her face and neck with the rough towel and took a comb out of her pocket. The teeth snagged in Dora's wet hair. She folded the towel and put it on the wooden tray beside the bowl of soapy water.

Dora pulled the blankets around her and turning onto her side she settled herself for sleep. Lily kissed her cheek. 'I'm so glad you're,' she struggled for the right word, 'alive,' she mumbled.

'You've done a good job,' said the orderly. 'I should go and get her some clothes and when you come back, see if you can get someone to fetch her home in a car or taxi.'

When she stepped out of the guard-room Lily was swamped by Blyth and the twins. How easy it had been for Mary to just run off and leave her to deal with everything. Damn the Vines, damn Sailor and Algie too. But when she saw the children's anxious faces it was difficult to maintain her resentment. 'She's going to be all right.'

'Hurrah, hurrah,' said the Vines, dancing up and down.

'Lets go home,' said Lily, taking Sailor's arm. 'I think we've all had enough of the beach for one day.' Looking around her she could see no sign of Algie.

'He's pushed off 'ome,' said Mercy as if reading her thoughts.

Lily sighed. 'Mrs Carruthers told us to keep hold of him.'

Faith shrugged. 'He don't matter. Right little tyke 'e is. He burnt our dog. I 'ates him.'

'Needs a proper family,' said Sailor. 'Dahlia got no idea, either gives him soppy cuddles or belts him. Don't know why she took him on in the first place.'

'I suppose it might help if you had a bit of patience,' said Lily. Knowing that Sailor couldn't see her seemed to make it easier to be honest. Or perhaps having a real fright stripped away politeness.

'You ain't telling me nothin' I don't know meself,' said Sailor gruffly. 'The lad brings out the worst in me. It's not him that I hates it's what he turns me into with his tormenting ways.'

'It would help if he went to school wouldn't it?'

'Dahlia won't hear of it. Reckons they'll dig into his background and take him away from her.'

'There's so many orphans since the war,' said Lily, thoughtfully, 'I should think the authorities would be only too glad that someone was prepared to take him on.'

Mercy tugged at her arm. 'D'you reckon our Dora'll be all right?' she asked.

'Well,' said Lily, 'we'll have to look after her.' She turned to Sailor and said 'What shall we do about Algie? I can't see that we can just abandon him. Mrs Carruthers said we weren't to let him out of our sight.'

'He knows his way around, poor little bugger, he's had to learn, early. He'll turn up.'

They straggled on home with many stops for Blyth to climb on Faith or Mercy's back, or for Sailor to catch his breath. All the while Lily kept looking back for Algie. Her irritation with the children was fading, overlaid with relief at Dora's recovery. How could she have told Mr and Mrs Somers that their daughter drowned while she was buying winkles? It made her sound so careless. It sounded like the words of a silly seaside song. 'While I was buying winkles rum ti tum ti tum.' How could she have written to Harry and told him that Dora was dead? How could she be Dora's best friend and not have noticed her sadness?

All at once she wanted to be at home with Gran. To be a child again with everything certain. To yield up her responsibilities and sit waiting for her tea. For everything to be as it was before she'd opened the ditty-box and found the letter. Before that secret lay between them.

She had almost decided not to pursue the mystery of her mother but Dora's near-drowning brought all her questions to the surface. Had Mary Forrest intended to walk into the sea? Had she like Dora found life too much to bear? Or was she alive somewhere waiting to be found?

Chapter Twelve

Beattie stepped away from the table and surveyed her handiwork with satisfaction. Though she said it herself it was a handsome spread. The combined resources of both their china and cutlery stores had been required. Albert's mother's white damask cloth and serviettes had been starched to perfection. Beattie's cutlery gleamed after a good rub with the plate-powder. Three cheeses sat in readiness on the carved wooden board, Cheddar, Cheshire and blue Stilton. It was all colour and contrast: jewel-red strawberries, crisp emerald lettuce and celery, pink ham and a blue jug containing clotted cream.

The room smelled of lavender polish and the rich clove scent of pinks picked that morning from the postage-stamp patch of garden.

She was glad the Vines and the Carruthers had made themselves scarce. She wanted to enjoy the day with no unexpected hitches. It would be Olive and Samuel's first visit. Her marriage would be on display. After her sister-in-law's wonderful meals at the farmhouse in Romsey Beattie was anxious to display her own cooking skills.

She looked at the clock, half-past twelve: they should be with her at any minute. Albert had gone along to the harbour station to meet them. She clicked her tongue in irritation; why couldn't

Lily have stayed? She wanted her there to boost her confidence. Still, she'd promised to be home from the beach by three o'clock and with that she had to be content.

Her own nervousness surprised her. Putting on a spread was second nature. She loved seeing a well-laid table and family seated around it. But this was her first party as Mrs Pragnell, wife of a naval officer. Mrs Pragnell, once the orphan scullery-maid in Albert and Samuel's home. After all this time the insecurity still welled up in her.

As a key rattled in the lock, Beattie took a deep breath opened the kitchen door and greeted her visitors.

'Come in and welcome both of you. Albert, take their coats.'

Olive hugged her warmly. 'Lovely to see you Beattie. How well you look and what a spread. Oh Samuel, isn't this a treat. We've been looking forward to this for weeks.'

'Beattie, my dear. How are you?'

'I'm fine, Samuel,' she said accepting a whiskery kiss. 'Sit yourselves down and I'll go and strain the potatoes and Albert will pour you a drink.'

'My word Albert, you've fallen on clover here,' laughed Samuel. 'Seems a shame to disturb this wonderful table but I must say I'm starving.'

Beattie wanted to cry. Samuel and Olive had been so genuine in their pleasure at seeing her. How could she have been nervous? They were family.

Albert beamed at her, she could see the pride in his eyes. Whatever her background she'd given him a proper home life and some loving at long last. And she did love him. The mystery was why it had taken her so long to admit it to herself.

'Beer or lemonade, Olive?' asked Albert.

'I think I'll join you men,' laughed Olive. 'A beer please. Oh, no Albert, half a pint will be ample. I don't want to be squiffy.'

'No chance of that with Brickwood's,' snorted Samuel. 'You

need the Romsey brews for that.' He tucked his serviette under his chin and helped himself to a generous slice of ham.

Olive held out her plate to Beattie. 'Ooh! that Stilton looks just right. I haven't had any since your wedding. Wasn't that a happy day?'

The knot of unease in Beattie's stomach untied itself. The meal passed happily with many compliments to Beattie on her cooking. She and Olive were carrying plates into the scullery for washing when they heard footsteps in the passage and loud uncontrollable wailing. Mary Vine hurtled into the kitchen and into Beattie's arms.

'Merciful heavens,' she cried handing the plate in her hand to Olive. Beattie's initial irritation turned to alarm. The child rarely cried and never in this wild abandoned way.

'I've killed her,' she gasped and sobbed. 'I've really done it. Went and drownded herself. I been a cow to her and now she's gone.'

Beattie drew her chair away from the table and took Mary onto her lap. 'Sh, quiet, calm down. Here, blow your nose. That's it Olive, pour her a cup of tea. Take a few deep breaths. Right, have some tea.'

Albert and Samuel took their cups tactfully out into the yard.

Mary gulped the tea down greedily, the tears still wet on her face.

'Now, who are we talking about?' asked Beattie.

'Dora, she walked into the sea wiv all her clothes on and didn't stop. The water was over 'er 'ead it was.'

'Did nobody stop her?' asked Beattie, thoroughly alarmed.

'That posh woman what lives next door,' gasped Mary, 'she went in and fished her out but she was all floppy and 'er lips was blue. I know she's drownded.' Mary sobbed and sobbed.

'Listen Mary,' said Beattie, trying to make her voice full of certainty and confidence. 'Mrs Carruthers is a sensible woman. If she can't save her, she'll get help from the Point barracks down there. Bound to be a doctor on duty.'

'I've left the kids there, Blyth he'll be worried.'

'Lily's there, isn't she?'

'Yes, but she's all upset about Dora.'

'Lily will scoop them up and bring them home. Anyway the twinnies are ten now, they're not babies. They know where they live.'

'I wants to go to the lav,' said Mary, rushing from the kitchen and out into the yard.

'Poor child,' said Olive, who had been quietly getting on with the washing up, 'isn't she one of the family that's lost their mother?'

'She is,' sighed Beattie, 'and Dora the girl that please God, has been saved, is engaged to Mary's brother Harry who is out in the Far East. Poor Dora's been running herself ragged trying to help his family.'

'Do you think the young woman was wanting to kill herself? She must have been in a terrible state.'

'I wouldn't have thought so,' said Beattie, 'although she'd had a bad bout of tonsillitis a week or two ago. Lily was saying as her father's always nagging, mother's a bit of a drudge and there's a grandmother, an invalid but a right old tartar by all accounts. Poor Dora was caught all ways with nobody looking out for her.'

'Your Lily's a kindly girl,' said Olive thoughtfully. 'She'd have been a good friend, I'm sure.'

'As to Lily, she's very fond of Dora, but she gets caught up in her own affairs.'

'Beattie,' said Olive, touching her arm. 'We could stand here worrying about the whys and wherefores of little Dora, 'til the cows come home. Don't you think we'd be better off clearing up and looking out some clothes for the child. Albert and Sam could take a taxi down to the beach and find out what's happening.'

Beattie was grateful for Olive's quiet commonsense. This was not the first time that she'd underestimated her. That self-effacing manner hid a strength and wisdom she'd never appreciated before. 'You're right, Olive,' she said. 'I'll go and fetch some things of Lily's and put them in a bag.'

'Hasn't Mary been down in that lavatory a long while? Do you think she's all right?'

Halfway to Lily's room, Beattie sighed. 'I'll go down and see. Hope she hasn't locked herself in.'

As she crossed the yard Mary opened the door. The quick-moving feisty fifteen-year-old had gone. A frightened child had taken her place.

Beattie's heart was wrenched with pity.

'What we gonna do?' she asked.

'Listen my dear,' said Albert taking Mary's hand in his. 'What part of the beach were you at?'

Mary whimpered to a halt then gasped, 'Down Sally Port between the towers.'

'Sam and I will go and see what's happened. We'll take her straight to her home. If there's nobody in we shall bring her here. I'll drop a note through their door explaining the situation.'

'Best take some dry clothes,' said Olive. 'Beattie's just going to fetch them.'

'Pray God, you're not too late,' said Beattie kissing her husband.

'I'll see you soon, my love,' said Albert. 'Try not to worry. I'll be as quick as I can.'

'I'll get Lily's bed ready just in case,' said Beattie nearly in tears. 'Directly Dora gets here, we'll send for Doctor Marston. If she's to be in my care I want to make a proper job of it.' Beattie knelt down and got the stone hot-water bottle from the cupboard under the sink. It seemed a daft thing to use on such a sweltering day but doubtless the child would be feeling the cold after such a soaking. Not soaking, she chided herself, near drowning more like.

Poor Lily would be mortified at not spotting her friend's

distress. Beattie sighed, she was hardly blameless herself. Often, lately, she'd looked at Dora and seen a haunted look on the young girl's face, had noted how pale and thin she'd become and promised herself a word with her, later. It was always later, and in-between the word and the deed Dora had sought her own solution. While she was waiting for the kettle to boil Beattie listened to her sister-in-law talking to Mary.

'Have you had anything to eat?' Olive asked. 'What did you take down the beach today?'

'Bits of cake and sandwiches, we was eating them when Dora went in the water. She was just sat with us, not saying nothin', just staring at the sea. Didn't have a drink or no grub. Just starin' and starin'.' Mary gave a sob and sunk onto a chair.

'She was crying and Blyth sat on her lap. He give her a cuddle and a bit of love.' Mary bit her nails. 'I dragged 'im off her and then it 'appened. We wasn't taking any notice of her then she was gone.'

'It's a long time since you left the beach,' said Beattie firmly, 'lots could have happened. There might have been a doctor at the barracks. I bet someone sent for him. Any minute Mr Pragnell will be back with everyone safe and sound.'

'I been a real cow to her. Rotten I have.'

'Why is that?' asked Olive sitting down beside her.

'Me brothers.'

'Tell me about them.'

'Harry and me, he's a torpedo man out East on the *Lister*. Ever so clever. Me and Harry we was running the family. Then Dora turns up and he gets all mooney over her. He tells Dora to look after us. 'Zif I don't count no more.'

'How about the other brother?'

'Blyth.' A smile lit up Mary's tear-stained face. 'He's my treasure. It was me what looked after 'im always. Know why 'es called Blyth?'

'I did think it was unusual.'

'On account of my Dad. His ship went down at Jutland. We all thought he was drowned. But he weren't. Rescued he was and took to a place called Blyth in Northumberland. So when babes was born he said he had to be Blyth.'

'That makes him very special,' said Olive gently.

'Always been mine. Slept with me since 'e was little, me what 'e loves. This auntie what lives in Yorkshire she wanted to have him. But our Dad said he'd tan her arse if she came round here any more.'

Beattie caught Olive's eye and they both suppressed a smile.

'I hated Dora because Harry loved her and I thought Blyth was loving her, too, better than me. Then there was our Dad.' She began to cry again, great gulping open-mouthed sobs. 'Other Sunday he'd had a few and Dora was here and he got all silly, making up to 'er trying to kiss her. I know she wasn't playing up to him. She wanted to get away. But I was a right bitch and said I'd write to Harry.'

'D'you know what I think?' said Olive, taking Mary's little bitten fingers in hers. 'I think you'll be given a second chance to put things right.'

'You mean she ain't drownded or nothing?'

'She wasn't in the water very long,' said Beattie reassuringly, 'and there were plenty of people about. Any minute they'll all pile back here right as rain.'

'Why don't you have some food, while we're waiting?' said Olive. 'I'll set you up a tray with a little bit of everything on it.'

'Can I have one of them serviettes with a ring round it like the toffs where I work?'

'That will be my pleasure,' said Olive smiling at her, 'and you could sit out in the yard, in the shade, my lady.'

Mary gave her the ghost of a smile then followed Olive outside.

Back in the scullery she and Beattie set about finishing the washing-up.

'Poor little scrap,' said Olive quietly.

Beattie nodded. 'This may be just the thing that's needed to turn things round. Much as I'm fond of that kid she did lead Dora a dog's life. It's about time that family appreciated what that girl does for them. She's a gem. As for Lily it'll bring her up with a round turn too.'

'A bit of a harsh lesson,' said Olive.

'Maybe,' said Beattie. 'Now, while there's a bit of a lull why don't we have another cuppa. I could do with a five-minute sit-down before the next emergency.'

'Two minds with a single thought,' said her sister-in-law, smiling at her.

'Olive, you've been a brick,' said Beattie, as she set out two cups and saucers, 'I don't know what I'd have done without you.'

'Stuff and nonsense,' laughed Olive, 'a bit of help is worth a deal of pity.'

They sat in companionable silence either side of the empty fireplace drinking their tea. After a few minutes Mary returned with a well-cleared tray.

'You've made quick work of that,' smiled Olive.

'I ain't never had a tray before,' said Mary, smiling shyly at her. 'I wanted to . . .'

Her next words were unsaid as all three of them heard the key turn in the front door.

'They're here,' shouted Mary bolting down the passage.

But it was Sailor with the twins and Blyth.

'Where's Lily?' asked Beattie.

'Got in the taxi with your 'usband and some other chap,' said Mercy. 'Dora got took to the barracks. Nearly drownded she was.'

'That Dalalia, what lives next door to you, she got 'er out the water. This soldier carried our Dora up the beach and she sicked up all down the back of 'is uniform,' said Faith, relishing the drama her words produced.

'Thank God,' said Beattie thankfully. 'Sounds as if she was brought out just in time. Olive, dear, could you help Sailor out into the yard and pour him some lemonade?'

No sooner was Sailor safely parked on a seat in the shade than Blyth noticed Mary standing in the kitchen doorway. 'Where you bin?' he asked, accusingly, 'we was looking for ya.'

'I spect it was 'cos you bin so mean to her what made Dora want to drown herself,' snapped Mercy, glaring at her sister.

'Rotten you was,' echoed Faith.

Mary made a dive for the yard, pulling Blyth with her.

'Here,' commanded Beattie, handing Mercy a plate of sandwiches, 'take these home with you. I'll let you know when we get any news.'

'Some Sunday visit,' said Beattie as she sank gratefully into a chair. 'You'll be glad to get back to Romsey, Olive, for some peace and quiet.'

'I'm glad I was here,' said Olive, as she poured Sailor a glass of lemonade, 'glad to be of use. Poor Dora, what could have been going through her mind to make her do such a thing? She must have been desperately unhappy.'

'Any chance of that drink,' called Sailor, 'me mouth's like the bottom of a bird's cage out here. Come on girls, have pity on an old salt.'

'Well,' said Olive, 'you've certainly got some colourful neighbours.'

'You haven't met Dahlia,' laughed Beattie. 'Handsome I'd call her, with bags of style and confidence. But a real woman of mystery. Fancy her wading in and rescuing Dora.'

'Gold medal, she's got,' said Sailor as Olive guided his hand to the lemonade, 'Royal Humane Society for rescuing a bloke in France out of a river. Under fire it was too.'

'We've all got a lot to thank her for,' said Beattie, 'which reminds me. She must be in wet clothes, too. We should have thought of that. You wouldn't have a key would you, Sailor, so that we could get her some dry things?'

'No Missis,' said Sailor. 'Your Lily took charge of Dahlia's handbag to stop Algie getting his hands on her purse.'

'Who's Algie?' asked Olive.

'Little nipper what Dahlia acquired,' said Sailor. 'He run off somewhere in the midst of all the rumpus.'

'How old is he?' asked Olive.

'No more than seven.'

'I'd completely forgotten about Algie,' sighed Beattie. 'It's not going to be much thanks to Dahlia and her rescue work if we lose her child.'

From somewhere above them came the sound of laughter.

Beattie and Olive looked around, mystified at where the noise was coming from.

'Can't catch me, can't catch me, elephant's nest in a rhubarb tree,' yelled a child's voice.

'That's Algie,' said Sailor, 'he's up somewhere on a tree or a ledge of some kind.'

'Merciful heavens,' cried Beattie, 'Look, there on the bedroom windowsill. For the Lord's sake, Algie, be careful. Pull up the sash and get yourself indoors.'

'Won't open,' Algie cried, all bravado deserting him. He crouched with his hands gripping the top of the lower pane, his knees on the ledge and face pressed against the glass.

'Stand still, lad,' called Olive. 'We'll get you down in a jiffy. Beattie,' she said, 'let's get Albert's ladder up, quickly.'

Beattie and Olive dragged the ladder off the pegs on the back wall and carried it into the yard next-door, setting it in position against the house.

'It's too short,' cried Beattie, 'what'll we do now?'

'Just get me across that wall, woman and stop your blathering,' said Sailor, getting to his feet.

'But, Sailor . . .'

'Never mind the buts. I'm an old topman from the days of sail. Climbing's in your hands and feet, seeing don't come into it. Don't worry lad, old Sailor will get you down in no time.'

Olive stepped over the wall and took Sailor by the hand and led him to the bottom of the ladder.

'You gals hold it steady now, while I shins up it.'

Beattie could feel her heart banging against her ribs as she watched Sailor climb to the top.

'Listen to me, son, lower one leg down a bit 'til you feels me get hold of it. I won't drop you, no way.'

'I'm scared,' cried Algie.

'Course you are, lad, but you trust in old Sailor. You can do it.'

Still whimpering, Algie turned his head and looked down at Sailor. 'Can't,' he moaned, turning his face back to the window.

'Come on Algie, you're a big boy,' coaxed Beattie.

Sailor waved a hand impatiently behind him. 'Pipe down Missis. He's got to be guided by one voice only. No distractions.'

'There's no hurry, lad. You just take your time. Old Sailor ain't going nowhere.

Beattie clutched Olive's arm and the two women looked helplessly up at the little boy perched on the ledge and Sailor waiting hands outstretched.

Again Algie turned his head and then with fearful slowness he inched his left leg from the sill lowering it towards Sailor's outstretched hand.

'Very well done, lad,' said Sailor. 'Now give us your other one — that's it. This is what we got to do next. I've got your weight. You must let go the sill now and I'll slide you down between me and the ladder 'til your feet touches a rung. That's it, that's it. All over bar the shouting.'

Beattie and Olive watched as Algie and Sailor moved slowly to the ground.

'Thank God for Sailor,' said Beattie, 'and as for you young man, you gave us an awful fright.'

'No more than he gave himself,' laughed Sailor. 'Now ladies, I reckon that calls for a beer – you can give the lemonade to the sprog.'

Beattie felt giddy with relief. She sat down beside Sailor, who had a very subdued Algie on his lap.

Olive went into the kitchen and reappeared with a beer for Sailor and passed the lemonade to the little boy. 'Just heard a key in the door,' she said. 'It must be them back from the beach.'

'Please God, let little Dora be safe,' Beattie prayed, as she walked indoors.

Chapter Thirteen

'Do you remember walking into the sea?' asked Dr Marston.

Reluctantly Dora opened her eyes. She remembered very little of the last twenty-four hours – it had been a time of fear and confusion. There had been that hot little room and the bed with scratchy grey blankets. The walk on cotton-wool legs down some steps to a taxi followed by the feeling of safety as she sank into Lily's bed and lost herself in sleep. Awakening on Monday morning she had found her mother standing there, her eyes red-rimmed from crying.

'We were so frightened, Dora,' she'd whispered, 'thought you'd gone forever.' She'd said something about Gran being dead but it hadn't really registered. Now, later on in the morning, she was sitting up in Lily's bed trying to think about who had walked into the sea.

'Miss Somers, do you remember trying to drown yourself?' asked Dr Marston.

Dora struggled to speak. She wished he could read her mind and save her the effort of putting her thoughts together. There had been a girl who'd walked into the water, mesmerised by its clear green beauty. Was it her? Clumsily she managed to say, 'Somebody went into the sea.'

The doctor examined her fingernails pressing them making

them look pale and bloodless. It was a while before the colour returned. He pulled down her eyelids.

'Have you been feeling tired, recently?' he asked.

Again she looked into his eyes wanting him to speak for her.

'She had tonsillitis a few weeks ago,' Mrs Pragnell said.

'I think that you are severely run down, my dear. It's possible that you have anaemia. A good iron tonic and lots of rest should set you right. You're lucky that I don't prescribe eating raw liver, that would have been the treatment a few years ago. Since your parents are taken up with your grandmother's funeral, and Mrs Pragnell is willing for you to stay here, perhaps she can call around later and collect your medicine. I will drop by at the end of the week.' The doctor's grey eyes looked searchingly at her. 'Has something made you sad?' he asked.

The words stabbed at Dora like skewers, cutting through her confusion. She howled with grief. All her trying and pretending was swept away. At some point she was conscious of the doctor leaving the room and of Lily's Gran holding her until her tears were spent. Tenderly, she sponged her face and hands with a cool flannel and gave her a glass of lemon barley.

'You just cuddle down in that bed, my love, and I'll look in on you later.'

Thankfully Dora turned her face into the pillow and sank down into forgetfulness.

Even the sound of Dora's steady breathing did not reassure her. Lily had had a fright. Behind her closed eyes she could still see Dora's lifeless body and Mrs Carruthers leaning over her, wrenching her mouth open. Then all the brutal struggle to bring Dora round.

This second night, after the near-drowning, seemed worst than the first. After all the chaos and confusion of Sunday and all the different people in and out of the house Lily had been too exhausted to stay awake. Now in the stifling July heat, curled beside Dora like a comma, she found it impossible to sleep. Carefully she peeled her nightdress away from Dora's back and slid from the bed.

She padded out of the room feeling hot and thirsty. By a chink of light between the kitchen curtains she found the jug of barley water on the dresser and poured herself a glass. Lily sat in Uncle Albert's high-backed chair, by the empty fireplace, her mind teeming with anxious thoughts.

Dora's near-drowning had stirred up other griefs. It had stripped away the cushioning effect of time and brought back to her that other loss at sea. She saw herself, again, on her twelfth birthday when the telegram came announcing her brother's death off Jutland – Boy Bugler Forrest on HMS *Black Prince*. Her terror at seeing Gran overcome with grief and the realisation that she would never see Andrew again. Never see his freckled face and coppery hair, see him polishing off a huge dinner or hear him playing the bugle, his cheeks scarlet with effort. Later there was the memorial service in Victoria Park when each family's grief was gathered together in one huge sobbing pain.

She was gulping down the last of the lemon barley when Gran came in from the yard. At first she didn't see Lily and when she called out to her Gran was startled.

'Ooh, you gave me a fright,' she gasped, 'it could have been one fright too many. I was just walking around the yard trying to cool down. Pour me a glass will you, love – I'm really parched.'

After taking the drink from Lily she settled herself in the armchair opposite. 'We won't forget July the tenth in a hurry, will we? It could all have ended in tragedy. Thank God for Dahlia,' she said. 'A friend in need and no mistake.'

'A mysterious one,' said Lily. 'The doctor in the barracks seemed to know her, said last time he'd seen her had been in Cambrai with a spanner in her hand.'

'The plot thickens,' laughed Gran, who always loved a puzzle.

'I think she must have been over in France during the war. In fact Sailor said as much, earlier. Reckoned she'd got a gold medal for rescuing some chap out of a river. She must have been a nurse or something mechanical like an ambulance driver.'

'Didn't she look peculiar in that army uniform?' laughed Lily. 'When the soldier dropped her off in his car I couldn't believe it was her.'

Gran nodded. 'Well, I suppose they don't keep much of a stock of women's clothes at Point Barracks, specially now the war's over. They're a strange trio and no mistake.'

'Sailor did say that Dahlia didn't want Algie to go to school because there'd be enquiries made about his background. I was telling him off about being so impatient with him. He swiped him around the neck with his stick, he did. Really hurt him. I know Algie's not very likeable but all the same . . .'

'You should have seen him earlier when the nipper got himself stuck on the upstairs windowsill,' said Gran. 'Blind as he is, he climbed up the ladder and brought him down safe and sound. Put the wind up me good and proper. Him breaking his neck would have put the tin lid on the day.'

'Crumbs,' gasped Lily, 'living next-door to them is as good as going to the pictures.'

They sat together in a comfortable silence. It seemed a long time to Lily since last they'd been alone together. It was almost as if the awkwardness between them over her finding Dad's letter had never been. Gran's face was in the shadows, her expression unreadable. Drawing comfort from the darkness, Lily licked her lips nervously, then said, 'Gran, can I ask you something?' she said.

'Try me,' she said quietly.

'Tell me about when my mother drowned.'

The sentence hung in the air between them and for a moment Lily thought it was going to remain unanswered.

'I've been expecting this,' said Gran, 'expecting and dreading at the same time.'

'Because you know that I found Dad's letter? That I opened the box?'

'Why did you, Lily? You must have wished that you hadn't.' There was sadness in Gran's voice but no reproach.

'I don't think I would have done if Dolly Vine hadn't died and we'd not got caught up with her being brought home and everything.'

'Poor Dolly, touching our lives even from beyond the grave.'

'Dora was next-door telling them about their Mum and I was in here fed up that we couldn't go out and do things like we'd planned.'

Gran sighed. 'So it was the devil finding work for idle hands,' she said.

'I'd taken your gloves upstairs, to your bedroom, then I found the key and curiosity got the better of me.' Lily leant towards Gran and said almost pleadingly, 'Why has my mother's life always been such a secret? Dad never carried a picture of her, there was never a photograph on the mantelpiece. It was as if she was a family disgrace.'

Gran sighed. 'Mary was small like you with the same dark beauty. But that was only half the story.'

'Did you like her?'

'We were chalk and cheese. I should have felt some sympathy for her, being an orphan girl, as I was, but I can't say that I liked her. I want to be honest with you, Lily,' said Gran, 'and that may mean saying things that you don't want to hear.'

'Go on,' Lily said, 'just tell me.'

'Everything was tomorrow with Mary, cleaning, paying debts, taking care of things. Hated her own company and wanted constant excitement. What worried me was that your Dad was like someone else when he was with her. Didn't have a will of his own. As if,' Gran sighed, 'this is going to sound ridiculous, as if he was enchanted. She wanted the moon and he would not gainsay her. Mind you, she could be wonderfully entertaining – sang like an angel.'

Lily tried to fit the pieces together. Her mother had passed down her beauty but not her singing voice. That talent had gone to Andrew. From the other things that Gran had said she and her mother had little in common. Lily liked to be on her own sometimes, to read and daydream, and she liked things to be in order. But was the tidiness Gran's training? Why had her mother left so suddenly? Was she tired of her husband or was it her children? She was so frightened of the answer to her next question that she could hardly form the words. 'Did she love me and Andrew?' she asked.

'Doted on you both,' said Gran. 'But she was just too young for the responsibilities of a family, was only a child herself.'

'Why did Dad say, in his letter, that you thought he was escaping from a bad marriage?'

'They were both too young and too impatient,' sighed Gran. 'He hated living in chaos and she couldn't bear him going away. Oh, they had wonderful times when he came home. She'd be laughing and clinging round his neck. It was the dailyness that sunk them.'

'What d'you mean, Gran?'

'Well, you're old enough to know about feeling passion for someone and wanting to be forever in their arms.'

Lily was glad the room was in darkness so that her blushes were hidden.

'But between that passion lies: washing, cleaning, cooking, paying bills, dealing with illness, bad temper and boredom.'

'How d'you mean?'

'Well, there was never a meal ready and she was always in debt. Borrowed from the neighbours. Your father wouldn't sit down and talk things through with her. Just flew into a rage and stormed out. It was six of one and half-a-dozen of another.'

In asking the next question, Lily felt like someone riding a horse up to a fence and nerving herself to jump. It would be so easy to shy away but it was now or never. The subject had been broached, they were on their own and whatever the effort to ask or answer, their feelings would be hidden in the early morning shadows. She would have liked to have paced about the room as she normally did when agitated but forced herself to sit still. At any minute Gran could get up and leave and the opportunity would be lost. 'Why didn't you believe him when he said it was her body that he saw at the mortuary?' she eventually asked, her voice shaking.

Gran did not answer. The silence felt like a thick impenetrable curtain. Lily had not the courage to ask again. And then when she'd given up hope, Gran began to speak

'We were both exhausted, strung up with anxiety with two little children crying all the time. Each day got nearer to the time he had to go away. Both of us full of guilt, asking ourselves, why she had gone, where had she gone? When Constable Wilkes came with the news of a body washed up on the beach it was almost a relief.'

Lily tried to gauge what Gran was feeling by the tone of her voice. She sounded tired and sad.

'I offered to go with him but he said that it would be better for me to stay with you children. He felt you'd been passed from pillar to post over the last few days. Yes, he insisted on going on his own.' Gran got up and poured herself another drink.

Was she really thirsty or was she buying herself time, Lily wondered.

'I was worked to a pitch waiting for him to come back. I think you children caught my anxiety because you wouldn't settle and kept grizzling. Of course you were only eight months or so, who knows what you were feeling. Andrew was nearly five and desperate for his Mummy. By the time your father came back I was in no mood to wait. I asked him if it was Mary, the moment he stepped over the doorstep, not giving him a chance to gather himself.'

'Poor Dad,' murmured Lily.

'He just wanted to be on his own for a moment or two. He needed to grieve. I insisted that he swear on the Bible that the body he saw was your mother.'

Again there was silence. Lily wanted it to be over. She hadn't thought it would be like this. There was pain in Gran's voice, pain and regret.

'It was anger and fear that made me doubt him,' she said quietly, 'and grief on his part, that and exhaustion. And then before we had time to forgive each other he was gone halfway across the world.' Gran sighed and got to her feet. 'It was years and years before ever we could speak of it again: it lay like a wound between us.'

'Do you think she could still be alive?'

'Lily, you are trying my patience now. We've all had a shock and it's stirred up a lot of things best forgotten. You'd be better employed looking after your friend than asking me questions I can't answer.'

'Sorry, Gran,' said Lily, getting up and putting her arms around her grandmother. 'I didn't mean to upset you.'

She was pushed firmly away. 'I'm off to my bed now and the subject is now closed.'

Lily paced about the empty kitchen and wondered whether it was exhaustion or fear that had sent Gran to bed.

Mary waved out of the bedroom window at Blyth as he rode down the street on his father's shoulders.

'Going down the park with Dad,' the twins shouted up the stairs before slamming the front door.

It was early Sunday evening. A week since Dora had nearly drowned herself and by the way Dad and the kids carried on it was as if it had never happened. Mary wiped her nose on the sleeve of her blouse. She hated being on her own and she hated Dad. Oh, he was great for parties and sing-songs, for playing the fool, but when you had to face up to something he just slid away. He was as much to blame as she was over Dora. Trying to get her to kiss him, especially when he was in his sweaty old vest. He made her feel ashamed. When they'd told him about the accident he'd wept easy, boozy tears and wanted to go next-door and see her.

'Because of you she tried to drown herself,' Mary had shouted at him. 'Always trying to smarm all over her,' she'd raged at him.

'It was your fault, you narky cow,' shouted Faith.

'You was horrible to 'er you know you was,' snapped Mercy.

'If she'd've died it would be your fault, your fault.' Faith had started hitting her round the head.

Then they were both at it kicking and slapping. Normally Mary would have yelled and kicked back and got the better of them by sheer determination but she hadn't the heart for it. They were right, she'd made Dora's life a misery. All her little thoughtful acts and kindnesses she'd thrown back in her face. Why?

It was only Blyth climbing onto Mercy's back that stopped them.

He was red-faced and ferocious in his anger. 'Stinky, stinky pig,' he'd roared, pulling Mercy's hair.

His rage was so comical that it broke the tension. Laughing at his antics they had pulled him off Mercy's back and hugged and kissed him.

'Geroff, geroff,' Blyth had yelled, laughing and crying at the same time.

Mary had waited until last Tuesday evening before going next-door to see Dora.

She was sitting in the back yard. Sailor was there too and Mr Pragnell was doing a drawing of him. Mary thought him a strange man with his old straw hat and leathery brown face. His bleached blue eyes followed the sound of your voice but there was no life in them like the windows of an empty house.

'Blimey, Squire,' he complained, shifting his position, 'this sitting is thirsty work. I think we should have a stop for refreshments. I'm parched.'

Mr Pragnell laughed. 'Right you are Sailor, I'll get you a lemonade or would you rather a glass of stout?'

'Stout would be just the ticket.'

'Would you like to come indoors and cool off for a few minutes? Here, give me your arm. And you girls, would you like a lemonade?'

'Yes please,' said Mary shyly, glancing sideways at Dora.

Sailor shuffled indoors on Mr Pragnell's arm.

Mary perched uncertainly on the edge of the deckchair vacated by Sailor.

Dora had said nothing, had not even looked at her. She was wearing a pink flowered frock of Lily's and her hair was loose about her shoulders. How small and fragile she seemed to Mary, like a little girl. She had never seen her sitting so still before. Always she had been on the move, making the tea, cutting out clothes, ironing, sewing, laughing or singing. 'How you feeling?' she managed to say at last.

'I'm tired. Just want to sleep all the time,' said Dora, not looking at her.

Her voice sounded unfamiliar and far away. Mary sneaked another glance at her. She couldn't quite understand what the difference was. It was Dora and yet it wasn't. Like a photo is only a likeness of someone, so the pale girl in the flowered frock was only a likeness of the real Dora.

'I'm sorry I was mean to ya.' The words burst out in a rush.

'Doesn't matter anymore.'

'Dora,' gasped Mary, near to tears, 'I won't be narky no more, I promise.'

Dora looked at her as if she wasn't there, as if she could look right through her. 'Please yourself,' she said.

'Shall I write to Harry for you?' Mary asked, desperate for some response. 'Shall I tell him you was took bad?'

'D'you know what you can do?' said Dora staring at her. 'You can just go away. I'm not frightened of you anymore and I don't care whether you like me or not. One thing I've decided, though.' She stared at Mary and her eyes were hard like brown stones. 'I don't like you and if you was to walk into the sea I wouldn't lift a finger to stop you.'

Mary gulped. The force and meaning of the words stung her to tears.

'Got to go,' she managed to mumble to Mr Pragnell when he came back into the garden with a tray of biscuits and lemonade. And then she rushed over the wall into her own back-yard and shut herself inside the lavatory. She sat on the seat and wrapped her arms around herself, rocking back and forth, sobbing out her shock and hurt.

Her courage had not allowed her to call again. Tomorrow Dora was due to go home after her gran's funeral. So there was still time to call while Dad and the kids were down in the park. Defeated at the thought Mary flopped back on her bed.

Of course if Harry hadn't gone away things would never have got so bad. They would have sorted the family between them and Dora wouldn't have got in such a state with everything.

Mary opened the red Oxo tin where she kept her brother's letters and took out the one that had arrived on Saturday.

Dear Mary,

What a shock getting the letters from you and Dora. I know Ma wasn't getting any better but just to die like that with no warning. I felt so sick with worry being so far away. What rotten, rotten news. I just wish I could rely on Dad. Knowing he'll be as much use as a paper fireguard to his kids makes me feel so bitter. Thank God my Dora is there to help you cope with everything. Now I know what's been happening I'm not so worried about not hearing from her for a while.

I know you get the hump when I go on about Dor but it doesn't mean I don't still think the world of you. You know you're number one with me out of all the family. The kids would all have been in the orphanage if you hadn't kept things together. I expect, it won't be long before you'll be all spoony over someone of your own.'

Mary snorted it would be ages before she let herself get all soppy like Harry and Dora. All her desires were pinned on Marshall's High Class Butcher's shop and the gleaming glass kiosk. How was she ever going to dislodge that smug slug of a Beryl from behind that beautiful brass till?

I've been trying to get a picture of Ma in my head from how she was when we was both little before the twins came. D'you remember Mary, how she used to splash about with us in the sea and pretend she was a mermaid and put all those seaweed necklaces round us? They looked so lovely and fresh and green in the water and then when we laid them on the stones they turned all brown and manky. Like the difference between her then and the mad woman in the hospital tearing up all the paper. I wish we could just have a day back on the beach with Ma laughing and jumping over the waves to chase out the pictures of what she turned into.

Mary didn't think she would ever go on a beach again, never ever. She had been so frightened. Seeing Dora all white and floppy had panicked her. It had taken so much effort to keep going when Ma died but she'd done it. She didn't know how but she had. But in those few seconds seeing Dora stranded on the stones had stripped away all her hard-won composure and left her hysterical with fear. Now that she knew that Dora was safe, Mary didn't know what she felt. There was a hollow inside where the terror had lain leaving her tired and weepy.

She'd have to write to Harry but the Lord knew what she would put in the letter about Dora.

Chapter Fourteen

Beattie was enjoying herself hugely. She was seated in the saloon bar of The Duchess of Fife sipping her milk stout and gazing out of the window. Below her she could see the water being whipped to a froth by *The Duchess's* huge paddle-wheel as it churned the ferry towards the Isle of Wight. Too often she had been the figure standing on the shore or waving from the platform as her husband Joseph or son Alec set off to foreign places. Today the boot was on the other foot and she was the traveller. Slowly they swept out of Portsmouth harbour and past the Round Tower with little figures dotted on the edge of the shingle.

Their holiday had come not a moment too soon. A new month and new scenes, that's what they all needed. July had tested her courage. Never would she forget Dora's face with its absent look or her abandoned weeping. Then there had been Lily with her questions. Sitting with her in the sweltering gloom of the kitchen she had been wracked with anxiety. It was vital that Lily believed her mother was dead, all their lives depended on it. How could the young girl possibly understand the terrible dilemma that had faced her grandmother on the eve of Alec's marriage to Miriam? How could she know the agony of Beattie's deception? Of course, it could all be to no purpose, now. Mary

Forrest might truly be dead. After all it was well over a year since that heart-stopping meeting. Mary had been almost unrecognisable – almost but not quite.

Her thoughts turned to young Dora. Had she really meant to kill herself?

'Thank the good Lord she didn't attempt it early in the morning when the beach would have been deserted,' Albert had said.

'Perhaps she just wanted to be rescued and it was her only way of getting our attention?'

'Yes,' said Albert, 'I think you're right. Had she been serious she would not have chosen such a crowded time of day. Serious suicides don't want to be found. It certainly devastated her parents and all her friends. The Vines were very upset. Mary was very contrite when she came in to see Dora and even Fred seems to have been affected.'

'That cheap-skate matelot,' Beattie had snorted. 'I hope his conscience pricked him good and proper after the way he tried to slobber over her all the time. Who could be charmed by an article like him? Couldn't entertain the idea not even if he was hung with diamonds.'

Albert had roared with laughter. 'I think his ambitions would be somewhat hampered by the beer,' he said. 'The condition is known as Brewer's Droop, I believe.'

'Albert!,' gasped Beattie, 'I'm scandalised.'

'Not you,' laughed her husband.

Thinking about it again made Beattie smile as much in gratitude as amusement. Dear Albert, what a joy he was to her. She watched him sitting back in the wicker chair looking keenly about him. How handsome he was, with his silver hair just a shade too long curling around the edge of his collar and his Panama set at a jaunty angle.

'I'm dying to see Rosie,' said Lily, joining them again after a stroll around the deck. 'It seems years since we've seen her.'

'Only four months,' smiled Beattie. 'As for little Joseph, he'll have changed out of all recognition.'

'It'll be strange to see Dad out of uniform and in a different place,' said Lily wistfully. 'He even said in his last letter that he'd shaved his beard off. Won't be like my Dad at all.'

'Don't you think you might have changed, too?' asked Albert, smiling kindly at her.

'You're a young woman, now, getting to be a skilful seamstress with all the future before you,' said Beattie, leaning forward and speaking quietly to Lily. 'You're no longer the little girl who ran up the road her hair flying wanting to see what Daddy had in his kit-bag.'

'I suppose not,' said Lily sadly.

'I'm sure Michael Rowan doesn't see you as a child.'

Lily blushed.

'My adopted family,' said Albert. 'Just think, I've become a granddad without ever being a father.'

'Oh, I don't know,' said Beattie. 'You were a father to Miriam. It was you she wanted to give her away at her wedding.'

Albert squeezed her hand.

In the next few moments, with much thrashing of water *The Duchess of Fife* came alongside Ryde Pier and its passengers disembarked. Albert got a porter to carry their luggage and put it aboard the little train waiting to take them to Sandown.

Beattie was sure the journey from Ryde to Sandown was a delight as the little train chugged through the Isle of Wight villages and along the edge of the sea but her thoughts were all with Miriam and the children. She was famished for the sight of them. While Albert once again sorted the luggage, she and Lily scanned Sandown platform for the first sight of the children. And then in the distance she saw a little girl and a blonde woman holding a baby. 'Miriam, Rosie,' she cried holding out her arms.

'Granny,' called Rosie, dancing up and down with excitement.

Beattie felt a great leap of joy at the sight of the child. The little girl had grown taller. What a beauty she was with those toffee-coloured curls and hazel eyes. She hugged her fiercely, tears gathering in her eyes. 'Your Granny has missed you so much,' she said into her soft little neck.

'You coming to my house?' asked Rosie when at last Beattie had finished hugging her.

'Yes, I want to see everything.'

'Hello, Mother, it's so good to see you,' said Miriam kissing her and setting the baby in her arms.

'Joseph Andrew,' Beattie chuckled, 'you're the image of your Grandfather Forrest.' And, he was, as he looked up at her with his blue eyes and quiff of auburn hair. 'Looks to me by the length of you, you'll be another six-footer.'

'Miriam my dear,' said Albert, gently, 'the island air agrees with you. You're looking bonny.'

Miriam laughed. 'I haven't a second to spare,' she said. 'Busy from morning to night. But I'm happy, the nippers are well and Alec is thriving. Let's get a taxi and get ourselves to The Lord Tennyson and meet the landlord.'

Sitting in the taxi with Rosie on her lap Beattie looked curiously around her as the car sped sway from the station. Sandown bore no comparison to Portsea. It was a small hilly seaside town rather than a sea port. The driver took them down Station Road and along by the promenade. The sand stretched for miles and the sea was somewhere distant over the horizon. 'I bet the children love running along the beach,' said Beattie, looking at the groups of people making their way across the road to the sands, weighed down with shrimping-nets and buckets and spades.

'It's a shame,' said Miriam, 'I rarely get the chance to take them but this week I've got a bit of extra help so we could spend a few hours tomorrow if you like.'

'Wonderful place for sketching,' said Albert. 'I believe there's a cliff walk into Shanklin?'

'Yes, Alec likes to wander along there when he's got a hour or so, which isn't often,' said Miriam. 'Nearly there now,' she said as the taxi climbed up a hill.

'Hello family,' called Alec. As they stepped inside the pub he rushed up the stairs from the cellar.

'Hello, Son,' said Beattie holding out her arms to him. 'My word you've filled out a bit,' she added, holding him away from her. She smiled at him trying to put her finger on what the difference was. But it was no one thing but a mixture of changes. His hair was longer and curled around the back of his neck, the beard was gone. He'd discarded his uniform for moleskin trousers and rolled-up shirtsleeves and a fancy waist-coat. Yes, he had put on weight but it was about time that his skinny frame was properly covered. What shone out of him beyond the surface changes was a confidence and sureness. He'd found himself. Beattie smiled fondly at him. 'No need to ask if you're happy, Son,' she said, patting him approvingly on the arm.

Alec winked at her and then turned to Lily. He laughed delightedly and swung her round in his arms. 'My word, Princess, you've turned into a beauty. I hope that Michael appreciates you. Or he'll have me to deal with.'

'Oh, Dad, you are silly,' said Lily blushing furiously.

Yes, thought Beattie, these next few days will set us all to rights.

'You've come just at the right time,' said Alec, taking one of their bags and hefting it onto his shoulder. 'We've got an hour or so before we open at six.'

'Let's all go upstairs,' said Miriam, 'and we'll show you around and get out the teapot.'

'It's deceiving,' said Beattie when she had been into the two bedrooms and upstairs into the attic where Lily was sleeping. 'It looks so small from the outside.'

'It goes back a long way. There are two more bedrooms beyond that door and a separate bathroom. That's where the B and B's stay.' Miriam laughed at Lily's puzzled look. 'Bed and breakfast visitors. I hated the look of the inside when I first arrived,' she said, 'I wanted to jump back into the taxi. It was all dusty and gravy-coloured. Mrs and Mrs James, I think they had one pot of brown paint which they sloshed on from cellar to attic. Now, I'm trying to making our living quarters more home-like and separate.'

'Do you have to work in the bar at all?' asked Beattie, looking approvingly at the crisp white net curtains at each window and the pretty hand-sewn cushion covers that brightened the old brown sofa in the little parlour.

'It was a nightmare at first. The children were all unsettled and the staff had been used to pleasing themselves. We knew very little about the trade and they knew it. But,' she smiled, 'Alec has got a new man in now who wants to put the pub back on its feet and his daughter helps in the bar. And now, thank goodness, we've got a young widow for the evenings.'

'No shortage of them,' sighed Beattie.

'We're so lucky,' said Miriam smiling, 'and happy.'

'Well,' laughed Beattie, 'it's a tonic to see you all.'

'It's hard work,' said Miriam, 'but now I can come up here with the children in the evenings and it's a real little home.'

'Right,' said Alec, as he reappeared from the attic, after carrying up Lily's case. 'Let's go down to the kitchen and have that tea.'

'My word, Miriam,' gasped Lily, joining them at the door of the kitchen, 'what a spread.'

The kitchen was dominated by a large black-leaded range that almost filled one wall on top of which was a huge black kettle and frying-pan. Next to it was the door into the bar and on the wall opposite was a vast dresser crammed with dinner-plates and casserole dishes. There was a big brown sink set under a window that looked out over the cliffs to the sea beyond.

'We can see Southsea beach from there, way in the distance,' he said as he set about carving a joint of ham. 'So near and yet a different world.'

'Mmh! I like these pasties,' said Lily, 'what does the T P on the top stand for?'

Miriam blushed proudly. 'They're Tennyson Pies. I've made them a speciality of the house. Minced lamb, peas and potato but the secret is the mint sauce and a pinch of sugar.'

'And I suppose this is Forrest Pudding,' Lily laughed, catching sight of the trifle.

'I'm working on a pudding,' smiled Miriam, 'and Rosie is my chief taster.'

Beattie sat between her husband and son with Lily and Miriam, and the little ones opposite. It was a moment to treasure with her entire family around her. Alec now richly content, Miriam looking more confident than she had ever seen her, the children brown and bonny. Lily was almost exotic in her dark-eyed beauty and Albert a splendid silver-haired patriarch. She felt a sense of completion – a piercing joy. It was a glimpse of perfection.

'Would you like to give us a hand to open up?' asked Alec as he got up from the table.

'My pleasure, dear chap,' said Albert, pushing back his chair.

'Rosie,' said Lily, 'do you want to come up to my bedroom and help me unpack?'

Little Joseph banged vociferously on the tray of his high-chair not wanting to be left out. He held up his hands to Lily who lifted him into her arms.

The young widow arrived and after greeting Beattie had a hurried talk with Miriam before disappearing into the lounge bar.

'Let me give you a hand with these dishes,' said Beattie taking an apron from the back of the kitchen door.

Miriam sank into a chair. 'I'm too tired to refuse you,' she said. 'What with the heat and the excitement of seeing you all, I hardly slept a wink last night.'

Beattie pushed another chair in front of her daughter-in-law. 'You put your feet up while you can,' she said. 'After that lovely tea it'll be my pleasure to clear up.'

'Oh Mother, it's so good to see you.' Miriam sighed. 'Tell me all the gossip about Lemon Street. How's Chippy Dowell, and Ethel Rowan and everybody?'

It was a magical week. The high point was a picnic on the sands on the Wednesday afternoon. Lily paddled with the children, her skirt tucked up to her knees while Alec built sandcastles that Joseph promptly knocked over. Miriam sat in her deckchair intermittently dozing and chatting to Beattie. In the background sitting on the sands was Albert with his sketch-pad and pencil.

From time to time Beattie surreptitiously glanced at Albert's drawings. She marvelled at how in a few swift strokes he could capture the essence of his subject. The look between Alec and Miriam as he knelt at her feet and presented her with a wavy length of seaweed. Lily hand-in-hand with Rosie, turning to smile at Joseph riding on her shoulders.

Beattie nestled back into her deckchair and closed her eyes. How she would miss them when the week was over. What a help and support to them she could be if she stayed. How painful it was to accept that, in spite of their obvious affection for her, it would be the last thing that Alec and Miriam would want.

Hold your horses, she chided herself – two more days yet.

Days of sunshine and laughter packed with small incidents that she would treasure in her heart.

As they climbed back up the beach in the late afternoon Rosie took her hand. 'What shall we do tomorrow?' she asked.

Beattie smiled at her. 'You choose,' she said.

'The beach, the beach,' she cried.

Chapter Fifteen

'That Beryl's got herself engaged to the butcher's son. She was flashing her ring when I went in just now,' Cissie said as she took off her coat and set down the parcels of meat on the kitchen table.

Mary flung the forks undried into the cutlery drawer. 'That's spoilt everything,' she whispered fiercely. All her dreams of wearing a starched white blouse and striking the brass keys of the till behind the kiosk fled like soap-suds down the sink. She wanted to lash out and hit something, to scream out her disappointment. Instead she was faced with the porridge saucepan and Mrs Mullins' nagging. She stared out of the kitchen window desperately trying not to cry. That bleedin' Beryl was now set in that kiosk firmer than concrete. And she was stuck here, equally firmly, skivvying for those Clements, who didn't hardly know she existed. That little Charlotte was like a china doll with her big blue eyes and blonde curls. Once she had thrown a ball down the stairs and Mary had taken it back to her.

'What do you think you're doing?' Mrs Clements had snapped at her.

'Was just giving her back her ball. I wasn't doin' nothing.'

'She's got red hands,' said Charlotte looking at Mary as if she were some sort of curious animal.

'Cos I works 'ard,' Mary had muttered, feeling her temper rising.

'Don't speak to my child and get back downstairs at once,' said Mrs Clements, picking up her daughter and rushing with her along the passage towards the nursery.

Mary stabbed a knife into the kitchen table and watched the blade quiver wishing it was sticking out of Lettice Clements' shoulders or even better that rotten Beryl.

'Jesus! What you up to, now, you stupid little bitch,' yelled Mrs Mullins, pulling the knife out of the table. 'Your just clear up the kitchen and then you can scrub the floor.'

It was nine o'clock on a hot August Monday and already great wet patches were visible under the arms of Mrs Mullins' vast black dress. She dried her sweating face with a tea-towel then spooned a liberal helping of sugar into her cup of tea. 'Cissie,' she said, 'Nanny Harker wants you upstairs to bring down the nursery washing. Them kids 'as had the squitters for the last two days. There'll be a deal of washing to bring down. I'm off to see Mrs Clements.' She glared at Mary. 'That fruit cake's due out at ten. You let it burn and I'll dock your money.'

In unison Cissie and Mary stuck out their tongues at Mrs Mullins' retreating back.

'Poor Giles and Charlotte,' said Cissie 'they looked proper poorly when I went up this morning. Didn't touch their breakfast. Nanny Harker was ever so worried.'

What about me? Mary wanted to cry. Why give any sympathy to them toffs' kids? As Cissie hurried out of the kitchen Mary turned back to the sink and cried hot tears into the retreating water. She wished Harry was home, he would tease her out of her temper or buy her sherbet dabs or monkey-nuts. There must be something she could think of to cheer herself up.

A wave of anger hit her as she thought of Mrs Mullins. How she hated working for that grumpy old cow. Cissie got on with her all right because she was prepared to flannel her, saying how wonderful her baking was and sneaking out the empty stout bottles from her bedroom. Mary clashed all the time, refusing to be bullied. As she scoured away at the saucepan she vowed to set herself a month to dislodge Beryl by fair means or foul. If she failed she'd leave Lancaster Terrace and stay at home and let Dad do the worrying. Having set herself a time limit she began to feel more hopeful.

Cissie came downstairs and put on a big apron before sluicing the sheets in the scullery. Mary left the washing-up to drain while she swept the floor and set the chairs up on the table. 'Let's have a sing-song while old misery-guts is out the way,' she said.

'Margey, I'm always thinking of you, Margey,' they sang while they splashed and scrubbed.

'When all is said and done there is really only Margey, Margey my girl,' trilled Mary, as she rubbed the bar of yellow soap over the scrubbing-brush. She rinsed the floor-cloth and took it out in the yard and draped it over the empty bucket. 'How about "Lily of Laguna?"' Mary suggested as she stepped back into the kitchen.

'How about the cake?' said Cissie. 'Cripes, Mary I can smell it out here, you better be quick. She'll go mad if it's burnt.'

Mary dashed to the oven. Even with the folded-over oven-cloth the tin was fiercely hot and Mary dropped it on the table.

'Cripes,' gasped Cissie, 'you'll leave a brown ring on the table. She'll be raging when she gets down here.' The smell of burning filled the kitchen. 'Open the window. Quick!' She gasped as she fanned the air with a paper.

'I'll have to leave it there,' said Mary. 'It's too hot to take out of the tin. No point in movin' it, the damage is done.'

Mrs Mullins, who had slipped back into the kitchen unseen by the two girls, fetched Mary a swipe across the neck with a tea-towel. 'You bloody deaf or something?' she roared. 'What's the bleedin' good of telling you anythin'? We got the lunch to get and then this tea-party for Mrs Clements. I could pitch you out the door.'

'Then you'd only 'ave Cissie to 'elp ya,' said Mary, covering the stinging welt on her neck with her hand.

'I'll hang out the sheets,' said Cissie, scuttling out to the yard.

No good looking to you for help, thought Mary bitterly. Still, why should Cissie stick her neck out? She was in worse straits than herself, with no family to fall back on. Gradually Mrs Mullins simmered down and they got through the day. In between the cleaning and washing-up there were small compensations. Mary and Cissie were given the remains of the fish mousse left over from lunch, because Mrs Mullins 'couldn't abide salmon', and there were even a couple of spoonfuls of rich purple summer pudding with a dollop of cream.

At seven o'clock Mary loitered home. There was a slight breeze and as she passed each garden the scent of roses and honeysuckle wafted towards her. Normally she took a detour to look at the butcher's shop but it felt like rubbing salt into the wound to see that little kiosk that would never be hers.

Instead she strolled through Victoria Park watching the courting couples sitting spooning on the benches. Over by the conservatory she heard a familiar sound. She'd recognise that silly baby-like giggle anywhere. Stealthily she crept towards the two figures she could dimly see standing close together, under the shadow of one of the trees. It was Beryl and someone else.

Mary sneaked back behind a tree and had another look. That was never Leonard the butcher's son with her. It couldn't be. This fellow was in naval uniform – a Chief Petty Officer by the look of the brass buttons of his sleeve. He must be all of thirty or even older thought Mary, astonished. They were certainly getting very warm with each other. Blimey, the way he was kissing her, she couldn't pass him off as her brother. Mary wished she had a camera to record Beryl's treachery.

And then a wonderful idea presented itself.

At Sea May 2nd 1921

Dear Lily,

We are on our way to Singapore. While we were at sea we sighted a column of smoke and we were told it was a subterranean volcano seldom seen by travellers. Before our eyes an island was being formed at sea. There was a huge column of smoke and belching molten rock. When it stopped it's eruptions we saw that this island was about five hundred foot wide and about one hundred foot high where before there had been nothing. It was such a wonder to me I couldn't stop looking at it. Out here, stuck with hundreds of other sailors, there are days and days of sweltering boredom and routine and then, suddenly something breathtaking happens. I have named it 'Lily's Island' especially for you.

Lily lay on the narrow bed in the attic at the Lord Tennyson and read Michael's letter by candlelight, trying to visualise the scenes he described to her. She smiled to herself – fancy an island named specially for her. Climbing on top of the bed Lily peered out of the window over the sleepy houses of Sandown to the cliffs and the sea. She was on an island herself but not one made out of an erupting volcano. Dimly she remembered something about a land bridge between Portsmouth and the Isle of Wight that had worn away in the Ice Age, or something like that. It was difficult to think of that intense far-away cold when it was still swelteringly hot in her little room.

Tomorrow would be the last day of their holiday and by the evening they would be back in Lemon Street. It had been lovely seeing everyone again. The week had sped by filled with trips with Rosie and Joseph to the beach and helping Miriam in the kitchen, and even washing glasses behind the bar with Dad.

The four months apart had changed things. Dad and Miriam and the little ones had become a separate family now. Lily felt as if she'd been set adrift. She was no longer anchored with Gran and Dad but somewhere in-between all of them. It wasn't as if she could confide in Dora. She was ill and tired and couldn't cope with her own problems, let alone anyone else's. 'You'll be miles better, when I get back from the Island,' she'd said hugging her fiercely.

'I wish you weren't going,' Dora had said, 'I'll miss you.'

'I'll send you a postcard,' she'd promised. 'Would you like me to write to Harry for you?'

'Don't want letters,' said Dora, 'I want Harry.'

If only Michael were home things wouldn't be half so bad. She'd have someone to talk to. The trouble with writing was that by the time you got a reply to whatever was troubling you, life had moved you on to a new set of problems. Sighing, Lily turned again to her letter.

> *When I get home again we'll have to go to the Lord Tennyson. I should think your Dad will be rushed off his feet with all the thirsty holiday makers.*
>
> *I really miss you Lily and wish that we had had more time with each other to have given me more memories. But this is the great thing about writing letters we can share our souls with no-one but each other knowing what has passed between us. If you have anything that worries you please confide in me and I will do the same. I know I can't write back instantly but I will always be thinking of you and wanting what's best for you.*
>
> *I wish I had been less shy and held you more often. I keep looking at your picture and wish that I could magic you here beside me. As you say paper crosses are poor things compared with the scent of you and the feel of your lips on mine. We have so much to discover about each other, so much to look forward to.*

Lily blew out the candle and lay on top of the covers. She felt restless and excited. Turning the key in the lock she stripped off her nightdress and lay naked on top of the bed. She began to run her hands over her body as if they were Michael's hands, feeling the fullness of her breasts beneath her fingers. She whispered to herself pretending the words were his. 'Lily, Lily,' she sighed. After a few moments she found the soft secret place between her thighs and began to stroke herself to a delicious quivering pitch of excitement. Slowly, slowly she brought herself release and pulling the covers over herself dropped down into sleep.

The next morning Gran and Uncle Albert took the little ones out for the day and Lily did some ironing while Miriam was busy making pastry.

'Do you like it here?' Lily asked. 'Better than Portsmouth?'

'It's a bit of a whirlwind at times,' said Miriam, cutting out a circle of pastry to fit a pie plate. 'Your Dad and me, hardly have five minutes to ourselves. What with the pub and the bed and breakfast people there's not time to breathe. Still, everyone says in the winter it's ever so quiet so we'll be able to rest up for the next season.'

'So you wouldn't come back to Portsmouth?'

'No,' said Miriam firmly. 'I know it's your home Lily and you love it,' she added, reaching out and touching her hand. 'But this is our fresh start together your Dad and me. We're Mr and Mrs Forrest with our new life opening up for us. It's a lovely spot for Jo and Rosie to grow up in. Portsmouth has happy memories, of course it has.' Her smile was full of affection. 'Meeting your father, and Gran and Albert. Battling to become your friend.'

Lily blushed to remember how jealous and spiteful she had been to Miriam when she first realised what she meant to Dad.

'But let's talk about you. Tell me about Michael. I recall him from our wedding, he was a lovely fellow.'

'Never mind Michael, you can talk about him any day of the week,' said Dad from the kitchen doorway. 'We'll take a stroll, Lily. You'll be gone tomorrow and we haven't had five minutes together.'

They walked out of the pub and down the road to the cliff

walk between Shanklin and Sandown. There were bushes of huge blue hydrangeas and below them the sea stretched away to the distant horizon.

'I've come to hate it, now,' said Lily, 'since Dora's accident.'

'That doesn't make much sense,' said Dad, pausing to light his pipe. 'It was Dora's choice to walk into the sea as it was mine to join the navy. The sea is a part of our world both good and bad.'

'You didn't see her when she came out of the water,' said Lily fiercely, 'she looked terrible, she was only just alive.'

'But you can't punish the sea, my love. I'm very fond of little Dora, she's a good girl, kind and loving. What you have to think about is why she did it. At the time it was her state of mind that mattered not the state of the tide or the temperature of the water.'

'Didn't you hate the sea after Andrew drowned?'

'No,' said her father turning towards her. 'It was the wickedness of men, of war that sent him to his death. The sea is a part of our world, a wonderful part: it feeds us with fish; bears our ships from one country to another; invites us to play in it and sings to us. But there is a dark and greedy side where it becomes a graveyard, dragging men and ships to their death.'

They linked arms and continued their walk.

'What about when my mother drowned?' For a moment or so Lily didn't think that her father had heard her. Then he released her arm almost roughly and strode on ahead.

The path had narrowed and the fence between Lily and the cliffs was broken in places. Dad had now disappeared in the distance. Lily felt frightened by his sudden going away from her; she was also afraid of being alone on the cliffs. Somehow she had to go after him. Risk falling down the cliffs and falling out of favour with Dad — both possibilities dried her mouth and set her heart hammering against her ribs. Tomorrow would be too late. Turning her eyes away from the cliff edge and looking resolutely at the fields to her right, she forced herself to follow her father. 'You can't keep shutting me out, Dad,' she shouted, 'I'm her daughter.'

'You never knew her,' he said, jumping out at her from a hidden bend in the path. His face was shut against her, denying her any knowledge of what he was thinking.

'But I'm part of her,' Lily burst out. 'She held me and loved me.'

'You don't know what it was like,' he said walking to the cliff edge, leaning on the railing and staring at the sea.

I can't bear this, Lily thought. If I wasn't so frightened of falling I'd run away all the way back down the path and pretend that we'd never had this talk. Or, I could say that I was sorry and my loving playful Dad would reappear and we'd be friends again. But it wasn't just fear that kept her standing there, it was pride as well. Summoning up the last sliver of courage she put her hand on his shoulder. 'Dad,' she said, 'why is it so difficult?'

'Why after all these years have you chosen today to ask me? Is it what happened to Dora? Is that what's stirred up this hornet's nest?' He stared at her, his face full of bewilderment and pain. 'You tell me why you're asking now.'

'As I said, she was my mother, I've a right to know. Besides,' she looked away from him,' I opened Granddad's ditty-box and found a letter that you wrote to Gran just after the drowning, when you'd left her to look after us.'

Dad said nothing.

Lily willed him to look at her to say something, anything to fill the emptiness. What was he thinking? She had to know.

'I don't want to remember the person I was then.' He said in a voice she could hardly hear. 'You don't know about regrets yet, Lily, but I do.'

Lily thought of her jealousy and spitefulness to Miriam and how she had failed to listen to Dora's troubles.

'We want to be heroes. Don't want to face our shameful side.'

'I don't understand.'

'Mary was beautiful and it was me she had chosen. She was like a trophy rewarding me for being a handsome fellow. There was a glitter of excitement that blinded us to our differences.'

'Didn't you love her?' asked Lily.

'I thought so,' he said, staring at the ground.

'Did she love you?'

'She tried to in the beginning but she hated the routine of being shut up in the house and me always being away.'

'Did she love us, Andrew and me?'

'She doted on you, the pair of you,' he said. 'Often I'd come home the place would be in an uproar, no dinner and she'd be dancing you round the room.' He looked at her and smiled. 'Made up this little song, you know, it was to the tune of Bobby Shaftoe.' He wrinkled his forehead and then began to sing. 'Lily Forrest's gone to sea to get her Daddy home for tea, He'll dance her up upon his knee, and give her lots of kisses. Lily Forrest's bright and fair with pretty ribbons in her hair She saves her Mummy from despair pretty Lily Forrest.'

By this time they had walked a few paces further along the cliff path and found themselves a bench in the shade. Lily sat beside Dad trying to conjure up an image of her mother from what the photograph had shown and what Gran and Dad had told her. She closed her eyes and let the Bobby Shaftoe tune play in her head. Mary Forrest had been beautiful, had turned men's heads but why couldn't she have stayed? In the brief time that they were together her mother had loved her. Could that be enough?

'The magic went and we punished each other because we were disappointed,' her father said.

'Couldn't Gran help?'

'I think she tried to but we were both stubborn and proud. It was the thought of me going away again that was the final straw with her and one day she just walked away.'

'Do you really believe that she drowned herself?' Lily asked, watching her father carefully.

He faced her, looking into her eyes. 'When she left, she had no money. As you know she was brought up in an orphanage. What friends she'd had I went to see and they were as much at a loss as we were. Where could she have gone? You were six months old and you're now nearly seventeen: if she's not drowned where is she? Surely to God she'd have found some way of seeking you out?'

'Why did you say you were ashamed?'

'Well,' Dad looked away from her, running his hand through his hair. 'I could have tried to be more patient, tried to understand her. When I look back I see an impatient, cocky, heedless sort of lad, that I'm not proud to own as myself.'

'Did you recognise her when you saw her at the mortuary?'

'It's so hard,' said her father, staring down at his hands. 'Looking back across the years. I was so tired and anxious. It definitely was the body of a young girl with long black hair. She was all bloated and blue-looking and I was shocked and had to rush outside and be sick. It was difficult to recognise her as Mary or anyone. We walked the streets for two whole weeks and found nothing. I thought it was her, honestly I did, Lily. And when you think about it, it must have been.'

'Oh Dad, I'm sorry. I didn't think how it would be for you to remember.'

'Can we let her lie in peace, now?'

'Yes, oh yes.'

'Just remember that she loved you,' he said, 'and that I still do. I may have a new little family now, but you're still my dark princess.'

Lily took her father's arm and together they walked back to the Lord Tennyson. She felt as if a heavy weight had been rolled away from her — the weight of a secret.

It had been a simple family holiday but so much had changed between them all. The week together in Sandown had served to underline the changes for her. In calling her his dark princess Dad had been speaking of a role she had gloried in as a little girl. But now she was a woman and her ties with Dad were different. He had Miriam and his new family and she had Michael. Even Gran's life had changed with her marriage to Uncle Albert.

In his last letter to her Michael had spoken of wanting to share his soul with her. It made her realise how little she had shared with him of all the recent turmoil. Now, she felt ready to confide in him, to tell him of all her doubts and fears, even the pain of Dora's near-drowning and her feelings of guilt. There must be no holding back if they were to be true soulmates.

Dora sucked the black liquid through the glass straw. It tasted metallic on her tongue. She didn't know whether the iron tonic was making her feel any better. Certainly she was not so tired. But then she had not been to work for two weeks now. It was good to wake up without that heavy feeling of dread and without the sound of her grandmother's stick tapping on the ceiling. She knew that Dad missed his mother and would like her to say that she missed her, too. But the words wouldn't come. Even from Dora's earliest childhood Gran had been a critical discontented presence in the family. She'd always taken Dad's side in an argument and reduced poor Mum to an apologetic shadow. Dora had hated her and her death had been a wonderful release.

Even now she didn't know whether she had really meant to finish everything on the the beach that Sunday, it was so hard to remember. What she did know now, was that she had frightened everyone. For the first time in her life Dad had said that he loved her as he sat holding her hand, round at Lemon Street in Lily's bedroom. She'd hardly recognised the tearful desperately anxious man as Dad. Then there was Mary's visit. In spite of her exhaustion Dora had been well aware of what a dent it caused in her pride for Mary to apologise but she could not just accept the fumbled words. A spurt of anger had struggled beneath her tiredness and she'd sent her away. Now, she'd had enough of being waited on and she was looking forward to going back to work. Not that she had been idle. Miss Pearson had sent her around some jackets to finish and had said there was a pile of work waiting for her.

'Nobody else has quite got your thoroughness,' the fore-woman had said when she called around a few days ago.

Of course, nobody at Denby and Shanks knew of the events on the beach. Pernicious anaemia had been the official reason for her being away sick. She hadn't yet decided what to tell Harry. She was pretty certain that Mary would not have said anything. The telling-off she had given her had severely dented her pride. Mary would not want Harry to think that she had been persecuting his fiancée– that would certainly lose her the favoured place in her brother's affections. The wonder was that she had never stood up to Mary before. Still, she reasoned, as she broke off the cotton thread with her teeth and smoothed back the collar of the coat she was finishing, better late than never. At the sound of footsteps on the stairs, Dora looked up to see her brother Barney standing in the doorway.

'You all right, Dor?' he asked. 'Guess what?' he said. 'That posh woman Mrs Carrruthers is in the shop. Dad's getting all flowery over her. You know what he's like with toffs.'

Dora laughed. Her poor father for all his bluster was really quite shy.

'He told her how grateful he was that she'd rescued you and asked if there was any way that he can show his appreciation. "Need some transport," she says, "take me to the bicycle shed."'

'Perhaps she's going to have her wicked way with him,' laughed Barney.

'I think I'll go downstairs and say hallo,' said Dora, laying aside her sewing. 'I've never properly thanked her myself, besides,' she winked at Barney, 'I should go and protect Dad from her wiles.'

Laughing together they went downstairs and through the shop.

Dora was curious to see what Mrs Carruthers wanted in the bike shed. In the short time that she had stayed at Lily's she had become fascinated by her. Dahlia was like her name, a vivid showy flower reaching out to the sun. And she'd reached out to her for some strange reason that Dora couldn't fathom.

In the huge shed where the dockyard men left their bikes each day were bunches of tyres suspended from the ceiling, a work bench, and hanging around the walls various frames and wheels. As she and Barney walked in Mrs Carruthers was pointing to a tandem frame slung above the work bench.

'That would be just the thing,' she said, 'get it down would you, please.'

'Well,' said Dad, scratching his head,' that would need a deal of work. It would take at least a week or two and I don't know whether I've got the right size saddle for the back.'

'How did you come by it?' she asked.

'Two brothers from the local cycling club asked me to store it when they joined up.' He sighed. 'Never came back poor fellows.'

'Well at least we can put it to good use. I'm sure they'd like to think of a sailor blinded in his country's service having a jaunt around on it.' She turned around at the sound of Dora's footsteps. 'Oh, good-day to you Dora. I'm about to buy a bicycle from your father.'

'You are welcome to that for nothing,' said Dad looking doubtful. 'It'll need a deal of work doing to it.'

'No problem at all,' said Dahlia. 'I'm a good mechanic. If you'd let me loose in here with your tools I'd be much obliged.'

Dad puffed out his cheeks. 'Well, I don't know. . . .'

'Oh go on Dad,' urged Dora. 'I could help sometimes. I'd like to.'

'If it will put a smile on your face it'll be well worth it,' said Dad. 'Look Mrs Carruthers, I must go back to the shop. Perhaps you could drop in on your way out and we'll come to some arrangements.'

'I must be off too,' said Barney, 'See you later Dor. Bye Mrs Carruthers.'

Dahlia waved her hand dismissively.

'I love this shed,' said Dora, shyly. 'I love the rubbery smell of the tyres. I used to play down here when I was a little girl. Then later I helped Dad to clean up bikes that he'd put together from old parts. Mongrels he called them. He'd give me a cloth and metal polish to clean the wheel spokes.'

Dahlia nodded absently as she stood at the bench looking at the tools.

Dora couldn't remember whether she had ever thanked Mrs Carruthers for rescuing her. Better to be thanked twice than not at all, she supposed. Now would be good while Dahlia wasn't looking at her. 'I'm grateful that you saved me,' she managed to mumble.

'Are you sure about that?' asked Dahlia quietly.

'What d'you mean?'

'Well, you could have been furious with me for interfering. Especially if you were seriously intending to end it all.'

'I don't know whether I thought of what I did as killing myself or just wanting to go away.' For the first time, Dora felt, she was being asked what had been going on in her mind. Although she was strolling around the shed and not appearing to listen Dora knew she had Dahlia's attention. 'Everyone needed me to do things for them,' she said. 'Harry wanted letters, Gran wanted trays of food, at the shop it was jackets. Dad wanted someone to nag and Mum someone to stand up for her. The Vines wanted me to be referee to their fights, to take them out places, mend their clothes, be a mum to them I suppose. Mary was jealous 'cos I'd taken her place with Harry, her brother. And then her Dad wanted to slobber over me.' Dora scrubbed her mouth with her hand at the memory. 'I was like a bar of soap. I was working up a lovely lather for everyone else but me, I was disappearing down the plug-hole.'

'How are you going to change things.'

'Well,' said Dora doubtfully, 'things will be easier here now Gran's gone.'

'But that's not a change brought about by you,' said Dahlia, taking a cigarette packet out of her overall pocket and striking a match.

'I'm only going around to the Vines once a week on a Saturday, and Sundays are going to be for Lily and me to do things,' said Dora, the plan just coming to her.

'Now we're getting to it,' said Dahlia with satisfaction. 'How about the lecherous father?'

'I shall threaten him that I'll tell Harry if he tries it on again.'

'That's leaving it to Harry and it's all too protracted and long-distance,' said Dahlia, dismissively. 'A sharp slap in the face or knee to the groin. Pain, that's the best teacher. You, Dora, must be the one who decides when you're going to be kissed and by whom.'

'Blimey,' gasped Dora. 'That takes a bit of thinking about.'

'That's good,' said Dahlia. 'I approve of thinking. Drifting and letting others take the initiative, that's what muddies the waters. Do you want to change things with Harry?'

'I want him to see me as his fiancée, not a mum to his brother and sisters. I want him to ask me what I want for a change.'

'Splendid. That just leaves your parents: how will you tackle them?'

'S'pose just say what I can do and what I can't.'

Dahlia put down a a wheel-socket and turned towards the door of the shed. 'Getting it clear in your head is the first step.

Remember Dora, you are as much entitled to be happy as anyone else.'

'I'm really glad you saved me,' said Dora to Dahlia's departing back.

'Champion,' said Dahlia, turning around and smiling at her. 'I'd hate to think that I'd been wasting my time.'

Chapter Sixteen

17 October 1921

Dear Mr Pragnell,

   Please could you call around and see me in Hawke Street. I am in a desperate fix. It has been months since I had any work and there is nothing left for me to sell or pawn. Even my blanket is gone.

   I know my rent is owing but what can I do? If there is work of any kind that you could find me I would be most grateful. Sincerely Sergeant Clifton.'

'Poor fellow,' said Beattie, handing the letter back to Albert. 'We must put a parcel of food together and get a couple of blankets.'

'I'd better make haste,' said Albert, 'this letter is two days old. He's a good man and I must try and raise his spirits somehow.'

A sad start to a sad day, thought Beattie as she gathered together a tin of corned beef, a chunk of cheese, some bread and a spare tin-opener. In the afternoon she and Albert would be part of the huge crowd at the unveiling of the War Memorial beside the Town Hall Square.

He came back into the kitchen with two grey blankets tied up with string. Looking at his watch he said, 'It's nearly twelve. What time are we setting out for the service this afternoon?'

'We don't need to leave until two,' Beattie replied. 'With any luck you'll be back in time. I'll wait for you until then but after that I'll walk up on my own. I need to go for Andrew's sake if no one else.'

'Of course, of course,' said Albert distractedly. 'There will be other families going from the street I'm sure. The sooner I get around there the better.'

Beattie waved him goodbye and went back indoors. In some ways she would not be sorry to go on her own. It would give her a chance to pay her respects to Joseph at his own memorial in the park.

How lucky she was to have made a new life with Albert when thousands of other women were struggling on alone or having half a life with a demented or disabled husband. She thought of Ethel Rowan, Michael's mother, from across the street. The poor woman had cared for her elder son Arthur, shell-shocked and wheelchair-bound until his death aged twenty-five. Thank God Michael had been relatively unscathed by his war experiences.

But even those who had survived the war had little to celebrate. Whole families were crammed in one room, some even split up with mother and children in one place and father in another. Children queued for the Salvation Army farthing breakfasts and the Portsmouth Brotherhood was overwhelmed with vouchers for their free boots.

'Homes fit for heroes' – what a hollow promise that had been Beattie thought, as she set the iron to heat on top of the stove. She tried to concentrate on the job in hand but her thoughts kept straying to Albert and Sergeant Clifton. The morning dragged on and by half-past one she had completed the ironing and had a lunch of cheese on toast and a cup of tea. Albert did not return.

As she stepped out onto the pavement Chippy Dowell drew

level pushing his mother in the wheelchair. Mrs Dowell smiled at her before pulling her scarf around her mouth. 'Afternoon, Beattie,' she wheezed.

Beattie smiled encouragingly. 'Good to see you, Winnie,' she said 'and you Chips.'

Poor woman she thought, spent her life looking after her backward son and now she needs someone to care for her. There was a stale, cobwebby look to Winnie Dowell. A good wash and clean clothes, that's what you're crying out for, thought Beattie, who promised herself a visit the next day to see what she could do for the pair of them.

As they approached Victoria Park Beattie shivered. It was a cold autumn afternoon with lowering clouds. 'I'll see you up at the Cenotaph,' she said to Chippy and his mother, 'I've something to attend to in here, first.'

'Give him my good wishes,' gasped Winnie.

Beattie was touched by her neighbour's understanding. She left the path, near the pond, to look once more at the name of Petty Officer Joseph Forrest inscribed on the little stone pagoda. It commemorated the men lost in the taking of the Taku Fort in China in 1900. Over twenty years, she marvelled, since her first husband, Joseph, had been a living presence in her life. When the memorial had first been erected in the park she had gone there every week to touch the stone letters of his name and talk to him. Gradually Joseph's presence had faded and she'd been able to let go of him.

'Goodbye my love,' she whispered. 'I thought the world of you but now I'm happy again and cared for. Sleep well my darling.'

Ahead of her little groups of people were laying wreaths and bunches of flowers on the grass behind the entrance to the War Memorial.

'All the toffs and bigwigs got to lay their flowers first,' said an old man angrily, almost throwing his bunch of chrysanthemums on the ground. 'Cut them this morning from my garden. Our Charlie loved his chrysants.'

Everyone was directed out of the park by the side gate. The Town Hall Square was crowded. All heads were turned towards the vast white memorial. It was U-shaped. The high wall at the back had tablets set in it inscribed with thousands of Portsmouth names and the two low side walls each ended with a statue of a man crouched behind a gun. In the paved centre was a tall column draped in a Union Jack.

Beattie managed to wedge herself between two old military men, their civilian jackets studded with medals. Chippy and Winnie were somewhere, swallowed up in the crowd. Somewhere, thought Beattie, among all those names on the memorial would be Boy Bugler A Forrest of HMS *Black Prince*, her Andrew.

The road into the square was guarded by men from the Royal Navy and Royal Marines. On the steps leading up to the massive Town Hall, with its pillars, plinths and stone lions, stood the mayor and councillors resplendent in their civic robes. Beattie smiled to herself – the bigwigs as the man in the park had said.

The service started and she mouthed the words of, 'Oh God our help in ages past,' bowed her head for the official prayers, even watched the Duke of Connaught pull the draped Union Jack from the Cenotaph but her mind was elsewhere. She was sure that most of the people in the crowd were doing the same. Remembering all the dead was beyond the imagination of anyone. Behind each face would be the treasured image of an individual, husband, son or brother. Homely pictures of the son's first haircut, his schooldays, the husband his head thrown back in laughter at a family party, the brother on his bicycle. All of them snatched too soon from their lives.

After the Mayoress had set down her huge wreath and the dignitaries had departed to a civic reception in the Town Hall, Beattie's interest was rekindled. Through the arch cut in the wall of the memorial, families were coming out of the park with their tributes. She even spotted the man with the chrysanthemums. If she had not been so caught up with Albert's worries, earlier, she would have brought flowers for Andrew.

Gradually the crowd thinned and people began drifting away. Like many others Beattie lingered, reading the names on the wreaths. 'To Daddy, who gave his life for us, with love from Ruby and Tom,' said a note pinned to a bunch of Michaelmas daisies. 'Our Hero,' said another card. Then her attention was caught by a wreath with a cap ribbon from HMS *Black Prince* and the words, 'Chief Petty Officer Miller, to Dusty from his pals at the Ship and Castle.' She smiled – Andrew would have appreciated that.

As she walked back through the park someone touched her sleeve. It was Albert.

'Hallo, my love, how did it go in Hawke Street?'

Instead of falling in to step beside her, he led her towards one of the benches. The seat was wet with rain from the downpour of the night before. Heedless of this, Albert sat down and Beattie felt obliged to do the same. Whatever had happened with Sergeant Clifton it had upset him deeply.

'They wouldn't treat a dog like it,' he burst out, suddenly, 'it was shameful, shameful, what they did to him.'

Beattie felt wet and cold and thoroughly alarmed. 'Albert,' she said after he had remained silent for several minutes, 'put me out of my misery for the Lord's sake.'

'I wish he had been able to do just that, for Clifton,' said her husband reaching in his pocket for his handkerchief and wiping his eyes. 'Poor wretch, it was so degrading. Evidently the other men in the house had gone out and Clifton was at the end of his tether.'

'Oh, Albert,' gasped Beattie, taking his hand, 'how terrible.'

The poor fellow had tried to hang himself from the stairwell. Evidently the banister broke and he fell down into the passage, smashing his glasses and breaking his nose. When the other fellows returned they found him covered in blood with the rope still around his neck. One tried to see to him and the other fetched the police. 'I've just come back from the station, now. He's been charged with attempting suicide, to compound all his other miseries. Beatrice, it was quite dreadful. The poor man was so humiliated and ashamed he couldn't look at me.'

'What can you do?' she asked. 'There must be something.'

Albert took out a pair of wire-rimmed glasses from his pocket. The bridge had snapped at one time and had been repaired with black twine.

'He hasn't hurt his face has he?' asked Beattie anxiously, 'the glass didn't go into his eyes?'

'No,' said Albert, 'fortunately they slid off as he fell. I think he might have trod on them. The first thing is to get him a new pair. Woolworth's will suffice for the time being and then perhaps I can arrange for an optician to see him. At the moment, he's on his way to the asylum, for assessment. He may well be sent to prison.'

'How dreadful,' gasped Beattie, 'to be treated as a criminal.'

'I shall speak up for him of course, and try and get him a good solicitor. But it's such a savage and inhuman law. He'd have been better off slaughtered in France than facing this barbarity.'

'Let's go home Albert,' said Beattie, getting up and tugging at his sleeve. 'Sitting here and getting chilled will help no one.'

They walked in silence out of the park and down Queen Street, past the two naval barracks, one for officers and one for other ranks. Albert and Joseph would have been stationed on opposite sides of the street, thought Beattie inconsequentially. The discarded fiancé and the husband. It was a tribute to the pair of them that they had become close friends.

But now, all her anxieties were concentrated on Albert. He was so tender-hearted and was probably scourging himself with guilt for not having helped poor Clifton earlier. It would take all her powers of persuasion to lift his spirits. She was just debating some little treat for his tea when they turned into Lemon Street.

Beattie was astonished. Neighbours were out in the street laughing and cheering, even Chippy and Winnie Dowell. Cycling up and down the street were Dahlia, Sailor and Algie on a tandem. The little boy was perched on the cross-bar, his hands gripping the middle of the handlebars. Beattie had never seen him so happy, he had a grin from ear to ear. It transformed him from a distrustful changeling into a merry seven-year-old.

Dahlia was resplendent in breeches, gaiters and army boots. Topping off the whole outfit was a pilot's leather helmet. Behind her, Sailor was in his usual naval garb, his straw hat repaced by a grey woollen balaclava. He, too, was grinning. 'Tally ho, Tally ho, where's the fox?' he chuckled.

They did another circuit of the street.

'Should have been at the Memorial Service,' shouted Mrs Perks from number 7. 'Not respectful at all.'

Dahlia screeched the tandem to a halt beside her. 'What I've got respect for, madam,' said Dahlia firmly, 'is life. Our tribute to the dead is to live our lives to the full and take every moment to celebrate our existence. Anything else is blasphemy.'

'Hear, hear,' said Beattie.

Albert, oblivious of the spectacle, drew the key through the letter-box and disappeared indoors.

Chapter Seventeen

Mary was alone in the kitchen at Lancaster Terrace. Captain Clements and his wife had taken the children to meet Father Christmas at the Landport Drapery Bazaar accompanied by Cissie and Nurse Harker. After coughing and spluttering all morning Mrs Mullins had staggered up to her attic bedroom and given in to a bout of 'flu. 'Nothing for it,' she had said,' but to go horizontal. You gals will have to manage best you can. Mrs Clements will have to send around to the agency if I'm not right by the morning.'

This is the moment thought Mary as she crept up the stairs. Cautiously she opened the door into Lettice Clements' sitting-room and peered around her. She crossed the thick red-and-cream carpet to the little desk by the window. The wood was the colour of sucked toffees and was satin-smooth under her fingers. Mary laughed to herself, relishing the danger of her position. If Lettice Clements could see her now she'd boil over, her pointy face puce with rage. Mary would be out of Lancaster Terrace before her feet touched the ground. She looked at the little lamp beside the blotter on the desk. From a distance the glass shade looked like a blue-and-green pleated cloth. Beneath it was a metal base with a neck resembling plaited stems and leaves. Mary was enchanted. There was a cord with a little button switch.

Electricity intrigued her, the instant response between switch and bulb was magical. For several moments she stood there alternately tracing the swirly pattern on the shade with her fingers and switching the lamp on and off. A coal dropped into the fender from behind the brass fireguard, startling her back to the precariousness of her position. Looking around the room was a luxury she couldn't afford. There were things to do before the family returned.

At the back of the desk was a carved wooden letter-rack. Standing with regimental stiffness in the appointed slots were sheets of cream notepaper and envelopes. Quickly she helped herself and tucked the paper under the bib of her apron before hurrying down to the kitchen. It had been a struggle to resist writing earlier but she had to be sure of her ground. No good basing her accusations on just one sighting, she she had to be certain. After three occasions – once in Victoria Park, once late at night, coming out of the Captain Hardy, and only a few days ago close together in a side street near the Charlotte Market – Mary was ready. At the last glimpse they seemed warmer than ever. Mary even felt a tinge of sympathy for Leonard Marshall, poor bloke, anyone could see he was dotty over Beryl.

She spread a clean newspaper on the table and set out her stationery on top. As she got her school-prize fountain-pen from her pocket, Mary remembered the hours and hours spent copying pothooks on lined paper in the handwriting lesson. That had been time well spent. Just as she was about to begin her task she noticed the printed address on the top right-hand corner of the paper. Quickly she searched in the cutlery drawer for a pair of scissors. After cutting off the incriminating corner, and slipping it under the page, she sat at the table and wrote her message to Leonard.

Dear Mr Marshall,
    As a well-wisher I must tell you some upsetting news. I have seen your intended wife on three different times. She has been

*keeping company with a naval man and they have been really close
and spoony with each other.*

*You should have it out with her. Such a high class butcher as
you needs a respectful girl to be your missis not some young tart
what doesn't know when she's well off.*

Sincerely a person who have your best interest at heart.

Mary smiled to herself as she folded the paper. This would spike
Beryl's guns good and proper. She was distracted by a shrill
ringing of the front-door bell. At the same time she saw Cissie
coming up the yard. Hastily she crammed the paper in the
envelope and put it into her apron pocket. She allowed herself a
little gloat of triumph. Nobody would guess a skivvy like her
would be capable of such penmanship.

When she opened the front door Mrs and Mrs Clements
swept up the stairs without a word. Giles held his father's hand
and laughed up at him. The little boy had was clutching a toy
telescope. Charlotte in her white fur bonnet and muff was asleep
in Nurse Harker's arms.

'Send Cissie up with the nursery tea,' said Nurse. 'Mrs
Clements will ring for hers later.'

Mary hurried back into the kitchen.

'I got to meet Father Christmas,' Cissie burst out. She looked
flushed with excitement. 'Even give me a present.'

'Don't still believe in all that twaddle do ya?' Mary sneered
and then was instantly sorry.

Cissie had looked almost pretty in her enthusiasm for the
afternoon treat and now it had been tarnished. She dragged off
her coat in silence and took her apron down from the hook
behind the door.

'Take no notice,' Mary said, not looking at her friend, 'I was
just narky 'cos I was left here with moany Mullins.' She smiled
and part of Cissie's excitement seeped back into her face. 'Go on
tell us what he give ya.'

Cissie got out the nursery teaset and sliced some bread ready for toasting. She threaded a piece of bread onto the fork before answering Mary.

'Ever so pretty it is,' she said as she settled herself by the range. Reaching into her pocket she drew out a little red stick which when shaken became a brightly-coloured paper fan. 'Mrs Clements wanted me to give it to little Charlotte but 'er'usband said as I could keep it.'

'Baby will tear it in seconds,' he told her. 'Poor girl,' he says, 'she has little enough out of life.'

'What'll you do with it?' asked Mary idly, as she filled the china teapot and set out a plate of shortbread biscuits.

'Add it to my treasures,' said Cissie, as she put the heaped plate of toast onto the nursery tray and set off upstairs.

Mary thought of the time when Cissie had shown her the battered pink hat-box that she kept under her bed up in the attic. It had a few snapshots of her father in his sailor's uniform and a pretty young girl laughing into the camera, with Cissie a baby on her lap. There was a little ivory brooch with 'Martha' inscribed on it, a chipped plate with a picture of Brighton, and a silvery rattle in the shape of a teddy bear. In a yellowing envelope were Cissie's birth certificate, her parents' death certificates, and their marriage lines.

'What was it like?' asked Mary, setting the milk-jug and sugar-basin on the tray.

'It was ever so strange. Crowds of people there was and Miles was that excited. We had to get into this big grey thing with sliding doors. "Santa's Submarine", they called it. It went into a black tunnel and then you saw "Neptune's Kingdom" with all sorts of lovely shells and stuff. When you got to the end of the trip you was met by Father Christmas in a sort of snow house. Miles was in a ferment, he wanted everything. Nurse Harker had to give him a right pinching to shut him up. Then Charlotte was frightened by Neptune and created something dreadful.'

'I bet old Santa was cheesed off with the lot of you.'

Cissie laughed. 'He winked at me and whispered, "If my reindeer hadn't got distemper I'd bugger off out of here back to Greenland." Lettice was looking at him all beady like she does, so he give me the present. "Happy Christmas to you one and all," he said. Funny thing was, he looked just like that old sailor that sits in the library readin' the paper all the time.'

The bell from the drawing-room tinkled impatiently. 'You better hurry,' said Cissie. 'That'll be Lettice wanting her tea.'

'You go please, Cissie,' begged Mary. 'You know she hates me, calls me the guttersnipe.'

'Well,' said Cissie, 'you gotta take up the nippers' tray and see to Mrs Mullins. She must be spitting feathers by now. Always has potted-meat sandwiches at five. Blimey it's nearly quarter to six.'

There was little chance of further talk in the next hour as they hurried back and forth up the stairs with loaded trays. Fortunately for both of them the Clements had a dinner engagement.

Mrs Mullins declared she'd been on the point of starvation, when Mary took her tea to her. 'You gals make the most of tonight, 'cos I shall be back at my post tomorrow and looking for a good day's work out of the pair of you.'

'Hope they're not too late back,' said Cissie, standing at the back door yawning as Mary put her coat on, 'I'm ready for bed, now.'

'See you in the morning,' called Mary from the gate.

'Don't do anything I wouldn't do,' laughed Cissie before going back indoors.

Mary hurried along the road towards Marshal and Son High Class Butchers. She looked around her, anxious not to be seen, then dropped the letter addressed to Leonard through the brass letterbox. As she walked away she looked up at the bedroom windows above the shop. Was it her imagination or had the curtains moved aside for a second? Mary shrugged her shoulders. It was done now, all she had to do was wait.

She thought about Cissie's parting words about not doing anything that she wouldn't do and sighed. Mary doubted very much that little Cissie would ever stoop to such a dirty trick.

October 31st 1921

Dear Dora,

What with getting the news about Ma passing on and not getting a letter from you I'm really browned off. I miss you something awful Dor and it's ages and ages til we get back to Pompey. Someone brought this little poem on board the other day and it puts all our moans in a nutshell:

I'm tired of itch skin diseases.
Mosquitoes and vermin and flies
I'm fed up with tropical breezes
And sunshine that dazzles the eys.

Dora had hurried to work so that she could read Harry's letter in peace before everyone else arrived. She rubbed the chilblains on the back of her heels before turning over the page to hear more of his woes.

They sing of the East as enthralling
That's why I started to roam
But I hear the Occident calling
Oh Lord, but I want to go home.

Why haven't you written, Dor? I know you must have had a lot to do with helping the kids since Ma's gone but even a post card would cheer me up no end. Michael is always getting mail from Lily. You would tell me if you'd found someone else?

A wave of irritation washed over her. Harry's problems seemed so petty compared to those that she had been struggling with.

What wouldn't she give for a little of the sunshine he was carping about. Again her chilblains itched and she scratched them until they stung. She winced with pain. Of course if she had written and told Harry a bit about how she had been feeling lately things would be different. Why hadn't she told him, she wondered. When she looked back over the last few months of anxiety and despair Dora hardly recognised herself. Gradually with rest and the iron tonic she had begun to feel stronger.

From time to time Mrs Carruthers came around to the bicycle shed and Dora would sit on the bench and talk to her while she adjusted the brakes and saddles of the tandem. Dahlia was so clear-cut in what she wanted and didn't wobble and hesitate as she did.

'Stop asking permission all the time,' she'd chided her. 'You are entitled to make choices for yourself. If you lie down in front of that family of Harry's they'll wipe their feet on you. Set out your boundaries and stick to them.'

Emboldened by her talk she had tackled the Vine family about their arrangements for Christmas, early in December before they could take anything for granted.

'I'll be there for Christmas tea,' she said to Mary. 'You and Fred can get your own dinner and the twins aren't helpless.'

'Whatever suits you,' said Mary, meekly.

Dora knew that she had punished the girl enough but a little speck of resentment kept her from making her peace.

'When will we open our presents?' asked Faith. 'By the time you gets to us it'll nearly be over.'

'Four o'clock's still early, plenty of time for games and presents and all sorts,' Dora said, enjoying her new found firmness.

'I wants Snap and Tiddly-Winks and everythink,' demanded Blyth. 'You written to Santa, Auntie Dora?' he asked, catching hold of her hand and smiling up at her.

Dora smiled back. 'Yes I've written a long, long list.'

'What's on top?' he had asked.

'It's a secret,' she'd told him.

Now, sitting alone in the cloakroom of Denby and Shanks she wondered what would be top of her list of wishes. A few months ago it would have been getting married to Harry, now she was not so sure. It seemed ages and ages since he'd gone away and sometimes she hardly remembered what he looked like.

How she had wanted him then, in that time far away, before HMS *Lister* steamed over the horizon and out of her life.

Her thoughts crystallised on a magical Sunday in the May before he was due to leave. They had borrowed bicycles from her father and cycled through the town to Cosham, the little village beyond Portsmouth. They left their bikes in a hedge on the other side of the hill and dawdled through the fields, the sun hot on their faces. The hedgerows were smothered with Queen Anne's lace and bees droned in the clover. Harry helped her over a stile into a field full of sheep. At the sight of strangers they leapt and frisked away from them. In the far corner, sheltered under an oak tree, was a little hut on wheels.

'Do you think it belongs to a wizard?' Dora had asked, as they walked around it, fascinated by the little steps up to the door with its cobwebby window set in the top half and fastened with string and a wooden peg. 'Don't reckon it's used much,' Harry had said, 'there's a little bunk with an old mattress and a blanket. Look, there's a newspaper on the floor gone all yellow with the sun.' He'd pulled the peg out of the hasp and the door creaked open. It was warm and dusty inside with a faint smell that reminded her of a pet-shop. Harry held out his hand and Dora had stepped inside. It was she who spread the blanket on the floor. They looked at one another and by some silent shared agreement they undressed and lay down. It seemed as if she had stepped out of her life of permissions and approval and been set free. They lay looking at one another, kissing and touching with no sense of guilt or shyness, just an intense, wondering curiosity.

One movement flowed into another. There was a sharp tearing pain as he thrust himself inside her, his breath hot on her face. She had wanted that deep throbbing rhythm to go on and on but it had ended in a sudden jerking spasm that left her tearful and secretly disappointed.

Afterwards they had dressed and left the hut to sit under the shade of a tree and eat their sandwiches.

'I shan't never ever forget this day,' Harry had said, taking her hand and kissing her open palm. 'We was made for each other, you and me.'

'We're so lucky,' she'd said, looking into his blue eyes and seeing the image of herself in them. She'd stroked his coppery hair and promised to write to him every day.

And then the world rushed in, thought Mary, as she folded the letter back into its envelope. It wasn't just the physical distance, though, for in the beginning their thoughts had spilled out on paper. Funny thoughts, sad ones, plans and hopes for the future. But gradually she had let herself be swamped by other demands, not least Harry's family. He deserved better than the few scrappy notes she'd sent and she wanted more than his moans about prickly heat and boredom.

'Blimey, what's up with you, sat there with a face like a kite?'

Ruby Froggat burst into the cloakroom, startling Dora back to the cold December Monday.

'I was just thinking about Harry,' she said, taking off her coat and hat and hanging them beside the speckled mirror.

'Outta sight outta mind,' said Ruby, 'that's my policy.' She stared critically at herself in the mirror. 'I was thinkin' of gettin' me hair bobbed, like them Flappers, but it's so curly I don't reckon it would settle right. Probably end up looking like a bit of bleedin' coconut matting.'

Dora laughed. Red-haired Ruby was a whirlwind of a girl. Sometimes she swept in and upset everyone with her spiteful teasing, and other times she would have the whole workroom laughing with her. Linking arms they walked into the workroom and settled to their tasks.

The air was filled with the smell of hot metal and damp cloth, as old Mr Savours lifted the fourteen-pound steam-iron, and pressed the finished garments.

Mrs Markham stretched some felt over a wooden frame and tacked on to it the badge she was making. By the window two young apprentices sat doing basting stitches under the watchful eyes of Miss Pearson the forewoman, while two older women treadled away at their sewing-machines.

'D'you read about that breach of promise case in the *Daily Express?* It was some girl here in Pompey?' asked Ruby breaking the thread from a buttonhole in her teeth.

'Ooh yes,' said Mrs Markham her lips drawing together like purse strings. 'Violet Norris, a waitress at the Mikado Cafe in Elm Grove. Heartbroken she was.'

'Reckoned this Captain Sidney Cattermole had wrote her hundreds of letters. Paper said they was of an amatory nature. What d'you reckon that means.'

'Throbbin' with passion, I don't doubt,' said Mr Savours, almost disappearing behind a cloud of steam.

Miss Pearson coughed disapprovingly.

Unabashed Mr Savours continued, 'Going out with a waitress he reckoned it was love on a plate.'

Everyone chuckled and even Miss Pearson gave a thin smile.

'Keepin' it warmed up for him 'til he returned,' said Ruby winking at Dora.

'I read as he sent her a cheque for £20 to get herself an engagement ring,' said Mrs Markham, filling her needle with scarlet thread.

'Blimey,' gasped Ruby, 'I'd be well set up with twenty quid.'

'It was his mother that put the kibosh on it,' said Dora, remembering the case. 'Said he was too ill to know his own mind and that marrying a waitress would be most unsuitable.'

'Right old tabby, she was,' said Ruby. 'I hope that Violet keeps the money.'

'Wouldn't happen to you, Ruby,' laughed Dora, 'you're much too sharp.'

'Comes of sleepin' in the knife-drawer,' her friend retorted.

Dora smiled. She realised how much better she felt and more a part of everything. A few weeks ago she would have been sitting at her table crouched over her sewing in a fog of misery. Now she was eager to join in the workroom banter. At dinner-time she was joining Lily for pie and chips in Driver's Cafe. Being up in the beehive they saw little of each other during the week and she looked forward to having a chat.

At last from across Half Moon Street the dockyard bell sounded and every one put down their work and rushed down the stairs. As Lily and Dora linked arms and turned the corner into The Hard someone tapped her on the shoulder.

'Miss Somers isn't it?'

Dora looked up into the face of a young soldier. 'Yes, I'm Miss Somers. Who wants to know?' she asked.

'Rifleman Finch, Bert Finch,' he said, searching her face, as if wanting to commit it to memory.

She looked at him. He was tall with startling blue eyes and probably blond hair from what little she could see under his cap. She wanted to go on looking at him but politeness made her turn away. How did he know her name?

'You probably don't remember me,' he said. 'I carried you up off the beach, that day when you had your accident.'

'That was good of you,' she murmured, blushing and not knowing what else to say.

He coughed. 'It's good to see you looking better.'

'Would you like to have some dinner with us? We're just going around to Driver's,' asked Lily.

He shook his head. 'Sorry, I'd like to but I've to get back to the barracks. Perhaps another time,' he said, smiling down at her.

'Perhaps,' said Dora, returning the smile.

Lily set off for Nesta Armitage's house in Asylum Road. It was over a week since the tiny white-haired woman had been at work and Lily was assigned to take her a present and a Christmas card signed by everyone in the beehive. In two weeks, Lily's six-month trial in the gold-wire workroom would be at an end and she would not be sorry. With a bit of luck she might be able to persuade Miss Pearson to let her go back to tailoring with Dora and Ruby. She was bored with making cuff curls, cutting out cardboard patterns and making the tea. Clemmie, Nesta and Freda were highly skilled and produced wonderfully intricate work on the epaulettes and sword-knots and other pieces of military regalia but they were poor teachers. Lily became frustrated with their scrappy information and lack of patience. It was as if they were jealously guarding their craft from outsiders.

'Please Miss Hatcher, could you just sit with me for five minutes and take me through each step,' she'd asked.

'Just watch Miss Ivers,' Miss Hatcher had snapped.

'Short end over round top pick up twice, then over one, under one, over one. Now, follow and pick up one then over twice then over and under to finish.' Clemmie Ivers had mumbled as she crouched protectively over her work. Lily tried to follow the older woman's flashing needle. The little coal-fire heated the room to an unpleasant fug and Lily was overwhelmed by the smell of stale perspiration from Nesta Armitage, overlaid by cheap cologne. She supposed that she had made some progress but the stuffy room and the gloomy company had blunted her interest. They always seemed to take the heavy end of the stick in their conversation and laughter was a very rare commodity.

On Christmas Eve afternoon she would much rather have gone down to Charlotte Market with Dora than visit a tetchy old spinster but Gran had promised not to decorate the tree until she returned. With that treat ahead of her she wound her scarf around her neck and set off.

She got off the bus at Milton Park and made her way to Asylum Road. It was over a mile long with the mental hospital at the other end. Looking at the numbers on the houses Lily realised she was in for a long walk. Eventually she rapped on the knocker of number 305 and Miss Armitage let her in.

The hall was bare of any rugs and was covered with cracked green lino. Miss Armitage, coughing hoarsely and swathed in a grey blanket, led the way into the front room.

'Can't spare you more than five minutes, Miss Forrest, only I've to go up to the cemetery to take this holly wreath to Mother's grave.'

'Please don't worry,' said Lily, happy not to prolong her visit. 'Miss Hatcher sent me with your Christmas card and present.'

'Very kind I'm sure,' sniffed Miss Armitage. 'I'll just get you a glass of lemonade and a piece of seed cake. Don't want you saying as I stinted on the refreshments.'

'There's no need at all,' said Lily hastily, 'I know you're in a hurry.'

Miss Armitage shuffled away and Lily looked around her. It was a large cheerless room with one armchair with faded chintz covers pulled up to a mean little fire. Along one wall was a single bed draped with a crocheted cover beside which was a rickety drop-leaf table. Another smaller table stood beside the armchair with an array of medicine bottles. Above the mantelpiece was a yellowing photograph of Miss Armitage beside a fierce old woman in a large hat with a veil. Lily stood in the middle of the room wondering where to put the card and the present. It must have been a long miserable week for her workmate, being ill and alone in such cheerless circumstances. Lily resolved to be warm and sympathetic when Nesta came back.

Eventually, when Lily was thoroughly chilled, Miss Armitage shuffled in with a cloudy glass which she placed on the rickety table, and invited Lily to perch on the bed. The plate had been wiped rather than washed and contained a small hard square of cake. Lily struggled to swallow what turned out to be a very thick orange liquid and bit into the cake. It tasted dry and musty and in order to swallow it she had to keep sipping the viscous drink.

Lily licked her lips and tried to summon up some saliva to dispel the sickly orange taste. 'Don't you want to open your card?' she asked, putting the half-finished cake back on the plate.

'I'll save it to open tomorrow,' she said, putting the envelope on the bare mantelpiece.

Her faded blue eyes dared Lily to feel sorry for her, and all her earlier good intentions crumbled. She determined to leave as soon as she decently could.

'Aren't you going to finish the cake I took the trouble of cutting for you?' the invalid challenged.

It was only the thought of the pancakes that Gran would have waiting for her that helped Lily to swallow down the last two mouthfuls of cake and drink. 'Well, I'd better get back to my Gran,' said Lily brushing the crumbs from her coat. 'Happy Christmas, Miss Armitage. I hope you feel better soon.'

'Goodbye Miss Forrest,' said Miss Armitage, almost pushing her out of the door.

Lily put on her gloves and felt as if she were flying down the road, so great was her relief. She wished she could have been more sympathetic towards Miss Armitage and there were plenty of reasons to pity the old spinster – spending the Christmas alone in that cold house not the least of them. And then, there was the thought of that card to be opened and set in isolation on the mantelpiece. But there was something repellent in Nesta

Armitage that discouraged even the most determined well-wisher: a furious pride that challenged the slightest sign of compassion from anyone.

'Hey! Stop, stop, it's Lily Forrest isn't it?'

'Heather Neal,' gasped Lily, delighted to see an old friend from school.

'What are you doing up here?' asked the tall, jolly-looking girl, wearing a nurse's cloak and holding the hands of two bedraggled-looking women.

'Visiting a woman from work,' said Lily, 'I'm an apprentice at Denby and Shanks.' She smiled at Heather, remembering her from school as a kindly older girl. 'How long have you been up at the asylum?' she asked.

'Only six months but I love it. Hard work and poor pay but you really feel you make a difference, most of the time.' She turned to her two charges. One was a tall woman with a black beret and thick glasses. They reminded Lily of old-fashioned dimpled windows. The other patient was small with long black hair streaked with grey.

'This is Charlotte,' said Heather, introducing the big woman who reached out and pumped Lily's hand enthusiastically.

'Hallo, hallo, hallo,' she cried in a strange high-pitched voice.

Lily hoped her instinctive revulsion was not apparent to Heather. She had been so clever at school. How could she waste herself on these drab, disordered women?

'And this is Amy,' said Heather, touching the younger woman's shoulder.

'Hello Amy,' said Lily, forcing herself to smile.

The woman looked up into Lily's face. If she were not dressed in the shapeless grey hospital clothes, Lily thought, she might be made to look quite pretty. She had large dark eyes and as she looked at her Amy's face broke into a smile.

'What's your name?' she asked.

'I'm called Lily,' she said, smiling back at her.

They stood for a few moments looking at one another and Lily felt suddenly afraid.

'I brought them over to the shop because they haven't got any visitors. Charlotte goes around pestering people and Amy starts to cry.'

'Haven't they got any relations? It seems a shame at Christmas-time,' said Lily, unable to draw her glance away Amy's dark eyes.

'I think Charlotte's got a brother somewhere but Amy's a bit of a mystery.'

'What do you mean?' asked Lily, warily.

'It's a long story,' said Heather, 'and I think that's your bus coming up now. You'd better catch it. They've only one every half-hour. Anyway, if you're up here again we might see each other.'

'Happy Christmas Heather, and Charlotte and Amy,' said Lily, waving the three of them goodbye.

'Come and see me,' called Amy.

Lily looked out of the window. Charlotte bounded into the shop but Amy watched the bus until it disappeared. When she could no longer see her Lily had a strange, unexplainable feeling of loss.

Chapter Eighteen

It was just before six and Beattie was sat in the kitchen, her diary in her apron pocket. She loved the first hours of Christmas morning with everyone asleep and the air full of expectation. Later the usual patchwork of friends and family would gather around the table. This year they were herself, Albert and Lily combined with Dahlia, Sailor and Algie and finally Ethel Rowan and Chippy Dowell.

Two large chickens were sitting on the shelf in the larder with their snug lining of sage-and-onion stuffing. In their raw plucked state they gave no hint of the transforming golden succulence performed by heat and lard. The potatoes floated in a pan of water ready for parboiling. Hidden secretly away in a blue cotton shirt-tail tied with string was the pudding, waiting to release its spicy fragrance into the room.

Beattie washed quickly, sipped her tea and then began to write.

So many Christmasses. I'd like to search them all and find the absolute heart of its magic. Even the meagre celebrations at the orphanage, the desperate Christmas after Joseph died and our attempts at jollifications during the war all of them still held that flicker of something powerful and mysterious. It seems that it's not

*only my yearning to step outside the humdrum and the routine
but that of humankind every where. We all need to hallow a few
special hours each year, to lighten the darkness and draw in the
stranger.*

*How many people living and dead come into my thoughts at
this time. It's like an invisible gateway through which, once a year,
old friends and family pass and this is multiplied a thousand
thousandfold throughout the world. I don't know if I believe in
God but, certainly, I believe in Christmas.*

The lid rattled on the kettle, startling Beattie out of her
reflections. Quickly she made fresh tea and carried two cups
up the stairs. Setting them on the dressing-table she slipped out
of her nightdress and slid naked into bed beside her husband.

Albert stirred sleepily and drew her into his arms. Beattie ran
her hands down his warm back pressing her fingers over the
bones of his spine. He kissed her gently on the lips. Slowly they
began their lovemaking, stroking, murmuring and whispering.
Her body moulded itself to his and they roused each other to a
state of melting contentment.

'Happy Christmas, my darling,' said Albert kissing her neck.
'Now, you have a little doze and I shall bring us up a second cup.'

'Thank you, my love,' said Beattie sleepily, 'what time is it?'

'Seven o'clock.'

'Can you get the range going? We'll need it good and hot and
the birds inside by eight if we're all to sit down to dinner at one.'

'Right ho, my dear. Now you snuggle down, I won't be long.'

She had been worried about Albert and his depression over
poor Sergeant Clifton. Fortunately Clifton had opted for
summary trial in the local magistrates court and with his old
commanding officer's testimony was released to Romsey to work
on Samuel's farm. Any lingering doubts had been overcome by
Albert's enthusiastic wooing of a few moments ago. Sometimes
she wished that he could grow a tougher skin and not be so

constantly wounded by the misfortunes of others. Beattie sighed. If that happened he would no longer be her Albert.

After drinking her tea she rushed back downstairs and was immediately caught up with the preparations for dinner. She rapped on Lily's door at nine o'clock with her jug of hot water. 'Happy Christmas my duck. Come and have a bite of toast before I clear the table.'

Flushed with sleep Lily came to the door and kissed her. 'Happy Christmas, Gran,' she said hugging Beattie warmly. 'Just give me time to wash and dress and I'll see to things while you and Albert get to church.'

'Won't you come with us. We can all set to when we get back.'

'No thanks, I'd like to sit and write to Michael.'

Before church the stockings were taken down from the mantelpiece and the presents exchanged. Each of them exclaimed at the magnificence of their book or scarf or gloves and then issuing instructions over her shoulder Beattie picked up her gloves and set off with Albert for St George's.

She sniffed appreciatively at the combined scents of chrysanthemums, wax polish, mothballs and wintergreen chest-rub which made up the smell of Christmas in church. Afterwards she couldn't have remembered which hymns they sang or what was the message contained in the Reverend Merchison's rambling sermon. It was enough to be there with Albert. Afterwards they greeted friends and neighbours at the church door then hurried home, their breath smoking in the cold air.

Lily had done marvels in their absence. A white sheet had been thrown over the greatly extended table and chairs brought down from the studio. Cutlery had been unwrapped and set out that had not been used since the wedding. The chickens were in the oven and the sprouts and carrots all prepared.

'Ooh you've set my mouth watering,' said Beattie smiling at

her granddaughter. 'Half-past eleven, plenty of time to have a sherry and toast the cook.'

The morning flashed by and in no time the guests had piled into the kitchen and settled themselves around the table.

Lily, flushed and pretty in her red bridesmaid's dress, coaxed Chippy to have a glass of beer.

'Mother don't like me to touch the stuff,' he protested, 'she say I acts daft when I'm sozzled.'

'It's Christmas Day, Chippy and she'd want you to be cheery wouldn't she?'

'Come on lad, we've got to drink a toast to the cook,' said Sailor, 'my nose is twitching and my mouth watering.'

Since his mother's death a couple of weeks ago Chippy had been dazed and tearful. He hadn't been back to work in the dockyard where he swept up wood-shavings in the shipwrights' shop and carried messages. If he didn't shift himself soon, the job would be given to one of the hundreds of men desperate for work. His next-door neighbours told Beattie that he wandered up and down stairs each night calling for his mother.

'Come on old chap,' said Albert, filling his glass for him. 'Let's toast my dear Beatrice and that handsome dinner set before us.'

All eyes were drawn to the vast willow-patterned meat platter placed in front of Albert. Almost overflowing the dish were the chickens, their bronzed breasts hung with garlands of chipolatas. Forming a defensive border around the bird were a row of crispy roast potatoes.

'The cook, the cook,' everyone cried, clinking their glasses and smiling at Beattie.

She in turn smiled fondly at Albert as he made elaborate play of sharpening his knife on a steel before squaring up to his task as carver. She passed a plate to Dahlia, resplendent in a green satin blouse and long black hobble skirt, like some exotic bird adrift in a flock of sparrows.

'Have some sprouts,' offered Ethel Rowan, passing her the vegetable dish.

Beattie was pleased that Michael's mother had come. It would be good for Lily to get to know her. She was a quiet woman, easily overlooked but once she'd overcome her shyness Beattie knew that Lily would enjoy her company. She had once been a schoolteacher and shared Lily's love of books.

Dahlia busied herself cutting up Sailor's food. 'The chicken is between twelve and quarter-past, sausage at half-past, veggies next and spuds at quarter-to,' she told him, quietly as he picked up his knife and fork. Beattie thought it an ingenious method of finding his food and giving him that little bit of independance.

Algie, in a new grey jumper, ate wolfishly with hardly a pause for breath. Beattie felt a sense of failure as she looked at him, the one child she had not been able to like. There was a constant watchfulness and suspicion in his eyes, a coldness and immediate withdrawal and flight if closeness was ever attempted. Dahlia was either harshly punishing or soppily sentimental. The nearest they had ever got to a falling-out had been when Beattie pressed her about sending the boy to school.

'I'm not having him turned into cannon fodder, a little son of the empire. Saw too much of that in France. If he's not in the system he won't be known about and he'll be safe.'

'What about learning to read and write and finding out what's in him, Dahlia? You can't just lock him out of life. He needs a boyhood with friends of his own age.'

'Sailor and I are all he needs for the moment,' she'd said firmly.

'I wonder what Michael and Harry will be eating,' Lily said, smiling at Ethel Rowan.

'Probably something with rice I should think. It's hard to imagine isn't it.' The two of them sat somewhere in the sweltering heat thousands of miles away. And yet I can remember

Michael's father writing to me one Christmas from China and it was freezing, they were on the jetty having snowball fights.'

'They've moved the *Victory* from its anchorage in Gosport and are putting it into dry dock you know, Sailor,' said Albert. 'It'll be a risky undertaking.'

'By God yes,' said Sailor, his fork halfway to his mouth. 'I should think the sea-worms will have had a picnic all these years on her timbers.'

Beattie let the talk flow on around her as she ate her dinner and made sure that everyone else had plenty. She thought about the little family in Sandown and wondered how they were faring. Alec had said that they relished the quiet of winter at the Lord Tennyson, after the hectic bustle of the summer season. Rosie was happy at school and Joseph was toddling all over the place.

'My old mum had wrapped up some presents for the children,' said Chippy, suddenly. 'I left them in the front room. I'd best go get them.'

'There's no rush,' said Ethel. 'Why don't you have your pudding first? Your mother told me that was your favourite food of all on Christmas Day.'

Albert and Ethel cleared the plates and Beattie took the pudding out of its cloth and set it on a warm plate. She doused it liberally with rum, stuck a sprig of holly in the top and struck a match. Everyone cheered as she carried the flaming pudding to the table; even Algie was entranced. Ethel followed behind with a jug of custard. It was Chippy who found the silver threepenny-bit on his plate and he crowed with delight. 'Just wait 'til I tells Mother,' he said, swigging thirstily on his second glass of beer.

After a cup of tea and mince-pies the spell was broken. Ethel insisted on helping Lily and Albert with the washing-up. 'Beattie, my dear,' she said when all the plates and glasses were safely put away, 'that was a wonderful feast. I shall have to move my buttons if I eat anything else today. Thank you so much. I shall go home now and write a few letters. If you want to see those photos, Lily, why don't you pop across in an hour or so?'

'I'd like that,' said Lily, smiling shyly.

Chippy wanted to go home to get the children's presents. Algie followed and Sailor got his stick and declared that he would stroll up and down a bit to 'let his vittals settle.'

Dahlia rose unsteadily to her feet. 'I've got an appointment with a bottle of gin,' she said. 'Tell Sailor he might as well stay here if he wants any tea and that goes for Algie. Want to blot out the rest of the day. Too many absent friends. I feel them like ghosts around me. See you on the morrow.'

Beattie nodded. She couldn't fathom Dahlia at all. They were both respectful of each other but there was a secret side to her neighbour that hindered a closer friendship. Albert and Sailor had formed a firm alliance based on the common bond of naval service. But Algie worried her. He needed stability and a chance to mix with children his own age. His life of drifting around lonely and bored was bound to lead to grief.

'I'll see you later, Gran,' said Lily, following Ethel out the door.

'Be back by seven both of you,' said Beattie, 'and we'll have a game of whist with Albert.'

Beattie closed her eyes and let her thoughts drift. Lily had had a tempestuous few months: what with Dolly Vine's death, finding the letter about her own mother, and then Dora's near-drowning. She sensed that she and Alec had talked together in the summer for when they got back from their holiday she was a different girl.

Even Dora was heaps better. She'd put on weight and had a bit of colour in her cheeks and there was a glimmer of confidence that hadn't been there before. Of course that was partly due to rest and the iron tonic but Beattie sensed she was beginning to find her feet. Her days as a willing doormat were over.

As for Mary, if anyone needed loving and guiding it was her.

Ever since her mother had been carted off screaming to the asylum, Beattie had had a protective interest in the girl. She doubted she'd last long as a scullery maid. Mary was far too slapdash. She was also fiery and independent, not qualities that endeared her to employers. What she needed was some little outfit that she could run herself. Beattie sighed, fat chance of that.

'What are you thinking about, my love?' said Albert coming in from the yard. 'You look positively ferocious.'

'Wasted talent and the unfairness of life.'

'They are enough to put the damper on anyone. But you know I've got some good news. Ethel is going to write to Sergeant Clifton. What with Olive's cooking and a bit of physical work in the open air that should do wonders for him.'

'Does this mean the cloud is lifted? You no longer feel responsible for half the world and its worries?'

Albert had the grace to look shamefaced. 'Well, I think I shall give myself the day off. I'll take it all on again tomorrow.'

'Good,' said Beattie. 'Now let's you and I have a glass of port, if Dahlia's left us any, and enjoy the peace and quiet.'

Chapter Nineteen

November 1st 1921

Dear Little Dora,

Why didn't you tell me your troubles? Hearing it all second-hand through Lily and Michael made me feel such a cheap skate for not noticing anything was wrong. I've given Dad a right roasting and Mary. Dora I think the world of you. There isn't nothing I wouldn't do to set a smile on your face and make you happy. Please, my little sweetheart just look after yourself and leave my lot to get on with it.

Sent you a little parcel. Hope it gets there for Christmas. I got some green Chinese silk, a bamboo bracelet and some shells from the beach at Ceylon. I am trying to picture you wearing a dress made of the silk what I got you. Nearly wore out that picture of us at Easter Fair with looking. The place where I popped the question. Wish I could magic you here Dora so I could hold you tight and tell you how much I love you.

Dora sighed. He sounded just like the old Harry that she remembered. She wished that she had written about everything earlier. Now he would get her letter telling him of her despair just as she was getting over it. She determined to write a happy newsy note directly she got back from the Vines that night. Sipping her tea Dora returned to his letter.

247

We been playing soldiers all day. We were divided into the red force and blue force. Blue defended the road to Hong Kong and the red had to attack them. As one of the attackers I was charging about all over the place, falling over and barking me shins. A bit of excitement tomorrow as we are off to Stone Cutter's Island where the Hong Kong Pirates live. We have orders to clean out their lair. Must rush now my Love to get this letter to the mail boat that leaves in a few minutes.

Tons of Love, Your Fiancé Harry.

Dora smiled to herself as she folded his letter back in the envelope. It had been a good Christmas just like the ones before Gran had lived with them. Now with her death they were released from her glowering presence. They had all sat around the table talking and laughing. Mum looked years younger and Dad didn't mention the shop once. The pair of them had started going to the pictures once a week. Now they were out along the sea-front walking off their dinner and Mark and Barney were on the bikes somewhere.

Dora opened her dressing-table drawer and took out the dress length that Harry had sent her. She held the material against herself and looked into the mirror. The pale colour seemed to light up her face and bring out the green glints in her hazel eyes. Dora smiled at herself, she was almost pretty. She stood for a moment running her hands over the silky cloth, revelling in its smoothness and imagining herself standing in the completed dress on Farewell Jetty with Harry stepping ashore and into her arms. Regretfully she folded it up and laid it back in the drawer.

Hastily she gathered up her presents for Harry's family. For once she was looking forward to seeing them. Blyth's face would be a picture when he opened the blow football game and she was sure the twins would love the little satin camisoles she made from a remnant in the market. With Mary she'd taken especial care: it would be something of a peace-offering as well as a Christmas present.

She remembered the morning she had called to tell Mary that her mother had died. The young girl had sat there in a ragged nightdress, miles too short and drawn together across the chest with a safety-pin. Dora smiled as she wrapped up a soft pink wincyette nightie with smocking on the yoke, long sleeves and the name 'Mary' worked in white silk thread on the pocket.

The only person left out of the present-list was Fred. She still nursed a burning resentment towards him from the day he lurched towards her in his sweaty vest full of ale and fumbling lust. No, she would not forgive him.

As she passed the mantelpiece, on her way downstairs, Dora looked at the card from the soldier who had rescued her in the summer. Inside he had written:

'*To Miss Somers wishing you a Happy Christmas, Regards Bert Finch.*'

She wished that he hadn't sent it. Thinking about Bert Finch made her feel unsettled. The last thing she wanted was for Lily to see the card and say how handsome he was and how interested in her. There had been a few days, she had to admit it, when she'd thought about him and even hoped to meet him again but those fancies were dispelled by Harry's latest letter. No, she was Harry's girl. No matter how handsome, Bert Finch was simply not in the running.

Shaking her head as if to rid herself of the troubling image of Bert, Dora put on her winter coat and wrapped a scarf tightly around her neck before setting off for Lemon Street. Already at half-past four the sky was beginning to darken and the warmth had gone from the day. She wondered idly what the children might have got for her. There had been excited whisperings the last time she had been with them, rustling of paper and things hurriedly hidden under cushions. Mary would have been working all day so the dinner would have been cooked by Fred and the twins. Dora rounded the corner and the two sisters rushed up to her.

'Have you seen our Blyth?' they asked. 'We been looking for him all over. Mary'll carry on cruel if we've lost him.'

Lily, with her Christmas dinner settled snuggly in her stomach, lay on her bed reading Michael's letter. She took out a sheet of paper with beautiful pen-and-ink drawings of some Chinese fishing-junks. The one from Foochow interested her most with its sails ribbed with strips of bamboo and a little curved roof-cabin on its deck. The fisherman wore a hat of plaited straw and looked like a figure from one of Gran's willow-patterned plates. The largest one was the Hong Kong fisher with a high prow and large patched sails. Later she would show the drawings to Uncle Albert sure that he would be equally admiring of Michael's talents.

Again she turned to the most interesting part of the letter.

Last week things came to a head between Harry and I. Since hearing about his mother and not getting any letters from Dora he had gone completely off the rails. One night came back on board drunk and shouting, falling all over the place. I accused him of being just like his Dad and that made him furious. In the end I told him about Dora wanting to end it all. The shock seems to have pulled him around and my black eye was almost worth it to see my chum back to his old self. I hope Dora writes to him soon and puts him out of his misery.

Lily felt guilty. She liked Harry well enough and could see how her friend was enchanted. He had a happy, laughing nature and was a handsome blue-eyed fellow. But like Michael she could see something of Fred in him. Shrugging her shoulders as if to discard the troublesome Vines from her mind Lily returned to her letter.

> *I was stunned by your news about your mother, Lily. What an awful shock for you. I could imagine you looking at everyone in the street or on the bus and asking yourself, 'Is that my mother?' As you say the worst thing must have been having to keep it all a secret. You were very brave tackling your Dad about it especially when it meant having to admit to taking the letter out of the ditty-box. The worst thing must be: knowing just enough to weave all sorts of things in your head about her but not enough to find out anything for certain. Although I can't really say or do much to help you in this I felt honoured that you trusted me with your secret.*

'Lily if you don't go over to Mrs Rowan's soon it won't be worth going,' called Gran, after tapping the door and startling Lily back to the present.

'Right ho, Gran,' she called, putting the letter away, all except the drawings.

'Lily, dear, come in and welcome,' said Michael's mother, holding open the door. 'I've just this minute found that album I was talking about.'

Watching Lily looking at everything, Mrs Rowan laughed. 'I just love the sunshine and try to bring it into the house,' she said, 'especially on gloomy winter days.'

The arm chairs had bright orange antimacassars and yellow, red and gold velvet patchwork cushions. On the walls were pictures of her sons Arthur and Michael from their earliest chubby-toddler days, and a wedding photograph of their parents. From what Lily could see Mrs Rowan had never been a pretty woman. She was tall and rangy with a long freckled face and blonde hair. In the picture she and her new husband were seated on a gate by a country church smiling at each other. What struck Lily was the look of dazed delight on Mrs Rowan's face, making her seem almost beautiful in her white dress, with her hair threaded with daisies. 'I couldn't believe my good fortune,' she said coming to stand beside Lily. 'Such a lovely, lovely gentle man.'

'You must miss him and your son.'

'I do,' she said, looking up at the photographs. 'There are many times when I feel sad but the early despair has passed, thank goodness.'

'I'm glad,' said Lily. 'Michael worries about you. He tells me things about when he was little and you all sounded so happy together.'

'It's all in this little album.' Mrs Rowan pulled out a chair at the table for Lily and sat down beside her. The pages were black and the writing under the sepia pictures was in white pencil. Each one was precisely dated. 'I did enjoy making this for you,' she said. 'I was wondering what to do with all the extra snaps and I thought you might like them.'

They smiled at one another.

'Thank you, Mrs Rowan,' said Lily, 'it was ever so kind of you.' It seemed such a weak reaction. On the surface it was a simple gift, a little book with cardboard covers. But it was so much more. Mrs Rowan was valuing her friendship with Michael, taking it seriously and sharing his childhood with her.

She rested her hand lightly on Lily's shoulder. 'You are a good girl, Lily.'

The next hour seemed to flash by as they looked at the pictures of Michael and Arthur on beach picnics, standing proudly with their sailor dad or with their mother in Victoria Park.

'It's strange, isn't it?' said Lily, 'how some people change completely and you hardly recognise them from when they were little. But, Michael, his expression, the way he looks so curious and interested in everything, is there even as a baby.'

Mrs Rowan looked at the picture of herself with her son taken at the school gates when he was six. 'I love photographs,' she said, 'they're only glimpses but they bring back the moment. I look at them often and often.'

Lily was about to ask her something but there was a crashing on the door and they both hurried up the passage to answer it.

Outside were Dora and the twins. 'You seen our Blyth?' they asked. 'We been lookin' for ages and it's getting dark.'

Mary was desperate to get home. Christmas working for the Clementses was no different than any other day with Mrs Mullins yelling and the dishes piling up. It was the first Christmas without her Mum, well not really, thought Mary. Last year she'd been in the loony-bin and might as well have been dead for all the use she was to her family. But this year she wasn't anywhere where they could see her. She shivered when she thought of her alone and cold in the ground.

With a bit of luck she might be able to run home at five. The Clementses were going to Craneswater Park to Lettice's parents so there was no tea or supper to get ready. Still, she reflected as she put the clean meat platter back on the dresser, they'd had the best dinner she'd ever tasted. By the time it was on the table at three o'clock she was nearly fainting from hunger. Mrs Mullins had pinched some paper hats from upstairs and for once they had a proper white cloth. Their plates were piled high with turkey and stuffing, cranberry sauce and sprouts. Nobody spoke, there was a more important task for their mouths than idle chat. Mary chewed and crunched, relishing the different flavours, not wanting the meal to end. She loved the golden crispness of the potatoes, the succulence of the turkey and the rich, sour-sweet taste of the cranberry sauce. The three of them sat in sated silence after the pudding and custard, too full to move.

Mary wondered whether Dad and the twins had cooked their dinner of chicken and spuds to the timetable she'd left them. Had they opened their presents? Mary had sneaked into the Clements' drawing-room three mornings running and got enough mandarins to put one each in the toes of the twins' and Blyth's Christmas stockings. She'd got a new golden 1921 penny for each of them, a handful of almonds and raisins, and a toffee everlasting-strip from the sweet-stall in Charlotte Market. Nellie Moyes from the toy-stall had given her three Kazoos and some broken party-blowers all for threepence. With a bit of glue and patience she'd managed to get the blowers looking good as new. Even got a sixpenny packet of Woodbines and a box of matches for Dad and wrapped them up in green shiny paper. Her prize gift was the game of tiddly-winks for Blyth. She'd managed to bargain for it from Nellie after mending two dozen other broken blowers for her stall.

'Got nimble fingers, you 'ave, my girl,' she'd said approvingly. 'I could use you here with me.'

Mary wondered what Dora would make of the writing-set she and the twins had put together for her complete with a blotter and stamps. She surprised herself in her need for forgiveness, for things to be right between them. Harry had given her a right roasting when he found out about the trouble on the beach, said he was ashamed of her. That had really hurt.

Mary filled the sink with hot water from the kettle and began to stack the plates. Please, please let it soon be going-home time. She smiled to herself as she washed and drained the glasses. Drinking sherry, if Dad knew he'd be at the kitchen door in a flash. And how about how she'd soft-soaped Mrs Mullins with the necklace. It had been a mixture of two broken ones on the jewellery stall and had taken ages to thread together with the large beads in the centre graduating to tiny little ones near the clasp.

'I got you one of my mum's necklaces,' she'd said, 'I thought the beads would match your eyes.'

The cook ran the green beads through her sausage-pink fingers and smiled. 'You know Mary, if you was to apply yourself,' she grunted breathily, 'you might amount to something.'

'Course the necklace was too small to go around Mrs Mullins fat neck but it had had the desired effect and the atmosphere in the kitchen was greatly improved. Cissie had been enraptured with the card Mary had made for her with the capital letter 'C' written all swirly and entwined with flowers like in the old manuscripts.

'You ain't 'alf clever,' she'd said, her face pink with excitement.

Mary had had a bag of chocolate coins from Cook, which she knew had been pinched from the Clements children and a pincushion with her name picked out in fancy pins from Cissie.

'If you gets the chance you could come down to our house, later,' she said.

'Ooh ta,' said Cissie gratefully, 'Old Mullins will just get sozzled and I'll get lonely and sad. You're a real friend.'

Of course in the Clements' drawing-room the presents were piled high around the tree that sparkled with lighted candles. The sideboard was full of bottles and on the top was a huge bowl of fruit and a plate of nuts. As she scrubbed the meat-tin later in the morning she wished she was little again with someone to fill her stocking. Being grown-up wasn't a bit what it was cracked up to be. It was all chance what family you got yourself born into. She thought of Charlotte and Miles upstairs, all dressed up, their cheeks bulging with chocolates. Captain Clements, his uniform stiff with gold braid, people saluting him, and Lettice wrapped in her fur coat.

Then there was her family sunk at the bottom of the heap with nothing ever changing except for the worse. Sometimes she could understand why Dad got drunk and her Mum had gone off the rails. She just hoped he'd not got too drunk at work again. There'd been two warnings – the next time he'd be out.

As she hurried down the street Mary wondered when her letter to Leonard Marshall would bring results. Beryl's eyes had looked red-rimmed the other day and she had been really snappy when Mary pointed out that she'd spelt sweetbreads wrong again. But she was still wearing her engagement ring.

At last she was finished and Mrs Mullins let her go. 'Be here sharp at seven tomorrow, they've got the old folks back here for luncheon at one,' she'd said, 'and Happy Christmas girl, you done well.'

As she turned into Lemon Street Mary saw Dora and Lily and the twins. 'You haven't passed Blyth on your way, have you? they asked.

'We can't find Blyth anywhere. You haven't seen him have you?'

Chapter Twenty

Full of excitement, Blyth had skipped down the street hand in
hand with Chippy wondering what sort of presents his mummy
had left for them. Course, Algie had wriggled his hand out of
Chippy's grasp straight away, because he didn't never like to be
touched. Blyth wondered if he was excited, too. It was difficult to
know because his face was always shut tight with no laughter or
crying showing.

Chippy's house was cold and dark and smelt of wee. They'd
followed him into the kitchen where he lit the lamp then
wandered about calling for his mum. Blyth knew that Granny
Dowell, Chippy's mum, was up in the sky with Jesus. He
wondered if she would call down from heaven and tell them
where the presents was hid. They did a bit more wandering
about and Blyth stepped on a plate with something soft and
squidgy on it that stuck to his shoe. When they were out of the
kitchen everything was dark and gloomy. Blyth slipped his hand
out of Chippy's and went back down the passage to open the
kitchen door and let the light shine out, but the door kept
swinging shut making it seem darker than ever. He was just
getting a chair to wedge it open when Chippy started to howl
like an animal. Algie laughed but the hairs prickled on the back
of Blyth's neck. He wanted to go home. Mary would be

back soon and Dora was coming. Daddy was going to roast some chestnuts on a shovel.

Chippy flung himself down on the floor, his back against the front door.

'Let's go upstairs and look for them presents,' said Algie hitting him on the arm.

'I wants to go home. It's dark and we won't be able to see nothin',' said Blyth, trying to stop his voice wobbling.

'There's candles and matches in the kitchen,' said Algie going back down the passage.

In desperation, Blyth launched himself at Chippy. 'Gerrup, gerrup,' he screamed, pulling him by the shoulder away from the door. Every time he got a grip on Chippy he slipped back against the door howling and wailing.

Algie came back with a lighted candle in a saucer-like holder with a handle on it. The light shone up on his face making it glow in the darkness. Blyth began to feel even more frightened. Algie came up close to him and kept swinging the candle near his face and then swinging away from him. Some of the wax gathering in the saucer spilled out and ran onto Blyth's neck. It was hot and he cried out in pain. Ignoring him Algie began to climb the stairs, shielding the flickering candle with his other hand.

Blyth ran back into the kitchen and tried to get out of the back door but he couldn't get the latch to move. The big bolt was drawn across the top. Again he dragged a chair across the floor and stood on tiptoe, his fingers waving helplessly below the bolt. Stepping down, he trod on something that suddenly shifted beneath his foot and squawked. Big and furry, Chippy's cat rushed past him. Blyth wet himself in fright. He ran back into the passage ready to hurl himself at Chippy, to bite, kick or scream, anything to make him open the door.

'Blive. Blive, up 'ere I got sommink to show you,' called Algie. He appeared at the top of the stairs with the candle stick in his hand. 'I found the presents. Lots of them, all wrapped in paper. Come up 'ere quick.'

Blyth was torn between having a last go at Chippy and following Algie to see what he'd found.

'Come on, don't be a yellow-belly. Up here, up here,' commanded Algie from the top of the stairs.

Shivering and wiping his nose on his sleeve Blyth climbed the stairs.

Algie went into the front bedroom and Blyth followed him. On the dressing-table were two more candles in saucers. Algie lit them with the candle from the kitchen then put all three of them together back on the dressing-table.

Blyth looked around him. He couldn't see any presents. The smell in the room made his eyes water. Someone had wet the bed and there were dirty old clothes all over the place and plates on the floor with dried-up food on them. 'Where's the presents?' asked Blyth.

'Dunno,' said Algie. He was standing with his back to him watching the candles. He had a funny look on his face, sort of fixed with no blinking. As if he wanted to remember what candles looked like for ever and ever.

Blyth wanted to go, he wanted to go.

Algie seized a pillow and threw it at Blyth. Anxious not to be a yellow-belly Blyth threw it back. Algie caught it and found a little hole in one corner and made it bigger; he threw it up into the air and feathers erupted into the room. Blyth forgot to be frightened and hopped up and down trying to catch them. His nose was running and some of the feathers stuck to his face making him sneeze. Picking up another pillow he managed to find a hole, too, wiggling his finger inside trying to widen the gap but the sound of the matches striking against the box and the smell of burnt feathers diverted him.

Laughing and prancing about Algie waved the matches slowly in the air watching them flicker and holding them until they almost burnt his fingers. Blyth had never seen him look so excited. He went over to the curtain and held a match to the hem watching the flame climb up the folds before striking another one. Soon all four were ablaze. 'Wheee,' he cried, grabbing Blyth and dragging him round the room in a mad dance. 'Whee, whee, whee.'

It wasn't a game any more. Blyth's mouth went dry with fear. He shoved his way out of Algie's grasp and dashed to the door. As soon as he opened it there was a whooshing sound and the flames galloped faster and faster up the curtains. On the floor by the window was a bundle of old clothes. Soon they were on fire and flames were licking round the bottom of the bed. Blyth grabbed hold of Algie by the back of his jumper and tried to make him come with him to the head of the stairs. Impatiently Algie pushed him away.

'We gotta go,' screamed Blyth, biting his fingers as he ran for the door.

'You go, yellow-belly,' sneered Algie as he climbed onto the bed and bounced up and down on the mattress. He wasn't Algie any more but some wild creature that terrified Blyth.

The fire seemed to be running towards him. Blyth slammed the door and leapt down the stairs, tripping in his haste. Everything was turning over and over as he fell down into the blackness.

Chapter Twenty-one

Mary was tired-out and ratty by the time they got to Chippy's house. 'If he's not here we'll 'ave to get old Wilkes to look for him,' she said. 'Blimey, wasn't much to ask you two,' she said, glaring at the twins. 'Just keep an eye on 'im. Christmas Day and all.' She banged the knocker impatiently. From inside came the sound of wailing and crying. 'Well Chippy's there even if our kid ain',' she said peering through the letterbox. 'You got Blyth in there?' she shouted.

'Mum I wants you, tell me where you are,' wailed Chippy.

'You tell me if Blyth's there then I'll fetch you mum,' said Mary in a coaxing tone.

'The nippers is upstairs playing about,' said Chippy. 'Can you really find me mother?'

'Who's up there with him,' demanded Mary.

'That Algie, he's took a candle upstairs so's they can find the presents.'

Mary's stomach lurched. She looked up at the bedroom window and saw smoke pouring around the windowframe, and screamed, 'Blyth, Blyth!' She ran at the door, kicking and screaming.

'Uncle Albert will have a key,' said Lily, trying to pull Mary away.

'Anythink 'appens to Blyth I'll kill you,' she screamed through the letterbox.

The twins began to cry. Dora took hold of their hands. 'We'll run down the dockyard and get police to call out the fire engines. Come on girls, you're good runners, the pair of you.'

'I'll get Uncle Albert, you get your Dad,' said Lily anxious to do something.

'He won't be no good,' Mary snapped, turning back to the door.

'You'll blooming well have to make him good,' said Lily. 'Hit him or something. He's Blyth's Dad, he's got to help.'

Dora was glad to get away. She could feel panic rising in her throat. Another minute outside that burning house and she would have screamed. The twins gripped her hands and they ran out of Lemon Street. All the while Dora looked about her for Sergeant Wilkes, a sailor or soldier, or anyone to help them, but at four o'clock on Christmas afternoon the streets were deserted. They were hurtling into Queen Street when Mercy let go of Dora's hand.

'I got the stitch,' she gasped

'Don't matter,' said Faith, 'we can't stop. Our Blyth could be all burnt up be now.'

'Stop it,' shouted Dora, coming to a breathless halt. 'We just can't think like that. Policemen will phone the station, they'll be there in two shakes.' Time was going by, they dared not stop. They must get help. 'You two follow me,' she said, 'I'll run on ahead.'

Blyth, Blyth, Blyth, the name pulsed in her head as she ran beside the dockyard wall past the endless blur of bricks. Blyth, Blyth, Blyth: she was afraid to stop saying it. The name beat in her feet as they pounded along. And then she was at the gate, sweating and breathless.

'Calm down, Missie, what's the rush?' said the policeman. 'Come inside, sit down and catch your breath.'

She followed him through the dockyard entrance to the gate-house and sat on the chair he held out for her. 'Fire,' she gasped as soon as the words would come. 'Two little boys up in the bedroom.'

'Address?' barked the policeman reaching for the telephone.

'Nine Lemon Street.'

'Be through to the station in Park Road in no time,' he said over his shoulder. 'That you Percy? Fire number nine Lemon Street, two nippers up in the bedroom. Right you are.'

'How long?' she asked.

'Ooh ten minutes, twelve at the most,' he said reassuringly, 'unless they're already out, then they'll call up the station at Eastney.'

Dora took up the name again, timing it in and out with her breath.

The policeman stepped out of the gate-house and looked down the street. 'Hallo, what's this, the walking wounded?' he said as Faith, with Mercy trailing behind her, came into view.

'I fell down and hurt me knee and me 'ands,' she sobbed.

Dora got up and lifted her on to the stool and looked at her knee.

'It's only a graze. We'll wash it when we get back.'

'Stings like buggery,' sniffed Mercy.

'That's ripe language for a young lady,' said the policeman with pretended shock. 'What that needs is the touch of a policeman's hankie. It works every time.'

Mercy stretched out her leg and watched with interest as he wound a spotless handkerchief around her knee.

'You ready, now?' asked Dora having got her breath back. Mercy nodded.

'Take your time,' said the policeman, 'Don't want no more accidents. You girls have done a good job the lot of you. Steady now.'

'Thanks ever so much,' said Dora shyly.

'All in a day's work,' he said, smiling down at the twins. 'By the time you get home I reckon it'll be all over and the nippers safe and sound.'

'Cross your heart?' asked Faith.

'Cross my heart,' he said.

Let it be true, prayed Dora.

Mary's hands were slippery with sweat as she pulled the chain through the letterbox, turned the key and rushed indoors.

'What's up, what's up?' said Dad rubbing his eyes.

'Blyth, he's at Chippy's and the house is burnin'.'

'You lost me, gal,' he said, laughing foolishly as he got slowly out of the armchair. 'Dunno what you're on about.'

'Fire! Fire!' she screamed at him. Desperately she cast about for something to hit him with. Anything to waken that fuddled brain. On the table was a jam-jar stuffed with chrysanthemums. She threw them at his head. He recoiled at the sour stagnant odour as the water trickled down his neck. There was surprise in his face turning slowly to anger as he brushed the flowers aside.

'No call, for that, Jeesuuss, gal. Good mind to wallop ya.' He raised his arm and she snatched it, digging her fingers into his flesh, screaming into his face. 'Blyth's in Chippy's bedroom. It's on fire. Fire, fire. Dad, for God's sake!'

'What my little lad? In a fire, where, where?' He blinked and ran his hand over his eyes. He was suddenly all attention.

'Chippy's house. Smoke pourin' out the window. You gotta do sommink.' He startled her as he rushed out of the house and across the street. Mary followed her heart hammering in her chest. Could he really do anything?

Albert was at Chippy's door trying to get inside.

'Christopher!' He roared through the letterbox, 'Get away from the door and let me in at once.'

As Mary crossed the street there was an enormous bang.

Chippy's bedroom window exploded outwards showering the street with splinters of wood and glass. Above them smoke and flame belched out of the gaping hole. 'Christ Almighty,' Dad gasped, running past her back indoors, and reappearing with a kitchen chair. 'Out the way,' he shouted, smashing the chair against the downstairs window.

'Albert, leave the door, I'll get it,' he shouted before climbing in to the front room.

The noise brought other neighbours into the street. Some of them held drinks in their hands, others wore paper hats from Christmas crackers. They stood in bewildered little groups shivering in the winter dusk.

Mary paced the pavement chewing her hand.

Lily and Gran held her between them as she made to follow her Dad through the window. Mary could feel Lily trembling. They were both as frightened as each other.

The front door opened from the inside and Fred pushed the weeping Chippy into the street. 'I'll search downstairs first,' he said before shutting the door.

Mary rushed at Chippy. Smacking him round his face and head. 'Your fault, your fault,' she screamed, beside herself with fear.

Lily and Gran dragged her away and Ethel Rowan put her arm around the terrified Chippy and led him back to her house.

Gran shook Mary until her screaming stopped. 'Calm yourself child. Come on now, deep breaths. You gotta get a hold of yourself.'

Mary was now sobbing in her arms.

'You and me are going to wait here for Blyth and Algie,' said Gran, her voice slow and steady. 'Little lad will be frightened, he'll want his sister to pacify him. You've got to be strong. Do you hear me now?'

Mary nodded.

Albert called through the letterbox. 'Where are you, Fred?'

He turned back to Mary, Lily and Gran waiting in an anxious huddle.

'No one downstairs, he's going up.'

'Bloody hero, that's what he is,' someone said.

It was strange hearing someone speak well of her dad, thought Mary. It comforted her. She gripped Lily's hand and felt an answering squeeze.

There was the sound of coughing and of footsteps thumping down the stairs. Everyone strained forward. The front door opened again and Albert went towards Fred and helped him from the house.

Gran grabbed the chair lying on the pavement where Fred had left it.

With singed hair, face striped with soot and sweat Fred staggered out of the house. Gran helped him into the chair. He gasped for breath. In his arms was a charred bundle of cloth covering a small still body.

'I got him,' he wheezed, his eyes bright with triumph.

'Good old Fred,' the neighbours began to cheer.

'Is is really him?' cried Mary, stepping fearfully towards her father.

'Lily get a glass of water, quick,' snapped Gran.

Lily dashed into the house her heart pounding if she'd stayed a minute longer she would have screamed. The sight of the little scorched body horrified her. It couldn't be Blyth, she couldn't bear it. Her hand shook as she turned on the tap and the water flowed over the top of the glass and down her hand and inside her sleeve before she came to herself again. She ran out of the house and by the time she reached Fred half of it had slopped down her dress.

He held out his hand, raw and blistered, and took the glass from her. 'His Daddy's got him,' he wheezed. 'Touch and go it was. Bedroom's a furnace, couldn't see a thing.' He took a shaky gulp of water. 'On my knees, running me hands over the floor.

Felt his leg, hauled him out the door with me. Tangled up in this here curtain.' He handed Lily back the glass before lifting the cloth aside from the top of the bundle.

Almost immediately Gran folded it back in place but not before Fred and Lily had seen Algie's charred face.

Mary screamed. 'It ain't him. It ain't Blyth.'

Lily wanted to be sick. Neighbours fell silent. Those with paper hats took them off.

Fred leant his face on his arm and sobbed.

'It's only Algie,' said Mary, tugging at his sleeve. 'You gotta get back in and get Blyth. Algie don't matter.'

'He matters to me.' said a voice from the crowd. There was a gasp as Dahlia walked across to Fred. 'Give me the child,' she demanded, holding out her arms.

Mary said nothing.

'I'm sorry' croaked Fred, his face a ruin of soot and tears. 'Too late I was, too late.'

'I'm grateful to you,' she said, touching his arm before taking the little body and carrying it back across the street.

Lily could hardly look at Dahlia. She felt ashamed for herself and all of them just standing there almost echoing Mary's words, 'It's only Algie.'

She looked at Mary who was totally unaware of Dahlia's distress. She was still jigging about. As soon as the body had been transferred out of her father's arms she was at him again. 'You gotta get him Dad, please, please.'

Lily looked to Gran to stop her. But she had followed Dahlia back to her house. Couldn't Mary see her father was near collapse?

Fred finished the glass of water and rubbed his eyes against the sleeve of his jersey before staggering to his feet.

'Fred, Fred,' called Albert. 'I've got the key. Let me go.'

'He's my lad,' whispered Fred through blistered lips, 'my place to go.' As he stepped back through the downstairs window there was the clanging of a bell in the distance.

Seconds later the fire engine halted at the kerb. Fred opened the door and fell onto the pavement.

'I'll go for Dr Marston,' someone said.

'Shut that door,' roared the fireman, ''til we've got the water, or the whole place'll go up.' He turned to his crew. 'Line of hose. Extend the ladder.'

'The hydrant's over here,' said Albert as two firemen carried the stand-pipe off the engine.

Dora and the twins ran up the street behind them. 'What's happened? Where's Blyth?' they cried. The twins rushed over to Fred and knelt on the pavement beside him. 'Daddy, Daddy you all right?'

Dora looked at Lily. 'What's happened?' she asked.

'Let's go home and make some tea,' said Lily, desperate to leave all the fear and excitement. She linked arms with her friend. 'We'll bring some cups out for Fred and the firemen,' she said.

'I know Blyth's not been found but what about Algie?' asked Dora, her eyes anxiously scanning Lily's face.

'Home, let's go home, first.'

'If anything's happened to either of them I shall feel . . .' Dora's voice trailed away.

Lily wanted to cry. Dear Dora, the only one to think about Algie.

'Hey, Hey, what's going on. I can smell burning. What's afire. Somebody for Jesus' sake tell me what's going on?' It was Sailor hurrying up the street as fast as his stick would take him.

Albert took the chair left by Fred and helped Sailor on to it. 'Where have you been, old chap?' he asked.

'Folks in the next street hauled me in for a mince-pie.' Sailor creased his brow and turned his head from one side to the other to try and gauge what was happening. 'You tell me the truth, now, Albert. No soft-soaping, I needs to know.'

Mary was frozen. She held her arms around herself to try and stop the shaking. Her teeth wouldn't stop chattering. Although exhausted she couldn't stand still. The twins were helping Dad indoors. All three of them were crying. Neighbours were patting him on the back as he passed by them. What did it matter if Dad was burnt and exhausted, she thought furiously. He'd get over it. Couldn't they see that Dad didn't matter? Nobody mattered but Blyth. She watched the fireman climbing up the ladder with the hose under his arm.

'Turn on,' he called over his shoulder, and drenched the room from floor to ceiling before climbing inside. Below him the other fireman was taking a hose through the front door. Choking black smoke billowed into the street. Mary paced about, coughing and crying. She stared up at the black gaping hole trying by the force of her will to draw her brother out of the house.

Chapter Twenty-two

She found her sitting in the armchair staring into the empty grate. Cradled in her arms was Algie still swathed in the curtain. The smell of burning filled the room. Beattie went and stood beside her, resting her hand on Dahlia's shoulder.

'He's gone,' she said, her green eyes swimming with tears.

'It would have been the smoke. He would have been smothered before ever the flames touched him,' she said, taking Dahlia's hand and holding it in her own. 'I'm so, so sorry.'

Dahlia bent to kiss the child's uncovered face then pulled the curtain over it, tucking it securely behind his shoulders. Taking a firm hold of herself Beattie picked up the little boy's hand that had slipped loose from the folds and placed it beneath the curtain. It was the first time she had ever touched Algie without him brushing her aside. Always, he had kept people at a distance.

'Playing with matches when I first saw him. Always loved fire and now it's taken him,' said Dahlia.

The image of the child gleefully leaping about after scorching old Towser's tail leapt into her mind. Why in God's name had Dahlia not impressed on him how dangerous his antics were? And then she remembered Algie's screams and the thwack of the leather belt as Dahlia hit him, followed a long time afterwards by her sobs.

'When was that? she asked, 'that you first saw him?'

'This lodging-house up at Tipnor. Millie had written to me from there saying she needed me. His mother she was.'

Beattie nodded.

'She had come as a young girl of sixteen as a maid to work for my mother. A fairy child she seemed, small and blonde, her skin almost transparent. I loved her from the first moment I saw her. There was never, never anyone else. When she was seventeen she got into trouble with some lout from the village. I said that I'd look after them both, she could keep the baby and we'd care for it, the two of us.

'My mother was scandalised. Gave Millie the sack there and then, monumental bust-up there was, resulting in me storming out for good.' Dahlia shook her head. 'But in the end she went to Queenie.'

Beattie's head was in a whirl. There was Dahlia in some posh house, head-over-heels in love with a servant and in the midst of all that was Queenie Wheeler. It was like some story in *Peg's Papers*, only she doubted they dealt with such bizarre topics.

'Dahlia,' she said, 'you're going too quick for me. You're saying that this Millie became pregnant and then she wanted to get rid of the baby? And you were going to live with her and care for the child?'

'Yes,' said Dahlia. 'It meant leaving my parents and finding somewhere to live and a job of some sort.' She shrugged. 'When I spoke with Millie I just swept all these difficulties aside. I was twenty and in love and thought I could take on the world.'

'Why did Millie not want that?' asked Beattie, anxious to understand.

'The child was conceived through rape,' said Dahlia. 'I don't think she felt she could take to it after that. Besides, she was not much more than a child herself.'

The story of Millie did not shock Beattie, it was too commonplace. Even Dahlia's infatuation for the girl she could accept, though she found it difficult to understand. It was the presence of Algie while this tale unfolded that disturbed her. Quite why, she couldn't grasp. 'This Queenie,' she asked. 'Is she now your landlady, Queenie Wheeler? The two Queenies are one and the same?'

Dahlia nodded. 'She was another maid in our house. Sharp and aquisitive, things were always going missing. She said she'd see to Millie's little problem for half-a-crown. Nearly bled to death she did. Got the doctor just in time. Queenie disappeared after I threatened to set the police on her.'

Beattie covered her eyes. What a desperate picture Dahlia's words conveyed.

'I nursed Millie 'til she was better. Happiest time of my life, loving and caring for her. She was so delicate, almost ethereal. I wanted to protect her from the world. It seemed a miracle that she loved me, too. And then one day I went up to London. I still had this hope we could have a life together. I was looking for a flat for us somewhere. Thought that London would be more anonymous. When I returned she had up and left.'

So that was it, thought Beattie. Algie was taken on because of Dahlia's love for his mother, not for himself. But if Millie had loved her in the intimate sense that Dahlia implied, how had she become pregnant again? Surely men were anathema to her, particularly after the rape? She shook her head at the complications of the human heart.

'She was greedy for love and sensation,' said Dahlia as if reading her thoughts. 'Hated her own company. Loved anyone who would give her a good time.'

Beattie had an image of Millie as a pale flittering moth. 'But you,' she said quietly, 'for you it was different?'

'Yes. The only one ever,' said Dahlia staring past Algie into the fire. 'Even in France where I could have had my pick. Danger's a powerful aphrodisiac you know.'

Beattie didn't want to know. She looked at the child, who

had been caught up in the heat of adult passions, lying cold in this woman's arms.

'It was years before I found her again,' Dahlia continued. 'My parents were dead and gone, the war was over and suddenly a letter arrived. I was packing up the estate. It was to be sold. Everything to go to my brother in India. When I got her note I came down to Portsmouth, at once, and found her in this lodging house in Tipnor. She had pneumonia. Laying in bed in rags. Algie like a little wild animal, sitting in the corner of her room eating scraps of bread.' The words tumbled over each other, painting a desperate picture. Dahlia dried her eyes on a crumpled tea-towel and continued.

'Then in the next room was Sailor, poor devil, trying to hold it all together. Millie was his youngest sister. They were in this house owned by some drunkard and Sailor was whittling away his savings trying to feed them. Place was filthy, hardly any furniture and no means of heat. I cleaned up as best I could and bought medicine. Millie seemed pathetically pleased to see me. After a week or so she took a turn for the worse. I sat up with her all night. Must have fallen asleep. Next thing I knew, I was awake and choking with the room filled with smoke. It was the timberyard next door – it had caught fire somehow. I knew she was dead. Somehow, Sailor and I got the boy with us and rescued what we could. It was about five in the morning. We kept away from the police and the firemen.'

She looked at Beattie. 'I wasn't sure that Algie had set the fire and I didn't want to find out. Terrified of them taking the child away. I had some foolish notion that I could make it up to him for his mother's death. Outside, down the road, was a builder's hand-cart, we loaded it with our stuff and sat Algie on top and started walking. Don't know how we landed up in Lemon Street. We were almost sleepwalking by the time we got here.'

What a strange trio they had seemed then, thought Beattie, remembering looking out of her bedroom window at them on that cold April morning. They had become her neighbours. Albert had befriended Sailor. But she had never managed to kindle anything between herself and Dahlia. They were too different to have any common ground between them. And Algie? If his mother, Millie, had resembled a fairy, Algie had seemed a changeling child, living at a distance from human closeness and warmth. He had challenged her to like him and make that little bit of effort on his behalf and she had failed.

'I remember staring at the house through the window and there was a feeling of emptiness about the place. Sailor was handy with locks so I took a chance.' Dahlia gave a bitter laugh. 'It put the wind up Queenie Wheeler, good and proper, when she came snooping around and found me as her tenant.'

Beattie looked around her. The kitchen looked almost unchanged from when she had been in there shortly after Dahlia had moved in. There were still the pale patches on the wall where Beattie's family pictures had hung, and there was still the same feeling of emptiness. No personal pictures, snapshots or mementos of any kind softened the bare room or gave any feeling of homeliness. Beattie looked across at Dahlia. 'Nearly a year you've been here,' she said.

'Yes,' she answered, 'and what have I achieved for any of us?' She looked down at the child in her arms. 'Poor scrap,' she said, 'how little he's had of life. So few happy moments.'

Beattie sighed. What a needless waste of life. Even leaving the child to the authorities could hardly be worse than this. And then she saw the desolation in the eyes of the woman opposite her. She dredged her mind for some carefree incident to salve Dahlia's regret. 'I remember one time,' she said, 'when you got the tandem. I turned into the street after the service at the war memorial it was. Algie was sat on the handlebars his head thrown back laughing. I shall never forget it. A moment of pure joy. I think you'll have to try and fix that in your mind to cancel out what followed.'

'Thank you,' said Dahlia, tears pouring down her face.

Beattie stood looking down at the child. The smell of charred cloth filled her nostrils. The sight of him lying there like so much rubbish offended her. 'I think we should cover him with a clean sheet,' she said. 'The doctor will want to examine him, and the police. It's the least we can do to mark his passing. I'm sure the police doctor won't mind.'

'I don't know if there is one, clean, that is,' said Dahlia, vaguely.

'I'll fetch one from next-door,' said Beattie, 'I won't be two ticks.'

'Don't hurry,' she said quietly. 'I need a few more minutes alone with him.' Dahlia's voice was choked with tears.

Wearily Beattie stepped back into her own yard and walked upstairs into her bedroom. She lit the lamp and took a fresh sheet out of the chest-of-drawers. Holding the sheet up to her face, she inhaled deeply the smell of soap, trying to cancel out the stink of burning. An image of that little pointed face, the eyes watchful, the mouth set in a straight line, and the boy's feet poised for flight, flashed before her eyes. A child that no one would miss. Dahlia was distraught, now, but it was Algie's mother that she really mourned.

Would he be missed by Sailor, she wondered. After all Algie was his nephew. The boy had teased the life out of him up, tripping him up, stealing his money, hiding his stick. And yet, look how he went up that ladder after him. And afterwards Algie had sat on Sailor's lap, the only time she'd seen him sit with anyone.

Before leaving the room she pulled aside the curtain and looked across the street. Albert was talking to a fireman and Sergeant Wilkes. The ladder was being taken away from the window and a hose run out along the pavement to drain into the gutter while another was reeled in like a large swiss-roll. Dr Marston was walking towards Dahlia's house. She hurried down with the clean sheet, her heart lurching with anxiety. Where was Blyth? Please God let him be safe. Immediately she was swamped with guilt. Poor Algie, that was something he had never been in all his short life.

Chapter Twenty-three

Coughing and spluttering, Blyth found himself at the bottom of the stairs. It was dark and Chippy was still wailing for his mum. He began crawling towards the kitchen. where the lamp was. In there he would be out of the dark and not feel so frightened. His heart was jumping in his chest and his mouth felt all dried-up. In there he could get a drink of water. At last he bumped up against the door. Still coughing he got to his feet and searched around for the handle. With a shaky sigh of relief he walked into the lighted kitchen. He looked around him for a cup but could only find a little chipped bowl on top of a sheet of newspaper. He stood on his tiptoes and tried to turn the tap in the sink. It dribbled a few drops into the bowl. Blyth drank them thirstily.

Getting the water made him think of something Daddy had said. He'd told him that fire and water didn't mix. Perhaps if the fire chased him down the stairs he could stand on a chair and get into the sink and cover himself over with water. Which was stronger he wondered anxiously, the water or the fire? From somewhere in the house there was a loud bang. He felt as if his heart would leap out of his body, it thumped so hard. Quickly he dragged the chair up against the sink and climbed inside. It was smelly and he'd knelt against a slimy grey dishcloth which made him feel sick. It was cold in the sink and his teeth began to chatter. He was about to turn on the taps when he realised that he was sat next to the window. His hands were all slippery and shaky. It took him three goes to manage to pull down the latch. The window swung open into the yard. It was dark outside. Blyth teetered on the sill and then he thought of the flames sweeping across the bedroom, of Algie screaming, and he jumped. He landed awkwardly knocking against a bucket that clattered down the yard.

From the next-door house emerged Ma Abraham, the shop lady. 'Who's there?' she screamed. 'Come any nearer and I'll have yer liver.'

Blyth trembled. By the light coming from her kitchen, he could see that she was carrying something in her hand. Was it a knife? Ma Abrahams had always frightened him. She had a voice like a man and even a wispy beard. Daddy had said that her bark was worse than her bite. But then she had a dog so she didn't need to bite. And then to reinforce his fears Caesar bounded over the wall barking furiously. Blyth rushed down to the lavatory and was just about to shut the door behind him when Caesar followed him in. He leapt up at him panting and licking his face.

'Come back here you mangy devil,' screeched Ma Abrahams, 'or you can sleep in the yard.'

Blyth pushed the dog into the corner and shut the door behind them. It was cold and dark and stinky but at least he was safe from the fire and Ma Abrahams. He sat down on the floor and wedged himself against the dog. It formed a warm throbbing cushion around him. Gradually the heat transferred itself from Caesar to Blyth. He began to feel warmer and less frightened. Soon he and the old dog had established a rhythm and were breathing in unison. Exhaustion overcame fear and the boy lost himself in sleep.

He awoke to a light flashing in the lavatory window and someone knocking on the door. The noise set Caesar barking and scrabbling to get out. At first Blyth was confused as to where he was. He felt stiff and cold and his throat hurt.

'Come on, sonny, over here to me. That's it, I got you.'

Dazzled by the torch Blyth stumbled out of the lavatory and was swept up into the arms of a fireman. The big man with the brass helmet carried him back up the yard towards Chippy's house. 'No, no,' he croaked, struggling to get out of the restraining arms.

'The fire's all gone, lad, don't cry. I'm taking you home to your mummy.'

'No, no, she gone to Jesus,' said Blyth crying harder than ever. 'Mary, I wants Mary.'

By this time they had passed through the kitchen and were back in the passage. This time there was no Chippy and the front door was wide open. As they stepped into the street he heard some one scream, 'Blyth, Blyth.' He turned his head and there she was rushing across the street, pulling him from the fireman's arms.

'My little lad.' It was Daddy looking all black and burnt-smelling with tears making little rivers down his sooty face.

Between them they carried him back home. And there they were all of them, Faith and Mercy, Auntie Dora and Lily all wanting to hug and kiss him, even old Towser wagged his tale.

He was so happy. It was all too much. He burrowed his face into Mary's neck and burst into tears. And then he couldn't stop shivering.

'Come on my babes,' said Mary, 'let's get you washed and up to bed.'

'I'll stick the kettle on and make a hot-water bottle for him,' said Auntie Dora. 'Here,' she said picking up her bag. 'I got a present for you.'

'Don't never want another present,' sobbed Blyth, 'never, never, never.'

Chapter Twenty-four

What with having such an alarming Christmas, Mary had forgotten all about the note that she had posted through the letterbox of the butcher's shop all those days ago. Having her brother back safe and sound drove everything else out of her mind. Even her ambition to oust Beryl from the kiosk and take the job herself seemed like a dream: far away and without substance.

Life seemed to have divided into two halves. The time before the fire and the time afterwards. Before she'd had plans and dreams. Lots of things had seemed possible. And now? The only things she trusted were those that she could see and touch. Now, was the only reality. The past and present seemed equally insubstantial.

Each time she opened her eyes in the morning and saw Blyth lying snug in his bed was a fresh joy to her. No, she didn't hope or wish for anything but all of them staying safe.

Things seemed to have settled down a bit in Lancaster Terrace and Mrs Mullins was on the verge of being nice to her. She sat at the kitchen table spread with newspaper and helped the cook clean the silver with a saucer of pink plate-powder. She applied the paste to the hot-water jug and rubbed vigorously.

'How is the little shaver, now?' asked Mrs Mullins as she set the gleaming sugar-basin back on the tea-trolley.

'He's fine,' said Mary. 'Back at school as if nothing's happened. But he's started peeing the bed again and 'avin nightmares. Says he's frightened to close his eyes.'

'Poor little lad. Here Cissie,' she said, 'I reckon I've just heard the postman. Nip out into the hall, stick the letters on the tray and take them up to Mrs Clements. Carrying on top ropes she was because she hadn't got her invitation for some do or other.'

Cissie put down the silver egg-cups she'd been labouring over and hurried away. 'I reckon your Dad must be quite a hero going into the blazin' house after that little boy,' she said.

'S'pose so,' said Mary, feeling a twinge of guilt at how ready she'd been to push him back into the fire again when he'd failed to find her brother. Poor Dad, he'd had to stay in bed for the last few days, his hands swathed in bandages. But in Lemon Street he was a hero. Neighbours who had never given him the time of day sent along bowls of soup and bits of cake. His cough was terrible. Even the manager of the Sailor's Home Club had been round to congratulate him and give him a week off. Funny, really, he'd been on the verge of being sacked before the fire. Really, she thought, our Dad's been on the verge of something all his life.

She was polishing the sugar basin when Cissie reappeared.

'Mrs Clements wants to see you straight away. She's in ever such a temper. Sommink in a letter what she's just read. Says, "Fetch that Vine girl up here this instant." She calls out to 'er husband. "Charles," she says, "this is unsupportable. The guttersnipe has exceeded herself." Reckon you're for it now.'

Mary was not going to let Cook and Cissie know she was frightened.

'Save us a crumpet for when I gets back,' she said coolly. Taking her time she climbed the front stairs to Mrs Clements' sitting-room. Whatever the stuck-up Lettice did couldn't be as bad as what she'd suffered over Blyth. Worst she could do was give her the sack, narky bitch. One thing Mary was certain of, she wasn't going to cry or let her think she'd got the better of her. Taking a deep breath she walked without knocking into her employer's room.

'Hasn't anyone taught you to knock before entering any of the upstairs rooms?' said Lettice, coldly.

'You was expectin' me,' said Mary boldly.

'Nevertheless it is courteous to knock.'

It was a shock to see that Captain Clements was in the room, too, in his best uniform. The sight of him further diminished her respect for his wife. What did she need him with her for? Just to give her scullery-maid a tongue-lashing.

'Do you recognise this?' said Lettice, handing her a piece of notepaper with the corner missing.

Mary took her time studying her letter. She was rather proud of it. The handwriting was immaculate. For a minute or so she considered denying any knowledge of it. But what was the point? They was on to her. 'Yes, I seen it before,' she said, looking Mrs Clements straight in the eye, ''cos it was me what wrote it.'

'I would like you to read it aloud to my husband.'

'Right you are,' said Mary. When she got to the bit about Beryl being 'A young tart who didn't know what was good for her' Captain Clements had a fit of coughing and rushed out of the room. She finished reading and looked up to see Lettice trembling with rage. Just as she had imagined her when first she'd pinched the notepaper, she was puce in the face. The veins were sticking out in her neck and her pale eyes were all goggly with indignation.

'What a despicable thing to do,' she hissed through clenched teeth. 'To write a poison-pen letter is a wicked enough offence without compounding it by stealing my notepaper and putting the reputation of this house in jeopardy.'

Why couldn't she just give her the sack now, thought Mary, instead of making such a song and dance about it. Still, that was the toffs all over. In Lemon Street there would just have been a good screaming-match or a fight and everything would be over and done with.

'What have you to say for yourself?'

'She had it coming to her,' said Mary, 'carrying on with that sailor behind 'er fiancé's back. Then prancin' about in that kiosk as if she was Lady Muck. That was putting Leonard in the jeopardy good and proper.'

'Shut up, shut up, you stupid girl. I don't want to hear about it. It's all too sordid. What have you to say about trespassing in my room and stealing my stationery?'

'I took your paper 'cos there wasn't none at home and I'm sorry I was found out.'

'Very well,' said Lettice, looking at her as if she'd just crawled out of a piece of cheese. 'You leave me no choice. You are dismissed without references. You are to leave immediately.'

'Suits me,' said Mary, turning on her heel and slamming the door with all her might.

She skipped back down the stairs with a giddy feeling of release.

'Whaa!' gasped Cissie. 'What you goin' to do now? Won't get a reference and that Miss What'sername at the Servants' Registry won't send you after nothink.'

'Burnt your boats, now, you have,' said Mrs Mullins. 'Just as I was making something of you.'

I was making something of myself thought Mary, but kept silent. The triumph of slamming out of Lettice Clements' sitting-room was beginning to fade. What was she going to do? She'd have no money for nothing. Dad was hanging on to his job because of being a hero, but that would soon fade once he was back to his old tricks of watering the rum and being late all the time. They scraped by with Dad's wages and his small navy pension, almost two quid with Mary's two bob thrown in. The sixpence she kept for herself and tried to boost with taking Dad's empty bottles back to the shop and getting the halfpenny each on them together, with the occasional penny earned for doing a neighbour's ironing. It was the only household task she really enjoyed. Something where you could really see the difference when a rumpled frock was brought up nice and crisp. If she and Dad both got slung out they'd be on their bare bones good and proper.

One thing Mary was certain of, she was not going to apologise. She laughed to herself. Who was she kidding, thinking an apology would make any difference? Old Lettice had really taken the hump this time.

'Your temper will be your downfall, my girl,' said Mrs Mullins, as she pushed the tea-trolley with its gleaming silver over to Cissie to take back into the dining-room.

'S'pose we'd better get the muffins on the go. Don't want to send you away starvin' as well as jobless, do we?'

Later Mary bit into the steaming muffin which she'd lavishly buttered. Enjoy it while you can, gal, she said to herself. What was the good of making plans or having schemes. Just as you was getting to grips with life you got socked in the teeth. Make the most of the good bits, that was going to be her motto now. Plans was useless.

Lily stared out of the window. It was New Year's Day. She was glad to see the back of 1921. It had been such an awful year. Or was she too swamped by the fire and Algie's death to remember the good things? What were they she wondered. There was Gran's wedding, and the new closeness between herself and Michael. They had been on the edge of something when he went away but fear and shyness had held them back. If he were here now alone with her in her room there would be no reserve between them. Everything now was just in their heads and on paper. She longed to touch him and have him touch her.

She lit the candle and took out his last letter to her and began to read.

November 10th 1992

My Darling Lily,

I do hope you've got my present and that it arrived in time for Christmas. We have just got back from a place called Bias Bay where we were to capture pirates who had been robbing the big ships that tranport gold bullion to Hong Kong.

It was a big adventure, at first, with several of our ships creeping into the bay just before day break. The villagers were sat eating at little tables on the beach. At the sight of us, they leapt up and ran scattering food everywhere. We set their boats alight and the adventure was over. Those poor people Lily. I'm sure they had nothing to do with the piracy but were just used by more cunning people who hid among them. Some ran up the beach to their village and others into the sea. One old man waded almost up to his neck and tried to put out the fire with handfuls of water. He turned towards me, tears running down his face. I felt ashamed. What do the profits of these big Hong Kong Merchants matter beside the total ruin of that poor man. His face haunts me.

Lily shivered and drew her green shawl closer around her shoulders. Poor Michael, she wished she could be with him to hold him close and talk about other things. But there were pictures in her head, too. Images that she could push to the outskirts of her mind during the day but which flooded her thoughts at night. Dora's blue-tinged abstracted face as she lay on the beach; poor blubbering Chippy only last week, and then Algie. The shout of excitement when Fred staggered out of the door with the child draped over his shoulder. In that moment they forgave him everything. The short-lived triumph in his eyes and then the disappointment. It was the wrong child. Their terrible indifference as Dahlia stepped forward to claim him. Even Mary's rage was better than that callous disregard.

Lily peered at the clock on the dressing-table; it was two in the morning. Later at eleven it would be Algie's funeral. She was glad she had the excuse of going to work but Dora had taken the time off especially. Lily could not have gone under any circumstances because she wasn't sorry. Pretending she felt, would be the final betrayal.

Being kind and loving seemed to come so naturally to Dora, almost like breathing. Whereas she was so often jealous and grudging and critical. Ever since her accident Dora had been close to Dahlia and seemed to have gained confidence from the friendship. Lily was both fascinated and afraid of her. Dahlia lived by her own rules and was afraid of no one. She felt sometimes that Dahlia was mocking her or found her petty and not worth bothering with. Her large green eyes looked so directly at her as if she could read her thoughts and found them dull and shallow. If she were honest, she knew her discomfort with Dahlia sprung from her inability to impress her.

Lily returned to her review of the last year. It hadn't been all bad. There were good things too. The lovely holiday in the Isle of Wight when she'd walked and talked with Dad and they'd cleared the air between them. It had been very difficult for him reliving that awful time when her mother disappeared, but afterwards there had been a new feeling of closeness between them. The relief of Dora's recovery and having her friend laughing and teasing again. Seeing her schoolfriend Heather and the two patients. The meeting had been brief but she could still see Amy's face in every detail. She remembered the woman asking her name and when she said 'Lily' it was as if she had been given a present. Strange how that little incident lingered in her mind. Remembering her uncaring judgement of the two women Lily felt a twinge of guilt. She turned her thoughts to her new friendship with Michael's mother. That would please him no end. But still there remained the mystery of her own mother. Or was she building a fantasy on what had been an ill-founded suspicion born out of grief and strain. No, her mother had drowned and, as Dora said, she must count herself lucky to have had Dad and Gran.

Lily picked up her pen again. She must finish her letter to Michael, seek to cheer him up, then snatch a few more hours sleep. Opening her writing-pad she repositioned the candle and completed her account of the fire.

> *The glorious moment was when the big fireman ages and ages later stood in the doorway with Blyth in his arms. Mary almost exploded with joy. He was swept up into his sister's arms and with everyone crying and laughing along with Dora and poor singed Fred was borne away like a prince.*

Well, she thought as she screwed on the cap of her fountain-pen, they were done with 1921. She and Michael were now at the halfway point of his commission. Only eighteen months until he would be home. Lily yawned, she'd just fold the pages and slip them into the envelope, have another look at the presents Michael had sent her and then tuck down under the blankets.

She crept across out of bed, shivering as her toes came in contact with the linoed floor. Taking the candle in its saucer from beside her bed, she stood it on the dressing-table before opening the top drawer. Inside was a delicate ivory fan, each little blade carved with leaves and flowers. Lily laughed to herself. It was the last thing she needed in an English January. There was also a handkerchief embroidered with a willow-pattern bridge and a figure in a kimono. Michael had got it from an orphanage in China. Under the strict eyes of the nuns, little girls not much older than her sister Rosie spent hours toiling over their sewing. The best present was the little silk-covered snapshot album. It was filled with scenes of the Far East and pictures of Michael looking so handsome in his white tropical shorts. He was smiling out at her in another picture, standing in the sea somewhere, holding up a fish, and wearing a bathing-costume. Lily studied it carefully, looking at his dark eyes and his mouth with the beautiful full lower lip. The wide dark hair on his chest and the way it grew in the shape of a cross before it disappeared from view beneath his costume; his long sun-tanned legs. She sighed, feeling desire for him stirring in her breasts. They had so much to discover about each other and so long to wait. Shivering again she shut the drawer, hurried back to bed and blew out the candle. Away beyond Victoria Park she heard the Town Hall clock strike three. What would 1922 have in store for her, she wondered as she settled down to sleep.

Dora set her black hat straight with the help of the workroom mirror. She wished she didn't have to go but Dahlia had asked her.

'The last thing I shall ever ask of you,' she'd said. 'I'm dreading it. Would have been more fitting if he'd perished entirely in the fire. The thought of that child confined in a box and shut away in the cold earth is unbearable. If I could have got away with it I'd have had a bonfire.'

Dora kept Dahlia's feelings to herself. They would have shocked her mother and probably Lily's Gran, too. But she understood. The crackling, flaring heat of a bonfire would have suited Algie. It was surprising what she had come to see and be aware of since knowing Dahlia. She was unlike anyone she'd ever known before. To her anything was possible. Yes, thought Dora, pulling on her wool gloves, Dahlia's done more for me than all Dr Marston's bottles of iron tonic.

She promised Miss Pearson to be back by two o'clock and walked down Queen Street towards Dahlia's house, the very route she'd hurtled along just a few days ago with Faith and

Mercy. Whatever misgivings she had about the funeral, thank God it wasn't Blyth's, she thought guiltily. He was now well on the road to recovery, his cough almost gone, and in danger of being cuddled to death by his sisters. Even Fred was looking less grey and exhausted and enjoying the role of hero in the family.

What a lot she would have to tell Harry when she wrote tonight – and all about his family. She would save her promotion to forewoman at Denby and Shanks 'til last. The job should really have gone to Ruby as she was senior to her by six months. But I'm more reliable and more skilled, thought Dora in a new burst of confidence. There was bound to be a bust-up between them, but now I can take her on she thought proudly.

Outside Dahlia's house her spirits plummeted. Screwing up her courage she knocked on the door.

It was opened by Sailor. 'Come in, gal,' he said, gripping her hand. 'We didn't never think to see this day,' he said in a voice shaky with grief.

Dahlia was dressed in a black satin coat Dora had never seen before, and a green velour hat with a matching silk band. Her eyes were bright with unshed tears but her skin seemed dull and muddy. As she got up to greet her there was none of her usual firmness and purpose.

Dora went to hug her but Dahlia stepped away from the embrace.

'Don't touch me, or I'll fall apart,' she said.

They were startled by a loud rapping on the front door. 'That'll be the hearse,' Dahlia said. 'Thank God for motor transport, quick and relatively silent. I couldn't have borne the black plumed horses and their rattling harness. Good morning, gentlemen,' she said with some of her old briskness. 'Please put this case in the back, if you don't mind, and kindly knock next door for the Pragnells.'

Taking a deep breath Dora took hold of Sailor's arm. At first she was taken up with greeting Lily's Gran and Uncle Albert and helping Sailor into the hearse but then once settled she turned and saw the coffin. The sight of the little wooden box stabbed her with pity. There was a moment of fluttering panic and then she had control of herself. Poor Algie, she thought, sealed in his own world, unreachable by love.

At a nod from Dahlia the hearse drew away from the kerb. There were no neighbours with bowed heads and few drawn blinds. Dora felt hurt on her friends' behalf. They were an oddity: Sailor, Algie and Dahlia, and as such had never been fully accepted. Gran leaned forward and took hold of Dahlia's hand. Sailor had started to cry.

Albert took out his handkerchief. 'Here, dear fellow,' he said passing it to him. Dahlia gave a shuddering gasp and gripped Dora's hand tightly. 'I'm dreading this,' she gasped.

'It will be over soon,' said Gran, patting her arm.

'Thank you,' said Dahlia, staring out of the window.

It seemed an endless journey to Dora. Desperately she tried to think of something to say. She felt squashed, wedged between Dahlia and Sailor, who couldn't seem to stop crying. Every so often her eyes strayed to the coffin fixed between the silver railings. Each time the sight of it stabbed her afresh with its smallness and the pity and waste of it all. When she thought she could bear it no longer, and would have to leap out and run away, the car purred in through the cemetery gates.

His white surplice blowing in the wind, the vicar came forward and opened the door. 'Mrs Carruthers, please let me help you,' he said. Dora was uncertain what to do. Sailor needed supporting and Dahlia looked as if any moment she would fall to the ground.

'Come on shipmate,' said Albert, taking Sailor's arm and walking with him into the little chapel.

Gran shored Dahlia up on one side and Dora held the other. She was thankful the service was in the little cemetery chapel; as they were so few in number, they would have been lost in an ordinary church. So involved was she in helping her friend to her seat that she failed to notice that the vicar had already started the service. Dahlia gasped and gripped Dora's hand as one of the funeral men set the coffin on its stand in the aisle. Another man placed a wreath of holly and ivy on top.

'We are here to remember the life of Algernon Flowers, a child snatched from this world by fire. A life cut short by a terrible accident. Who knows what Algernon might have become if he had been accorded more time? But,' he sighed dramatically, 'it must be a comfort to his mother to know that Algernon is safe now in the arms of his Saviour.'

Dora began to feel angry. It was as if they'd come to the wrong funeral. Who was this peculiar person called Algernon who cuddled up to Jesus? Certainly not Algie, he would hate it.

They began to sing 'All things bright and beautiful', their voices ragged with pent-up feelings. Dora prayed for it all to be over.

As the funeral men came back to carry the coffin to the graveside, and Albert and Gran were busy with Sailor, Dahlia tugged Dora's sleeve.

'I'm off now,' she whispered.

'Where you going? When will you be . . .'

Dahlia turned back to the hearse and opening one of the doors took out the suitcase. She handed Dora a letter then held a gloved finger to her lips. While the other mourners took the path towards the freshly dug grave Dahlia walked briskly in the opposite direction.

At the graveside the vicar opened his prayer-book and looked around him enquiringly. 'Should we wait for Mrs Carruthers to compose herself?' he asked.

With the exception of Sailor, they all looked back up the path to where Dahlia could be seen hurrying towards the gate some distance away.

'Done a bunk has she?' said Sailor, tugging Albert's arm.

'I think she needs to be alone for a while,' Albert replied.

'If you don't mind, Vicar,' said Gran firmly, 'I think we should get on with the service. None of us wants to prolong the agony.'

Dora shuddered as the little coffin was lowered into the ground. Algie would feel so cold and trapped in there. One of the funeral men nudged her and handed her a clod of earth. As it drummed against the lid of the coffin Dora gripped Sailor's hand. Where would Algie be now, she wondered. If only she believed in heaven.

Chapter Twenty-five

Beattie was cold, tired and furious. 'What do you mean, Dahlia's jumped ship?'

Sailor let Albert guide his hands to the bowl of soup before answering. 'Reckons she brings bad luck on people that she's close to. Reckons we'll all get on better without her. Took Algie's passing very bad.'

'Well that's as may be,' grumbled Beattie, slicing furiously at the loaf. 'What's going to happen to you? What's happening to the house?'

'She left a letter,' said Dora, handing Beattie a thick white envelope with Dahlia's large untidy writing on it.

'You'd better read it out to us, I haven't the patience.'

'I had enough of reading out letters at Mrs Vine's funeral,' said Dora quietly. 'I've only got an hour. Promised to be back at work by two.'

'Beatrice, will you please sit down and eat your soup,' said Albert firmly. 'I will read the letter. And then we'll all have some tea with a good dash of rum. It'll put fresh heart into us. Isn't that right, Sailor?'

'Good rouser is rum.'

Grudgingly Beattie took her place. The funeral had upset her more than she had expected. A child's death was always shocking, especially since Algie seemed to have had so little out of living. It reminded her of all the other lives cut short. Her grandson Andrew and Joseph. At least with a body and a funeral you had a leave-taking and a certainty that they were dead. And if you wanted, a place to lay flowers. With no body to bury or ritual to mark the passing you continued in a useless limbo of hope, way past any possibility of the person being still alive.

'Are we ready?' asked Albert as he opened the envelope and settled his glasses on his nose. He look steadily at Beattie and she nodded.

'Ah, there's a letter inside for you, Dora.'

Quickly she took it and slipped it away in her handbag.

Albert unfolded the paper and cleared his throat.

Dear Friends,

Doubtless you will have been dismayed at my flight. The sight of Algie being consigned to the earth, was more than I could bear. He could never stand still and was a child of light and movement. I wrote this letter early in the morning and looked out of the window at a wonderful sky, the colours ranging from palest pink to deepest orange. If I could choose a fitting place for Algie's spirit it would be in the sunrise and sunset. Forever riding the clouds and moving across the heavens.

Albert paused to get out his handkerchief and clean his glasses.

'That's beautiful,' said Dora, reaching out and taking Sailor's hand.

'Mmm,' gasped Sailor, nodding his head.

Beattie nodded, grudgingly. Damned Bohemain, she thought. Fine words, fine feathers and no substance or staying-power. What in God's name was going to happen to Sailor?

Like him I seem to be a person not at home in this world. A Jonah bringing disaster in my wake. I have decided not to return

*to Lemon Street and hope that you, his friends, will care for
Sailor in my absence. I have written to Mrs Wheeler and paid
our rent for the next two months and enclose twenty pounds for
Sailor's immediate needs. As to my possessions do with them as
you wish.*

*Do not worry about me. I shall fetch up somewhere and find
myself a life of sorts. I hope in time that you will forgive me.*

Sincerely Dahlia

Beattie could stand it no longer. She got to her feet and slammed
out into the yard. Bloody Dahlia, who did she think she was
picking up people and putting them down as if they were
playing-cards with no thought to their needs or feelings? She
paced about the yard in a fury.

'Mrs Pragnell, please stand still a minute.'

Beattie turned to see Dora with her coat and hat on standing
in the doorway.

'Look,' she said, 'I know you're upset but there's something
you've got to remember.'

'Got to?' said Beattie indignantly. 'I haven't got to do
anything.'

'Well, I have to speak for my friend,' said Dora, refusing
to be intimidated. 'It was Dahlia who pulled me out of the
water last summer and listened to me and gave me courage.
She took on Algie and Sailor, rescued them from the fire and
tried to make a life for them.' She put her hand on Beattie's
arm and smiled hesitantly at her. 'Look, you're Lily's Gran
and you've been good to me but I have to speak as I find.
Must go now.'

Beattie's anger was beginning to cool when Albert came out
to speak to her. He smiled at her and she almost laughed when he
took out his handkerchief and waved it like a flag of truce. 'Are
you feeling calm and reasonable?' he asked, catching hold of her
hand and kissing it.

Beattie snatched it away, her temper flaring. 'I don't want to be calm and reasonable. I could give her a good shaking.'

'Beatrice.' Albert's voice was deceptively quiet. 'If anyone needs a shaking it's you. You are too old to have a tantrum. If you wish to stamp about in this childish fashion you can do it alone. I think Sailor needs a little reassurance. You must make your own decisions. He and I are going next-door. I shall probably spend the night in there. I hope I shall find you in better spirits tomorrow.'

After a few more minutes in the cold yard without her coat Beattie began to feel ridiculous. She went back into the empty house and busied herself in a frenzy of washing-up, cleaning and polishing. What was her anger all about? Of course there was the justifiable resentment of having to take on the responsibility of Sailor without having been asked. But that wasn't it. Being taken for granted, being good old Beattie, yes that rankled. It was something more. Dahlia had just up and gone, had been answerable only to herself. Something Beattie had often thought about but never done. Always she was tied by responsibility to others. No, that wasn't true: there had been a period between Joseph's death and taking on Alec's children when she could have broken free. But there was another element besides courage and that was cash. Where would she have gone, what would she have done? From whatever source Dahlia had money and that bought freedom. Beattie set the iron to cool in the sink and folded up the ironing-blanket. No, she was not a lone adventurer whatever she liked to think. Being brought up in an orphanage had taught her that. She needed family ties. No, Beattie Pragnell, she said to herself, you were being a dog-in-the-manger. You wouldn't have the desire or the courage to go, so you were angry with Dahlia for being different and for playing by her own rules.

Albert did not come back and Beattie felt too foolish to seek him out next-door. Lily dashed in for her tea and out again, saying she was going to visit Michael's mother and play Snap with Chippy.

It was a lonely night without Albert. She missed the warmth of his body next to hers. It was also the time when they shared their thoughts with each other. Albert was like a spirit-level or compass needle. Instinctively he guided her to act from her better nature. Not that she always agreed with him. But their fallings-out and fallings-in were often exhilarating and rarely serious. This time was different. She had been childish and unreasonable and totally ignored poor Sailor's plight. Albert had been very angry.

Directly he lifted the latch and walked into the scullery the next morning, she rushed into his arms.

'Oh, I've missed you and I'm so sorry Albert,' she cried.

'Over and done with, my darling,' he said kissing her soundly. 'I missed you. Hardly slept a wink. Sailor seemed to drop like a stone. I thing the poor chap was exhausted. I've left him sleeping, still.'

'Where did you bed yourself down? Things seemed pretty bare and comfortless in there.'

'Oh, in the chair by the fire. Sailor wanted me to use Dahlia's room but it was in some disarray and I hadn't the energy to set it to rights.'

Beattie sniffed. 'I don't think being a housewife was ever one of Dahlia's accomplishments.'

'A motor mechanic was more her forte,' laughed Albert.

''Morning, you two lovebirds,' called Lily as she sat herself down at the kitchen table. 'Is there any honey left?'

Beattie smiled at her. Her cheerfulness and normality was a tonic. Perhaps they would all get back to their old routine after all, if they could just weather the immediate problems with Sailor.

'Happy Birthday, Miriam,' Lily said as she drizzled the honey on to her porridge.

'Heavens, yes,' said Beattie, 'and Anniversary to the pair of them.'

'Something to celebrate. Just what we need,' said Albert, following her to the table.

'Yes,' said Beattie. 'Let's have something special for tea. Dinner is going to be a bit of a scratch affair with soup and sandwiches. We've to sort out something for Sailor. He can't manage on his own next-door so we'll have to see what can be done.'

'How about Chippy?' said Lily, pouring herself a second cup of tea. 'He seems much better. Michael's Mum thinks it was all the beer he drank on Christmas Day that set him off.'

'What's he got to do with Sailor?' asked Beattie, pouring herself a second cup of tea.

'Well, couldn't they muddle along together? After all, Chippy could be Sailor's eyes and he could be Chippy's brain.'

'Muddle along would be the word for it,' laughed Albert, 'but it's not without its merits.'

'Why don't you invite Michael's mum and Chippy?'

'Good idea,' said Beattie. 'I'll get some boiled ham and I think there's still some of Olive's Dundee cake left and Samuel's parsnip wine.'

'Oh, I'm going to Driver's with Dora, at dinner-time,' said Lily, 'I think she's got something to celebrate.'

'Tell her from me, that I'm sorry about yesterday,' said Beattie. 'I'm proud of her, the way she's turned herself around. You'd hardly recognise her from the little mouse of last summer. What's the celebration?'

Laughing, Lily put her finger to her lips. 'It's a secret. Tell you later.'

The day seemed to rush by with Albert taking Sailor out to buy him some shoes.

Beattie concentrated on thoughts for the evening party suggested by Lily. She called over to Ethel's house and found her with Chippy, cutting his hair.

'Beattie, good to see you,' she said. 'Could you put the kettle on? I'll just tidy up the neck Chippy, and then comb it level. Look almost back to your old self. Your Mum would be proud of you.'

Beattie suggested the tea-party.

'I loves parties,' said Chippy, grinning from ear to ear.

'Shake that towel out in the yard and put these bacon rinds on to the bird-table.'

'He looks tons better,' said Beattie, pouring out the tea.

'I think he's turned the corner,' said Ethel. 'He loved our day out in Romsey yesterday.'

'How's Sergeant Clifton?'

'He's fine,' said Ethel, and Beattie was surprised to see her neighbour blush. 'But now there's a problem. Mr Pragnell wants to give the cottage to the new cowman and his family. Of course it was kind of them to have him at all but now he'll have to move on.'

Beattie sighed. 'We thought the peace was the end to all our problems, didn't we? And yet it seems to be just the beginning. Everything's turned upside down and not an atom of security anywhere. People set adrift, damaged bodies and minds.'

'Oliver was saying what finally drove him to think of ending it all was meeting his old officer in Charlotte Market.'

'What had happened to him?'

'Well, old was the wrong word, really only in his thirties. But gone completely grey. He was stood at a street corner on crutches, selling matches. Oliver said he thought the poor fellow had consumption. Sweating he was, with a dreadful cough.'

'Eager enough to sign them all up to the colours at the start of things,' said Beattie, feeling a spurt of rage.

'Having a jelly at your party?' asked Chippy, coming back into the kitchen. 'I'm itchy after me haircut.' He shrugged his shoulders and Ethel fetched the clothes-brush, undid his collar and helped brush the loose hairs from around his neck.

'I should think we could manage that,' said Beattie picking up her shopping bag. 'Anything I can get you Ethel?'

'A blue-bag if you would and a packet of starch. I'm like the cow's tail, all behind this week.'

'Well,' said Beattie, 'we're all at sixes and sevens since the fire. One of the reasons I've invited you over for tea. It'll be a while before number nine is cleaned up. The front bedroom needs a complete new window and stripping and redecorating. As to the rest of the house it needs a thorough overhaul.'

'We need to pool our ideas,' said Ethel. 'While I'm glad to look after Chippy in the short term I do have other things I want to do, and I think he needs to get into a proper routine. Even get back to work if the job's still there.'

'See you for the party,' said Chippy, following Ethel to the front door.

Beattie hurried past number 9 with its boarded-up windows. The fire seemed to have underlined the changes in her life since marrying Albert . . . When she'd been a widow other people's needs were a welcome distraction from her own. Now, with a husband, and Lily almost independent, she wanted time to do other things that didn't involve Lemon Street and all its problems.

Chapter Twenty-six

November 25th 1921

Dear Mary,

We have been having a rare time here in Malacca. The Malacca Club is a great place open to the ship's company as well as the officers. There was a holiday because of our arrival. There are rubber plantations further up country and some of the owners and their wives and children came to the club to welcome us. Free drinks all round, Dad would have been in his element. I think some of those plantation owners wanted to find husbands for their daughters. They were a plain horsey looking bunch of girls, except for one of them who was immediately snapped up by this petty officer signalman who's got a wife and three kids back home. Poor cow she's in for a big disappointment. He's a bit of a Casanova. Let's hope it's only a broken heart she's left with.

I am getting on champion with the model ship I'm making for Blyth. S'pose I shall hardly recognise the little chap when I get back to Blighty. What age is he now? Is it five or six? I expect he'll want a trip around the real ship and see the torpedo shells and such like.

How are the twinnies? Did they tell you they wrote me this letter between them full of drawings of them in the park with Dora for their birthday. I really fell in clover when I met her. She is pure gold.

*How about you? Are you still crossing swords with that fat
old cook? I couldn't believe the Captain's mississ is called Lettuce.
She sounds a right fussy mare.*

*Here, I nearly forgot. Got this young A.B. called Matthew
Miller known of course as Dusty. He's a lively lad. I think you
would get on great guns with him. To cut the cackle, Dusty
would like someone to write to. Don't seem to get any letters
except from his Mum. I've put in this note from him. See what
you think.*

Love to all the family Your Brother Harry.

Mary picked up the note addressed to her and put it away under
her pillow to digest later. It was now two weeks since she'd lost
her job and time was hanging heavy, especially now that Blyth
and the twins were back at school.

Dad was still at home but getting better every day. Soon he'd
be able to leave off his bandages and go back to work. What she
was going to do with herself was not yet clear. She'd been a
disaster as a scullery-maid and had no desire to improve her skills
in that direction. Nelly Moyes who ran the toy stall at the market
had offered her a shilling a week for helping her out on a
Saturday.

'Can't spare you no more, my duck,' she said in her
gravelly voice. 'But it'd be good experience. You got the gift
of the gab and nimble fingers. And you can reckon up
quicker than me. Chew it over for a few days and let me
know.'

Mary would be sixteen next week on the seventeenth of
January. She would have to give out several hints before Dad or
her sisters would remember. The only people who gave her cards
without prompting were Lily and her gran. Course she couldn't
expect Blyth to know and it would be a miracle to get anything
from Harry on the right day. Faith and Mercy had had that
birthday tea in the park with Dora. She would have done

something special for Blyth as well only it was around the time of her accident.

Underneath all her prickliness towards her, Mary really wanted Dora as a friend. She knew that if she could just be chummy with her for five minutes and not all narky and suspicious they could be pals. Dora had made her a lovely nightdress at Christmas, which they'd found in a bag in the road after all the panic of the fire, along with the twins' presents and Blyth's blow-football game. Mary sighed. After all, there wasn't a great load of people queueing up for the job of being friends with her. There was Cissie but now she didn't work with her any more it was difficult to keep contact. She supposed she could write to her. Mary laughed to herself at the thought of Lettice picking up an envelope written by the 'guttersnipe'.

'There's a cup of tea waiting down here for you, my gal,' called Dad.

'Down in a minute,' she shouted, getting to her feet. If Dad had made it, it would be a miracle she thought. Probably a pot the twins brewed ages ago. She flung the blanket back over the bed and straightened the pillow; as she did so the envelope crackled underneath. Mary smiled, she wouldn't read Dusty's letter now, she'd leave herself something to look forward to later.

Dad was washed and dressed and the place was cleaned up. Well, she doubted anyone else would recognise the difference. But by Vine standards it didn't look bad. The washing-up was stacked in the sink, there was a fresh sheet of newspaper on the table and he'd emptied his ashtray.

He smiled sheepishly at her, waiting for her approval.

She reached out a hand and touched the teapot: it was hot. 'You've not done bad,' she said coolly, as she poured the milk from the bottle into her cup. There was a plate in front of her with a slice of bread-and-butter with jam thickly spread. The bread was cut on the slope and graduated from about an inch thick at one end to less than a quarter at the other. She took up the sticky knife beside the plate and cut the slice in two before starting to eat. Dad poured the tea into both their cups, spilling some on the paper.

'Couldn't find no saucers,' he said apologetically.

'Bloody hopeless, you are. Can't never get things right.' The words were almost said when she looked up at him and saw the desperate eagerness in his face. ''Ain't got no saucers,' she said, looking down at her cup.

'That's all right then.'

'What you goin' to do today?'

'Go up the Home Club, tell them as I'm ready to start back tomorrer. What you got planned for yourself?' he asked, as he sat there opposite her holding his cup in both hands.

'Straighten up this place. Dunno,' she shrugged, watching her Dad struggling to make himself a cigarette. Although his fingers were healing he could not as yet bend them very far. By holding the packet of papers in his hands he had drawn out a single one with his teeth. It lay in a wet curl on the table. The challenge of picking up a few threads of tobacco from his pouch and shaking the rest free was proving almost impossible.

'Here,' she said trying not to sound impatient, 'you're spilling it on the floor. We'll have to get Towser on the baccy if you drops much more.'

'Thanks Gal,' said Dad, passing her the pouch and the packet of papers.

Mary laid a thin line of tobacco on the paper and licked the edge before sealing it. 'Reckon if I gives you this ciggie you could start calling me Mary?' she asked.

'Thank you, Mary,' he said, his blue eyes twinkling. 'P'raps you be kind enough to strike us a light.'

While she took out a match he went across to the mantel-piece and brought back a small creased envelope.

Mary lit his cigarette and he drew on it hungrily before

passing the envelope over to her. 'Read it,' he said, passing it to her.

Inside the envelope was a small piece of paper with a few words scrawled in pencil and two one-pound notes. 'Blimey,' Mary gasped, setting them down on the table before returning to the letter.

Dear Pal,
   We read about you trying to rescoo them kids from the fire and rekon yor a hero. Weeve ad a bit of a collekion and hope the cash will come in ooseful.
   All the best, Nobby, Spike and Knocker.

'What you going to do with it?' asked Mary, 'treat your pals up the George?'

'No,' said Dad, 'I thought you might come with me while I reports in about me job. Then we could go down the market and get some grub for all of us. Maybe we might set ourselves up with a set of china and a tablecloth. You bin working with the gentry up there in Lancaster Terrace. Be able to set me right about milk-jugs and saucers and such like.' He winked at her. 'After that there might even be a few bob left for a certain Mary's birthday that's coming up soon.'

She wanted to cry. Instead she said. 'I reckon we might buy you some Woodbines. Save us all the trouble of rolling your ciggies.'

'No Ruby, that won't do,' said Dora firmly.

The work-room fell silent. Miss Pearson continued her inspection of the new apprentice's tacking. There was a feeling of expectancy – Dora could almost taste it.

'What's wrong with it?' Ruby's voice was dangerously quiet.

'The collar doesn't sit right. The stitches in the middle have been drawn too tight. They'll have to come out.'

'Who says?'

'I do,' said Dora, fighting to keep her voice steady.

'Well I'm not doing it. Who are you to tell me, anyway?'

Dora was beginning to feel angry. 'You were here when Miss Pearson told everyone that I've been made up to forewoman. I've every right to tell you.'

'Well you can do it yourself. A bit of pressing and it'll come up good enough.' Ruby flung it back at Dora and looked around to see what reaction her defiance had caused. Miss Pearson had her back to both of the girls and continued sewing. Mr Savours paused with an iron hovering over a wet cloth. Mrs Markham had a strand of gold wire between her fingers ready for threading.

'Please, everyone,' said Dora, 'don't let me stop you. Now, Miss Frogatt,' she said slowly and calmly. 'Good enough is not the standard here and you know it. Where's your pride? Either remove the stitches and redo them or you'll receive a formal warning.' She took the jacket and put it down on Ruby's work-table before resuming her seat and taking up her own sewing.

'Miss Somers,' said Miss Pearson, getting to her feet, 'I have to go over to the shop. I shall be back in half an hour or so.'

'Who the hell d'you think you are, Miss Hoity-Toity?' roared Ruby. 'Making a show of me with old Pearson.'

'You made the show, Ruby,' said Dora, refusing to lose her temper.

'I've a good mind to give in me notice. Plenty of other places I could go. I could leave this minute,' said Ruby, tossing her head.

'I didn't see many tailoring vacancies in the *Evening News* last week,' said Dora. 'And there won't be many that will take you on with no references. Storming out will feel good for five minutes. How will it feel having to come around later and beg for your job back?'

'Don't be daft, Ruby,' said Mrs Markham. 'Don't cut off your nose to spite your face.'

'Look Ruby, I know you've been here longer. I didn't ask for the job but I've got it now and I'm going to do it as well as I can. There'll be no favourites and you all start with a clean slate. You know you can do better. It's up to you. Dinner-time, now, everyone. See you all back here at half-past one.'

Ruby's temper had cooled to be replaced by the sulks. She left the work-room, slamming the door behind her.

'End of round one,' said Mr Savours. 'I reckon you were saved by the bell.'

'You were in your rights what you said, Dora. She had it coming.'

'I don't know about you,' said Dora, anxious to avoid a post mortem, 'but I'm ready for my dinner. I'll see you all later.'

'Blimey', said Lily as they sat in Driver's Café eating steaming bowls of beef stew, 'I wish I'd been there.'

'My knees were knocking,' said Dora. 'But I knew if I gave in to her I'd be lost before I'd even started.'

'You haven't half changed, Dora. Harry will hardly recognise you. When I think what you were like in the summer, almost afraid of your own shadow.'

'Surprised myself,' laughed Dora, taking another slice of bread.

'That chair taken?'

Still laughing Dora looked up to see Bert Finch about to sit down beside her. To her own annoyance she could feel herself blushing. 'No,' she muttered, staring at the table-cloth, 'we were just going.'

'No, we weren't,' said Lily, smiling at Bert. 'You've got half your bread-pudding yet to eat and I want another cup of tea.'

Dora threw her a furious look.

'How are you young ladies, then?' said Bert, settling himself beside Dora and reaching across her for the salt-cellar.

Dora could hardly swallow, so conscious was she of the

pressure of Bert's khaki-clad leg against hers. Covertly she looked at him as he tucked into his steak-and-kidney pudding. He had taken off his cap and set it under his chair. His blond hair curled crisply above his collar and there was a faint pink line across his forehead where his cap had pressed. He had long tapering fingers curled around his knife and fork. He took small mouthfuls and ate slowly. After a while he took out his handkerchief and dabbed his mouth. Dora was fascinated by his full soft lips.

'Don't you want that pudding?' Lily said. 'Pass it over, I'm starving.'

'You're looking very well, Miss Somers,' said Sergeant Finch, smiling at her. Dora blushed.

'Her name's Dora,' said Lily, helping herself to Dora's pudding.

'I know her name,' he said quietly, 'it's for her to say whether I can use it.'

'I'll think about it,' said Dora, getting to her feet. 'See you after work,' she said to Lily.

'And what time is that?' he asked, looking directly at her.

'None of your business,' she said, attempting to sweep out of the café but colliding with a girl behind her.

'Here, watch what you're doin'. Nearly dropped me scone.'

'What you doing encouraging him?' said Dora, furious with Lily.

'Stop pretending,' laughed Lily, 'you know you like him.'

'But I'm engaged to Harry.'

'Haven't got a ring though, have you?'

'Well, how can we buy one with him thousands of miles away?'

'Could send you the money to get one, couldn't he?'

'Don't need that. We're promised.'

Lily laughed and Dora wanted to hit her. 'You never said what we'd do to celebrate your promotion,' she said changing tack. 'How about the pictures next week? You can choose.'

'All right,' said Dora, cooling down. 'We'll take Mary, it's her birthday.'

'If we have to,' Lily said. 'See you tonight. Don't be late, I've got to hurry home.'

Dora was in the cloakroom taking her comb out of her handbag when she remembered Dahlia's letter. There were five minutes to go before dinner-time was over. She sat down on one of the rickety chairs and opened the envelope.

Dear Dora,

Don't think too badly of me. It took as much courage to go as it would have done to stay. Dora, I have watched you in the last few months taking hold of your life and standing up for yourself. I am full of admiration. Be very sure that it's Harry that you want to spend your life with. Marry him because you love and desire him not to be a mother to his brothers and sister or because you've drifted into it.

I have given you the tandem so that you and Lily can have fun together get out of Portsmouth and see something of the countryside. Give Sailor an outing sometimes if you can.

We're bodies as well as minds and spirits. Whoever awakens you Dora Somers will have a whirlwind to contend with. Listen to your heart, be passionate about the person you're going to spend your life with.

Don't let timidity hold you back. Fortune favours the brave.

With love from Dahlia.

Dora dropped the letter back into her bag as if it were on fire. She turned on the tap and splashed her face with cold water then dried it on the roller towel. Taking a deep breath she re-entered the work-room.

The afternoon was long and quiet. Ruby re-did the collar and threw it on to her work table. 'That's perfect, Miss Frogatt, thank you,' she said, well aware that Ruby was making faces behind her back. At six o'clock Dora stepped out of the work-room door and looked expectantly about her. She walked slowly down the street, hoping at any moment to have the opportunity to ignore Bert Finch.

'Miss Forrest, I think we would both agree that your time in the Epaulette Room has not been a success.' Miss Pearson smoothed an invisible crease on her skirt.

Lily swallowed nervously. 'I tried my best,' she said. 'Miss Hatcher never seemed to have enough time to sit down and teach me.'

'The impression I received from Miss Hatcher was of a young woman full of opinions and lacking a certain respect.'

Lily blushed as much from temper as embarrassment. It was all so unfair. Freda, Nesta and Clemmie were a bunch of old witches or a coven to be more exact. But they had more power in Denby and Shanks as skilled needlewomen than she, a mere apprentice. 'I'm sorry,' she mumbled.

Miss Pearson spread her hands in a dismissive gesture. 'We have had to think again how to provide the Epaulette Room with a new apprentice.' She gave Lily a wintry smile. 'Mrs Markham has generously offered to work with Miss Hatcher until we can find someone else.' She took up a pin-cushion and began to take out the pins and stab them one by one back into the cushion.

There was a dryness in Lily's throat as she watched those pale slender fingers at work. What had she decided? Would she be dismissed? She looked up into the cool grey eyes of the other woman.

'You will return to the work-room under the direction of Miss Somers and you will serve an extra six months before becoming qualified.'

Lily sighed with relief, she'd kept her job. Yet she burned at the unfairness of Miss Hatcher's criticism. She had been eager and willing to learn but had come up against a wall of prejudice and a reluctance to pass on their skills.

'I learned from you, Miss Pearson,' she burst out. 'You were patient with me and took time to show me and . . .'

'Maybe, maybe.' Miss Pearson got to her feet and went past the stacked shelves of suiting to open the door of her tiny office. The interview was at an end. 'You will collect your things and return to the work-room tomorrow at eight o'clock.'

Lily rushed up the stairs to the beehive and flung open the door. 'I'm collecting my things,' she gasped, snatching her coat from its hook on the wall by the kettle and taking her scissors and apron from the work-table. Drawing herself up to her full height, she said, 'You will happy to know that I am going back to the work-room with Miss Pearson.'

The three women said nothing and continued to bend over their work.

Lily hated to be ignored, and their lack of interest made her reckless. 'I have hated every minute of it here.'

Miss Hatcher did not look up. 'I hope you've got everything, Miss Forrest,' she said icily. 'I wouldn't want you to have to come back.'

Lily was furious. She had wanted to turn on her heel and vanquish them with a crushing remark. Since nothing came to mind and as they had dismissed her so thoroughly she had no choice but to go. Well, she wouldn't have to listen to any more carping criticism, no more smell of stale wee and mothballs, she was free.

'Good riddance,' said Dora, linking arms with her as they left the work-room that evening. 'It's Saturday tomorrow, if it's dry we could try out the tandem, what d'you think?'

Lily laughed. 'We could get make ourselves some cycling britches and check caps.'

'We could borrow some from Mark and Barney. Could bowl along the sea-front and see your Auntie Hester.'

By the time Lily arrived home her temper had cooled and she was more than ready for the jam roley-poly that Gran was just taking out of the cloth as she walked in.

'Ooh I'm full up fit to bust,' she gasped after her second helping.

'It's your night for treats,' smiled Gran. 'There's a fat letter from Michael, on your pillow. But first you can wash up. We're off to the first house at the Theatre Royal, taking Sailor and Chippy to the pantomime.'

'How are they getting on together next-door?' Lily asked, as she began to clear the table.

'Well, I think they'll stagger on for a few more weeks. The rent is paid up until March. But Albert wants to move Chippy back to number nine when it's cleaned up, perhaps with Sailor. Don't forget to fill the hot-water bottles.'

Lily rushed through the dishes, the thought of Michael's letter speeding the task.

By seven o'clock she had stirred up the fire, flung off her boots and settled herself in Gran's armchair. Eagerly she tore open the envelope, unfolded the many sheets of paper and began to read.

December 1st 1921

Dear Lily,

Some exciting news. I had to go and see the Captain this morning in my best uniform to be told that I am now promoted to Acting Petty Officer. Good news for me but bad news for the poor Petty Officer I'm replacing who died after being bitten by a sea snake while out swimming. In a year's time, if all goes well I shall be confirmed in the rate. So it's goodbye bell bottoms. Also goodbye to sharing a mess with Harry. He has now been made a Leading Hand so it's celebrations all round. I am writing to

Mother so you will both have the good news at the same time.
The rest of the letter is for you alone.

Lily felt a thrill of pride: Michael a Petty Officer at twenty-three.
She returned eagerly to the letter.

> *At last some time to myself. I am almost alone in the mess*
> *with the exception of two others who are sleeping off a hearty*
> *meal at the Malacca club. Your picture is on the table in front of*
> *me in the dress you wore for your grandmother's wedding. I wish*
> *that I was a poet to tell you how beautiful you are. The books*
> *here offer no inspiration at all: 'Potentialities of the Torpedo', or*
> *'Engine Room Efficiency.'*

Lily laughed. She was glad Michael was not going to compare
her to a wrench or a spanner.

> *The only other book is the Bible and here I found some*
> *treasure in The Song of Solomon. 'Thy lips, O my spouse, drop*
> *as the honeycomb; Honey and milk are under thy tongue; and the*
> *smell of thy garments is like the smell of Lebanon.'*

Lily felt her face grow warm. She was stirred by the rhythm of
the words and their beauty.

> *'I am come into my garden, . . . my spouse: I have gathered*
> *my myrrh with my spice . . . Open to me, my love, my dove*
> *. . . for my head is filled with dew and my locks with the drops*
> *of the night.'*

Lily closed her eyes. The words painted a vivid sensual picture.

> *I ache to touch you and hold you close. Still another eighteen*
> *months until we're together again. When that happens I shan't ever*

want to let you go. Lily will you marry me? It will make me so happy if you say yes. This question must come as no surprise to you. Even before I went away we knew we had reached a special understanding didn't we?

I shall be twenty-five the October after we get home and then I shall be entitled to seven and six a week marriage allowance. I know that love is the most important thing and that we have plenty of that but after Mother had such a struggle to manage after my Dad died I'm determined for us to be as secure as possible. Anyway we will need a little time to see if after all this time we still feel the same when we see each other in the flesh.

I have sent you an ivory ring that I bought in the market. It fits my little finger so I hope it will not be too big. It is not a proper engagement ring but it's a token of my love until I'm home and we can get engaged properly.

Lily hugged herself with joy. She paced the room, restless with desire, turning the ring round and round her finger. Michael wanted to marry her, he wanted to love her and hold her close. She went over to the dresser and took the Bible out of the bottom drawer and leafed through it until she found the Song of Solomon. The words were full of mysterious images.

'*I rose up to open to my beloved; and my hands dropped with myrhh, and my fingers with sweet smelling myrhh, open the handles of the lock.*'

The blood rushed up into Lily's face as she puzzled out the secret sexual meanings behind the words. How far away Michael seemed and how much she wanted him.

Chapter Twenty-seven

The four of them hurried along the dockyard wall, their breath
smoking in the chill January morning. Albert had his pencils and
sketch-pad in the pocket of his overcoat. Chippy in his role of
Sailor's attendant swung along beside him wearing a new
balaclava helmet knitted by Ethel.

'Hold up,' snapped Sailor, 'we ain't in a race. The *Victory*
won't get docked in five minutes.'

Beattie had set aside the time to go to the January sales at
McIlroys and Marshall's Corner. They needed new sheets and
she wanted to get some material to run up a little dress for Rosie.
But Albert had so wanted her to be with him.

'It marks the end of the sailing navy, Beattie, the one that
Joseph and Sailor and I joined as boys. We must honour the ship
on its last journey. My grandfather was a midshipman at
Trafalgar and Sailor's great-grandfather was an upper-yardman.'

'So was Joseph's granddad. I know they were the great heroes
but a lot of them ended up breaking their bones or collapsing in
the rigging. Seen a good few begging in the streets.'

'What I wouldn't give to be back there,' gasped Sailor, trying
to keep up with them.

'Hang on Chippy,' said Beattie, giving Sailor a chance to
catch his breath. 'Must do up my shoe buckle.'

'To have all that energy and speed. To race up the yards, agile like a monkey, squandering your strength because you knew after a night's sleep it would be there again to draw on.' He sighed. 'Ended up busting me ankle and taking up gunnery. Never the same excitement.'

Beattie had no grandfather to boast of. Whether her own family had been sailing folk or ever lived in Portsmouth was unknown to her. But she had always felt a strong connection with the sea. The sound of the waves lapping the shore had always soothed her. It must have been one of the first sounds that she heard. How long had she been there in that little boat stranded on the beach at Sally Port? The baby found tucked in a dying sailor's tarpaulin. Was he her father? She would never know. But he had wanted her to live, that much was certain. And of her mother she knew nothing There had been a kindly woman called Ruth but she had not been a relative, of that she was certain. At least Lily had always had a father and grandmother. How little she knew of the life of a foundling.

'The steam-hammer's getting louder, we must be nearly at the yard,' said Sailor excitedly. 'Now Albert, don't forget you're to tell me every last detail. How the old girl looks, how they gets her moving, what other ships are about.'

'We're at the gate now,' said Albert, handing his invitation from the Marine Artists' Society to the burly dockyard police-man.

'Lieutenant and Mrs Pragnell,' he said reading from the card. 'Who are these other two people?'

'This gentleman lost his sight in the service of his country in the African Wars,' said Albert, placing his hand on Sailor's shoulder. 'And this is Mr Dowell who attends to him. His eyes, as you might say.'

'A bit irregular, but just this once.'

'I take full responsibility for my party,' said Albert, looking steadily at the policeman.

'Off you go then,' said the policeman, reluctantly. 'Number two basin.'

Walking through the dockyard was like entering a walled town populated by a vast number of skilled craftsmen: shipwrights, sailmakers, mastmakers, blacksmiths and carpenters and their labourers. Walking amongst the sailors, maties and bowler-hatted foreman brought back a host of memories. Standing at Farewell Jetty waving goodbye to Joseph as his ship sailed away from her, then dawdling back to the empty house, taking his shirt to sleep with her and clinging to the smell of him in its cotton folds. The joyous homecoming with the sound of the Marine band and the families cheering when all that waiting was forgotten. There were, too, the heartwrenching groups of women with their prams and tribes of children walking through the gate, when the ship was lost, to memorial services at the dockyard church of St Anne. Beattie had been waving and waiting all her life. And now like the *Victory* she was an old lady taken into safe anchorage with Albert.

'There's the Mast House where I sweeps up. I'll just go and see Mr Cramer, he's the foreman.'

'Chippy, you stay with us. Perhaps on the way home. Don't forget you've got a job to do here, you're Sailor's eyes, remember.'

'Right you are,' said Chippy, grasping Sailor's arm.

As they walked on Albert named the various buildings to Sailor. 'Just passing the Anchor Pound and now the Rope House,' he said. 'Over a mile long I believe.'

'We're here,' said Albert, excitedly shepherding Sailor to a safe corner amid the crowd of onlookers, sailors, families and dockyard workers. 'I can see her, set against the last streaks of a fading sunset, all pinks and pearly greys. There's a great deal of movement around her. Two divers in big brass helmets have gone into the basin. There's a hawser attached to *Victory*'s capstan and there's the boatswain just ahead of us directing operations with flags. To her left is an admiral's barge with all the brass hats and such.'

'Poor old girl,' said Beattie, 'she's had a real battering, look at the gold work, it's chipped off and her sides look all bashed about. Seems to be waddling in the water.'

Sailor and Albert talked earnestly about her bow being hogged, fastening sickness and deformation of the keel, but it all passed over her head. The sight of the once-proud warship being drawn into the dock put her in mind of Chippy's mother being helped into her chair. She felt tears welling up and dashed them away with her hand.

'Want to restore her to as she was at Trafalgar,' Albert was saying. 'It will cost thousands.'

There was something humiliating in Victory's exposure to all eyes as she staggered slowly into place. Thousands of pounds for new masts and rigging and yet there were men begging on the streets and widows desperate to know where the next meal was coming from. Nippers bare-arsed and bare-footed. Doubtless at five some of those nippers would be outside the dockyard gate begging the maties for the crusts left from their sandwiches. Men and their ships were a mystery to her.

She looked up at the admiral's barge and the high-ranking officers bedecked with gold braid, epitomising the Nelson Spirit. All the epaulettes, sword-knots and sleeve rings represented thousands of hours of fine needlework, hundreds of tiny eye-straining stitches. For all the people in the centre of the canvas there were always the supporting groups in the background, whatever the profession – the swordmakers, fletchers, saddlers, gardeners, wigmakers and seamstresses.

Beattie was tugged out of her thoughts by Chippy worrying at her sleeve.

Chippy tugged at her arm. 'Can we go and see Mr Cramer now?' he asked, jigging up and down impatiently.

She walked over to Albert who was absorbed in his sketching, all the while commenting to Sailor on what he could see. 'Chippy's wanting to go, now. We'll see you back at the house.'

'No, Chippy,' said Albert, 'we must all leave together or we shall annoy the policeman. I've taken responsibility for all of us. Please, content yourself for ten minutes and then I'll be with you.'

Looking at his crestfallen face, Beattie rummaged in her pocket and pulled out a couple of toffees.

'Here Chippy, suck on these, we won't be long.' She stamped her feet and walked about to warm herself up. The sunrise had completely gone leaving grey lowering skies. For some reason the sight of HMS *Victory* had dispirited her. The old ship had reminded her of her own increasing years. Where had the dark-haired, laughing girl who had bathed naked with Joseph at midnight and made love to him under the pier gone?

'Right,' said Albert putting his charcoal back in its box and closing his sketch-pad. 'For your patience, you shall be rewarded. A drink at the Ship Anson, I think. First we'll call at the Mast House and see the famous Mr Cramer.'

Chippy almost danced back down the road. He was warmly greeted by his old foreman.

'What a surprise, Chippy son. How are you faring? Good enough to come back here?'

Chippy beamed from ear to ear.

'How about a bit of a sweep-up for old time's sake?'

'How is he now?' asked Mr Cramer, taking a generous pinch from his snuff-box.

'I think he's more than ready,' said Albert, 'don't you, Beatrice?' He turned and introduced her. 'My wife Mrs Pragnell and Sailor our neighbour.'

'Yes,' said Beattie. 'He could do with the routine, if you could spare him, Sailor.'

'Gladly, I shall be glad of the peace and quiet and for him to leave off a-pinching my arm. Poor chap, we're chalk and cheese and that's the truth of it.'

'There's going to be a deal of work in here when *Victory* gets her new masts,' said the foreman before sneezing explosively. 'There'll be a load of wood chips created. We'll need someone to haul them away in a basket to the hoop-makers furnace.' He smiled. 'He'll be Chippy by name and Chippy by nature.'

Beattie smiled and slipped her hand through Albert's arm. 'The best news I've heard for weeks,' she said, smiling up at him.

Chapter Twenty-eight

They'd all remembered. Mary couldn't believe it. There was a lighted candle in a jam-jar beside her plate, along with a pile of cards and a plate of dripping-on-toast.

'Open mine Mary,' shouted Blyth, his face pink with excitement.

The envelope had 'Mary' written on it in wobbly blue crayon and inside a huge red face with a tiny body and little matchstick arms and legs. The eyes were round like brown marbles and the mouth was a red gash with huge tombstone teeth. All over the card was her name in large drunken letters.

'It's lovely,' she said hugging him fiercely. 'I shan't never forget my name with this to remind me.'

It felt strange to be the centre of attention. To be surrounded by all of them smiling and wanting her to be happy. She blinked at the candle and the light flickered as tears threatened.

'We done cards for ya,' said Faith, 'done one each.'

'And they're different,' said Mercy.

'Let's all farm into the toast what you gals made while it's nice and hot. Then we got the cards to look forward to,' said Dad.

Mary smiled at him and he smiled shyly back at her. She knew there would be no card from him as his fingers were still not able to hold a pen.

They all crammed round the table laid with the new blue-and-white striped china. There was even a milk-jug and sugar-basin.

'What you goin' to do tonight?' asked Faith, licking her finger and dabbing up the last toast crumbs from her plate.

'Dora and Lily's going to take me to the pictures. We're goin' on the tandem to the pictures down the Shaftsbury in Kingston Road.'

'How come Dora got the tandem? Thought it belonged to Sailor and that Dalalia,' said Dad.

'It b'longs to Dora now,' said Mary, sprinkling some salt onto her dripping toast. 'She give it to Dora before she scarpered.'

'Can I have a ride?' asked Blyth.

'Not today, babes. But you ask Auntie Dora, she'll probbly take you out with Sailor.'

'You ain't going out to pictures before you've had your tea tonight?' he asked. 'We got jelly and cake and singing.'

'Course not,' she said, passing him the last half-crust.

'Right kids, it's ten to nine, you'd best get your skates on.'

'I'll just open their cards,' said Mary.

The twins stood together staring anxiously at her.

Faith's card was a surprise to her. It had a picture of herself wearing a crown and sitting on a puffed-up pink cushion. She was looking out of a window, a telescope to her eye. And, there in the distance was Harry. Instead of HMS *Lister* written on his cap were the words 'Happy Birthday'. 'Come here,' she said, and hugged her sister's thin straight little body.

Mercy's card consisted of birthday greetings-in rainbow colours and 'Tuesday January 17th' – in giant letters and numbers. Mary was surprised they were both so different. Always she'd lumped her sisters together as the twinnies, without a thought of them as individuals. 'Mercy, that's lovely,' she said. 'I likes the little stripey letters must 'ave took ages.'

Mercy blushed.

'Right you lot, scarper,' said Dad, following them to the front door and shutting it behind them. 'Sixteen eh,' he spread his hands disbelievingly. 'My Mary a young woman on the brink.'

'On the brink of what?' she asked. 'Ain't got no job and no prospects.'

'What about Nellie Moyes and her stall down the market?'

'Only Saturdays.'

'It's a toehold. You don't know what could come of it.'

'What' laughed Mary, 'I becomes a millionaire and marries an admiral.'

'That little stall could be a goldmine,' said Dad, pouring his tea into the saucer and blowing on it. 'Always be kids wanting toys. Poor old gal, she's let it get all run down. Needs some fresh stuff. Bits of things what you wouldn't find anywhere else.'

'What d'you mean?'

'You're a clever gal. Look at them tops what you made for Blyth with rainbow stripes on. Was only scraps of wood with a chopped-off bit of dowelling stuck through the middle. Remember how he loved it and all the other kids wanted one. And you took them party-blowers apart last Christmas and made 'em up good as new. And the little boxes for the twinnies what you covered with pictures. Still keep all their little treasures in them.'

'Never thought you noticed,' said Mary, secretly excited but trying to appear off-hand.

Dad shrugged. 'Didn't used to notice nothing. Only where the next pint was coming from. I just needed a bloody good shake-up to set me right.'

'What, like the fire?'

He nodded. 'Christ, Mary,' he said, 'When I thought I was going to lose my little boy. It was like God was punishing me. Saying, Fred you never paid your family no heed and I'm going to take him back. I never wanted to go back in that second time. It was only you shoutin' an a carryin' on what did it. I was frightened of the fire and of finding him gone. If he'd died,' his voice had sunk to a whisper, 'you'd have blamed me regardless of the rights and wrongs of it. Never would have forgive meself, never.'

Mary couldn't look at him. Instead she stared at Mercy's card, the letters blurring before her eyes.

'Even though I was hurt bad and hardly breathin' I saw the look on your face when I come out the second time without him. Good as said, what's the good of lookin' to him for help. And gal,' he said, his voice breaking up, 'I don't blame you one iota.'

'Dad,' she cried flinging herself into his arms. 'Dad, dad.'

'It's all right my gal,' he said, holding her tight. 'Been a right waster most of me life. No wonder you had no time for me. Served me right. Took a fire to pull me round.'

Mary rested her head on his shoulder. It was ages since she'd sat on his lap. Must have been when she was not much older than Blyth. 'What we gonna do, Dad?' she asked.

He gave a shaky sigh. 'Well, we got to pull ourselves up by our boot straps, as your Granny Ada would say. Let me go from the Home Club, they have. Can't hackle the job no more. Hands ain't up to it, and I forgets things. Thank God for the navy pension and old Albert not nagging me for the rent. But I won't flannel you, things ain't looking good.'

'What d'you reckon you could do?'

Dad shrugged. 'Fetching and carrying, driving a broom around a floor. Hundreds out there wanting the same.'

Mary began to feel frightened. She'd decided to help Nelly on Saturdays and had resigned herself to seeking out some cleaning work. But another anxiety nagged at her. 'They won't split us up, will they? If you don't get nothin' they won't take Blyth?'

'It's not goin' to come to that,' said her father as she got up off his lap. 'We're just treading water, we ain't sinking not by a long chalk. Dora's fetching round a few quid what Harry sent for us.' Course when they get hitched we'll have to say goodbye to his money. It'll get the girls some new shoes. They're walking on cardboard. The soles have give up the ghost. We just got to pull together. Twinnies can do a bit of doorstep scrubbin' and runnin' messsages. Twelve they'll be this May, have to do their share.'

Mary gave a shuddering sigh. 'So we ain't in Queer Street yet?' she said.

'No, ducks, we're just around the corner.' He smiled and drew an envelope out of his pocket. 'All this gloomy talk and I forgot to give you your present.'

Mary opened it up and found a necklace with her name worked in gold-coloured wire.

'You'll have to fasten it yourself,' he said, looking down at his hands.

Mary knew it would fall to pieces in a few weeks and probably leave a green tidemark around her neck. But it didn't matter. Dad had remembered and he'd listened to her and understood the importance she attached to her name. He watched her anxiously as she fastened it in place.

'Happy Birthday, Mary,' he said kissing her on the cheek.

'Thanks, Dad,' she said, kissing him back.

'Hark!' he said his finger to his lips, 'reckon I heard the letterbox rattle, must be more cards for the birthday girl.'

'I had the best ones already,' she said. They sat together while she opened cards from Dora, Mrs Rowan, Lily and her Gran. Then Dad got to his feet and put on his coat.

'I'm going down to the yard to see if they got anything,' he said. 'Be back for dinner. What we got?'

'Stew and dumplings,' said Mary, setting her cards along the mantelpiece. 'More dumplings than stew.'

All the cards reminded her of the letter from Dusty that was still under her pillow. She lay on her bed and reread it for the hundredth time. His handwriting wasn't a patch on hers but he sounded a decent enough bloke.

Dear Mary,

I have heard so much about you from your brother Harry that I can feel I know you already. He says you have a bit of a temper that gets you into trouble. That's what happens to me. I don't mean to fly off the handle but when I think things is unfair I just lose my rag.

There's the Chief Petty Officer who is a proper old woman always breathing down my neck. Waiting for me to put a foot wrong and then he's on me like a ton of bricks.

Still it's not all bad. Your Harry is teaching me boxing and says I could turn into a very useful fighter. My mother won't like that at all. She hates fighting. My Dad and brother were killed in the war and I think she would like to wrap me up in cotton wool. That's why I joined the navy. To have a life of my own and a bit of adventure.

What would be my dream is to work with aeroplanes and to learn to fly. I think the closest I shall get to that will be strapping a kite to my back and jumping off a mountain. What are your dreams?

I don't know much about girls. I never had a sister. Do girls dream of adventure? I'm glad I can write to you before we meet because I am not good at talking with women. I blush and trip over my tongue. I am not much to look at. I am six foot tall and a bit on the skinny side. Anyway I thought I would tell you the worst then if I sound too dreary you can tear up my letter and no harm done.

I hope you will write to me and we can be pals if only on paper.

Yours Hopefully, Matthew.

Mary liked the sound of him. Perhaps she would write; after all she didn't have much else to do.

After a noisy tea-party with jelly and jam tarts, with everyone singing Happy Birthday, Dora and Lily called for her to go to the pictures. Dora lit the paraffin bicycle-lamp and the three of them set off on the tandem. Mary had to stand on the step on the back wheel and rest her hands on Lily's shoulders while Dora sat in front and steered. Her two friends had borrowed Dora's brothers' cycling britches and checked caps and looked like girls from adventure stories.

Dora parked the tandem by tying it to a lamppost, and took off the cycle lamp and blew it out. The two of them treated Mary to a front seat in the dress circle and a bag of sweets. It was a Keystone Cops picture and they sat giggling and munching toffees. They came out of the pictures weak with laughter.

'What next?' asked Dora, as she re-lit the cycle lamp. 'Shall we have a penn'orth of chips between us?'

They whizzed along between trams and other bicycles, singing at the tops of their voices. After swooping around the corner of Edinburgh Road they swept down to the fish shop in Queen Street. Mary went in for the chips and they stood outside laughing and talking.

'Blimey, Mary,' said Dora, 'you put so much salt on, looks like a snow-storm.'

'Here,' said Lily. 'We haven't given you your birthday bumps yet.'

To the amusement of some passing sailors, Lily and Dora took an arm and a leg each and bumped Mary gently up and down on the pavement sixteen times.

'We'll cycle you home,' said Lily to Dora, 'then we'll walk back to Lemon Street together.'

'How will I get me leg over the bar in this skirt?' asked Mary.

'Pull the back through to the front between your legs and safety-pin it to the waist-band. Here, I got one in my pocket,' said Dora handing it to her.

After throwing the chip paper away the three of them clambered back on the tandem and made off. 'Daisy, Daisy give me your answer do,' they chorused as they swooped from side to side.

Mary was having fun. Not something she'd had for ages.

Dora put the tandem in the shed and stood waving to Lily and Mary as they ran back down the road. She stood outside the front door too restless yet to go indoors. Things were working out well. At last she and Mary were on the same side. I'll write and tell Harry, she thought. It will be a change for him to get some good news about his family. She was enjoying her work, too. It was satisfying to get recognition for her skills. Ruby was still sulky about her promotion but seemed to have settled down to a grudging acceptance of her authority. It was nice to have Lily back in the work-room. She hoped that Ruby would soon come out of her sulks. When in the mood she could be very funny and lighten up the tedium of the day. The other afternoon, when Miss Pearson was over at the shop, she'd had them in hysterics demonstrating the tango with Mr Savours.

As she stood there mulling over things in her head Dora became aware that someone was watching her. He was under the lamppost opposite, standing there smoking. She was about to open her handbag and get out her keys when curiousity got the better of her.

'Hello Dora, fancy meeting you.'

It was Bert Finch.

Almost before she'd had a chance to say anything he was across the road and standing beside her. 'What you doing here?' she asked, backing away from him.

'Waiting for you,' he said.

Even in the darkness she knew he was smiling. 'Why? Did you want to frighten me out of my skin? Well you have.' She knew that wasn't true. It was excitement not fear that was making her mouth go dry and the blood rush into her face.

'I'm really sorry, little Dora,' he said in a light teasing tone. 'I saw you earlier but you were with your friends. I didn't want to intrude.'

'So you scared me half out of my wits instead,' she protested. 'I've a good mind to call my father.'

'But you won't,' he said, taking her arm and drawing her into a doorway.

Dora felt on the edge of something. Instinct warned her to draw back. She was engaged to Harry and had no business loitering about after dark with a man she hardly knew.

'I've never forgotten you,' he said. 'At the right place at the right time I was. Saved your life. Doesn't that deserve a little gratitude?'

Standing there in the shadowy doorway she could hardly see Bert Finch. And yet all her senses were alive to him. She could feel his rough uniform coat brushing against her, smell him: the mixture of beer and tobacco and something else. Did desire have a particular scent, she wondered. Could he smell it on her beneath the soap and eau de Cologne.

As she hesitated he dipped his head and kissed her. She was surprised and drew away but he held her firmly by the shoulders. His lips were soft and tasted of salt. When she offered no resistance he ran his tongue over her lips and pressed it persistently between them. They were deep, drenching kisses that made her tremble. 'You know we are going to be lovers,' he whispered against her neck.

Dora tried to shake her head.

'Your body knows it even if your head doesn't.'

'I must go,' she said. 'I can't. I shouldn't. Look Bert, I'm engaged.'

'Where is he then?'

'He's away in the Far East.'

'What do you think he's doing? Sitting on board playing tiddlywinks?'

'I don't know.'

'Well, I think we should meet up again somewhere where you can show me just how grateful you are.'

'I don't know, Bert.'

'I'll meet you by Clarence Pier at five o'clock on Sunday. You'll be there,' he said confidently. 'I can teach you about love Miss Dora, and you are going to be a very willing pupil.'

Once safely indoors, Dora couldn't understand what had possessed her to let Bert Finch kiss her like that. Thank goodness her brothers weren't around and her parents were in bed. There was nobody around to see her flushed cheeks. She paced about the kitchen, even looked out of the window that faced down towards Lennox Row where Bert Finch had gone striding away. It must stop before it began. No she wouldn't go to Clarence Pier. She'd go and see Harry's family. Dora lit the lamp in her bedroom and stood before the mirror looking at her cheeks rubbed red by Bert's beard. She ran her fingers over her lips. How had it happened?

Reflected in the mirror was the little wooden box on her bedside table in which she kept all of Harry's letters to her. She opened the lid and took out the letter that she'd received only that morning and read the last few lines.

My dear Dora with her nut brown eyes and violet scent is waiting for me across the sea. One day we'll have a little home together and be man and wife. That dream keeps me going all these thousands of miles away. When the ship ties up at Farewell Jetty she'll be waiting for me. My dear, true Queen of my Heart.

'Oh Harry, please hurry home,' she whispered before blowing out the candle and settling down to sleep.

Lily's stomach was clenched in anxiety. For two pins she'd run back home. It was guilt that had worn down her resistance when

Heather invited her to join the sewing group at the asylum. Guilt at her unkind judgement of Amy and Charlotte. But why was she keeping it a secret from Gran? She would be pleased to think that Lily was helping to sew things for the hospital fete. She laughed, remembering her words whenever she thought her granddaughter was being selfish.

'If you don't grow up to help other people you're not worth the upbringing.'

At seven o'clock on a January evening Asylum Road seemed long and dark.

Heather was waiting for her at the hospital entrance. She looked so much a part of the place in her long navy cloak and white lace-trimmed cap. 'I'm so glad you came,' she said, taking her arm and shining a torch ahead of them as they crossed the grounds towards one of the large low buildings. 'We're in Weston Villa,' she said. 'Amy's so looking forward to seeing you.'

'I'm surprised she remembers me,' said Lily, beginning to have second thoughts.

'When you never have visitors every little meeting is precious,' said Heather pressing the bell at the villa entrance. 'Don't be anxious because we'll be locked in. It's just so that none of the confused patients wander off and get lost.' She smiled at Lily's doubtful face. 'I remember you were good at sewing and patient and kind to the little ones, at school. That's all you'll need here.'

A large grey-haired woman came and unlocked the door and locked it again behind them. Lily was overcome by the heat and the smell. It was a mixture of carbolic soap, body odour and urine. It frightened her.

Heather took her arm. 'We're through the ward and in the visiting-room.'

The big nurse disappeared behind a screen. 'Come on Pearl, that's it, lift up your arms and let me put on your nightdress.'

Opposite the screen was a woman in a full-size metal cot. She was naked and screaming, 'Bugger, you bugger, bugger, bugger,' at the top of her voice.

Lily gripped Heather's arm.

There was a fire blazing at the end of the ward behind a high brass guard. Beside it in a battered armchair was a little woman, sat tearing up strips of paper and putting them into a cardboard box. She looked up as Lily and Heather passed by. 'Can't stop, got to be done,' she said, as if it were work of great importance.

Lily was overwhelmed. She felt as if she'd been hit by a giant wave and knocked off her feet. This was a world stripped not just of clothes, but dignity, privacy and all the things she took for granted. Let other people deal with these deranged women. People like Heather and the big nurse behind the screens. Always when she was frightened she wanted to take to her heels; to run and run and put a distance between herself and the cause of her fear. But they were locked in.

Heather turned and took her arm. 'Lily, come on, we're through here in the laundry room.'

'I want to go, I must go. Heather it's all too horrible, I can't,' Lily was gabbling and trying to push Heather's arm away.

'Lily I'm so sorry,' said Heather, 'please come and sit down. How stupid of me, I take it all so much for granted. Come on. Amy's waiting for you.'

'I'll just say hello and then . . .' They went into the laundry room; it was clean and cool and quiet. It smelt of starch, and around the walls sheets and blankets were stacked in orderly rows.

'Sit down and get your breath, it's all been a bit of a shock. I'll bring us in some tea and then Amy and the others will be back from supper. Are you feeling better now?'

Lily nodded, unable to reply. She still wanted to run away but not so desperately as before. Slowly her breathing steadied. It would only be an hour or so and then she could go home. Never would she come back again. She'd write to Heather, make some excuse. Having calmed herself she began to look around. On a long table were cotton-reels and pieces of different-coloured cloth. Skeins of raffia, bits of cardboard and a pin-cushion. What would they make, she wondered, what would Amy and the other patients be capable of?

'Take off your coat Lily, and give it to me. I'll hang it up outside. Here, drink this tea, it's hot and sweet.'

Gratefully, she took the cup and sipped the scalding liquid. Someone tapped on the door and her heart leapt with fright.

It was Amy and two other women.

'Hello Lily. I wanted to see you again.' Amy was dressed in a long grey frock with a white collar, covered by an apron. Her face was alight with pleasure and her brown eyes shone. Shyly she held out her hand.

Lily didn't understand the sudden affection that she felt for the woman opposite her. 'I'm pleased to see you, too,' she said, taking Amy's hand. They stood for some moments looking at each other and smiling.

'These are my friends,' said Amy, introducing Lily to her companions. 'Dorcas and Marigold, pretty, pretty names.'

Lily shook their hands. Both the women were plain and nondescript, with grey hair cut too short as if it had been trimmed around a pudding-basin. In contrast Amy, even in the unflattering clothes, looked appealing. Her long hair was caught back off her face with a piece of bandage and her dark eyes were in startling contrast to her pale heart-shaped face.

'Let's all sit down and see what we can make,' said Heather.

'Like this,' said Amy taking up a skein of raffia. 'Yellow, colour of the sun.'

'I could cut out some circles of cardboard and you could wind the raffia around it,' said Heather. 'It would make a mat for a teapot.'

'We can do that,' said Amy, shuffling her chair next to Lily. 'Right, Dorcas and Marigold, there's some pretty pink gingham, we can make some pot-holders. I'll cut them out and show you how to sew them together.'

'Sew together,' echoed Marigold in a gruff voice.

'What's your favourite colour?' asked Amy as she and Lily began to wind the raffia in and out of the cardboard ring.

'I don't know really,' said Lily. 'I like them all for different things.'

'What colour make you feel happy?'

'Red, I think.'

'Warm and rich like Christmas.'

'Yes,' said Lily.

The work progressed slowly with Marigold and Dorcas constantly needing their needles re-threaded. At the end of an hour and a half they had one red-and-yellow teapot stand and half a pot-holder to show for their efforts.

The large nurse reappeared with three cups of hot milk. 'Right, ladies,' she said, 'when you've finished your drinks you're to come back to the ward and get ready for bed.'

Lily and Heather tidied away the sewing projects into a cardboard box. The needles and pins were counted and Heather took charge of the scissors. 'In case of accidents,' she said.

As Lily put on her coat ready to leave, Amy came up to her and kissed her on the cheek. 'Sweet dreams,' she said.

'Sweet dreams to you,' said Lily kissing her back.

Hand-in-hand Dorcas and Marigold shuffled away. 'Sweet dreams,' they said.

As they walked through the door Amy turned and smiled. 'See you again,' she said, 'you promise me?' There was a questioning tone in her voice.

'Don't promise unless you mean it,' said Heather quietly.

The door was opened onto the ward and once more Lily was afraid.

Amy watched her face.

Now the smell from the ward was different, the carbolic was

predominant with another sweet sickly odour that she couldn't identify. Lily tried to swallow down her fear. She smiled at Amy. 'Yes,' she said, 'I promise.'

Amy smiled and waved to her. 'You my friend,' she said.

Lily looked straight ahead of her as she walked back down the ward. The screens were now around the naked woman from earlier on and from behind them came the refrain: 'And bugger, bugger, bugger you.'

Relief speeded her steps as she and Heather left the hospital. 'Those poor women, I had no idea,' she said. 'Where do they all come from?'

'It's a different story with each one,' said Heather. 'Most come from Portsmouth. Some have mental problems following an illness or even childbirth. Loss of memory, alcoholism, inherited problems. Others can come from all over the country. Amy, I don't know where she came from and neither does she. It's not even her real name. It's Amy short for Amnesia. What her name is nobody knows.'

She became serious. 'Listen, Lily, I know seeing them all this evening was a shock. And I'm sorry I'd not prepared you. We do what we can and with more nurses we could do better. For some reason you've become important to Amy. I hope you haven't promised just out of politeness.'

'No,' said Lily, 'I'll be back next week.'

'Good,' said Heather, 'I thought I could rely on you.'

Chapter Twenty-nine

February 15th 1922

Dear Mother,

I am just dashing off a quick note while Alec puts the birthday girl and her brother to bed. It's been a very happy exhausting afternoon with two of Rosie's schoolfriends in to help her celebrate. She was thrilled with the little dress you made and it fits her a treat. The book Lily sent is sure to become a bedtime favourite, thank you both so much.

I feel as if I am losing her just a little, as she is in love with her teacher, Miss Baker. Last week she came home and asked me all about being in a family. She was most upset that you didn't know who your Mummy and Daddy were. 'Did she lose them?' she asked. The idea of an orphanage was quite beyond her understanding.

Alec told her that one day you would tell her all about it and tell little Joseph all about his Granddad Joseph who ran away to sea on a sailing ship. A real family history. What do you think?

Before I forget thank you and Albert and Lily for the cards and presents for Rosie. The dress is lovely, she'll be so proud of the sailor collar.

I do wish we could be with you. Now that Rosie has started school and Alec is busy painting the outside of the pub we don't have a moment to spare.

Much as I miss you all I am feeling really settled here. It's hectic in the summer but in the winter it's lovely and quiet. There are only twenty in Rosie's class and she's coming on so fast.

Joseph is now a sturdy little boy who loves banging things and shouting. At the moment he is busy lining up my pegs into what he calls a 'Puffer tain'.

What with taking Rosie to and fro to school; Alec redecorating and Easter not far off I don't know when we're likely to get to see you. But be sure you're always in our thoughts.

Love to Lily and of course dear Albert,

Lovingly Yours Miriam.

Beattie turned to Albert who was busy with his ledgers sorting out his tenants' rent arrears.

'Why don't we have a day in the Isle of Wight and see Alec and Miriam and the children? It would be a change of scene and do us the world of good.'

'I'm sorry, Beatrice,' he said firmly. 'I must have some time for my painting. It's been sadly neglected of late with all the problems of the fire, attending the inquest, the funeral and now getting all the repairs done. I've not had a moment to myself.'

'Well, I thought . . .' said Beattie huffily.

Albert caught hold of her by the shoulders and looked steadily into her eyes. 'Why don't we both have a day doing what we like and then in the evening we'll go out together for dinner, just the two of us.' He danced her around the room. 'Then we can recapture our first careless rapture,' he said teasingly.

Beattie had to laugh. 'Don't be so whimsical,' she said.

'There's a lot to be done to number nine before it's habitable again: new window-frames top and bottom, and reglazing, the ceilings replastered. I had a letter from Oliver Clifton from Romsey. He wants to come and see me. Says he'll be happy to camp out along there and do a bit of decorating in lieu of rent. What do you think?'

Beattie smiled. 'There's something brewing between him and Ethel. I'm sure of it. But, yes, it sounds a good idea. How d'you think he'd get on with Chippy?'

'Well, Ethel took him with her last time she visited Oliver and they got on well. Of course that leaves Sailor on his own.'

'From what he was saying the other day,' said Beattie, beginning to clear away the breakfast things, 'Chippy's a bit of a mixed blessing. Always talking and he moves things around so that Sailor never knows where anything is and is often falling over bits and pieces that Chippy leaves about.'

'Ideally the three of them in number nine would be the answer. That would get Sailor out of Queenie Wheeler's clutches. The three of them would, I think, be able to pay me a reasonable rent, with Sailor's pension, Chippy back in the dockyard and Oliver maintaining the place.'

'Well, there's one thing,' said Beattie, 'our new neighbours, whoever Queenie was to find, they couldn't be any stranger than Sailor and Dahlia and poor Algie.'

'I wonder where she is, now?' said Albert.

'Who knows,' mused Beattie. 'I don't fancy going to the island on my own. I've rather got out of the way of being on my own. So used to being at everyone's beck and call. I need to find myself a passion like your painting.'

'You've got the answer there,' said Albert tapping the letter in her hands. 'Writing your life story for your children.'

'Do you think so?' she asked doubtfully.

'It's a wonderful tale. Being found on the shore, almost lost before your life was started. A child of the orphanage who learned to read and sew and speak up for herself. What a story you have to tell.'

Beattie smiled. 'I suppose you're right.'

'I know I am,' said Albert. 'There's a verse in the Bible about it.'

'Had enough of the Bible at the orphanage. Killed religion for me.'

'Where is it?' he asked. 'It was in the dresser drawer. Ah! Here we are. Deuteronomy, I think. "Do not forget the things your eyes have seen, nor let them slip from your heart all the days of your life. Rather tell them to your children and your childrens' children."'

'Oh, Albert that's beautiful. Are you sure you haven't just made it up?'

'No, my darling. Even I have not quite that eloquence.' He took a piece of paper from his desk and copied out the words for her. 'Let that be your text for the day,' he said handing the paper to her. 'I'm just calling in to see Sailor,' he added, going into the passage to get his coat, 'then I shall be busy all day with the tenants. I'll get something to eat on The Hard somewhere. You have the whole day before you – enjoy it.'

Beattie sat at the kitchen table thinking of what Albert had said. 'Do not forget what your eyes have seen, nor let them slip from your heart.' The words clicked through her mind like beads on a string. How could she convey to her family what it had been like?

The empty monotony of her childhood. The treadmill days of cleaning, sewing, hymn-singing and prayers. And yet as Albert had said she very nearly had no life at all.

She would be sixty-six in two days' time. If she was going to set about her life story she'd better get a move on. As she washed up and cleared away the breakfast and made the beds her mind was teeming with images. She opened her wardrobe and took out the hat-box. It was crammed with notebooks. The early ones in pencil print with no full stops, even the marks where the lead had broken. Beattie was overwhelmed with remembered pain. She sat on the bedroom floor and wept for the angry little girl with the bitten fingernails and hunger for life. Watching other children with families. Feeling almost branded as an outsider in her rough ill-fitting institution clothing. The lack of everything that she now held precious: closeness to another human being, privacy, colour, music, spontaneity. When she could cry no more she dried her face on her apron and replaced the books inside the hat-box and closed the wardrobe door.

Revisiting her past was going to be a more painful business than she had imagined. It was to pick at scabs and re-open old wounds. And yet, how she had longed to know where she came from. Who her mother was: what fantasies she'd woven around that word. What hopes she'd had of being found. And her father? Was he the dead sailor on the beach or a distant prince or pirate? Questions, questions, questions.

'Gran where are you? I'm starving. What have we got for dinner? Gran, are you all right? What are you doing sitting on the floor?' asked Lily smiling at her.

'Waiting for you to help me up, my duck,' said Beattie, letting her granddaughter pull her to her feet. 'As to dinner, it'll have to be cheese on toast. I'm all at sixes and sevens. Been day-dreaming.'

'What about?' asked Lily as she went down the stairs ahead of her.

'That would be telling,' said Beattie, following her into the kitchen. 'You'll have to wait a while 'til you get to know my secrets.'

Chapter Thirty

Dora woke on Easter Sunday with a sick feeling of dread. Did Lily really believe that she was going on a promised trip with her parents? She'd told Mum and Dad she was meeting Lily. Since that first Sunday meeting with Bert Finch in the deserted sports pavilion her life had ceased to be her own. Never had she told so many lies. It wasn't as if she even liked him. She wrote letters saying that the friendship was all wrong and she never wanted to see him again. But they were never posted. Then, full of self-disgust, she would sneak out again to meet him.

He had become, as he'd predicted, her lover. Dora could not believe how green and foolish she'd been, that first time. Even as they'd crept into the deserted changing-rooms she had thought it possible to leave again without giving in to his persuasion. But she had underestimated her own appetite once it had been aroused. He held her face in his hands while he kissed her forehead, her eyebrows, her lips. Tender, sipping kisses that made her tremble. His blue eyes searched hers holding her in thrall. She felt like a small animal irresistibly drawn to a hunter's lure. With teasing slowness his hands unbuttoned her coat and stole beneath the folds of her camisole. She had gasped with pleasure as he helped her out of her clothes and ran his hands over her body. He would rouse her to an unbearable pitch of longing, stroking and kissing her. Then he would enter her and they would climb together faster and faster until she cried out in ecstasy. He would hold her until her breathing steadied and she was sated.

The excitement alternated with shame and terror. What if anyone found out? What if she became pregnant? The open kindly Dora was constantly on the run from the greedy, lying Dora of those snatched meetings with Bert Finch. She yearned to have her life back as it had been with her work and family and friends, open, happy and uncomplicated.

'We'd promised ourselves a trip out over the hill,' Lily had said, crossly. 'I told Aunt Hester I'd bring her back some primrose plants. Gran's made us some seed cake and there's even your favourite blackberry jam left for sandwiches and ginger beer. Oh, Dora I could shake you.'

'You can still have the tandem. Take Mary,' Dora had suggested.

'What would I want to do that for? She's a kid. You're my friend or I thought you were.'

'We'll go out on the Saturday evening,' said Dora, desperate to avoid an argument. Lily was so sharp it wouldn't be long before she found out she was being lied to.

And then there was Harry. His letters lately had been so full of affection and plans for the future, which shamed her. Lately she'd been feeling the same panic and despair that had over-whelmed her on the beach last summer. But even that escape was denied her. She was terrified of death, knowing that she was full of wickedness and would burn in hell.

Tears formed in her eyes as she stood barefoot at the sink filling the kettle. She had been feeling so happy with herself, so purposeful and confident. If only Bert could be sent away somewhere. She knew she hadn't the strength of will to end it. The thought of not seeing him again, not touching him, plunged her into despair. If only she could pray but she couldn't get her thoughts to stay still long enough. She was on a mad merry-go-round and could find no way of stopping it.

Later she stood at the Town Hall waiting for the bus to Portsdown Hill; she looked anxiously around her not wanting to be seen. They had decided to meet up at the tea rooms at the top of the hill and walk into the fields beyond. Bert had suggested she catch the nine o'clock bus before the crowds gathered wanting to go up to the Easter Fair. No, she could not go to the Fair with Bert. It was there two years ago that she had gone with Harry. It was at the Easter Fair that he had proposed to her.

He was waiting for her, a tall blond soldier, helping her from the bus. She took his hand and followed him into the tea-room gardens. Tomorrow she'd think about Harry and Lily. Tomorrow, she promised herself.

Mary's face lit up at the invitation. 'That'd be champion,' she said. 'Dad's taking the kids up the Fair. What time?'

'About ten-thirty,' said Lily, 'see you in the morning.' Well, she thought sourly at least someone is happy with the arrangements.

'Can I have a picnic for tomorrow?' she asked Gran.

'Course you can, my duck, whe're you off to?

'I'm going on the tandem to Stake's Wood with Mary. I'll try and bring Aunt Hester back some primrose plants.'

'I didn't think you were that pally with Mary,' said Gran, giving her one of her searching looks.

'I'm not really,' said Lily. 'It just that every time I make plans with Dora, lately, she makes some excuse.'

Gran frowned. 'That's not like young Dora to let you down. You'll have to seek her out and have a proper sort-out between you. Go around to her house. I thought she was looking a bit peaky lately.'

'Who'll be at the front doing the steering?' asked Mary the

next morning, as Lily tied a bulging shopping-bag onto the carrier behind the saddle.

'I'll start us off and then we can take turns. We'll probably have to walk up the hill.'

'Or stand up on the pedals,' suggested Mary.

'You'd better put this ginger beer wedged up right in the basket, with this bit of blanket. You don't want any explosions,' said Gran. 'Better safety-pin your skirts around the front. Don't want to catch them in the spokes. Albert, will you check the tyres and the chain? And, Lily take the pump with you. It's a hefty stride back from the hill if the tyres go flat.'

'I'll give you the bus fares home just in case,' said Uncle Albert. 'You can leave the tandem at Cosham Station if necessary.'

Lily set her straw boater on her head and took her place at the front after Uncle Albert was satisfied that they were road-worthy.

'Bye,' called Mary, after they'd had a practice ride up and down the street.

'Bye.'

It was a long ride out of the town through Copnor and Hilsea. At Cosham they got off and pushed the bike through the railway level-crossing and on up the High Street. People were swarming up the hill urged on by the sound of the fairground hurdy-gurdy.

'Let's try cycling up there,' said Mary. 'I go on the front.'

'Let's have some ginger beer first,' said Lily, feeling hot and thirsty.

'Ready?' asked Mary, handing back the bottle and wiping her mouth with the back of her hand.

'You sure you want to be on the front?' asked Lily. 'It'll be ever so hard to push the pedals up the hill.'

'I'll stand up,' said Mary confidently.

After a shaky start they wobbled on, both of them standing in the pedals. A tram rushed past very close nearly driving them into the kerb. Lily felt the sweat break out on her face as they cycled on. Her muscles ached with the effort of keeping going. At the top they stopped.

Mary turned around, her face red and shiny with sweat. 'Cycle down the other side?' she gasped.

Breathless, Lily nodded.

'Whee,' they cried as they sat back on the saddles and swooped down the long slope past Widley church.

They turned down Crookhorn Lane away from the main road and pushed the bike across a field full of green shoots.

'What d'you reckon that is?' asked Mary, looking about her.

'I'm not very good with plants,' answered Lily. 'Could be wheat or barley.'

'Ain't half hungry. What time is it?'

'Must be nearly twelve. We didn't set off 'til half-past ten and I should think it took us a good hour to get here.'

'My guts is rumbling,' said Mary. 'Let's untie the bag and stick the bike in the hedge. Then we can climb over the stile into the next field.'

'The other side of that is the woods.'

'Ain't never been in the country,' said Mary. 'Feels funny with no houses and people and nothing.'

Lily shut the gate behind them and they walked into Stake's Wood.

Mary looked fearfully around her. 'It's all cool and quiet like in church. Boo!' she shouted and a couple of pigeons rose up suddenly in front of her and flew up into the trees. Mary leapt back in fright. 'Made me jump they did.'

'Let's sit on that fallen tree trunk. It's too wet on the ground,' said Lily, spreading out the bit of blanket that Gran had given them over the log before unpacking the picnic.

Nothing more was said as they cracked the egg shells against a stone and sprinkled salt into the eggs. Steadily they ate their way through blackberry-jam sandwiches, seed cake and a couple of ginger-snap biscuits.

'Better save a couple for the return journey and some of the ginger beer for when we climb back up the hill.'

'Country's not half bad,' declared Mary, 'I'm going to have a scout around.' She brushed the crumbs from her crumpled blouse and set off further into the wood.

'Don't get yourself lost,' said Lily, 'I don't want to push that bike back on my own.' She yawned drowsily. 'If you see any clumps of primroses let me know.'

'Right you are,' called back Mary, striking into the middle of the wood.

After packing up the remains of the picnic Lily settled herself on the ground and leaned back against the fallen tree trunk and closed her eyes. The sun filtered through the trees and dappled her face. A light April breeze riffled through the wood and she fancied that she heard tiny scurryings amid the ferns and undergrowth. The air was fresh and spicy. She dozed contentedly, weary after the ride from Portsea and pleasantly full. It was a pity that Dora hadn't come, there was so much they would have talked about but Mary was proving a better companion than she'd expected. She wasn't half as prickly as she used to be. Was it because she was growing up or because she and Dora were being nice to her? She closed her eyes and dozed with the sun warm on her face. Although it had seemed silent at first, the wood was full of little scurrying sounds, water trickling and the call of birds.

'Where are ya Lily?'

The voice startled her. She awoke to the sound of someone crashing through the undergrowth towards her. 'Here, over here,' she called.

'Found you some primmies bit further on,' shouted Mary. 'What ya got to dig 'em up with?'

'There's a little spanner in the tool-kit on the back of the tandem.'

'That's two fields away.'

Lily felt in her skirt pocket and pulled out a nail-file. 'This might do,' she called out, waving it in her hand. She hurried towards Mary's retreating figure.

In a dip of the ground beneath a silver birch tree they found a a large clump of primroses. Lily bent and dipped her face into their creamy petals. 'They smell all woody and fresh,' she said, digging around the base of a couple of plants. With a bit more digging and gentle tugging they came away from the rich black soil. 'Better put them in the sandwich bag,' she said.

'Sshh,' said Mary 'look, there's a robin over there.'

They watched the little bright-eyed bird hopping along the top bar of a gate leading out of the wood.

'Just gonna find somewhere to have a wee,' said Mary, climbing over the gate and pushing her way through the hedge.

Lily took advantage of Mary's absence to duck down behind a tree. She was just smoothing down her skirt when Mary reappeared, her face flushed with excitement.

'Just found a little hut. Let's go and look inside.'

Lily wedged the primroses and the bag in a bush before hurrying after her.

It was a very rough shed made of logs. There was a door fastened with a peg and string. It had a tiny cobwebby window in the side. Mary went towards the door.

Lily pulled her away, whispering urgently. 'Might be a big dog inside.'

'That window's too high up,' Mary whispered back. 'Look down there, that knot-hole, we could peep through there.'

They knelt in some wet grass and Mary was the first to peer into the shed.

'It's a bit dark,' she whispered. Then she pinched Lily's arm in excitement. 'Two people in there getting all spoony with each other. Blimey they got no clothes on.' She moved aside for Lily to take a look.

There were two figures lying on a blanket on the floor of the hut. It was a shock being so close to them. Watching the tangle of naked limbs Lily felt a mixture of curiosity and shame. She wanted to look away but something kept her eye to the wall. The man turned his head and whispered something to the woman. He stretched out his hand and picked up a saucer with a lighted candle-stub in it, moving it to a safer distance. In that moment Lily had a clear view of his distinctive blond hair and the army jacket on the floor. Startled she moved away and in so doing she knelt in a bed of stinging-nettles.

Eagerly Mary took her place.

'We must go back,' whispered Lily, rubbing her stinging knees. 'That man's a soldier, he could turn nasty. I'm going back to the wood,' she said. 'Do what you like but I'm off.' She ran back across the field, her heart pounding. Her knees were burning and she was close to tears. What she had seen through the gap in the wall disturbed her. The couple were like two animals in their writhing and groaning. But was she any better spying on them? Lily felt soiled by the incident. She had glimpsed only the side view of the soldier but it was enough to recognise him as Bert Finch.

The day was spoilt. She wanted to cycle away as fast as she could – but for that she needed Mary.

Mary continued to stare through the knot-hole. The man had now climbed astride the woman and she had twined her legs around his waist. From her position at the window Mary was looking over the man's shoulder directly at the woman. She raised her head to kiss the man and her hair fell back from her face. It was Dora.

Mary felt as if she'd been punched in the stomach. Jesus Christ! Our Harry's Dora. What should she do? Her first thought was to rush in there and shout and scream and kick.

Call her all the dirty names under the sun. Harry's Dora! Pure gold, he'd called her. Spoke about her as if she was the bloomin' Virgin Mary. If she rushed in that bloke might give her a good hiding. She stood there chewing her hand trying to get her breathing to slow down. Should she tell Lily? No, they were as thick as thieves. Lily might even know about this other bloke. Besides she knew Mary didn't like Dora. She started to cry, great gulping sobs. It wasn't true about not liking Dora. She'd just begun to trust her. The three of them had had that trip to the pictures on her birthday. They'd sat there in the dark laughing and eating toffees like real pals. Dora had ruined everything.

Mary pulled her blouse free of the waistband of her skirt and wiped her eyes. No, she wouldn't tell Lily. She'd just say as she had a headache and wanted to go home.

'Perhaps you've had too much of the sun,' said Lily, full of concern. 'Here, have the last of the ginger beer. Shall we leave the tandem at the station and get the tram home?'

'No, I'll be all right,' said Mary. 'Only I'll sit on the back and p'raps we'll walk up to the top of the hill.'

Lily didn't seem at all disappointed at leaving early. Could she have recognised Dora, Mary wondered. She shrugged her shoulders and helped Lily tie the bag behind her saddle. The ride home would give her a chance to think what she was going to do with this powerful information. It was a long ride back to the hill and neither of them had the energy to pedal up it. Even walking up and pushing the tandem with the sun in their faces was hard going.

As they free-wheeled down the other side they saw the crowds still pouring up to the Easter Fair. She wished, now, that she had gone with Dad and the nippers. At least she might have won a coconut, she thought sourly.

'Come in and have a cup of tea,' said Lily when at last they cycled into Lemon Street. 'I'm looking forward to lying down. My legs are like lead.'

'Your Gran there?' asked Mary. She liked Lily's Gran. She could talk to her. Didn't lay down the law or go blurting out things what you told her. Listened as if what you said was important. She sniffed hard, feeling the tears coming. What she would like would be to sit on Gran's lap like she'd done when Mum got took to the Asylum. She'd felt safe there. Impatiently she rubbed her hand across her nose. Wasn't a bleedin' kid any more. Have to sort it out on her own.

'No,' said Lily, 'she and Uncle Albert have gone along the sea-front to meet up with Auntie Hester and Uncle George. Won't be back for ages.'

'Think I'll go indoors for a bit,' she muttered, 'ta for the outing. See ya later.'

Throwing her hat into a corner of the room she dragged off her boots and lay on top of her bed. Feeling cold she took the blanket from Blyth's bed and covered herself. It smelled of him, grubby and biscuity.

She was startled by a tap on her door.

'What ya want?' she called out.

'It's yer old Dad.'

'What you doin' home? Thought you was takin' the nippers up the fair.'

'Ethel and that Oliver Clifton have took them along with Sailor and Chippy,' said Dad sitting on the end of the bed. 'Proper firm's outing.' He laughed. 'You needn't give me that beady look. I've not been on the booze. Took back all them bottles in the shed and they got half-a-crown to spend.'

Mary looked at him. He was in an old grey jumper and flannels and looked decidedly sober.

'How come you're back early?'

'Got an 'eadache.'

Dad leaned forward and pushed her hair away from her face. 'Looks like you been crying. What's up, me tater?'

The use of her childhood nickname brought on the tears.

Dad cuddled her up to him and sat there until the tears were done.

'It's that Dora,' she burst out. 'I seen her with this other bloke. They was all spoony together.'

'Where was this?' asked Dad, taking out a packet of cigarettes and matches from his pocket.

'In this hut in the woods. They didn't 'ave no clothes on or nothink.'

'That's real spoony,' said Dad. 'How d'ya know it was Dora?'

'We was looking through this knot-hole and this bloke was on top of her and it was like we was lookin' over his shoulder. She leans up to him and her hair falls away from her face and I seen her. Dora all right.'

Dad blew a reflective smoke-ring. 'Must have been a bit of a shock.'

'Well, she needn't think she's got away with it I shall write to Harry and . . .'

'Hold your horses, who says it's any of your business?'

'Well it is. Harry's my brother and she's being a deceivin' mare.'

'What d'you think your brother's going to do when he gets your letter?'

'He'll tell her to sling her hook.'

'And how will he feel about you telling him?'

'Well, well . . .' Mary began to struggle.

'Think he's goin' to write and say thanks very much?'

'Well er no, but . . .'

'First he won't believe you. He knows you're jealous. And if he does he'll hate you for it.'

'But she's, she's—'

'Don't matter what she is, my tater. I know it's hard but you got to keep your nose well out.'

'Well we gotta do somethin'.'

'How about you write that letter and Dora finishes with this chap? By the time he gets your letter everything could change. And there's somethin' else you're not taking into account.'

'What's that?'

'How d'you know what your sainted Harry bin up to out East?'

'What d'ya mean?'

'Lots of temptation for a young lad. Young chinky girls comes on board to do the washing and sewing. Sometimes sets up ashore with the lad, becomes his sea-wife so to speak.'

'Did you have a sea-wife?'

'If you're not careful you'll put your nose in one too many knot-holes, my girl, and somebody will chop it off.'

'But Dad—'

'Look, here's what we're going to do. I'm going to make us a nice cuppa and that Ethel sent over some ginger cake. I'll say no more. You're free to do what you like, me tater, but if you take the advice of an old sailor you'll keep well out of it.'

Mary sat on the edge of the bed chewing her hand. Okay, so she wouldn't write to Harry but that didn't stop her sending a letter to Matthew.

Chapter Thirty-one

'June already,' said Beattie, putting down the Sunday paper beside her deckchair, 'How the year has flown. I can't believe that Lily will be eighteen tomorrow. Another twelve months and Michael and Harry will be back.'

Albert turned from watching some children building sand-castles and said, 'She is quite the young lady now, isn't she?'

'Yes,' said Beattie, sighing to herself. 'And if that little ivory ring on her left hand is anything to go by she won't be with us for much longer.'

'Shall you mind? Michael seems an admirable young man. Ambitious too. A petty officer at twenty-four is very good going.'

Beattie wrinkled her forehead. 'She's had so little experience of life, Albert. Michael has been her only sweetheart and most of their courtship has been from opposite ends of the world.' She scooped up a handful of shingle and sifted it through her fingers. Never any pretty shells in Pompey, she thought, just these boring ones like old toenails.

'There's a lot to be learnt from a letter. One confides to paper what one fears to say. You must know that.'

'I agree with you. But a young woman changes so much between sixteen and eighteen. Lily lives so much in her imagination.'

'If you look back over the time that the two of them have been apart she's dealt with some harsh reality in these last two years. She and Dora coped magnificently with Dolly Vine's death. They supported the family, saw the body brought home and Dora attended the funeral.'

'Don't forget it was the Vines that nearly pushed her over the edge or under the water so to speak.'

'Lily rose to that occasion, too' said Albert, 'brought the children safely home and was a tower of strength to Dora.'

'It's all such a gamble isn't it, child-rearing? You try to give them the set of beliefs that you have found of value and then they bump up against friends and colleagues who view life so differently. And you never know from where or when the tests are coming. But you're right, Albert, of course you are. She's a granddaughter to be proud of.' She smiled at him. His face was growing pink in the afternoon sun and if they didn't shift themselves soon he'd have a nose like a ripe strawberry. 'There's the fire as well. And being taken down a peg or two over the Epaulette Room business.'

'I think she has matured a lot and all credit goes to your early teaching, my dear,' said Albert, kissing her hand.

'They're good girls all three of them,' said Beattie, squeezing his hand in return. 'Poor little Mary. I hope there's something really good in store for her. What a battler she is. Thank God Fred seems to have pulled himself together. For the first time that family has some chance of survival. Doing well with the toy stall. Last time I was at the market Nelly Moyes seemed very pleased with her. What with Sailor and Chippy and Oliver Clifton settled in number nine everyone seems to have turned the corner.'

'I was touched when they invited us in for tea,' said Albert.

'That bread,' laughed Beattie, 'cut like a children's slide. An inch at one end down to almost nothing, and tea, you could have varnished a table with it.'

'Perhaps it was varnish,' said Albert. 'Oliver is so good to Sailor – putting rails everywhere so he can find his way around. He's a born leader, got that little household running like clockwork. Wants to get Fred roped in somewhere now his hands are getting better. Just need a bit more work.' He chuckled. 'D'you know what they're going to call themselves?'

'I haven't the faintest idea,' said Beattie, dropping the shells back on the beach.

'The Lemon Street Volunteers,' laughed Albert. 'Want me to find them a shed to keep their hand-cart and paint-pots in. Goodness knows what part Sailor plays in all this. I think it's pushing the cart and standing guard over it.' He took Beattie's hand and kissed it. 'And now that we've reviewed our friends and neighbours how about those newly-weds in number twenty-five? Do you think they'll stay the course?'

'I think so,' said Beattie reaching out and taking his hand.

'You don't regret giving up your independence, do you?' he asked her.

'Not one jot,' she said firmly. 'Just wish I'd said yes sooner.'

'So do I,' he said winking at her. 'All those Sunday mornings we've missed.'

'That's been such a surprise and a delight of course,' she said, blushing under his teasing look. 'I thought once you got to our age it all faded away.'

'And how have you found sex at sixty, Mrs Pragnell?'

'Slower and more affectionate,' she said. 'Savouring instead of grabbing. Wanting to give pleasure as well as receive. Not always having to complete the journey. Having nothing to prove and yes, seeing the ridiculous as well as the sublime.'

'I hope you'll put that in your family memoirs,' he said, taking her hand and pulling her up out of the deckchair and into his arms. As they kissed each other before leaving the beach they were cheered by a couple of young sailors.

'Good for you, granddad,' one of them said cheekily.

Albert waved his straw boater in acknowledgement.

They walked arm-in-arm along the promenade towards Clarence Pier past day-trippers and giggling girls eyeing young sailors. Beattie thought about her recent obsession, the writing of her life story for her grandchildren. At first it had seemed rather stilted and factual rather than about her feelings but now, after several scrapped attempts, she had found her voice. Re-examining the past was painful but also surprising. She was amazed at her own daring. How old was she when she had written: *'I am not just a thing I am a girl, I am Beatrice?'* Or the line stabbed through the paper with the force of her temper: *'I will reed no won will stop me!!!'*.

And now, she was coming towards the end of her life. At sixty-seven she had what? Another ten to fifteen years at most. How many more sunsets was that, she wondered looking at the apricot streaks in the sky. How many springs and autumns, how many tender moments of lovemaking. Would she live to see Lily married with a child in her arms? Would Dora find happiness with Harry and would little Mary meet someone to love her as she deserved?

And as for Albert? How very fortunate she'd been that he had waited for her. Little had she known when Joseph died, and the future had looked so bleak, what Albert would come to mean to her. He had been her friend for so many years and she had been content with that. Now he was so very much more to her. More she realised than Joseph, her first love, could ever have been. It was good that he had been the husband of her early years. He was all noise and passion, quick-tempered and proud of his in-exhaustible strength. How beautiful he had been with his wild red hair and blue eyes. He had only to look at her and she desired him, quivered to have him touch her.

She had treasured his letters bringing the world through the letterbox. The smells and colours of the East, the searing cold of Alaska, the baffling customs of other peoples and his observations about life on board with his mess-mates. His anxiety to know how young Alec was faring and his tender solicitude for herself. Oh Joseph, she sighed I wouldn't have missed you for the world.

But how would he have weathered the challenges of old age? Someone so proud of his strength and beauty. So sensitive to the slightest suggestion that he was less energetic, less handsome and less responsive than the image he had of himself.

'My darling where were you?' asked Albert nudging her arm. 'You looked to be in seventh heaven.'

Beattie smiled. 'Far, far away,' she answered. 'You know that I was a foundling.'

'Yes and very glad I am that you were found.'

'So am I,' she laughed. 'I could have very easily been a lostling and missed everything.'

Chapter Thirty-two

She was not pregnant after all. Dora was almost crying with relief as she took one of her monthly squares out of her dressing-table drawer. This was the time to finish with Bert before she was tempted again. Why did she keep seeing him? All that lying and letting people down. She felt awful about Lily's birthday: she'd completely forgotten about it. Well, she was meeting Bert in an hour's time. She would tell him straight away then go around to Lemon Street with a present.

Lily suspected something and Mary had been funny with her lately, just as they had begun to be friends. She nearly died when Lily said that they'd been peering at them in the shed. Thank goodness she'd only seen Bert. But what had Mary seen? She wouldn't put it past her to write to Harry.

Those moments with Bert hidden away in the woods had been the most tender of their whole affair. He had kissed every part of her, even the soles of her feet. She had cried at his gentleness and he had held her like a child. But then, the moment she had stepped outside, she was overwhelmed with regret. She remembered the time in the shepherd's hut with Harry, his fumbling passion and now her betrayal.

Dora brushed her hair and a pale guilty face looked back at her from the mirror. All the hiding and scheming was sapping her energy. It was like last year when she was tearing around trying to please everyone. Now she pleased no one, not even herself.

If she were honest she didn't even like Bert. He was coarse and deceitful. She didn't like what she became when she was with him. It was hard to recognise the greedy reckless Dora as herself. But he roused her to an almost unbearable pitch of excitement with his kissing and stroking. The awakening of her body seemed to be at the expense of some other part of herself. It was as if she were exchanging gold for tin, enticed by the temporary glitter.

Always there was the danger of discovery. They no longer met at the sports pavilion as they had in the winter. It was occupied most evenings by the naval cricket teams. They'd hidden under the railway arch down by the harbour but it was cold and dark and smelt of dogs. Tonight, the very time that she had decided to finish everything, he had managed to borrow a sergeant's house for an hour or so while he and his wife were visiting relations.

'We'll have a proper bed. Never loved you in a bed have I?' he'd said. 'Made for bedding, you are.' Bert had laughed, making her feel suddenly cheap and worthless.

All the things she took pride in: her job as tailoring forewoman; her engagement to Harry; her role as Auntie Dora to little Blyth, were of no consequence.

Bert would be sulky when he found out that she had the curse. He expected her to be always available. That sulkiness would be to her advantage – it made him less attractive to her. But she was disappointed too. It would have been wonderful to make love for the last time in the privacy of a proper house. Just for the last time.

In her pocket was a letter from Harry. The envelope felt like a leaden weight of reproach. Dear Harry who loved her and wanted only what was good for her. She paused at the deserted bus-stop at The Hard and took out the letter. She tried to draw strength from it, still hoping to turn back or to go forward and end things with Bert.

March 17th 1921

My Darling Dora,

Not long now and we'll have only a year left out here. How I miss you.

What a shock to here about the fire at Chippy's house. I went away on to the beach here and had a good cry when I thought of nearly losing little Blyth. Fancy our Dad being the hero? I have written to him. It feels as if a big weight has dropped off me hearing about him looking after the kids at last. I didn't like hating him Dora and it's such a relief to know that at last he's pulling himself together. Sad about his hands I hope he will get the movement back. You know he was wonderful with ropework could tie knots at the speed of light.

I'm really proud of you getting promotion my sweetheart. That makes two of us. I shall be made up to Leading Seaman by the end of the month. You haven't really said how you feel about living in Gosport and me going into submarines. I know there have been accidents but they're getting safer all the time. I know that it's a year after I get back that I'll qualify for Marriage Allowance. But I don't want to wait. Let's get married straight away and get on with our lives.

You know I daydream about walking home from the base at Dolphin to you in a little house, waiting there with my tea all ready. I would kiss your sweet face then close the door and shut the world away.

Dora began to cry. Ruined, everything was ruined. Gasping and sniffing she held her handkerchief to her face. For a few paces she turned back towards the dockyard gate. No, if she was going to finish with Bert she must do it properly. I want to go back to the simple, even boring routine of writing to Harry, seeing his family and Lily, she thought as she put the letter back in her bag. I'm being destroyed by all this lying.

Her steps had now reached the end of the High Street in Old Portsmouth and she carefully looked away from the curious glances of the groups of soldiers leaving the Point Barracks for a night of liberty. Around the corner in Broad Street she looked at the neat row of sergeants' quarters, looking for Bert's face at any of the windows.

'You know Lance-Corporal Finch?'

Startled, Dora turned to look at the woman who was clutching at her arm. She was poorly dressed. The straw hat was broken and her black jacket was shiny with age. Her long skirt was frayed at the hem and one of her shoes had a flapping sole.

'Well, I don't know. I . . .'

'Either you knows him or you don't,' challenged the woman.

'Ma, I'm hungry,' whined a little girl holding on to the woman's skirt.

'Once we finds your Dad we'll be able to get some grub down ya,' said the woman, glaring at Dora.

From the corner of her eye Dora saw Bert duck down beneath one of the windows opposite.

'You could ask at the soldiers' quarters over there,' she pointed towards the barracks, away from Bert on the other side of the street.

'Right, come on Bessie, we'll run your Dad to earth and he can give us one of his fairy stories about why he hasn't been home lately. That's after he's parted with some money.'

'I seed him in that window over there,' the child said, 'he was waving to the lady.'

'Did you be God?' snapped the woman. She glared at Dora.

The little girl had let go of her mother's skirt and was running over to the house where she'd seen her father.

'You his latest tart, then?' challenged the woman, her face uncomfortably close.

'Well, no I thought I was his . . . I didn't know about . . .' answered Dora miserably.

'Thought don't come into it with Bert, it's all fucking with him.'

The word hit her with the force of a slap.

'I asked you a question. You his latest tart?'

Dora nodded unhappily, looking down at the pavement.

'Well,' said the woman, pinching her arm. 'I'm Mrs Finch and I think I'm due some compensation. I been on short rations with his brats, while he been lining your purse.'

'But I never knew,' mumbled Dora. 'He didn't give me any money he . . .'

'Fucked you for nothing. Silly cow.'

The word stripped her of any dignity. Tore away all the romance, making her feel cheap and tawdry. She tried to run but the woman had hold of her arm.

Perhaps money would get her to loosen her arm. Acutely aware that they were the subject of interest by the passing soldiers, Dora fumbled in her bag. 'You'll have to let go. I need both hands to get at my purse.'

'I'll get it for you,' said Mrs Finch, letting go of her arm and quickly dipping her hand into Dora's bag. She emptied the coins into the pocket of her skirt then flung the purse onto the ground.

'And here's something for you, dearie,' said the woman, as Dora straightened up from picking up her purse. She drew back her arm and swung at her punching her in the face, knocking her to the ground.

Dora staggered to her feet as Bert and the child came out of the house.

Stepping around her as if she were a stray animal, Bert grabbed his wife by the shoulder and shook her roughly. 'Sall.

You're making a show of me,' he snarled. 'Come inside with the kid. Leave her, she don't mean nothin'.'

With her nose bleeding and tears streaming down her face Dora hurtled across the street through the Sally Port Gate and on to the beach. She sat there with her arms around herself, blood dripping onto her skirt, wanting to sink beneath the shingle. Wanting to feel and be nothing.

May 1st 1922

Dear Mary,

I am writing off straight away to explain why I can't do what you asked me. You must be wild at what your Harry's girl has done but I can't do nothin. More than my life's worth. Telling your brother what happened would be butting into his private life. Blimey Mary he'd have my head off me shoulders. I am the youngest in the mess still serving Boy's Time. I have to look lively, do my job right and not fall out with anyone.

You're Harry's been good to me. Training me up for the Boxing Tournament and helping me with arithmatic. I am going to tear up your letter in case it falls into the wrong hands. There's more than a year to go before we gets back to Pompey by that time things could have sorted themselves out with that Dora girl.

Anyway I want to thank you for writing to me and go on to the rest of your letter. You seem to be a girl with a lot of ideas. This toy stall in the market is a good start for you. It must give you a chuck up to see the nippers wanting bits and pieces what you have made yourself. You will see I have sent you a couple of flicker books that might go down well with the kids. I got one off a stall in Singapore and took it to pieces and worked out how it was done. It's just lots of little drawings, with very tiny changes, from one to the other, then when you flick the pages the figures seem to move. I have sent you one with the man in the rickshaw and the other with two boxers. If you think they're any good you

*could try some out yourself. I will send you some more with my
next letter. If I get anymore ideas I'll pass them on.*

*You asked me what was my big dream in life. Well I would
like to fly an aeroplane. What about you? Most girls seem to
dream about weddings and babys but I think you are wanting a
bit of adventure before settling down.*

Please write again soon.

Your Pal Dusty.

Mary smiled to herself. Dusty sounded as if he'd make a good pal
and she liked the bit about her being an adventurous girl. And he
was right about the marriage bit. Bloomin' slavery that was. At
first she was aggravated that he wasn't going to do anything
about Dora but she'd no wish to get him into trouble. And as
Dad said, Harry would hardly be grateful for the news.

Anyway things were looking up in the market. She was
working with Nelly on Fridays as well as Saturdays and her bits
and pieces, as Dusty put it, were going down a treat with the
kids. She was now getting half-a-crown a week and an extra
shilling for glue and paper and such like for her 'materials of
trade' as Nelly called them.

Dad was busy with Sergeant Clifton with his decorating
outfit. His hands was getting better and he'd only been pie-eyed
once since the fire. Even the twins were stirring themselves,
out washing doorsteps on Saturday mornings. Perhaps Faith
would help her to make some flicker books. Mercy's drawing
wasn't so good and she didn't want to sit still for more than five
minutes.

Thinking of drawing reminded her of the card they'd put
together for Lily's birthday. She'd run it along now, might even
get a bit of cake.

'What you doing?' asked Blyth, wandering into the room. 'I
wants to play wiv the boys in Cross Street, they got a cart and
stuff.'

'How about us taking this card what we made along to Lily? It's her birthday.'

'They give us cake and lemonade?'

She looked at the hopeful expression in her brother's eyes. 'You got hollow legs,' she said, giving him a hug.

'Gerroff,' he protested, an expression of disgust on his face. 'That's soppy girl's stuff.'

Mary missed his old impulsive bursts of affection. Since being at school for the last year he was eager to be tough and boyish. Only at night when he'd had a dream about the fire would he let her hold him. Still, she reasoned, he'd be six next month, her baby brother no longer.

'Come on then,' she said spitting on her hankie and rubbing the dirt off his face. 'We'll go and see what they got.'

'She's gone around to Dora's,' said Gran when they knocked on her door.

'Can we come in and sing Happy Birthday to you?' asked Blyth hopefully.

'Would we like Blyth to come in and sing to us?' she said to Mr Pragnell who was standing behind her in the passage.

'All right, old chap,' he said, 'come and sing for your supper, and Mary you're welcome, too.'

All Lily's anger at Dora vanished as the woman punched her in the face. For a moment she was frozen with shock. She had followed her with increasing anger and bewilderment all the way from Unicorn Gate but had never expected to see her friend caught up in such a scene.

Lily rushed through the Sally Port on to the beach. 'Dora, Dora, no please, please don't cry. Here give me your hankie, I'll dip it in the water.'

She was crying too as she ran down over the shingle to the water's edge. 'Please, take your hands away. Let me look.' Dora's nose was red and swollen. Lily dabbed the trickle of blood away and then concentrated on the skirt. 'It'll have to be soaked in cold water when you get home.'

Dora covered her face with her hands, again, and was continuing to cry. 'Ca – can't go home like this. Can't go anywhere.' She had pressed herself into a corner formed by the Round Tower joining the old town wall. The beach was dotted with people: fishermen, soldiers, children lobbing stones into the water. Lily was anxious to get her away from them and back home to Gran. She'd know what was best to do.

'Look you can come home with me,' she said, kneeling on the stones and taking hold of Dora hands. 'Your Mum thinks you're with me anyway. Stay the night. Uncle Albert will drop a message round.'

'So ashamed,' Dora gasped. 'Bad, bad, bad.'

Lily held her, rocking her in her arms. She didn't know what to say. The scene in Broad Street had shocked her. Women fighting in the street like . . . Her brain slid away from the word whore. But Bert Finch's wife, if that awful creature was really Mrs Finch, had called Dora his tart. And Dora had not denied it. So the girl in the hut in the woods had been Dora. It was unbelievable.

'Your Gran won't want me in the house. You won't want to be my friend.'

Dora was shaking with shock. In spite of the warm evening her hands were frozen.

Lily took her friend's face in her hands. 'Dora look at me,' she commanded her. 'We all love you. Come on home with me. Please, it's my birthday and you're my best friend.'

'I've let you down.' Stumbling and crying, Dora let Lily help her to her feet.

'What do you want to do, wait for a bus? Could you walk home with me?'

'Walk.'

'Look, love, you're not badly hurt. It's more shock than anything. We'll try and walk quickly to warm you up.'

Once they were clear of Broad Street and walking towards The Hard Dora seemed steadier. Lily walked arm-in-arm with her friend, not knowing whether to chat idly or to say nothing. Her head teemed with questions. As they turned the corner into Lemon Street they saw Mary and Blyth talking at the door with Gran and Uncle Albert. 'Let's turn back for a sec until they've gone,' said Lily.

'I should go home and not get you caught up in all this,' said Dora, pulling at her arm.

'Come on. They've gone now. You can stay home with Gran tomorrow. I'll bring you some work back at dinner-time. Give your face a chance to settle down.'

'Merciful heavens,' gasped Gran as they stepped into the passage. 'Dora, my dear, you have been in the wars.' Her kindly concern brought on fresh tears.

'Uncle Albert, could you go around to Dora's shop and say she'll be back tomorrow after work.'

'No sooner the word than the deed,' he said, reaching for his hat.

'Dora, my duck,' said Gran, 'you don't have to say a word. Just you sit there and I'll get you a nice cup of tea. Lily you fill a hot-water bottle and we'll get her into bed. What you need is Dr Sleep.'

Later when Dora had borrowed one of Lily's nightdresses and was safely in bed Lily and Gran sat together in the kitchen over a belated birthday tea. She smiled at Lily as she poured her a glass of Uncle Samuel's raisin wine. 'Happy eighteenth, my duck,' she said, 'Not your best birthday but not your worst by a long chalk.'

'No, that was my twelfth after Jutland when Andrew was killed.'

'Six years – where's it all gone to? Still, Michael will be back for your next one.'

'I can't think about that, now. I'm so worried about Dora. This woman Gran, she punched her in the face and called her a tart and . . .'

'Look, Lily. I don't think Dora would want me to know that, do you?'

'I didn't mean to only I'm so . . .'

'My guess is that the worst is over. Things have come to a head and now Dora will need to recover and take stock. She'll tell you what she wants you to know when she's good and ready. Then you can listen and forgive and forget.'

Later Lily crept into bed beside her friend. As always Gran had put things in perspective. She just hoped it was all over with Bert Finch and that they could get back to their old easy friendship.

She was awoken in the early hours by Dora coming back into the room with a glass of water. 'You awake, Lily?' she whispered.

'Yes, you all right?' Lily asked anxiously.

'You must think me dreadful. I'm so ashamed I can only tell you 'cos it's dark and you can't see me.'

'You don't have to tell me anything,' said Lily, secretly hoping she wouldn't be taken at her word. 'You're still my best friend whatever you've done.'

'I don't know. It was as if I was someone else. Mad or under a spell or something. Honest Lily, I didn't even like him.'

'I don't understand.'

'He drew me to him even though I didn't want to go. Made me want him. Sort of stole me from myself.'

'How do you mean?'

'When we went to Driver's that day and he sat down beside us it was like he'd set light to me. Even though I wasn't looking at him I could feel him next to me and wanted to be close to him. Thought about him all that afternoon and when he wasn't there in the evening I was disappointed. You remember Mary's birthday? When you two had gone he was waiting for me, jumped out on me he did. Kissed me, made me all dizzy and not wanting him to stop. Said he'd meet me on the Sunday after. Even though I said I wouldn't, I knew I'd be there.'

'But,' protested Lily, 'kissing is one thing but, well . . .' Her voice trailed away. She didn't want to appear to condemn Dora. It was such a huge step from kissing to naked love making – another from imagination to reality.

'As I said he sort of stole me. He brought out this greedy bit of me that wanted him so bad I tossed everything aside. When I was with him it was like I was living deeper and faster. Then when I wasn't with him I couldn't hardly bear thinking about what I'd done – all the lies I told, and Harry. How am I going to face Harry?'

'I don't know,' said Lily, 'but if I saw and recognised Bert, that day in the woods, Mary might have recognised you. After all, she was there longer than me.'

'Wouldn't she have come raging in?' said Dora.

'Might have thought Bert would have hit her or something. But that's not to say that she won't write to Harry.'

'She's been funny with me again after being so happy on her birthday.' Dora sighed. 'Could be anything but I'll find out soon enough. Given all the time it takes for letters to get there and back, reckon if I haven't heard by the end of August . . .

'He might be so upset it'll take him a while to think about it.'

'D'you think I should write and tell him, make a clean breast of it?' asked Dora. 'I know it'll break his heart.'

'Is it all really truly over?' said Lily. 'That's the first thing.'

'Oh yes,' said Dora. 'When his wife spoke to me she rubbed all the shine off what we'd been doing. Made me face it fair and square.'

'It's hard to know,' said Lily. 'Once it's written down he can keep going over it, torturing himself. And even if he forgives you and wants to trust you again it's still there in the back of his mind.'

'I hate myself,' said Dora, breaking into tears. 'I've ruined everything.'

Lily stared into the darkness, feeling helpless. 'I know it doesn't feel like it,' she said, 'but the worst is over. His wife has ended it for you. All you've got to do now is get back into your old routine.'

'Couldn't even finish it myself. Had to have her make a show of me,' Dora sniffed.

A worrying thought came into Lily's mind. 'I've got to ask you something very personal,' she said, grateful that Dora couldn't see her face. 'There's no chance, is there, that you could be – might end up having a baby?'

'That's the only good thing about tonight. I came on just before I went out,' said Dora. 'At least I've that to be grateful for. And you of course,' she said, squeezing Lily's hand. There seemed to be a hint of the old Dora in her voice. 'I'll go into work tomorrow afternoon. If you could just cover for me in the morning I'll go home and change.'

What an awful birthday, thought Lily as she was drifting off to sleep. Thank goodness next year I'll have Michael's return to mark the day.

Chapter Thirty-three

Lily hurried along Asylum Road with her parcel of goods for the September Sale of work. She'd had a snatched lunch with Gran and was rushing to be at her stall by half-past one.

'Why is it such a mystery?' asked Gran as she helped her pack away the sewing needle-cases, pin-cushions and dressing-table mats.

'I don't know,' Lily had answered, feeling shy about her pet project. 'I promise I'll tell you all about it when I get back.'

'Well, you've worked hard Lily and all credit to you. Here's half-a-crown to swell the funds.'

As Lily sped along she thought about Amy and their growing friendship, how her face lit up whenever they met. How little she had in her life and how much importance she attached to Lily's visits. It was impossible to imagine a life without memories and one enclosed within the walls of the asylum. Gradually she had become used to walking through the ward with its wild sounds and noisome odours and became less frightened of the lost, disordered women. Although there had been many meetings of the sewing group she and Amy had only completed four tea-pot stands. Dorcas had achieved one hemmed dishcloth, while Marigold contentedly stitched and then unpicked the same grubby piece of green gingham. Sometimes they would sing together such songs as 'Annie Laurie' and 'All things bright and beautiful.' Dorcas and Marigold were willing but tuneless. This was the only time that Amy became distressed. She had a clear true voice and the others' lack of melody irritated her. The solution was to let her sing on her own which she did with great enjoyment.

Lily had taken to bringing little gifts each week, careful to include them all. Today she had promised to bring some ribbons to put in their hair. It would be a challenge to know where to fix them on Marigold and Dorcas's pudding-basin haircuts but she was looking forward to plaiting Amy's hair and threading through a scarlet ribbon.

The gatekeeper waved her through and she walked up the long main drive which was lined with stalls in different stages of readiness. Heather's stall was not far from the gate and Amy rushed up to greet her.

'You got the ribbon, Lily?' she asked excitedly, waving a steel comb and wooden hairbrush.

'Let's get the sewing out first,' said Lily. 'You can help me unpack.'

'You have done well,' said Heather looking admiringly at all the different items.

'You too,' said Lily, examining the satin-covered coat-hangers and tiny drawstring lavender bags displayed on top of the large hospital sheet.

'No, Jimmy, it's not tea time,' she said sternly to a small man with thick horn-rimmed glasses who had just bitten into his second jam tart from the cake stall. Unabashed he took another one and ran off into the grounds.

'Hair, hair,' demanded Amy.

'Yes please do it for her,' said Heather. 'I've to fetch Dorcas and Marigold. It will keep her occupied while I'm away.'

As she was plaiting Amy's hair, Lily looked around her. It

was a warm afternoon and she was grateful for the shade under the trees. Already a small crowd had gathered outside the gate waiting impatiently for two o'clock to come. The stalls displayed a wide variety of things, from children's soft toys to vegetables from the hospital farm. The patients assisted the nurses with varying degrees of success. Some wandered off into the grounds and others kept taking the goods and thrusting them into their pockets. The more reliable patients were deployed on the hoop-la and tombola tables. Some swings and slides had been set up and a striped tea-tent with tables and chairs dotted around.

Amy seemed soothed by the hair-plaiting and began to sing softly to herself. Lily was only half attending to the words as she concentrated on getting the ribbon smoothly threaded and tied in a bow at the end. She smiled to Dorcas and Marigold as they sauntered down the drive towards her. As she put down the brush and comb Amy started on a fresh tune. Lily recognised it as 'Bobby Shaftoe.' But the words were different. She was about to ask Amy to sing it again when the gates were swung back and the crowds swarmed in.

Heather had an apron on with a large pocket of change, and she and Lily were busy selling for the first half-hour. Then there was a lull as the crowd moved further up the drive in search of other amusements.

At the same time a thin white-haired man in dinner-jacket and bow-tie approached them, playing a violin. Amy was charmed, and hummed along to the music.

'What would you like me to play, pretty maiden?' he said to Amy.

She blushed and looked at the ground.

'What about "Bobby Shaftoe?"' suggested Heather.

Amy took hold of Lily's hand and began to sing: 'Lily Forrest's gone to sea to get her Daddy home for tea.'

Lily stared at Amy in shocked disbelief.

Still smiling at her, Amy continued to sing. 'He'll dance her up upon his knee and give her lots of kisses.'

'No, no,' whispered Lily, panic rushing up to her throat.

'Lily Forrest's bright and fair with pretty ribbons in her hair. She saves her Mummy from despair, Pretty Lily Forrest,' Amy was singing and swinging her around.

Her heart was thumping and she felt sick. Tears welled in her eyes. She thrust Amy away from her and ran blindly into to the grounds.

Behind her she could hear her shouting after her. 'Lily, Lily, come back, come back.'

Acid rushed up in her throat as she crashed into a laurel bush and sunk to her knees before being violently sick. She couldn't stop shaking. How could Amy have possibly known those words unless . . . No, she couldn't cope with the awful implications. And yet why else had she felt such an instant warmth towards her?

She must get away, give herself time to think what to do. Gran. Her name was like a lifebelt to Lily's panic-stricken heart. Fumbling for the clasp of her handbag she got out her handkerchief and dried her mouth.

Heather must be wondering where she had got to and Amy must be distraught. It wasn't fair to abandon her like this. Lily climbed out of the bush and smoothed down her hair and brushed the leaves from her skirt. She made her way back towards the stall but the sight of Amy setting crying by herself stirred up a fresh wave of panic. A nurse was passing by and Lily touched her arm. 'Please could you tell Nurse Neal that I'm not well and I'm going home. I'm Lily Forrest.'

'Why can't you tell her yourself?' asked the nurse.

'Going to be sick,' gasped Lily, rushing through the crowds and making for the gate.

As she rushed pell-mell down Asylum Road she'd no idea where she was going. All she was conscious of was wanting to put a distance between herself and the woman she had always been so desperate to know. Your mother, your mother, your mother – the words pulsed in her head. A stitch in her side halted her as she found herself approaching Crowell Road, the home of Auntie Hester and Uncle George. No she mustn't stop, it was Gran she wanted. Once the stitch was fading she hurried past their house and on out to the sea-front. Lily put her hand up to her face and found that she was crying. Lemon Street was at least four miles away, right at the other end of the sea-front. The thought of the distance exhausted her. She could catch a bus from the South Parade Pier. No, she was too het up to stand still and wait. She had to keep moving. The promenade was crowded and she was constantly having to weave in and out of the path of other people. Her shoes began to rub her heels and she stopped to take them off and continued running in stockinged feet. She remembered doing scout's pace at school and struggled on, running twenty steps and walking twenty.

Sobbing, sweating and exhausted she struggled along to The Hard and past the dockyard wall.

'My God, Lily, what's wrong child?' cried Gran, as she almost fell into the passage.

Lily could say nothing but clung to Gran as she helped her into the armchair in the kitchen. She was gulping and crying but she was safe. Like a small child, she sat there and let herself be fussed over: given warm sweet tea, scissors to cut off her torn stockings and a bowl of hot water to soak her blistered feet. As Gran knelt in front of her drying her toes Lily gasped, 'I found her, my mother, I found her.'

For a few moments nothing was said, while the water was carried out to the sink and the towel put away. Gran settled herself in Uncle Albert's armchair, opposite her, then said, 'Tell me again, Lily.'

'I didn't know it was her, for a long time, but today she sung to me. It's her, Gran, my mother, up at the asylum.'

'What possessed you to go up there in the first place?' There was sadness in her voice. 'God, child, if only I'd known where you were going I'd have nipped it in the bud straight away.'

Lily was frightened and confused. It wasn't at all the reaction she'd expected. 'Why would you have stopped me? You always wanted me to help people.'

Gran said nothing.

'It was her,' she said. 'Dad told me about this song she used to sing to me. Lily Forrest's gone to sea to bring her Daddy . . .'

'I believe you Lily. I've no doubt that it was Mary Forrest that you saw.'

'Gran what d'you mean?' cried Lily. No, she couldn't mean that? 'You've seen her?'

'Yes, Lily I've seen her. But that was three years ago and more.' She took Lily's hand and looked searchingly at her. 'Whatever I did,' said Gran looking at Lily, 'I did for the good of you all.'

'How, how can it be good for me to pretend you didn't know?' Lily demanded, thrusting her hand away.

'It was that Christmas just before your Dad and Miriam got married. I went up there to see Dolly with presents from her children. I saw this woman who looked like Mary and when she spoke I was certain.'

'How could you do it? Keep me from knowing even when I found the letter last year and asked you about her? You lied to me!' Her heart was pounding, she wanted to leap out of the chair and shake the answer from her. How could Gran who had so instilled honesty into her have lied about something Lily so desperately wanted to know?

'Think, think Lily,' Gran demanded. 'Your father was about to marry Miriam, the mother of Rosie. She was carrying another child, for God's sake. Do you realise what could have happened? Your father could have gone to prison for bigamy. Would you have wanted that for your sister and brother?'

'You could have told me. I wouldn't have wanted to get Dad in trouble. I would never have . . .' Her voice trailed away.

'You were fifteen then and fiercely jealous of Miriam. How could I be sure of what you might have done?'

'So you just left her there and said nothing. Didn't even go and see if there was anything she needed.'

'How could I without questions being asked?' said Gran, looking pleadingly at her. 'Don't you think the authorities might have put two and two together? Might have wanted to know if I was related?'

The door opened and Uncle Albert came in. He stood looking at both of them. 'Shall I take my tea upstairs?' he asked gently.

'Did you know about all this?' shouted Lily.

'About what, my dear?' he asked, perching on the arm of Gran's chair.

'That my mother is alive?'

'Yes,' he said. 'I did.'

'So both of you have lied to me.' She was shaking with anger. 'And Dad, does he know? Did he marry Miriam knowing that my mother was in the mad-house?'

'No,' said Gran, 'he didn't know and he is not to know.'

'Liars, liars you're liars.' She leapt from the chair and hurled herself at Gran, her arms flailing. A stinging slap halted her. Lily looked in astonishment at Uncle Albert and then she crumpled on to the floor. She lay there sobbing. Alone, she was alone. They had all deserted her. All that time when she could have known her mother. The tears kept coming, she felt as if she were dissolving in grief. Dimly she became aware that she was being helped back into the armchair. She could smell the paint and turpentine on Uncle Albert's shirt.

'Lily, I wouldn't have hurt you for the world.' Gran was kneeling in front of her and the pain in her face stung Lily to fresh tears.

'I feel so tired and mixed up,' she gasped. She wanted to be angry with Gran but she couldn't. Her mind was in a turmoil. Nothingness, to drop away into sleep, that was what she wanted.

'Lily, my dear woman,' said Uncle Albert,' you have had a very great shock. I think that you need to rest and be taken care of while you decide what you want to do.'

'I'll make us some tea,' said Gran struggling to her feet. 'And then it's bed for you my lady. We'll talk again tomorrow.'

They both fussed over her as if she were an invalid. Gran helped her into her nightdress as if she were a little girl. Lily lay in her bed exhausted but unable to sleep. She closed her eyes and the tune of 'Bobby Shaftoe' beat in her head.

Chapter Thirty-four

The madness was over and she had got her life back. Dora could not believe that all the wanting and scheming was at an end. There were still moments when she flayed herself over her shameless behaviour and putting her life with Harry so much at risk. At first she had feared seeing Bert again, avoiding Driver's Café and Old Portsmouth, but as the months went by and there were no sightings of him her confidence returned.

She and Lily went out a few times on the tandem: along the sea-front to her Aunt Hester's and once over the hill as far as Droxford. Dora went around to Harry's family each week, played Ludo with Blyth and the twins, even laughed and joked with Fred. Only nine months and Harry would be back home and they would be planning their wedding. She settled down for an evening of letter-writing in her bedroom. Positioning her cup of tea next to her on the dressing-table she took up her pen.

October 5th 1922

My Darling Harry,

I do love you so much and I'm counting the days until we're together again. Last Saturday I went over to Gosport on the ferry and saw all the sailors hurrying to and fro out of HMS Dolphin, the submarine base. I tried to think of myself as a

*submariner's wife living over there and I liked the idea. It would
be good to be away from our families to start out on our own.*

*It's so good to write about your lot and not have some awful
news to tell you. They all seem to be bobbing along at the
moment. Fred is working with this Oliver Clifton who's taken
over number nine with Chippy and the blind bloke I told you
about. Well Fred takes old Sailor up to the Workshop for the
blind in Cosham, during the week on the tandem. Ever so proud
of himself, is Sailor, learning to make baskets. I think Sergeant
Clifton gets a bit cheesed off with your Dad because he's a bit
slap happy when it comes to decorating but they rub along quite
well.*

I'll leave Mary to give you her own news.

Dora stirred her tea. She and Mary were back to their usual
uneasy truce. The brief friendship after Mary's birthday had not
been repeated. Had she seen her in the hut with Bert? Dora didn't
know. Certainly Harry's letter gave no indication of knowing
about it. Anyway, whatever Mary said to him she knew that
Harry would always suspect his jealous sister's motives. And as
Dahlia had once said to her, 'Don't waste your energy on what
might never happen. Sufficient unto the day, my dear.'

Where was she? Dora missed her. There was no one with
whom she could talk in quite the way she had with Dahlia. It was
like playing a fast game of ping-pong.

Whatever Dora said was questioned and batted back with
another question. No one had listened to her more closely or
made her laugh so much.

She returned thoughtfully to her letter.

*The twinnies are growing up, getting quite pretty. They're still
thick as thieves together but sometimes they fall out, even beginning
to have separate friends.*

Biggest change in Little Blyth. He's insisted that he move his bed into Fred's room because girls are soppy. Fred has promised to take him camping next year and has begun to show him how to do knots. It's all been a bit of a shock to Mary but she's forever dreaming up new schemes for the toy stall. What does that young lad Dusty make of her letters?

Lily seems to be full of secrets. Had a bust up with her Gran but won't tell me about it. Other than that everything is boring and normal. Dad still worrygutting about the shop and Mark and Barney saving up for a motor bike.

Must sign off now.

Love and kisses my darling, from your Dora.

October 20th 1922

Dear Dusty,

Ta for your last letter and the other flicker books, they're going down a treat. Nelly and me are stocking up for Christmas. We even got a club where customers put by a few coppers a week for presents. She got me making dresses for the Christmas Angels for on top of the trees. You asked me what she looks like. Well she's sort of old and a bit shrivelled up looking. Got creases on her face like the skin on baked apples. Sideways on she looks a bit like Mr Punch with her big nose and pointy chin. Knitted herself this bright green pixie hood and green gloves with no fingers so's she can still count up the money. Thinks our Dad is Rudolph Valentino and gets all silly when he talks to her. Mind you he's as daft as she is.

'Hello, my sweetness,' he says, 'are you going to give me one of your radiant smiles. Make a poor man happy with the riches of your beauty.'

'Is that my prince,' she cackles, 'what have crossed the burning desert for the touch of my lips.'

Course people thinks it's side splittin'. Dad likes her 'cos she treats him to a beer afterwards at the Market Tavern. Although he's pretty good now he still gets pie eyed now and then. Last

Saturday night I locked him out 'cos he and Nelly went up the pub and left me to return the handcart back to the market and put all the stuff away. I was spittin' feathers I can tell you.

No more news about Dora. I think her and that soldier have gone off the boil. You might be right about not telling Harry though it browns me off to think she's got away with it. Mind you I think she knows I've rumbled her so I gives her a beady look from time to time just to rattle her cage.

Saw little Cissie what I told you about the other day. Seems the Clements is off to Singapore and she's got herself a job in a funeral parlour. Mind you it's not as bad as it sounds 'cos she gets to live over the shop and the bloke and his wife is quite good to her, lots of grub and that. Only trouble is when the people comes in what wants someone burying she can't stop crying.

Hurry up and gives us your news. It will be funny when we meets up won't it?

Just think we been friends for months now. Paper pals I calls it.

Take care of yourself, Regards Mary.

7th October 1922

Dear Michael,

If I don't pour all this out to you I shall go mad. There is no one else to tell.

I found out a few days ago that the Amy I've been seeing in the hospital is really my mother. It was such a shock. And yet, I felt as if I had known all along, even from that first moment, last Christmas when I first saw her. I am looking, now, at the photograph I have of my mother and it so obvious that Amy is her. How did I never seen it before.

But it is all so complicated. You see Gran has known about it for the last three years. She found her when she was visiting Dolly Vine and said nothing. I'm trying to believe that she acted from the best intentions as it was on the eve of Dad's wedding to

Miriam. If it had been known that my mother was still alive, Dad could be sent to prison for bigamy. But I can't forgive her for not telling me.

I have no one but you that I can trust. One minute I feel rage at what has happened and the next sadness. There's a hard revengeful bit of me that wants to to punish someone. It can't be Miriam because she is totally innocent and I'm convinced that Dad acted in good faith and still has no idea of what has happened. It's Gran and Uncle Albert. It feels like in gaining my mother I have lost Gran. And now, I have this secret that could destroy everyone's happiness.

I haven't been back to see my mother. Heather has written to say that she was very upset when I ran away and keeps asking for me. I can't believe that with all this churning in my heart I am still living here, going to work and seeing Dora and everyone.

My only hope in writing this letter is that by the time you reply to it I shall have sorted it all out somehow or another.

All My Love, Your Lily.

Chapter Thirty-five

Beattie sat on the concrete bench at the Eastney Promenade to catch her breath. She'd been foolish to think of walking all the way back from Hester's but she needed time to think. The last two weeks had been painful. Lily had accused her of deceit and betrayal. But what else could she have done, then? The discovery that Mary Forrest was still alive had taken her breath away, coming as it did on the eve of her son's second marriage. Her main concern had been getting Alec and Miriam safely married and their children protected. Lily's right to meet her mother had seemed a minor issue at the time. Especially as Mary Forrest would not have recognised her daughter and was far from capable of looking after her.

Beattie sighed. The priorities at the time had been so clear-cut. But now she could see the flaw in her reasoning. She had denied Lily the right to see her mother, had failed to trust her. Would she have coped with the knowledge? Beattie didn't know. She had matured a lot in the last two years. What would she do with it now? It was possible that she would go to the police. Lily was capable of sudden reckless actions, even now. Beattie prayed that her granddaughter was too fond of her father to want to ruin his life. But the loss of trust between herself and Lily would not be easily repaired. It had been the cornerstone of her granddaughter's life. Without that support Lily was floundering.

Beattie sighed again. Why had she dragged herself along to Hester's when she was so dog-tired? The answer was cowardice. She just couldn't stay in the same house as Lily without wanting to interfere. No, no, no, she tapped her umbrella fiercely on the shelter floor. She must stand back and let her wrestle with this problem alone.

'You've brought her up to be resourceful,' Albert had said, as she lay in his arms earlier that morning. 'No, you must give her time to think it through.'

'What if she never forgives me?' she'd sobbed.

'My darling you have to trust her. Forgiveness, if it's worth having, has to be worked through. She'll have to put herself in your shoes with the problems that surrounded your decision. And she must know that I advised you pretty strongly against telling her. Left to yourself you may have gone the other way.'

'It's so easy to see your mistakes when you look back isn't it?' she'd said. 'In the heat and press of the moment you long to have the decision made and the path taken.'

'Sometimes,' he said, taking her hand and squeezing it, 'you just have to travel hopefully. In the meantime take yourself off to Hester's. It's a beautiful Sunday — go and look at the sea. I find that always helps. Don't hurry back. I'll potter with my painting and cook our dinner for six o'clock. You need diversion. Take George some of Samuel's raisin wine.'

Beattie had stood at the water's edge and thrown pebbles into the sea. The fresh wind had tugged at her hair and gulls clamoured about her. For a few blessed moments her anxieties had seemed to float away.

Now, with the daylight beginning to ebb her worries crowded in on her. She got up to continue the return journey. A sharp pain in her chest made her gasp and she sank back on the bench to catch her breath. Beattie felt dizzy and almost sick.

How was she to get home? She was at the Eastney end of the promenade – quite a stretch from the South Parade Pier and the buses that would take her back to Portsea. It was cold and a wind was riffling the waves. Beattie looked about her for someone, anyone, to help. What if she died out here?

No good getting hysterical she chided herself. You've got two bad choices: stay here and die of cold or get moving and die of over-exhaustion. Or alternatively do nothing and die of indecision. She opened her bag and searched its contents. Amid the assortment of her purse, spectacle-case, safety-pins, smelling-salts and shopping-lists she found her tiny emergency bottle of brandy. She unscrewed the top and swigged back a good mouthful. In the distance Beattie spied two marines striding along towards her. The brandy began to warm her up and she once more got to her feet. The pain seemed to have receded and her breathing eased. As the marines approached she hailed them by waving her umbrella. 'Young man, please could you help me?'

'Ma 'am,' the younger of the two men ran up to her. 'What can we do for you?'

'I need to get home to Portsea but I don't feel well enough to make it to the bus stop.'

'What about a taxi? I could run back to the rank at the Pier and send one down for you. Horace here will stay with you. How would that be?'

'Very kind, Corporal,' said Beattie, noticing the red chevron on his sleeve.

'Got took bad did ya?' asked the marine called Horace.

'Lost my breath. I think I'd been overdoing it and what with the cold wind . . .'

'Your lips look blue. Probably heart trouble,' he said dolefully.

Beattie stared down the promenade praying the taxi would hurry. Her companion was doing nothing to raise her spirits. When she had almost given up hope she saw a black cab in the distance. 'You've been very kind. I'm most grateful to both of you,' she said as the driver held open the door for her. Saluting smartly, the men took their leave.

'Lemon Street, driver, please,' she said, 'number twenty five.' As the cab sped along towards Portsea Beattie began to feel better. She decided not to worry Albert by mentioning the incident. 'Can you drop me in Queen Street,' she asked the driver. 'I'll walk the rest of the way.'

Slowly Beattie walked towards her home. Albert had been right: a change of scene had helped to clear her mind. She recognised that there was nothing she could do but wait for Lily to make the next move. The thought of Albert waiting for her with the dinner simmering away on the stove and her slippers by the hearth filled her with a deep thankfulness. The little scare on the promenade she would keep to herself.

Chapter Thirty-six

Mary stood on a chair and lit the lamp in the kitchen. It was five o'clock in the morning. Christmas Eve, her first Christmas working in the market. Her brain was fizzing with all she had to remember.

'Get yerself kitted out proper,' Nellie had advised. 'Good warm shoes, yer feet gets frozen stood about and don't ferget yer woolly hat. Bleedin' cold first thing. Watch them nippers crowding round the sides, little thieving tykes half of them. Still,' she'd wheezed, 'we gotta give the kids a bit of magic. Lots of holly hung along the top with ribbons and a star. Gotta have a star. You done them fairy dolls, wings and dresses all different?'

Mary had nodded.

'Wants your Dad down here early even if you have to set a rocket behind him. Needs time to set up proper. Once the crowds comes it's too late.'

Mary filled the kettle, hacked a piece of bread off the loaf and pushed Towser out into the yard. While the water boiled she spread a liberal helping of dripping on her crust. She was stood in her nightdress and bare feet chewing appreciatively when her father crept up behind her.

'Booh,' he shouted. 'See,' he laughed as Mary leapt in alarm, 'I didn't need no rocket after all.'

'Blimey Dad, nearly choked me you did.'

Within half an hour they were hurrying through the empty streets to Charlotte Market. Nellie was already stamping about on the pavement surrounded by mysterious heaps and bundles. 'Bout time,' she snapped. 'Now Fred, get the lantern lit and tied firm to the top strut by the sign, "Nellie Moyes, Books and Toys". Then you gotta get us some holly off Jonas over there. Mary go down the tea stall, three cups and don't stint the sugar.'

'Blimey Nellie, I don't think I can stand much more of ordering about,' groaned Dad theatrically as he blew on the steaming cup of tea.

Nellie rolled her eyes. 'If only I'd had you sooner Fred Vine I'd have brought you up with a round turn. What you needs is the love of a good woman.'

Dad chuckled. 'On a cold morning like this the love of a bad woman is what's needed. Someone to warm up me bed. You're just a sergeant in long drawers.'

'Ow d'you know about me drawers?' chaffed Nellie.

'Ooh. A sailor only needs the sniff of red flannel,' said Jonas, dropping a bundle of holly at Nellie's feet.

The morning flew by puntuated by Nellie's raucous cries, 'Come on Missis, lovely fairy, set yer tree off a treat. How about some soldiers for your fort, sonny? Beautiful kasleidacope, give it a shake and you gets 'undreds of lovely patterns.' Suddenly she fetched a young lad a sharp crack on the head with one of the Christmas Annuals. 'Get them marbles out your pockets or I'll hang you upside down. Fred, quick get 'is ankles.'

Mary with a money bag strapped around her waist, was frantically bundling up comics, wrapping dolls and parcelling books.

'I fancies a bit of a look round,' said Nellie, when there was a lull in the selling. She hobbled about from stall to stall exchanging greetings and filling her shopping-bags.

Mary smiled up at her father who had just persuaded a

harrassed woman to top off her tree with the last of the fairies. 'What we gonna get Blyth?' she asked.

'A cowboy outfit, he's mad on Tom Mix and Buck Jones and what about a smoking outfit? You know: liquorice pipe and sweet cigarettes.'

'I fancies a kaleidescope,' said Mary.

'You mean a kasleidecope don't you?' laughed Dad.

'Innit lovely down here. All that fruit all polished and shiny, the naptha lanterns and everyone lookin' forward.'

'Yes, my gal. That's Christmas for ya. It's the little chink of hope in the darkness.'

'You make it like poetry.'

'And I'm sober,' he laughed, 'all except for a rum toffee.'

Mary smiled as she dipped her hand into the bag that Dad held out to her. 'How we gonna get our grub together for tomorrow?' she asked.

'Dora's got a list and promised to fetch it for us, said she'll probably see us up here sometime.' He looked searchingly at Mary as she busied herself taking out fresh stock and filling in the gaps on the stall.

'You still wild with her over that soldier?'

Mary sucked on her toffee and served a girl with a game of Ludo before saying anything. She hadn't really had much time to think about Dora lately, what with working for Nellie and sorting out the family Christmas. 'I'm not as mad as I was,' she said grudgingly, 'and I s'pose if Harry's happy that's all that matters.'

Dad nodded and then they were plunged again into a frantic clamour of customers.

'You're growing up, my tater. A gal to be proud of in spite of her old Dad.'

Mary glowed.

Nellie came back laden with shopping. Her face was rosy and her breath laden with sherry. 'Right you two, the dinner-time rush is over. Here's shilling, go and get youselves a bite over at Charlie's.'

Arm-in-arm Mary and Fred shoved their way past ragged children diving under stalls for blemished fruit, the Salvation Army band, and men on crutches selling matches and bootlaces.

'Poor buggers,' said Fred dropping a penny onto a soldier's tray. 'Here pal, come over with us and I'll stand you a cup of soup. Charlie, soup and bread for two and a drop in a cup for this soldier, here.'

'Much obliged,' said the man, hobbling towards the stall.

Mary sipped the hot meaty liquid and looked about her. She thought of Dad's words, 'A chink of hope.' Last year she'd been desperate to get that job in the kiosk and to dislodge the snooty Beryl. Now she was a marketeer with Nellie. Last year she hadn't known how nimble she was with her fingers, had not had the excitement of seeing children crowding around the stall, wanting her tops, and flicker books and fairies with their gauzy, sequinned wings. She'd not been pals with Dad and she'd not even heard of Dusty. In less than six months HMS *Lister* would be nosing into Farewell Jetty and Harry and Dusty would be coming ashore. What would they think of each other, she wondered as she broke the last of the bread into the tin mug.

October 10th 1922

Dearest Dora,

Just think this time next year I shall be settled back at home. We may even have got ourselves married. I could be sat in front of the fire with my pipe and slippers or we could be out to the pictures in Gosport, the Criterion isn't it? By the beginning of next April we will be turning around and steaming back to good old Pompey. I keep saying the names of the last ports of call before we get home: Aden, Suez, Port Said, Malta, Gibraltar and then into Farewell Jetty.

I don't never ever want to see anymore rickshaws or elephants;

tropical rain storms, snakes; junks or jungles. I've had my fill of
foreign travel. Michael is another kettle of fish altogether. There he
is drawing or painting and writing in his diary. I just want to
be sitting in The George with my best girl on my arm and a pint
of Brickwoods beer in my glass.

I've had this little picture in my mind of how it's going to be
when I step onto the jetty in Pompey. You'll rush into my arms
and we'll be laughing and crying and kissing, the marine band's
playing and the sun's shining. What d'you think it will be like
have you pictured it, too?

Dora put Harry's letter back in her handbag and spooned her
ice-cream out of the tall sundae glass. She was sitting at one of
the marble tables in Pitassi's Ice-cream Parlour in Edinburgh
Road, rewarding herself for having fought her way through
Charlotte Market and completing the Christmas shopping. Her
thoughts returned to Harry's letter. Yes, she had imagined that
first meeting a hundred times and not always in such glowing
terms. The worst scene had been standing with her eyes down-
cast in shame holding Bert's baby in her arms, then Harry
recoiling in shock and running back onto the ship.

Dora sighed, she didn't deserve such good fortune. To have
made such a bad mistake and not be punished. Lily said she'd
punished herself enough and it was at least half Bert's fault if not
more. But what if she settled down with Harry and everything
was rosy and then he turned up one day and threatened to tell her
husband? Blimey, she thought, I've not only crossed the bridge
I'm up over the other side. Dreamily she stirred the ice-cream
into a pink soupy state before taking another mouthful. The true
picture would be both of them shy and awkward, the rain pelting
down and Mary and the twins grabbing Harry and pushing her
aside.

'Can I have that sugar, ducks?'

Dora passed the basin to a blowsy-looking woman in a tight

fur coat. In one hand she held a cigarette, the ash falling into the sugar. Behind her in the booth opposite was Bert Finch.

'Jesus, Vera, you gonna be all day,' he complained, not appearing to have recognised Dora.

The woman shuffled back across the gangway to her seat beside him. Moodily he spooned the sugar into his cup.

Dora turned her head away and busied herself with the shopping. She had expected to feel some of the old excitement, guilt, fear even – instead there was disbelief. She felt nothing. He was nothing, nothing at all. Purposefully she gathered up her bags and slid out of the seat. As she turned in the gangway to leave the café Bert looked up. She watched the expression in his face change from surprise to a fake good-humour.

'Dora, what you doin' here?'

'I'm leaving, Bert, that's what I'm doing,' she said, meeting his confused stare.

Vera looked at her assessingly from behind a veil of cigarette smoke.

'Please yourself,' he said, a note of bluster in his voice.

'Yes,' said Dora calmly, 'that's what I'll do. I'll please myself.'

With the exception of Uncle Albert shut away in his studio, Lily was on her own. The Vines were down at the market and Gran was over at number 9 with Michael's mother and Oliver Clifton. She sat at the kitchen table with a small package in her hand. Inside the wrapping-paper was a new hairbrush and a length of green satin ribbon. It was almost half-past one on Christmas Eve. If she were to deliver it on time she would have to hurry. But Lily was hesitant. Before knowing that Amy was her mother the visits to the asylum had been a pastime. She had been frightened at first but gradually fear had given way to sympathy and then curiosity. Heather had told her how poverty, disease and abandonment had brought many of the women into her care.

She had gained a certain glow of satisfaction in helping to raise funds, seeing the happiness her visits brought to Dorcas and Marigold as well as Amy. But she'd had no obligation to continue seeing them beyond the summer sale. Now, if she made that one visit to her mother she would be honour-bound to continue. If only Michael had written but as always letters lagged behind events.

'Single to the White House, please.' Lily sat on the bus with the present in her hand. She could still hand the gift in at the gate and go home, she wasn't yet committed. As she walked up Asylum Road she thought about Gran and the distance growing up between them. She had been so harsh and condemning and Gran had been so frightened. How powerful and dangerous secrets were. Now she was the unwilling recipient in keeping the news from Dad. Of course she didn't want to hurt him or Miriam. She had grown to love her dearly and Rosie and little Jo. But Dad had shared his feelings about her mother last year on that holiday and there had been a feeling of trust between them. He had treated her as an adult. But if she didn't intend to be a daughter to Amy what was the point in writing?

The large iron gates of the asylum loomed into view. Taking a deep breath Lily approached the man in the gate office. 'I'm off to Weston Villa to see Amy.'

'Right ho, Miss. Do you know the way?'

'Across to the right of the main building.'

'Of course you used to come in of a Thursday evening,' the man smiled. 'Thought I recognised you.'

There was a moment after ringing the bell at Weston Villa when she could still have run away but she didn't.

'Lily, I am pleased to see you.' Heather came to the door with Marigold still clutching her sewing. 'You can help us put up the paper chains.'

It was as if she'd never been away. Guitily she realised she'd never contacted Heather or given her any explanation of her sudden flight.

'Amy's over there on the floor sorting through the box of decorations.'

'Amy, it's me,' she said going over to the kneeling figure. There was no response. Lily couldn't see her face, only her hair hanging uncombed about her shoulders.

'Amy,' she repeated, trying to keep the shake out of her voice. 'It's me, Lily.'

'Where you been?' Amy thrust her away. 'You left me, didn't want me.' She rushed at Lily, crying and beating her hands against her.

In spite of her fear, Lily held on to her. 'Amy, Amy, I'm here now.' She rocked her like a baby. 'Shh, shhh. I'm here, you're safe.' Slowly her fear ebbed away. It seemed as if Amy's tense body would never yield and then suddenly she was limp and exhausted. Her crying stopped. Lily took her into the ward bathroom and washed her face and hands.

'You going to do my hair like always?' Amy asked her.

'Like always,' said Lily. 'I've brought you a present.' She watched while Amy tore open the package throwing the paper on the floor.

'My brush,' she said. 'My brush, not yours,' she shouted at Marigold, who was about to pick it up.

'Come on sit over here,' said Lily firmly, 'I'll put your ribbon in.'

Slowly Lily began to brush her hair. The tangles loosened their grip and the long dark hair became smooth and biddable. Under the soothing rhythm of the brush the tight knots in her own mind began to unravel. It was all very simple. It was not she that needed a mother, it was Amy. Instinctively she wanted to care for her, to wash that lank hair and trim those nails. Amy needed her and she was not going to let her down. She smiled at her as she patted the ribbon on her hair and preened in front of the mirror like a little girl. 'Next time I come I'll get you a toothbrush,' Lily promised.

Amy smiled. 'You my friend,' she said.

'See you next week.'

'Bye Lily, bye bye bye,' said her mother, waving from the ward door.

Lily ran down the road all the way to the White House. Suddenly, she was impatient to see her grandmother. As she sat in the bus wedged between laden Christmas shoppers her anxieties continued to unravel. There were things she needed to put right and there wasn't a moment to spare.

'Hello Lily,' said Gran as she burst into the kitchen. 'Come and sit by the fire, you must be shrammed. I've put your slippers to warm by the fender. You thaw out while I give Albert a call. Think he's taken root up in that studio. I've got some freshly baked mince-pies for the pair of you.'

'They'll have to wait,' said Lily. 'I need to tell you something.'

Gran sat down in her armchair. 'Let's be having it,' she said. 'Anything in particular?'

'I – I went to see my mother today,' she faltered. 'She doesn't know who I am. But she needs me. I couldn't just walk away. It's strange but now I feel as if things have got changed around and I've become a mother to her.'

'You're growing up, Lily. You're on the verge of wisdom,' Gran said. She was smiling at her but Lily could see the fear beneath.

In that instant as she looked at her Lily realised how much she had hurt her grandmother in the last few months and how much she loved her.

'I'm so sorry,' she cried kneeling down in front of her. 'I've been so horrible to you and worried you so much. Oh, Gran.' She could say no more as the tears spilled down her face.

Leaning forward Gran took Lily's hands in hers. 'Listen, my duck,' she said quietly, 'I'll not pretend that I've not been hurt by some of the things that you've said because I have. And, deeply worried about what you might do in regards to your Dad's life with Miriam. But you had to come to your own understanding of things in your own time.' She rummaged in her apron pocket and handed Lily a handkerchief.

'I do love you Gran. And I know now that nobody could have been a better mother than you. But when I opened Granddad's box and found that letter saying that my mother might still be alive it knocked away all my certainties. Then when I saw her and found out who she was it was all too much.'

'And then finding that your Gran had deceived you by keeping her a secret must have put the tin lid on it.' Gran smiled sadly at her. 'That knocked my halo off good and proper.'

'Everything had been so safe and I'd taken it all for granted.'

'Now, Lily, I want to remind you of a chat we had a long time ago. I think it was the day when the Armistice was declared.'

'But what's that got to do with anything?'

'Mary's mother, Dolly, came in. Do you remember? She was all over-excited, dancing about and spilling the sugar?'

'Yes, I do,' said Lily.

'You were very disapproving and said how glad you were that she wasn't your mother.'

'I was thinking, coming home on the bus, how my life would have been if mother hadn't run away. Would she have been all rackety like Dolly Vine and would my life have been like Mary's – all muddly and uncertain?'

'You have to live the life you're given, not waste your energy on might have beens,' said Gran firmly.

'Anyway,' said Lily, 'what about that afternoon of the Armistice? How does it tie in with me and my mother?'

'We had a talk afterwards about wisdom and cleverness.'

'You said we could be born clever but we had to learn wisdom?'

Gran nodded. 'Anything else you remember?'

Lily smiled. 'Wisdom is hard-won through making mistakes.'

Gran leaned forward and took Lily's hands in hers. 'It's not just making mistakes, it's having the courage to learn from them. You're a young woman to be proud of Lily, and I love you dearly. And now, as I said earlier you're beginning to get a glimmering of what wisdom's all about.' She kissed Lily on the cheek and said. 'Is there anything else you want to say before I call Albert down for his tea?'

'There's just one thing,' said Lily. 'Only you and me and Uncle Albert and Michael will know about Amy. I shan't tell Dad or Miriam.'

'If you've shared that secret with Michael things must be serious between the two of you.'

'Yes Gran,' she said, kneeling down in front of the armchair. 'We want to be married.'

'Oh, Lily,' said Gran, her face wreathed in smiles, 'I'm so glad. Especially since it's Michael — a man that I really like, that's a wonderful bonus. You've done a lot of thinking, my duck, and made some good decisions. Let's get Albert down and tell him your news. It will make his Christmas. It's certainly made mine. Albert,' she called, as she hurried down the passage, 'we've got something to celebrate.'

Lily reached out and took one of the mince-pies. She was suddenly very hungry.

Chapter Thirty-seven

'Happy Birthday, my darling,' said Albert. 'And now, I'll take off your blindfold and reveal your present.'

Beattie clutched Lily's hand as they stood in the entrance to his studio. She could feel the excitement in her husband's voice. It had been months since he'd let her over the doorstep into his studio and his secrecy had been hard to bear. Now she looked at her present, on the wall opposite, a painting almost as tall as she was.

'Take your time before you give your judgement,' Albert said. Beattie could feel the nervousness in his voice.

The painting was a revelation to her. Carefully she studied it trying to take in every detail. It showed the beach at the Round Tower. Far away in the distance could be seen the outline of HMS *Victory* against a sky streaked with pink and gold. In the foreground was Michael's ship HMS *Lister*. The beach was crowded with women and children. Near the shore was Lily waving her green shawl, and in her shadow was another figure just like her in an old-fashioned dress, waving too. Beattie and Miriam and Rosie were there and behind them she recognised herself, as a young mother with Alec as a baby in her arms. Behind her another figure in a long flowing dress was waving a handkerchief. To the sides of the painting were little houses and through the windows could be seen women nursing babies, sewing sailors' collars, writing letters. Each face was caught in the moment the woman looked away from her task and out to sea, her thoughts with one of the sailors on the ships.

Beattie was astonished. She sat down on the old backless chair by the door.

'Albert,' she gasped, 'you've painted my life. It's wonderful.' Tears welled in her eyes. 'I don't know what to say.'

He was like a young boy in his eagerness. 'Let me show you,' he said taking her arm. 'Look there where the town wall meets the tower. In that little corner, there's a sailor. Look at his tarpaulin jacket. Can you just pick out the little bundle? And if you come over here and look really closely there's just the hint of a tiny hand.'

'Oh! Gran, isn't it magical,' cried Lily. 'I can see Dora in one of the windows stitching a buttonhole. And look there on the beach Mary and the twins and Blyth with a telescope in his hand.'

Beattie squeezed his hand. She was overwhelmed by her husband's skill and perception but also by his love. It was not only a tribute to her but to all women who made their lives with sailors. There was the admiral's wife waving from her carriage, the young girl pickpocket relieving a sailor of his money, and there with her skirts above her waist was the harlot, her face sharp with hunger.

'When did you get the idea for all this?' she asked.

Albert smiled. 'It was you, Beatrice. Do you remember when we came back from our honeymoon in Romsey. We stood by the harbour watching the mudlarks and you told me what Portsea meant to you. Don't you remember saying that you had the feeling of standing in other women's footprints?'

'I want to look at it 'til my eyes ache,' she said. 'I've never ever been so taken with anything.'

'Then every sketch and brush-stroke has been amply re-warded,' said Albert kissing her cheek.

'What are you going to call it?' asked Lily.

'Well,' said Albert, 'it's more a dedication than a title. See, on the frame at the bottom it says "For Beatrice a Woman of the Fleet".'

'Yes, I like that,' said Beattie, 'it sums me up nicely.' Turning to Lily she said, 'Why don't you go down and see if there are any cards on the mat. I haven't had my fill of looking yet.' She could feel a tightness in her chest and knew now that if she kept very still for a while it would, with luck, go away.

'Can I leave you here, my darling,' said Albert. 'I was up at dawn finishing your present and I badly need to wash – I smell like a turps bottle.'

'Go, Albert. You're leaving me in wonderful company,' she said pointing at her picture. She caught his sleeve. 'I don't know how to thank you.'

'I think we will find a way,' he said, kissing her on the cheek. 'Perhaps you could let Dr Marston have a look at you. Remember, my darling, I'm a doctor's son. This pain and breathlessness of yours needs looking at. Don't hide it from me. We must tackle it together. We've had so little time together and I'm greedy for more, aren't you?'

Beattie squeezed his hand, her eyes glistening with tears. Dear, dear Albert how she loved him. Please God, she thought, let me be spared for a little longer.

'Gran,' said Lily, handing her two envelopes. 'Here's a card from Miriam and one from Auntie Hester.'

She nodded and held out her hand, hoping that Lily wouldn't see the pain in her face.

'You read it out to me,' she gasped, 'I want to look at the picture.'

'Have a wonderful birthday, Dear Mother with love and kisses from all of us. We have kept some special news for today. I am expecting another baby either July or August. I hope that you and Lily will be able to come over nearer the time to lend a hand. I do want my family around me as they were last time.'

'Gran, isn't that wonderful? 'cried Lily. 'Oh, I'm so excited. I remember last time it was me that helped little Joseph into the world.' She rushed over and hugged her grandmother. 'I must go down and tell Albert.'

'Fetch me up a cup of tea,' said Beattie. She looked again at the painting, at the sailor guarding the tiny baby. Please God, I'm not finished yet. Just let me see my new grandchild, she prayed – that's not a lot to ask.

Chapter Thirty-eight

The waiting was almost over. The crowd at Farewell Jetty burst into wild cheering as the big battleship entered harbour followed by the two light cruisers, HMS *Lichfield* and HMS *Lister*. Mothers held their babies up in their arms: 'It's Daddy's ship, my darling.' Young lads whistled shrilly through their fingers. Those last few minutes while the little tugs nudged their charges against the jetty seemed the longest of the whole commission. Anxious eyes scanned the line of sailors drawn up to attention along the deck of each ship. Where is he? Where is he?

All the different sounds of homecoming clashed together: the fanfare of the Royal Marine band on the upper deck of the battleship, the bosun's shrill whistle, the shouting back and forth between the seamen and the dockyard maties as ropes were thrown and secured around the bollards on the jetty, the scream of the seagulls and the thump of the gangplanks being set in place.

Impatiently the crowd waited for the Port Admiral to be piped aboard followed by his entourage, then a sudden rush of sailors down the gangplank seeking their families.

Lily, Dora and Mary stood there tense and excited.

'It's him,' cried Dora, breaking away from her friends and running towards the gangplank. It was him. Her Harry standing on the jetty anxiously scanning the crowd. He was tanned and sporting a beard.

'Harry, over here.'

'Dora, Dora, Dora.' She was swept up in his arms and swung round and round. 'It's good to see you, gal. Ooh give us a kiss.'

She clung to him. His beard grazed her face and his lips tasted salty. I don't was this moment to end, she thought, or the kissing to stop.

'Let's have a look at you?' he said, eventually breaking free. 'I could eat you all up,' he laughed, kissing her again. 'You looks the same only different. I dunno, s'pose it's because I've had to make do with your photo. You're more a woman,' he whispered in her ear. 'You was a girl when I left.'

Dora inspected Harry with equal scrutiny. 'So different looking at you,' she said, blushing under his bold appraisal. Harry had grown into a more assured version of himself. He was no longer the larky Vine lad but a broad-shouldered man with strength and purpose. She reached up and touched his beard. The hair felt wiry under her touch as it formed a golden mat around his face.

'What's the plan,' he asked her. 'I've to go back on board to get my gear and then I'm home for fourteen days.'

'I've got a tandem parked around the corner,' she whispered. 'We've nearly four hours. I'm due back at work for two o' clock.'

'See you in two shakes,' he said, 'I don't want to waste a second.'

Dora watched him sprinting back up the gangplank then he disappeared below to get his kit-bag. Dear Harry, she didn't deserve her luck. How handsome he'd grown. When he'd kissed her it was as if he'd never been away. That same love and warmth and affection was there between them. All the waiting and wanting and worrying was at an end. They would make a new life together away from Lemon Street and his rackety family, away from Denby and the pernickety Admiral Shanks, away from her

Dad and his prophecies of doom. Mrs and Mrs Vine of Gosport. It was time for the Vine family to have a change of fortune.

'Are you Mary Vine?'

She turned to see a tall red-haired able-seaman holding a picture of her, and looking down into her eyes.

'Who wants to know?' Mary challenged, trying to cover her excitement. Blimey! He was more than she'd bargained for. It was taking her all her time not to start blushing.

'I'm Dusty, I mean Matthew Miller,' he held out his hand to her.

Mary shook it vigorously. 'Mary Vine, pleased to know you. Didn't tell me you was tall,' she said almost accusingly.

'Didn't tell me you had freckles,' he countered.

Mary smiled. Yes, she liked him. They would be able to knock sparks off each other. 'How long you got ashore?' she asked.

'About ten minutes or so then I'm off tomorrow night. I'm duty part of the watch today. Your Harry's off for a fortnight.'

'We'd best make the most of it,' said Mary. 'Let's go over there in that corner by the crane.'

'Lead me to it,' said Dusty.

Mary strode along beside him proud as punch. He was even better than his letters had led her to believe. There was a larkiness that didn't come over on paper.

'You're fiercer than I expected,' Dusty said.

'Gotta be,' said Mary, 'otherwise you gets took for a ride.'

'S'pose so,' said dusty, thoughtfully.

'Thought your Mum would be down to see you, from Kent wasn't it?'

'Canterbury, yes.' He sighed. 'It's a long way and we don't know nowhere where she could stay cheap. Anyway I'll be back there in a fortnight. In service she is, and don't get much time off.'

'I was a scullery-maid,' said Mary, 'but I didn't last long.'

'What ya do, pinch the silver?'

'Wish I had,' she laughed, 'we could have had a slap-up meal at the Queens. No, I pinched some notepaper.'

'That's a bit strong, to get rid of you for a bit of paper.'

'Stationery, Matthew, stationery,' declared Mary in Lettice Clements' ringing tones.

'Go on,' he urged her, 'put us in the picture.'

Mary gave him the full works: describing her first sighting of the kiosk in the butcher's shop, the querulous skinny-eyed Beryl, the wonderful Tiffany lamp in Lettice's drawing-room, the thick cream paper and envelopes, her own best swirly handwriting and then the day of discovery.

'Goggle-eyed with rage she was. Called me the guttersnipe. When I read out what I'd writ, old Clements her husband had to leave the room 'cos he was laughing fit to bust. But old Lettice she ain't got an ounce of fun. Cook reckons she's constipated.'

Matthew was red-faced and chuckling. 'You was wasted there, Mary. You should be on the Halls, make a fortune.'

'Happy with me market,' she said. 'Don't want nothing else.'

'Looking forward to seeing that and meeting Nellie,' said Matthew. 'I've got the weekend off. But now' he said, regretfully, 'I've got to go. What would you like to do tomorrow night?'

'Could we go to the pictures? There's a Pearl White film, *The Broadway Peacock*. But what would you like, Dusty?' she asked in a sudden fit of generosity.

'I'd like for you to call me Matthew,' he said.

Mary looked up into his dark-blue eyes and felt herself grow dizzy with excitement.

'Dusty's all right only it's nickname. Don't make you feel like a person, just a bit of naval gear like a marlin spike or a binnacle.'

'Better than guttersnipe,' said Mary smiling at him. 'Anyway, makes no difference to me, Matthew.'

'It does to me,' he said. 'You and my Mum will be the only two to call me that.'

She felt a warm gleam of happiness. He had made her feel special.

Matthew got to his feet. 'Must go or I'll be in the rattle.' Mary never had known what in the rattle meant but it didn't sound good. 'Shall I call for you at your house, tomorrow?' he asked.

'Yes, about half-six. Twenty-three Lemon Street.'

'I do know your address,' he teased, 'I've written it enough on your envelopes.'

They stood outside the dockyard gate and he dipped his head down and kissed her on the cheek. 'See you tomorrow, Mary,' he said smiling at her.

'Bye Matthew,' she called.

Then he was gone, back through the crowd. Mary held her hand to her cheek on the spot where he'd kissed her. She had a sweetheart and his name was Matthew Miller. Suddenly she had everything to look forward to. Mary was about to walk back home when she remembered that Dora and Harry would probably be there wanting to be alone. I know what sailors are, she thought, chuckling softly to herself.

Lily watched Michael hurrying down the gangplank. She had rehearsed the moment a thousand times. He looked so smart and assured in his number one Petty Officer's uniform with the gold badges on the sleeves. It was a second or so before he saw her and so she was able to examine his face minutely, watching the blend of anxiety and eagerness in his eyes as he searched for her. He was taller and thinner and she had forgotten the exact grey-green shade of his eyes, the crinkly lines of his forehead as he scanned the crowd for her, and the cleft in his chin. How strange it felt to see him as he was in reality and not the figure of her imagination or the faded photograph. Soon she would be able to touch him, to be held in his arms, to be close enough to have the scent of him on her skin. Her mouth was so dry she was afraid she would not be able to speak. He turned and saw her at the moment she was about to call his name.

'Lily,' he said and held out his arms to her.

'Michael, oh Michael.'

He began to kiss her. Lily closed her eyes, shutting out the crowds on the jetty, and immersing herself in the taste of Michael's lips, soft and persuasive against her own. She drew in the mixture of engine-oil, soap and sea that was her Michael. All she wanted was for the moment to last forever. To cancel out the endlessness of the waiting – for time to stand still. Slowly, reluctantly, they drew apart.

'Hallo, Lily,' he said shyly. 'It's good to see you.'

'You look different,' she said, 'but I don't know quite how, yet.'

'You'll have to watch me closely, and when you've found out what it is you can let me know.' He smiled down at her. 'I have to go back on board and get my gear, then I'm free for fourteen days. How about you?'

'I have today off and then back to work tomorrow.'

'Wait for me, Lily. I'll be as quick as I can.'

'Oh,' she frowned, 'it won't be quick enough.'

She watched him step nimbly up the gangway, salute the officer at the top and then disappear. Only a few more tantalising minutes and he would be hers. Everything had fallen into place. Gran and Uncle Albert had decided to spend the day in Romsey and Mrs Rowan was going with them.

'Tell Michael I'll be back at six,' she had said. 'Give him the key will you Lily?'

'Of course,' she had said demurely. It gave them at least five whole hours alone together.

'Right. Let's be off.'

She jumped at the sound of his voice, startling her out of her day-dream.

He hoisted his kit-bag up on his shoulder and took her hand in his. As they strolled through the dockyard gate and down Queen Street she could feel the warmth pulsing between their fingers.

'Where shall we go?' he asked as they turned into Lemon Street.

'Everyone's out today,' she said, avoiding his eyes. 'You can come to my house.'

He set down his kit-bag and turned to her. 'If you open the door,' he said, 'I'll carry you over the threshold.'

'No, no,' she said blushing. 'Ma Abrahams is looking. Quick, let's get in before anyone else sees us.'

The instant intimacy of their first moments was replaced by a sudden shyness. They stood about awkwardly in Lily's room. She wondered if the sight of her bed intimidated him. Would it have been better to have taken him into the kitchen? Should she offer to make some tea? She wanted him to hold her again and if she started fiddling about with the cups and saucers the opportunity would pass. Yet she didn't want to appear to take anything for granted.

'I'll take off my cap and jacket.' Michael turned away from her to put his coat on the little basket armchair. Afterwards he stood there without moving. Lily sensed that he was afraid. Impulsively she stood behind him folding her arms around his waist and resting her face against his back. Nothing happened. She closed her eyes and drew in the warmth from his body.

'Lily, oh, Lily,' he whispered, taking her hands and holding them up to his face. He kissed each finger in turn. She felt his body tremble and then relax before she, in her turn, kissed the bones of his spine through his cotton shirt. Michael swivelled around to face her. Again they kissed. They were tentative sipping kisses that slowly became more intimate. He parted her lips with his tongue and they clung more closely to each other. Michael drew her towards the armchair and pulled her down onto his lap. They had now moved beyond words and polite exchanges. Now there was another language to learn.

Lily was minutely conscious of him, the change from rough to smooth as she ran her fingers down his face, the throbbing of his heart against hers and the heat of his body. He undid his tie and took out his collar studs and unbuttoned his shirt revealing a dark mass of curly hair on his chest. She closed her eyes as he slid her blouse down around her waist and slipped his hand beneath the straps of her chemise.

Writing bore no comparison to the intensity of touching and stroking and seeing.

As if reading her thoughts he whispered, 'However much I dreamed and imagined you it was nothing. You're so beautiful. I love your hair, your eyes, your breasts. All of you, Lily, all of you.'

'Oh, Michael' she said. 'You're so handsome. I like the way the hair grows all dark and wiry on your chest. I know so much about you, Michael but it's all thoughts and feelings. I want to see you, all of you. I don't feel shy any more. I want to know you.'

Slowly they began to undress each other, punctuating their discoveries with kisses. They were in half shadow as the afternoon sun shone through a chink in the curtain, the light alternately revealing and concealing. Lily and Michael stood facing each other hand-in-hand, taking in the wonder and the difference in their naked bodies. By some unspoken consent they lay down together side by side. He ran his hands over her body circling her breasts, kissing and tasting her.

Led by her desires she drew him to her and lay beneath him. Michael straddled her body and leant down to kiss her mouth. She circled his waist with her legs and slid her hand between their bodies, touching him and guiding his penis inside her.

There was a natural resistance then a sharp momentary pain. It was a frantic dizzying experience. They were like a ship and a harbour, the one seeking the other. It was over before she felt fully satified. Michael got a towel from the rail by the dressing-table and poured some water from the jug on the wash-stand into the basin. He dipped one end into the water and knelt in front of her to wash the stickiness of their lovemaking away. He dried her gently and slowly, caressing her to a pitch of blissful completion.

As she lay in his arms she said, 'I sent you a letter once saying that writing wasn't touching. Do you remember?'

Michael smiled at her. 'Yes I do,' he said. 'When we're apart we pour our hearts out on the paper but it's the other things we long for isn't it? The seeing and touching. We exist on hopes and memories.'

'I said, then, that it was a day of endings and beginnings,' said Lily, 'with Gran getting married and the house moving and everything. Today is like that.'

'What are the endings?' asked Michael, kissing her hand.

'Childhood,' she said. 'All the judging and not understanding. Not seeing how much Gran has loved me. All the day-dreaming about my mother.'

'And what have you begun?' he asked.

'To see that life is not as simple as I thought. To become a friend to my mother. To appreciate all that Gran has done for me. To see that there's no end to learning. And,' said Lily, smiling and turning the ivory ring around her finger, 'to choose a life for myself as a woman.'